W9-AAB-917

An Irish Country Girl

ALSO BY PATRICK TAYLOR

Only Wounded
Pray for Us Sinners
Now and in the Hour of Our Death

An Irish Country Doctor
An Irish Country Village
An Irish Country Christmas

An Irish Country Girl

PATRICK TAYLOR

**Doubleday Large Print
Home Library Edition**

A Tom Doherty Associates Book

New York

AN IRISH COUNTRY GIRL

Copyright © 2009 by Patrick Taylor

All rights reserved.

A Forge Book
Published by Tom Doherty Associates, LLC
175 Fifth Avenue
New York, NY 10010

Forge® is a registered trademark of
Tom Doherty Associates, LLC.

ISBN 978-1-61523-874-3

Printed in the United States of America

**This Large Print Book carries the
Seal of Approval of N.A.V.H.**

To Dorothy

ACKNOWLEDGMENTS

Although my name may be on the cover and spine, no book is the product of a single individual.

Natalia Aponte, my agent and friend, made a suggestion over lunch that got me thinking about and finally writing *An Irish Country Girl*.

Tom Doherty of Tom Doherty Associates had the faith to allow me to follow my instincts.

Carolyn Bateman, my friend and editor, has read every word I have ever written. Without her skill and deeply professional advice, my sentences and paragraphs, plotlines and characters would be but shadows of their present forms.

Paul Stevens of Forge polished the final manuscript and made it shine.

Patricia Mansfield Phelan once more copyedited my work with her usual meticulous attention to detail.

Irene Gallo of the Forge art department created the concept, and the artist Gregory Manchess rendered the illustration that became the cover.

Sarah Howard, née Taylor, instructed me, literally, in the arcana of the tarot.

Dympna Bird's skill in the Irish language gave my characters' words the authenticity that I could not have provided. Corkman Dave Hyde corrected my misapprehensions about the game of road bowls.

To you all, I offer my most heartfelt thanks.

AUTHOR'S NOTE

Near the end of *An Irish Country Christmas*, Mrs. Kincaid, housekeeper to Doctor Fingal Flahertie O'Reilly of Ballybucklebo, bids farewell to her employer, his young assistant, Doctor Barry Laverty, and O'Reilly's lady friend, Kitty O'Hallorhan. It is a snowy Christmas Day in 1964, and they are leaving to attend an open house being held by the Marquis of Ballybucklebo.

Mrs. Maureen Kincaid, "Kinky" to her friends, has earlier welcomed a group of youthful carol singers into the hall of the doctor's house. What transpires next as she gives the youngsters hot drinks and sweet mince pies is where this work, *An Irish Country Girl,* starts. It is Kinky Kincaid's story.

All of this will make perfect sense to readers of the Irish Country novels who have already encountered Kinky, Fingal, Barry, and the village of Ballybucklebo. But if this is your first venture here, it will be uncharted territory, and a few words of introduction are called for.

The first three books in the Irish Country series are set in 1964 in County Down, Northern Ireland, in the small village of Ballybucklebo. They concern the adventures and misadventures of Barry Laverty, a brand-new medical graduate who has accepted a temporary assistantship to the unorthodox Doctor Fingal Flahertie O'Reilly. The young man and his mentor tend to their patients, many of whom are as eccentric as their senior medical advisor. Because O'Reilly is who he is, the two doctors also spend a considerable amount of energy solving the problems that arise in the everyday life of the village.

O'Reilly is fifty-six, widowed, a single-handed practitioner, a big man of distinctly odd attitudes, blasphemous, crusty—and a fine physician. His household consists of the demonically possessed white cat, Lady Macbeth; the dipsomaniac, Wellington boot–stealing black Labrador, Arthur Guinness; and the solid, reliable housekeeper, Mrs. Maureen "Kinky" Kincaid.

Having said that, some explanation is also needed for the readers who have come to know Doctors O'Reilly and Laverty, the village, and its inhabitants, because this book is different. But let me first thank you for your loyalty to Ballybucklebo. And please don't worry. Now that *An Irish Country Girl* is finished, I have begun work on the next Irish Country tale, which is set in familiar territory and peopled by the usual suspects.

Because this story is a departure, old friends and newcomers alike may be interested to learn how *An Irish Country Girl* came to be. For almost a year, one of my characters kept after me to try to answer a single question: how did she develop her most unusual trait? By the time I had the solution, I knew I had to tell Mrs. Kincaid's story, the one you are about to read.

I base my characters on people I have

known, but I never simply describe one person. Instead I take a physical characteristic here, a personality trait there, a speech pattern from elsewhere. When I was a young doctor doing locums for rural Ulster GPs, I met several housekeepers, remarkable women all. Kinky grew from them.

When she first appeared in *An Irish Country Doctor,* Kinky was in her mid-fifties, much smarter than people thought at first sight, a Cork woman—and fey.

Don't laugh. Some Irishwomen *do* have "the sight." My grandmother did, and I believe that, even after thirty-five years working in medical research. How else could she have sat up and announced, "Maggie's dead"? Her younger sister lived fifty miles away. Thirty minutes later the telephone rang. Maggie had died at almost exactly the moment Granny had made her pronouncement.

Kinky's ability to see things persisted in the sequels to *An Irish Country Doctor*, and I began to wonder *how* she was given the gift. That was the question that nagged.

Eventually I remembered another of

my housekeeper friends from my early days in practice. She had a marvellous way of recounting stories from Irish mythology, a subject that has fascinated me since childhood.

This friend came from Ballydehob (Mouth of the Two River Fords) near Skibbereen (Place of Little Boats) in West Cork. I have only to close my eyes to hear her saying in her rich brogue, "Now, Doctor Taylor, dear, in the telling of English stories you'd have begun, 'Once upon a time,' so, but in Ireland we say, 'And it is what it was . . . ,' or 'And this is what he said . . . ,' or 'It is what she did.' We do use them sometimes in the middle of the tale too, so." And off she'd go weaving her magic. When she spoke she held me in thrall.

She often spoke of the *Dubh Sidhe** (doov shee), the dark faeries, and in particular the *Bean Sidhe* (banshee), the woman spirit whose keening foretells a death. One story in particular concerned the

---

*Kinky, of course, is bilingual, speaking both Irish and English. When she uses *Gaeilge* (Irish) here, she tries to work pronunciations and explanations into the narrative. However, that sometimes interferes with the flow of the story, so I have included a glossary as a backup (see p. 299).

Saint Stephen's Day Ghost, or *Taidhbhse* (thevshee), who appeared on not one, but two Boxing Days.

Kinky came from a farm near the five-road-ends of Beal na mBláth, also in County Cork. What, I asked, might have happened there in the 1920s as an Irish girl named Maureen O'Hanlon grew to womanhood, fell in love, began to meet the denizens of the other world, and saw the Saint Stephen's Day Thevshee, not once, but twice?

Might that be how Maureen "Kinky" Kincaid was given the sight—or was it because she already had the sight that she was able to experience all that she did?

You will find out if you read on.

PATRICK TAYLOR
Cootehall, Boyle
County Roscommon
Eire

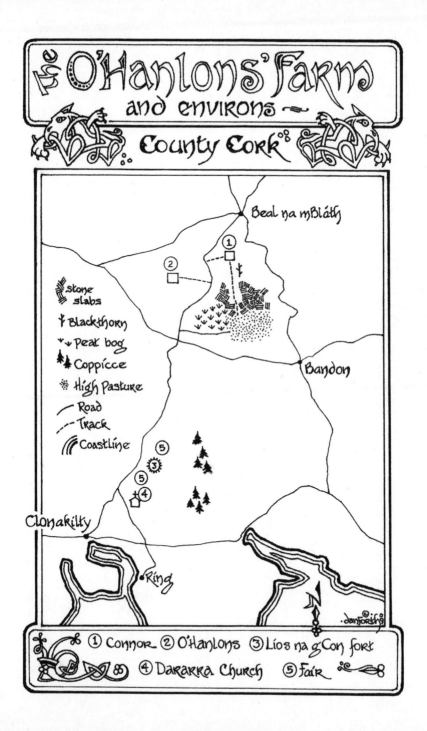

1

"Run along, make your calls, and enjoy His Lordship's hooley," said Mrs. Maureen Kincaid, "Kinky" to her friends, as she knelt in the hall and sponged Ribena black-currant cordial from a small boy's tweed overcoat. "I'll expect you all back by five, sir, not a minute later. I'd not want the Christmas dinner to be spoiled."

Her employer, Doctor Fingal Flahertie O'Reilly, said over his shoulder, "We'll be on time, I promise, Kinky." He strode off accompanied by his guest, Caitlin "Kitty" O'Hallorhan, and his young assistant, Doctor Barry Laverty.

Kinky shut the front door after them. She imagined that over the excited voices of the children she could hear footsteps crunching through the freshly fallen snow as Doctor O'Reilly led his little party to his big old Rover for the drive to Ballybucklebo House and the marquis' 1964 Christmas Day open house.

It was warmer in the hall with the door shut. Just as well with a dozen chilled little carollers inside drinking hot black-currant juice. She straightened up, inspected her handiwork, and smiled. "There you are, Dermot Fogarty. Good as new, so."

"Thank youse, Mrs. Kincaid." The eight-year-old bobbed his head. "If I'd got my new coat dirty, my daddy would've killed me, so he would."

She tousled his hair. Not for the first time she thought how harsh to her ears the County Down accent sounded, especially when she remembered the softer brogue of her own people down in County Cork.

She'd grown up there on a farm near Beal na mBláth and had left as a slip of a girl of nineteen to come north in 1928. That had been thirty-six years ago. She shook her head. It seemed like no time at all.

"Here." She refilled Dermot's mug, feeling the heat in the delft and inhaling the scent of the black-currant juice. "Try not to spill any more."

"Thank you, Mrs. Kincaid."

"Anyone else?"

Several voices replied, "No thank you, Mrs. Kincaid."

The kiddies were crammed into the hall and overflowing up the broad staircase of Doctor O'Reilly's house at Number 1 Main Street, Ballybucklebo, County Down.

"Then eat up, and drink up, and let's be having a bit of hush." They were quiet now, filling their faces with Kinky's home-made sweet mince pies and hot juice. She beamed over them. She liked children, would have loved to have had some of her own, but that hadn't been meant to be. She smiled sadly to herself.

She probably could have found another fellah here in Ulster, but och, he'd not have been the Paudeen Kincaid she lost so long ago. She saw herself in the hall mirror and thought she'd not been a bad-looking lass when she'd been with

Paudeen. Her silver hair, which she wore in a chignon now, was chestnut then and had flowed in soft waves to her shoulders. It was the worry about him one Saint Stephen's Day that had started the turning of it.

She'd been a slim girl then. Now, she knew she could afford to lose a couple of stone, although doing so wouldn't get rid of her three chins. But it was hard not to sample her own cooking, and she did love to cook. She always had, ever since Ma had showed her how all those years ago.

She shook her head, and sure if the years *had* passed, hadn't they been good ones ever since she'd come here, first as housekeeper to old Doctor Flanagan and later on, in 1946, to Doctor O'Reilly when he took over the practice? And hadn't looking after those two bachelor men been a satisfying job, and almost the same as rearing chisellers?

Doctor O'Reilly, learned man that he was, would not get out of the house without egg stains on his tie if she wasn't there to sponge them off or make him change it. He often called his Labrador, Arthur Guinness, a great lummox. Sometimes, she thought with affection, the pot does call the kettle black.

"Pleath, Mithis Kincaid?" A child's voice interrupted her thoughts.

She saw Billy Cadogan, a boy who suffered from asthma. He'd been a patient of the practice since Doctor O'Reilly and Miss Hagerty, the midwife, had delivered him ten years ago. "Yes, Billy?" He looked smart in what must be his brand-new cap and bright red mittens.

He held up his mug. "Pleath, Mithis Kincaid, can I have a toty-wee taste more? Ith cold thinging carolth round the houtheth today, tho it ith."

So, she thought, she should have known that Billy was the one lisping when they sang "We Wish You a Merry Christmas."

Before she could answer, Colin Brown chipped in, "Billy's right; it would founder you." Even today he was wearing short pants. His bare knees stuck out from under his overcoat, and his left sock was crumpled around his ankle. Colin was the lad who had single-handedly, as the innkeeper at the recent Nativity play, caused the mother superior to faint. Colin spoke again. "My Da says it's as cold as a witch's tit today, so he does."

Kinky frowned, then seeing the seriousness on the boy's face, realized that he was merely repeating what he had heard his notoriously foul-mouthed father say. "And what would you know of witches, Colin Brown?" she asked.

"Oooh," said Colin, "witches is oul' wizenedy women with wrinkles and warts on their green faces. They have black cats, they wear pointy hats and black dresses, ride around on broomsticks on Halloween night . . . they cast spells, and . . ."—he frowned—"and . . ." Then a smile split his face and his words came out in a rush. "And they get together in ovens."

"Colin means 'covens.'" That was Hazel Arbuthnot. She was Aggie Arbuthnot's twelve-year-old daughter. She had lustrous black hair, just like her mother. For a moment, Kinky wondered if Hazel had also inherited the family trait of six toes. No doubt Cissie Sloan, Aggie's cousin and the most talkative woman in the village, would know.

"That's right, Hazel, covens." Kinky heard the other children laughing at Colin's discomfiture. "And there's no need to laugh at Colin. He nearly got it right."

The giggling subsided.

"And some witches do cast evil spells and sour the milk, or make the crops fail or animals die—"

"Oooh." Several voices were raised, and Kinky heard sharp in-drawings of breath.

"—but some are good witches." She paused to let that sink in.

"Good witches?" Eddie Jingles asked. He'd had pneumonia two weeks before Christmas. He was better now, but his mother, Jeannie, had very sensibly wrapped him up in boots, thick trousers, a heavy anorak, a green scarf, and a blue-and-white-striped wool toque. "I never knew there was good witches. Are you having us on, Mrs. Kincaid?"

Kinky scowled at him, then let a smile play at the corners of her mouth. "Why would you think I was making it up, Eddie Jingles?"

Eddie blushed and lowered his head. "Sorry."

"Now," she said, "how many of you believe there are good witches? Hold up your hands."

Jeannie Kennedy's hand was the first to go up, then Micky Corry's. Those two had been Mary and Joseph in the Christmas pageant earlier that week. The last hand raised was Colin Brown's, but Kinky had expected that. Colin had a mind of his own.

"Good. So we're all in agreement then?"

"Yes, Mrs. Kincaid," a chorus of voices replied.

"I'm glad to hear it." She lowered her voice and let her gaze wander over the group, looking this one, then that one, right in the eye. "Because my own mother was a good witch, so. My very own mother, and she got it from *her* mother, my granny."

"Does that make you a witch too, Mrs. Kincaid . . . since your mammy was one?" Colin had his head cocked to one side, his eyes narrowed. "You've no warts on your nose, like."

"Don't be impudent, Colin Brown." She put her face closer to his, flared her nostrils, and widened her eyes. "Or I'll turn you into a tooooadstool."

The communal "oooh" was much louder.

Seeing the look on Colin's face, Kinky

softened. "I'm only pulling your leg, son, so, for I'm *not* a witch at all. I couldn't turn you into anything." Even if I did get the sight to see the future from my mother, Kinky thought, but that's none of their business. "And if I was . . . *if* . . . I'd be a good witch and lift spells or smell out bad witches or cure people with herbs or find water wells—"

"With a hazel twig?" Billy Cadogan interrupted.

"Or a Hazel Arbuthnot," Colin said, then sniggered and stuck his tongue out at Hazel.

"Less of that, Colin, or I'll not tell you any more," Kinky said.

"Sorry," Colin said. "I'll houl' my wheest. Honest."

"You do that, so," said Kinky. She let a silence hang, and hang, until Hazel said, "Pay him no heed, Mrs. Kincaid. He was just acting the lig. I don't mind. Go on, please tell us more."

Several other children added, "Please . . . please."

Kinky smiled. The sight wasn't the only thing she'd got from her family, and that was a story in itself. Her Da, God rest him, had been a famous *seanachie,* a story-teller, and Kinky Kincaid, when given an audience, liked nothing better than to spin a good yarn.

"So, it's a story you want?"

"Please." She saw the expectation on the rosy-cheeked faces.

"Very well," she said. "Take off your hats and coats and hang them there, now." She indicated the hall coat stand. "Then go on up to the lounge. The fire's still lit from this morning, and it's warm. Doctor O'Reilly won't mind, seeing it's Christmas Day. There aren't enough chairs for you all, so some will have to sit on the floor. Mind you're careful with your mugs of juice as you go up the stairs, now. Leave a chair for me, and don't be annoying the animals. Arthur Guinness and Lady Macbeth do be upstairs."

The hall was filled with a babel of excited voices as the children struggled out of their outer clothes.

"Now hush. Hush." Kinky had to raise her voice. "Do as I bid," she said. "I'll be up in a shmall little minute with more mince pies."

"Yo-o-o-oh."

She waited for quiet. "And then I'll tell you a story of faeries, and the banshee, and the Saint Stephen's Day Ghost, and if we've time—but remember I've a dinner to cook, so only if we've time—I'll tell you how the Saint Stephen's Day Ghost came back four years later."

2

When she went into the lounge, she saw one empty armchair to the side of the fire. Colin, Eddie, Micky, Billy Cadogan, and Dermot Fogarty were sitting on the carpet in a half circle facing the armchair. Colin was closest to the fire. Arthur Guinness, Doctor O'Reilly's black Labrador, lay flopped in the middle. The girls all had seats. At least, Kinky thought, the boys had *some* manners. Hazel was in one armchair. That wee opportunist Lady Macbeth, Himself's white cat, had already made herself comfortable on Hazel's lap. Jeannie Kennedy, Irene O'Malley, and the twins Carolyn and Dorothy Kyle had managed to squish themselves onto the sofa.

Kinky squeezed between Dermot and Hazel and offered the plate of mince pies to the boys. "Take two apiece," she said, "and then you'll not be interrupting, looking for more."

"Thank you, Mrs. Kincaid."

She'd let them eat for a while. Settle down before she started. That was one of the tricks she'd learnt from her Da. Wait until your audience is good and ready and eager to hear what you have to say.

She'd not wait too long though. She'd promised them a story.

Kinky moved to her chair by the fire, and as she walked she looked out of the bow window, through the swirling flakes, and across Main Street to the stone wall of the Presbyterian church opposite. Car tyres had dug dirty ruts in the drifts of the road, but the wall topped with the snow's royal icing sparkled in the forenoon sunlight. Icicles like sharpened crystal pencils hung from the eaves of the church roof. They absorbed and magnified the rays and dripped gently as the sun warmed the ice.

Two trotty wagtails, black-capped and grey-caped, strutted in tiny staccato steps along the top of the wall, wagging their long tails behind them. She'd always had a soft spot for those little birds.

She smiled at the arc of children around her. They were all still tucking in, fidgeting, settling down.

She knew how her Da must have felt when he faced an audience, waited for silence, and only then started to speak in his soft Cork tenor. He could hold them in the palm of his hand as he wove his tales, and just as Ma had passed on the sight to her, Da had seen the talent in his youngest daughter and had encouraged it.

"Always remember," he'd say to her, "when you're telling a *really* good story, there's no law to stop you making things up. If you've got their attention, they're not going to be thinking about whether you actually *know* what one of your characters was feeling and thinking inside. They'll believe you do if you say it convincingly. You're spinning them a dream, and we all do love good dreams, so."

Today she'd promised the children a ghost story, and that was what they would get. And wasn't she going to take Da's advice? There were gaps she was going to have to fill in from her own imagination— especially in the first part.

But hadn't she been there herself, four years later, when the story came to its conclusion, and didn't she know every last detail of that as a fact?

She scanned the room. It was quieter now. Every eye was on her.

"Now," she said, mimicking the words of the hostess in the BBC's popular afternoon kiddie show, *Listen with Mother.* "Are you sitting comfortably? Then I'll begin."

The girls giggled.

Kinky waited for silence. "Look at the snow out there," she said. "Do you think it's deep?"

"Yes, Mrs. Kincaid," Jeannie Kennedy said.

"It's deep enough I'll grant you, but it's only a sprinkle to the snow that fell on not one . . . not one, but two Saint Stephen's Days in Beal na mBláth."

Micky Corry held up his hand. "Please, Mrs. Kincaid, what's Saint Stephen's Day?"

These poor folks from the north. They

never were taught much about Irish lore. "Saint Stephen was a martyr. He was stoned to death."

"Oooh, yeugh," another girl said.

"His day is celebrated on what's known up here as Boxing Day."

"Is that the Feast of Stephen?" Micky asked. "When your man, King Wencless-lass, and his page went out?"

"Wenceslas." She corrected him auto-matically, wondering why northern children always got the name wrong. "And yes, it is the Feast of Stephen."

"The snow was 'deep and crisp and even' then, so it was."

"And on the days I'm telling you about, Micky, it was deep enough to bury a sheep." She paused and swept her gaze from one to the next. Their eyes widened. Eddie Jingles's mouth hung open. "It was deep enough to bury a man. But the trou-ble started six weeks before the first Saint Stephen's. It wasn't snowing that day."

She could see that all the girls were leaning forward. The boys fidgeted and nudged each other. Arthur Guinness yawned, put his great head back on his paws, sighed, and drifted back to sleep.

"I was there for both Saint Stephen's Days. I was only little for the first one. I was quite grown up for the second. I knew the fellah it all happened to, a fellah called Connor MacTaggart, a fellah who paid no heed to the Doov Shee, the dark fairies."

All the kids sitting at the table leaned even closer. The boys stopped fidgeting. She heard a girl say, "Oooh . . . the little people."

"Indeed," she said. "In Irish, the *Dubh Sidhe*, the dark faeries. And you should not ignore them. Connor found *that* out. Connor was a shepherd and a close friend of my big brother Art. They both played Gaelic Athletic Association games. He kept his sheep in his pasture, right on the bare top of a high hill near our fields, and he often passed our house on his way to and from his flock.

"He'd pop in to see us, and he always had sweeties in his pocket for the younger children. He'd never mind giving a hand if there was a heavy job to do. And if our sheep that grazed with his needed moving, sure wouldn't he laugh and say, 'It'll be no more trouble than giving you a smile, Fidelma.'

"Fidelma was the next sister up from me. She was daft about him." She saw how the boys scowled. They'd have no time for girls—not yet—but the girls giggled.

"I liked him well enough myself," she said, "and I remember him as if it were last week and not forty odd years ago."

She waited until the children settled down; instead of the English "Once upon a time," she began in the time-honoured fashion of Irish storytellers: "And this is what it was . . .

"Connor MacTaggart lived in the townland. He was a strong man, a brave man. He'd been in the First World War. He was a man who laughed a lot. He could play the *uillinn* pipes and dance slip jigs and reels 'til the dawn. He could drive a *sliotar*, a hurley ball, like no man for miles around. No man, nor no woman, had ever caught him telling a lie." She paused to let all that sink in and saw by the way several of the children were nodding their heads that they understood.

"No man nor no beast," she lowered her voice, "nor no creature of this world *or* the other scared Connor. He half believed in the faeries all right, but he didn't give a tinker's cuss for them."

She lowered her voice until it was just stronger than a whisper. "Do any of you know what it might mean if you heard hands clapping in the dead of night and there was nobody there? Or if you heard the sound of sheep being sheared, but there was no sheep nor no shearer?"

Every eye widened. No one spoke.

"Those're two of the noises the *Bean Sidhe* makes."

"The banshee?" Micky Corry grabbed himself by the throat and pretended to strangle himself. "Aaarrgh."

"Well, Connor said he'd heard of her alright, but he'd only truly *believe* in the banshee when he saw one."

Jeannie was shaking her head. Dermot was mouthing, "Silly man."

Kinky waited until they had settled down, then said in her usual soft tones, "So I take it you all know about the banshee, don't you?"

"Yes, Mrs. Kincaid."

"Well, so did Connor, but he decided to pay no heed to her nor to the Doov Shee, as you'll soon find out." She paused and smiled. She really had their attention now. "Not even when my Ma—"

"The good witch," Colin said.

"That's right. Not even after she'd warned him, not once, but three times."

3

"I remember him sitting in our roomy kitchen one Saturday in November. I was fourteen and there was no school on a Saturday for me. Ma was pouring cups of tea.

"That morning, when he'd been in his turf bog near the upper pasture, he'd noticed that one of our ewes had foot rot. He'd gone up with his donkey carrying two side baskets to bring down a load of turf that had been cut in the spring and left to season. Instead he'd loaded the sheep in one basket and brought it down for Da to look after."

"Excuse me, Mrs. Kincaid. How can you tell two sheep apart?" Dorothy wanted to know. "They all look the same to me. How did Connor know it was one of yours?"

"It was easy. Each farm had a colour, you see, and before you put the sheep into a common pasture you put a big blob of your dye into the wool over one hip on each animal. Connor's was a bluey-grey. Ours was green. A green blob said, 'I'm one of the O'Hanlon sheep.'

"I think Connor picked his colour to match his own eyes. They sat in a forest of laugh lines because the man always seemed to have a smile on his face. Life amused Connor MacTaggart. Apart from his sheep, the hurling, and the Gaelic football, I don't think he took anything else too seriously, and it showed on his broad face under black hair that stuck out like the bristles of a chimney sweep's brush from beneath his caubeen. He needed a shave, and the stubble on his chin was inky blue.

"I looked at him sitting at the table. He was a big man. More than six feet. He'd big shoulders under his tweed jacket. I'd seen him often enough with his sleeves rolled up, and his arms had muscles on them like you might see on a bull, and yet no one had ever heard of Connor lifting his hand in anger, or indeed his gruff voice either.

"He pulled a dudeen out of his pocket—and before you ask, Hazel, a dudeen's a wee short clay pipe. You'd not see one to-day, but most men smoked them back then. 'Do you mind if I smoke, Mrs. O'Hanlon?' says he to Ma, for he was a polite man, so.

"'Not at all,' says she, taking the teapot back to the shelf beside the range. For a tall, heavy woman she moved lightly across the red-tiled floor.

"I saw how the laugh lines deepened at the corners of her eyes, which were dark like anthracite. Ma's normally ruddy cheeks glowed redder still from the heat of the range. Her mouth curved in a smile.

"Connor stuck the pipe in his mouth, past what in those days was called an Old Bill moustache. I thought it made him look a bit like a walrus. He'd grown it when he'd been a soldier man.

"He lit up. 'Cold day today,' says he. 'My cottage was like one of those igloos this morning. I thought I might find an Eskimo girl had moved in, so.'

"Ma and I laughed. He could make folks laugh, could Connor.

"He'd have had room for someone to move in, for Connor lived on his own in a wee thatched, whitewashed cottage tucked in under the trees at the boundary of his land with ours.

" 'When I got up this morning,' says he, 'my fire was out, and on the bowl of water I'd left out the night before there was ice as big as the berg that sank the *Titanic*.'

" 'Go on with you, Connor,' says Ma. 'You're a terrible man for the exaggeration, so. Never mind icebergs. Why didn't you light your fire and put on more turf?' She held out her hands over the range.

"Her fingers were red from years of washing clothes, scrubbing floors, and kneading the dough for her baking. The knuckles were swollen with the arthritis that would one day stop her knitting. I think the warmth of the stove comforted her joints. They'd got worse since a couple of years ago. Sinead, my biggest sister, had explained to me that Ma was starting to go through the change of life.

"I saw her wince, but in all the years I lived at home I never once heard her complain.

"'Sure, I'd only a few lumps left in the house,' says Connor. 'My turf pile outside's running low and I shouldn't have let it. I know that. I went to get a full load this morning for my peat bog's near the pasture, but . . .' He shrugged.

"I knew he was too polite to continue, but it was obvious that with the sheep in one basket, he'd only brought half a load.

"Connor let go a puff of tobacco smoke. 'I've no desire to go back up there today, nor tomorrow either, because we're playing Dunmanway at the football and I'd not want to miss the match.'

"'Help yourself to some from our pile,' says Ma. 'Sure can't more turf come back anytime?'

"He smiled. 'That's very kind of you, Mrs. O'Hanlon, but I'd not want to be beholden.'

"That remark didn't surprise me. I'd once heard him tell my brother he'd be in no man's debt—not for anything. He was a proud man was Connor MacTaggart. Maybe a bit sensitive because he hadn't a lot of money, nor many prospects of getting any. Sheep farming's a hard life.

"Says he, 'I've no need to. There's a great big tree in the field beside my cottage. It must be fifteen feet high. I pass it morn and night on my way to and home from my sheep. If I fell it today, the chopping of it will warm me, and once it's down I'll get a fire going and have enough wood for the weekend. And a few more days' work with my axe and my saw, and I'll have logs for the winter and to spare, and I can make myself a new *shillelagh* too.'

"I saw Ma frown. 'A shillaylee? And what kind of a tree would it be, Connor?'

"'A blackthorn,' says he. 'That's the wood you make them of. What of it?'"

Hazel Arbuthnot pursed her lips, sucked in a breath, and shook her head. Her black hair rippled in soft waves. "Blackthorn? That's what Jesus' crown of thorns was made of, so it was."

"That's not the half of it," Kinky said. "You should have heard what Ma told Connor. She got very serious. 'Don't you dare touch that tree, Connor MacTaggart. Leave it alone entirely. Entirely, do you hear me now?'

"He laughed. 'Because the faeries, the Doov Shee, live under blackthorns?'

" 'They do, Connor,' Ma said, and I'd not seen her being so serious for a long time. 'Blackthorns are sacred to them, and they do make their homes there, so.'

" 'Och,' says Connor, 'I'm sure they'd not miss one. Ireland's as full of black-thorns as a hawthorn's full of berries in a hard winter.'

" 'Ordinarily,' says Ma, 'the Shee'll not mind if you pick the sloes in the autumn or cut a branch for a walking stick, not if you ask their permission first, but today's dif-ferent. You mustn't touch as much as a twig today.'

"I sat up very straight. 'Why not today especially, Ma?'

" 'It's the eleventh of November.'

"I frowned. 'What's special about No-vember the eleventh? I know it's Armistice Day, but why would the faeries bother about that?'

"Ma shook her head. 'They don't. They have things of their own to mark. Remem-ber the Shee are a very old race, and they still keep the old ways. Didn't we just enjoy Halloween on the eve of All Saints' Day?'

"'Yes, Ma,' I said.

"'Long before Saint Patrick, the last day of October was *Samhain*, the feast to mark the end of the harvest.' Her voice sounded hollow when next she said, 'And November the first was *Feile na Marbh*, the festival of the dead, when spirits walk the earth.'

"'Fayle na Marev?' I felt all goose-pimply, but when I looked over at Connor, he was tapping his teeth with the stem of his pipe—and grinning.

"'Now,' Ma said, 'I can't tell you why November eleventh came to replace the first for the festival of the dead for the little folks. I think it had to do with their refusing to recognize a change in *our* calendar made hundreds of years ago by a Pope Gregory. *Their* year is governed by the seasons and the solstices. It always has been. But whatever the reason, there'll be spirits abroad today and tonight.' She fixed Connor with a gaze that would have raised blisters on a plank. 'And if you don't want to join them . . . leave you that blackthorn alone today, and if you've any wit at all, Connor MacTaggart, leave it alone forever.'

"Connor nodded, 'Thank you for the advice, Mrs. O'Hanlon. I'll certainly think on it.' But I could tell by the tone of his voice she'd not scared him, even though she'd scared me. 'I'll have to be getting on home now,' says he. He rose and came to me. He put his hands in his pocket and pulled out some peppermints. 'Here you are, Maureen.'"

Kinky paused and looked at the children. "Maureen's my real name, by the way, but I don't use it much.

"'Thank you, Connor,' says I.

"'I'll have to be running along now,' says he.

"'And you'll take a load of turf? Won't you?' Ma asked. It wasn't often I heard a pleading tone in her voice.

"'It's very kind, Mrs. O'Hanlon, but sure I'll manage on my own.'

"And I knew, I *knew,* that Connor Mac-Taggart was going home and was going to pay no heed to Ma, and later that day, as sure as the sun rises in the east, he was going to fell that blackthorn."

4

Kinky shifted in her chair and looked at the eager faces. "Now imagine, children, how Connor called for his sheepdog, Tess, took hold of the donkey's halter, and strode down our lane whistling to himself. He was always whistling happy tunes like 'The Rakes of Mallow' or 'Courtin' in the Kitchen.' He was thinking he'd have time for a practice session on his pipes once he had the tree down, the fire blazing in his hearth, his supper eaten, and a wee half-un on the table.

"Wasn't it nice of Mrs. O'Hanlon to try to warn me? he thought to himself, but

God love her, the woman was wasting her breath. If older people chose to believe she was a wise woman, then no harm to them, but this was 1922. The Great War was over—hadn't he fought in it?—and the world had moved along. There were motor cars, electricity, wireless telegraph, moving pictures, aeroplanes, and all the other marvels of the modern age.

"Now don't you look surprised, Dermot Fogarty. It wasn't the Stone Age when I was a little girl. Hadn't Lilian Bland from near Belfast built her own aeroplane called *Moth* and flown it in 1910?"

Kinky smiled to see Dermot blush.

"And didn't she keep the engine going by feeding it whiskey—through her aunt's old ear trumpet?"

"Whiskey? Honest?" Colin asked.

"Honest."

Kinky waited for the laughter to die down, then continued. "Connor knew that things his grandparents would have thought magical were modern science in action now. Folks could choose to believe that the voice coming out of the loudspeaker was a spirit if they wished. But he knew it wasn't.

"'There's not much room for the little

people now, is there, Tess?' says Connor to the dog by his side. 'Faeries? Sure it's hard, having grown up here, *not* to believe in them a bit. But to be *scared* of them?' He shook his head and looked around. It was a grand crisp day.

"A great time to be striding along in County Cork leading the little donkey along the familiar road among the whins and the rowan trees, listening to the cries of a flock of curlew. There were no bright flowers in the grassy banks, but in the summer the road's edges would be alive with buttercups and thistles, honeysuckle and teasles. The white and red dead nettles had only stopped blooming a month ago.

"There was a gentle wind blowing from the direction of the O'Hanlons' farm behind him, and the scent of burning turf was borne on the breeze."

"Excuse me, Mrs. Kincaid," Dorothy said. "Is Cork like County Down?"

Kinky shook her head. "It is not. For a start it's about twice as big. The fields are bigger than the ones up here, and although there do be drystone walls, most meadows are divided by hedges of hawthorn and gorse. There are trees in the hedgerows and growing in woods of ash and sycamore, oak and beech. Cork is a very green place." She felt a lump in her throat, for she missed it yet.

Kinky swallowed, then continued. "It has a great long coastline and fine harbours like Cobh and Bantry, but we lived about ten miles inland from the sea, not on a loughside the way Ballybucklebo is, and our hills rolled down to the faraway shore. There were no drumlins the way there are here in County Down."

"What's a drumlin?" Hazel wanted to know.

Kinky smiled. "I once heard someone say County Down was like a basket of green eggs. You know how there are shmall little rounded hills all over the place?"

"Yes, Mrs. Kincaid."

"Those are drumlins. They were sculpted by the Ice Age, so, but Connor wasn't walking among anything like that. He was covering the mile between our place and his along a flat road that curved around the shoulder of a hill, and as he walked he thought he'd be glad to get home because it wasn't just a great day. No, it was a grand day for felling a tree.

"When he arrived at his cottage at the end of a short lane, Connor took the baskets off the donkey and pastured the little animal. He stacked the turf from the one basket, muttering to himself that there'd not be enough there for many fires, went into his shed, picked up his axe, and headed off.

"He wasted no time walking the hundred yards to the stile in the drystone wall around the field where the tree stood. He clambered straight over, the rough rocks cold against his hand. Tess followed after, her claws making a scrabbling sound.

"It was a clear winter afternoon with the bracken brown and the grass rimed with frost that crunched under his boots as he strode along. Tess startled a rabbit from a clump of yellow-flowered whins, and it scampered away with its ears aflop, its scut a white, bouncing button.

"Connor paused and looked up into cloudless sky so blue and so bright that he had to shade his eyes with his hand. Overhead a murder of crows flew east, and a flock of lapwing, green and crested, flapped along to the west, crying their sad *pee-wit, pee-wit*.

"'Begod,' says Connor to himself, 'but it's a fine day to be alive.'

"You'd have thought he was wearing seven-league boots by the length of the strides of him, and in no time he was standing under the tree. Its main trunk was fifteen feet tall and the other four trunks not much shorter. They were gnarled black, and their branches twisted, naked, and lifeless-looking. He lent his axe against a trunk, took off his jacket and waistcoat, and spat on his hands.

"He bent to pick up his axe, but from behind him he heard a whimpering . . ."

"The Shee . . . the faeries," Colin whispered.

"No," said Kinky, "it was Tess. Connor turned to see that his sheepdog, who normally came and sat at his feet, was still a good ten yards away. She lay with her belly pressed to the grass. Her porcelain blue eyes were fixed on him, and she made a high-pitched whining. 'Come, Tess,' says Connor, but divil the bit does she. Tess puts her tail between her legs and slinks away, looking over her shoulder at him and whimpering.

"'Come here, Tess.' Connor put an edge into his voice.

"She turned, edged sideways back toward him, but still ten yards away she lowered herself to the ground again and refused to budge.

"Connor was puzzled. He'd reared her from a pup. She was such a well-trained, obedient dog he might have entered her in a sheepdog trial, but those events didn't interest him. And here she was misbehaving? Och, well, never mind. 'Bad cess to you then,' Connor says, with a smile. 'I've no time to scold you today.' He spits again and picks up his axe.

"He hoisted it above his shoulder and eyed the first trunk, calculating where to strike. But before he could, he heard a voice. It was the voice of a woman, and it was as harsh as the sound of cinders under a door. 'Go you to your own place, Connor MacTaggart. Go you to your home.' Connor lowered his axe. He put a finger first in his left ear, then in his right. He shook his head. 'I'm hearing things,' says he. He laughed his deep booming laugh. 'I'd better go easy on the *poitín* for a night or two. I knew it could upset your eyes, but I never knew that whiskey could make you hear things too.'

"Connor, without thinking, for the act was so ingrained from his childhood, made the sign to ward off the evil eye and hefted the axe.

"'Connor MacTaggart,' comes the voice again. 'Stay your hand. This is a Shee tree.'

"'And if I don't?' asks he. 'I know the lore. You'll suck my cows dry of their milk, the milk'll go sour in the churn, the calves will be stillborn, and I'll have bad luck for a year and a day. Well, away you go. I don't keep cows and I'm not going to try to churn ewe's milk.' Connor laughed. 'And anyway we know now that it's germs in milk that make it go sour on a hot day, and Mr. McLoughlin, the veterinarian, told me that there's a program on now to vaccinate the cattle against brucellosis, and that's a germ too—it makes cows lose their calves.'

"Connor paused for a minute. He thought to himself that maybe he'd been a bit cruel. 'Look,' he says, 'I'm not saying you don't exist. I simply don't believe you have the power to hurt me. I'm sorry.' And then what do you think he did?"

"You thaid he was thcared of nothing, didn't you, Mithis Kincaid? He thertainly dothen't thound thcared."

Billy Cadogan's lisp didn't stop him joining in. She liked that. "I did say that, Billy," she said. "And he wasn't."

"I think he chopped away."

Kinky saw heads nodding in serious agreement with Billy.

"He did, but not just then. Connor lowered the axe, took two paces back, and walked slowly right round the tree. He looked at every branch, he peered among the roots, and then he stopped. Dead. 'So there you are,' says he, very quietly.

"He was looking at a hole between two roots; a hole such as might have been made by a badger. He bent down and breathed in three times through his nose. There was a faint scent of fox. Well, if the faeries were sharing a den with a fox, didn't he have the answer to both of them?

"He was absolutely convinced he was safe from any powers the Shee might have. But in case, just in case now, he *might* be wrong about that, only to be on the safe side, that was all, he was going to contain them.

"He walked a few paces into the field. If Connor could have made a harvest out of rocks on the MacTaggart farm, he'd have been a rich man indeed. He put down his axe and picked up a boulder, a boulder that it would have taken two ordinary men to lift, so.

"He was panting when he got back to the tree. The cords in his neck stood out like taut hemp ropes. He stood with legs braced apart over the hole and dropped the rock into its mouth. Says he, 'If you're for trying to give me a curse, I'll be long gone before you get that stone out.' Connor had to bend over and put his hands on his knees he was laughing so much. Faeries! Well, maybe he'd allow that they existed, but to be scared of them? Never. 'Unless you've got Jesus there with you— he was good at shifting boulders,' Connor yelled, 'you'll be down there for a while.'"

"Oooh." Jeannie Kennedy clapped one hand over her mouth, then said, "That's an awful thing to say. If your man Mac-Taggart gets punished, it might not be just the faeries after him."

"You're right, Jeannie." For a second Kinky regretted having embellished the story thus. "And all of you remember, you mustn't take the name of the Lord in vain."

"I won't," said Eddie Jingles. "Honest to God, Mrs. Kincaid."

The other children laughed, and Kinky could not hide her smile.

"See you don't," she said, and wagged her finger at him.

"Now," she said, "with the entrance blocked, Connor reckoned it was safe to go to work, but the voice was still saying something. It was muffled by the boulder. He had to bend over to hear.

"The voice had a strange, echoey sound to it. 'Connor MacTaggart, beware of the raven, the fox, and the spider. Beware when the snow flies.'

"'Och, I will so,' says Connor. 'Thanks for the hint.' And he shook his head. By what force could these beings harm a big, strong, modern man like him? Maybe they could influence superstitious folk by the power of suggestion, but not, not by all that was holy, Connor MacTaggart.

"He got his axe, took his stance, hoisted the axe above his shoulder, and swung."

5

"The blade bit into the trunk and the wood chips flew. One just missed hitting Connor in the eye. Sap oozed from the wound.

" 'By the wee man,' says Connor, 'no sap should be flowing at this time of the year. And would you look at the way it's reflecting the light of the sun? It's as red as blood, so.'

"He heard a noise, a *toc-toc-toc*. It was long, loud, and harsh. He turned and saw a black bird strutting toward him. Black as jet it was, with a heavy beak and shaggy throat feathers. Its eyes were small, dark brown, and piercing. It fixed Connor with its gaze, and it croaked, 'Toc.'"

"Excuse me, Mrs. Kincaid, but was it a raven?" Jeannie Kennedy asked. "My mammy says faeries like ravens, so they do."

"They do indeed, especially the queen of the dark faeries, the Doov Shee, the faeries who live under blackthorn trees."

Colin frowned, then asked, "So the crakey woman's voice that telt Connor to leave the tree alone was the voice of their queen. She's sent the bird to warn Connor off, so she has. Sure hadn't she just told him to beware of ravens?"

"She had," Kinky said, "but I don't think Connor was one bit fazed by the bird. He bent over, picked up a stone, and chucked it. He missed, but the bird didn't fly away. It fluttered up into the air over him, flapped its wings at his head, and darted its beak at his eyes.

"Connor threw up an arm to protect himself. He'd heard of mother crows swooping on intruders to protect their nests, but it wasn't nesting time. He felt the bird's beak stabbing at his bare arm. It broke the skin and he felt the hot blood. 'Enough!' he yelled, and he stepped back.

"Now, remember, Connor was a great hurling player. He grasped his axe as he'd hold his *camán,* his hurley. Then he swung and just managed to strike the raven a glancing blow with the flat of the blade, not enough to hurt it, but enough to make it fly to the ground and run around behind the tree.

" 'So,' says he, 'I've to beware of ravens, have I? If they've any sense, they'll beware of me.' He took a quick look at his arm. The wound was only a scratch. He'd had worse at the football.

"He stepped back to his work. 'I'll be as well hanged for stealing a sheep as stealing a lamb,' says he. 'I've started, so I'll finish.' He looked up to where dark clouds were rolling in from the north. 'I'll surely founder tonight for it's going to be even colder than last night. I will be needing a fire to keep me warm, so.'

"He swung again and again, and at every blow the axe bit more deeply, wood chips flew, and the sap flowed red."

She looked from child to child. Hazel

Arbuthnot had both hands clasped in front of her like a pietà. Micky Corry was chewing a fingernail. All wide eyes were on Kinky.

"The trunk began to lean to one side. Connor knew a few more strokes would have it down. He paused to catch his breath before finishing the job. He ran his thumb over the axe blade. Dull. Very dull.

"Well, no matter. He had a whetstone in his jacket pocket. He walked away from the tree, got out the stone, spat on it, and sharpened the blade. As he worked and heard the rough scraping of stone on steel, he noticed an animal scent.

"He glimpsed something russet-red moving on the far side of the tree. Connor tested the blade. It was sharp enough, so he put the stone away and went round to see what it was that had moved.

"The raven had disappeared, but in its place stood a vixen. She stared at Connor and did not seem bothered by the presence of a man. Her eyes were sharp, her muzzle pointed, and her mouth was curled into what looked very like a sneer. And the animal wasn't as browny red as he had first thought. It was more the blood red of the tree's sap—"

"It is the faeries, not crows and foxes," Micky interrupted. "It is! It is!" The boy was shaking with excitement. "I think they sent the raven, but the fox *is* the queen of the Doov Shee herself, that's what I think, so I do."

"So why would you think that? The queen of the faeries is a woman, not a fox." Kinky knew the answer, but she wanted to hear Micky's explanation.

"It doesn't matter because faeries can take on any shape they like, so they can, or change people into things. My Da told me about a fellah called *Tuan Mac Cairill,* and he was around here in Ireland way before *Cúchulain.* Your man *Tuan* got changed into a stag, then a boar, then an eagle, and then a salmon, so he did."

"I know the story," Kinky said, "and I'm sure Connor did too, but he wasn't the kind of man to pay much attention to Irish legends. Sure we know that already. He laughed at the fox, and he turned to Tess, who hadn't budged an inch. 'Get that fox,' he ordered, but Tess, who would have chased anything that moved once he'd told her to, stayed rooted to the ground. So did the fox, its gaze never leaving Connor's eyes.

"'Suit yourself then,' says Connor to Tess. What the blazes had got into the dog today? he wondered. She wouldn't come to him. She'd not hunt. Maybe she needed worming."

"If you ask me," said Carolyn, "I think Tess had more wit than Connor. I'd have run away by now, so I would."

"I think you're right, Carolyn, but there's nothing more stubborn than an Irishman with his mind made up. And to tell the truth, the trunk was beyond help now anyway, and I'm sure the Shee knew it. That was why the vixen had come only to watch. She knew it was too late to try to save her home. She might only want to know how to get revenge on the destroyer.

"'Shoo away, fox,' Connor says, and went at it once more.

"Four more axe strokes and the black-thorn started to topple, and as it did, Connor heard a sound that set his teeth on edge. It was a shrieking like the cry of a wounded hare. It rose to a crescendo, hovered, then died away as the trunk crashed to the ground.

" 'It always makes an awful noise,' says he, 'the last fibres tearing apart as a tree falls. It's nothing unusual.'

"The howling stopped. The crashing of breaking branches stopped. There was silence. Tess made not as much as a yip. No birds sang. The air was lifeless and did not whisper through the grasses. It was a stillness that Connor could hear, could feel.

"He shrugged and went back to work on the rest of the tree still standing. It took him very little time to fell the remaining, smaller trunks.

"He picked up his waistcoat and jacket. Although he'd been sweating from his exertions only a moment ago, Connor felt chilled. The stillness had passed and clouds covered the sky. They were so low they seemed to be growing out of the crests of the hills. A damp, raw wind blew, and a dank mist crept down the slope where Connor stood. The skin of his forearms was pimpled with gooseflesh. He slipped into his outer clothes.

"Connor went to the fallen tree. Taking

great care to avoid the long sharp thorns, he pulled one trunk free enough to give him room to work. In twenty minutes he had it chopped into manageable-sized logs. He laid them alongside each other in a bundle. He'd brought a piece of rope, and he lashed it round the bundle, then went back for his axe. 'Right,' says he to himself. 'I've turf enough for a fire tonight to make my supper and keep me warm, and heat my stirabout tomorrow—'"

"What's stirabout?" Irene wanted to know.

"Porridge," said Kinky. "Connor always had a plate of stirabout for his breakfast, 'but,' says he, 'it'll do no hurt to throw a few logs on the fire too and begin building my woodpile, so I'll start by getting these back to the cottage.' He laid the axe on top of the bundle and lifted them in his two arms. He didn't notice that as he did, some sap dripped onto the left side of his face, where it clung like a blob of red jelly. If he could have seen it in a mirror, he'd have noticed that it was shaped like a spider and the same colour as the vixen."

"And didn't you say the farmers marked

their sheep with coloured paint?" Dorothy asked.

"I did."

"Oooh. Did it mean the Shee had marked Connor as their own?"

"Maybe," Kinky said, "but Connor didn't even know the sap stain was there. 'Home, Tess,' says he, as he strode out. 'We'll get back now and tomorrow we'll rise up early and go and move the sheep in the upper pasture. They've been in the big field long enough. It'll still give us time to go and collect Art for the match; then on our way home we'll come by here and bring a clatter more branches for our woodpile. Doov Shee be damned. We'll still be warm when all the turf's done.' Tess tucked herself at her master's heel as they made for home.

"And the vixen followed them every step of the way, her gaze never leaving the red sap stain on Connor MacTaggart's face."

6

"As soon as he got home, Connor sent Tess to her kennel. He glanced back to the drystone wall and saw the vixen sitting on one of the flat coping stones.

"'You can smile at me all you like, fox,' says he. The animal was starting to irritate Connor. Foxes were meant to be scared of people, not pursue them. 'You'll smile on the other side of your face after I've told the foxhunters or the harriers where to find you. And, by God, I will, whether you are a fox or—and I doubt it yet—a Doov Shee. Get on with you, now.'

"But the fox just sat and stared.

"Connor bent and dumped the bundle of logs and the axe beside the small turf pile at the gable end of his whitewashed cottage. He straightened and looked at the place. It was a tidy little spot. The thatch of the steeply pitched roof was spotted with patches of moss, and the bundles of straw it was made of jutted out over the front wall. Four sets of red-shuttered windows, two to each side, flanked a door that was also painted red. He'd done that job three years ago and it was weathering well.

"He'd lived here, except for his time in the army, for all his twenty-three years. It was small, but when Da and Ma had been alive and his brothers and sister still living there, it had been a happy place. It had been his home.

"His home. The word meant a lot.

"He glanced back at the fox. 'All right,' says Connor, 'maybe I was a bit hasty. Maybe that ould tree was your home, yours and your cubs—for I do not think you're a faerie. So I'm sorry you've been evicted, but what's done is done. If you'll go away with you now, I'll not say a word to the hunt. I've done you hurt enough.'

"The vixen stared right back at Connor.

"'Go on with you,' he said, softening more. 'I suppose the tree had memories for you. This place does for me.' Memories of his elder brothers, both emigrated, one to New Zealand and one to California; of his sister Clodagh, married to a man from Belfast up in the north; and of Da and Ma, God rest them both, gone, both taken by the 1918 Spanish flu.

"Connor knew he was like the Red Indian fellah Chingachgook in one of the books Connor'd loved as a child. He might not be the last of the Mohicans, but he was looking like the last of the MacTaggarts of Beal na mBláth in County Cork, Ireland.

"And if he didn't get warm soon he would freeze, and then he would certainly be the very last and he'd not want that. He had plans to carry on the MacTaggart line—with a bit of help from Fidelma O'Hanlon.

"The thought of her made his smile broaden. He was going to ask her to go with him to the moving-picture house in Clonakilty. Art, who'd been up there last week, had told Connor they'd be showing a flicker called *The Kid* with Charlie

Chaplin. The kinematograph would be nice and warm inside—and dark.

"But that was next Saturday. Connor needed heat tonight. He looked up. There was no blue smoke coming from either of the chimney pots on top of the red-brick stack to put a bit of colour onto the dark face of the sky, but there would be by the time he had a few logs cut to size. He looked over and the animal was still there. 'Suit yourself, fox,' says he, 'but I've work to do.'

"And the fox sat and stared.

"Connor lifted the axe. He trimmed the branches away from the lengths of main trunk. The small ones would make grand kindling. He chopped the larger pieces into short lengths. He'd burn a few of those with the turf tonight. He stacked the rest in a pile, laid the axe on top—he'd see to it later—and carried the logs he had cut into the cottage.

"His kitchen was a friendly place, with its black-oak roof beams, grey tiled floor, and whitewashed walls. There were a couple of faded photos hung on the wall beside a large Welsh dresser, snaps of Ma and Da in their Sunday best. His good china, white plates with blue edging, stood upright on the shelves of the dresser.

"It was the work of moments to build a fire in the stone grate.

"He lit the kindling and as the black-thorn branches started to burn, Connor heard a noise. It was very faint and he had to strain to make out what it was. For all the world you'd have thought it was a baby crying. 'It's a grand evening for my ears,' says he. 'Voices. Falling trees that sound like wounded hares, sap crying like a baby because it's being forced from the wood by the heat of a fire. What'll be next? A ram bleating but sounding like the roaring of an elephant?' He laughed, and now the twigs were well lit, he banked the fire with four pieces of his remaining turf.

"A kettle, already filled, hung from a cast-iron gallows at the side of the hearth. He swung it over to have water boiled for his tea, chucked his coat over the back of a spindle-backed rocking chair, and left to go to the shed where he kept his tools. It wouldn't do to leave the axe uncleaned. The sap from the tree could start the blade rusting.

"The shed was lit by only a small window, but a hurricane lantern stood on the workbench. Connor laid the axe on the bench top, opened the lamp, and adjusted the wick. The smell of paraffin filled the small room. He fumbled in his trouser pocket and pulled out his dudeen and a box of matches, lit his short clay pipe and inhaled the sweet tobacco smoke. Before the match went out, he lit the lamp and closed the little glass door. The light brightened the room and cast his shadow, large and misshapen, against one wall.

" 'Right,' says Connor, 'let's be getting this blade cleaned.' He started to wipe, but the harder he wiped, the more the sap seemed to stick. He was just about to give up when the flame in the hurricane lantern guttered and almost went out. That was strange. The thing was designed to burn in the highest winds.

"The thought distracted him for a second, and losing his grip on the rag, the palm of his hand jerked forward.

"Connor felt the steel bite. The pipe fell from his mouth when he yelled, 'Aagh, Kee-rist!'

"Now I'm sorry, children," Kinky said, "but I know you all recognize that grown-ups do swear now and then, and Connor was no saint, and he'd hurt himself, so."

She looked around and saw sympathetic nods.

"It would not surprise you to hear that Connor dropped the axe, and as he shook his right hand, bright drops of blood spattered the bench top and the front of his waistcoat. 'Sweet mother of Jesus,' he growled, grabbed his right wrist in his left hand, and stared at the wound. The blade had sliced a cut a good two inches across the palm of his hand and—"

"That hurts," Colin Brown said. His face was screwed up into a frown. "I cut my hand on one of my Da's chisels last August, and Doctor Laverty had to give me stitches."

"And like yours did to you, Colin, his wound stung Connor sore. He stared at it for a moment, shook his head, and bent to retrieve his pipe. He knew he had better wash the cut and bandage it up. He blew out the lantern, left the shed, and crossed the yard. In the short time since he'd gone inside, the wind had come up from the east, cold and raw. It was a lazy wind, the kind that wouldn't bother to go round a man. It would just go straight through him.

"He heard a window shutter banging as it flapped.

"It wasn't until he had snibbed the shutter back against the wall and turned for the front door that he noticed the vixen sitting on the wall. Still staring at him. Still sneering. The half gale ruffled her red fur, so beneath it Connor could see the grey of the deeper hairs like the roots on the head of an old woman who used henna.

"Connor shuddered. 'That wind's like a stepmother's breath,' he said, closing the front door behind him. 'Thank goodness I got the fire started so at least it's cosy in here.'

"He crossed the tiled floor to the sink and turned on the cold tap. Since he'd had pipes put in the year before, he hadn't had to use the cast-iron pump with the curved handle that stood outside in the yard. That was a blessing.

"He stuck his hand under the flow, wincing both from the sting in the cut and the bite of the icy water. He forced himself to hold his hand there until the bleeding eased; then he bound the hand in a towel.

"There was a tin box in the cupboard above the sink. The faded scene on the lid was of a heavy-jowled, large-bosomed woman wearing a crown and a severe black dress. She rode in an open carriage. The picture was dated '20 and 21 June, 1887' and was in celebration of the English queen Victoria's Diamond Jubilee. As he lifted out a bandage from his first-aid kit, a huge gust hit the cottage. Smoke was blown down the chimney and his eyes watered. The shutter must have become unfastened again because it made an unholy banging against the wall of the house. It was going to have to wait.

"Connor walked to a corner of the room and looked up to where the timbers of the gable roof truss disappeared under the eaves. Sure enough, he saw what he wanted. A spider's web.

"He brought over a chair and scrambled up so he could get at the web, reached across, and pulled off as much as he could reach. Something scuttled up onto the beam."

"Yeugh. I *hate* spiders," Jeannie Kennedy gasped. "I'd have run a mile. I'm scared stiff of them. Horrible creepy-crawlies."

"Indeed you'd have run from this one," Kinky said. "And so would I. At first, Connor wasn't even sure it was a spider, it was so big."

"Eeuugh." Dorothy was frowning and pulling her head into her shoulders.

"It was like no spider Connor MacTaggart had ever seen. Its belly was as large around as the silver dollar one of the Yankee soldiers had given him in France for a souvenir, and it was fat. The hairs of its belly were a dirty yellow, and he was sure he could see lichen growing in red spots among the hair.

"Its thorax—that's its chest bit between its belly and its head—its thorax was pitch-black except for a pale red mark. Connor peered at the mark and wasn't it—"

"A skull," Mick Corry said confidently. "There's a moth like that called a death's-head hawk moth, so there is."

"Micky collects bugs," Carolyn explained.

"Well," Kinky said, "I'm sorry to disappoint you, Micky, but it wasn't a skull. It was the head of a fox."

Sometimes, Kinky thought, the old expressions are the best. You could have heard a pin drop in the upstairs lounge of Dr. O'Reilly's house at Number 1 Main Street, Ballybucklebo. She waited before continuing. "Its eight legs were striped yellow and black, and each ended in a claw. The creature stared at Connor, and he saw its eyes, hard and black as anthracite. He heard its jaws click. He, who was scared of no man or beast, shrank back. . . .

"It hissed at him like a cat, dropped down a gossamer thread, and scuttled across the tiles with its claws scratching before disappearing into a mousehole.

"Connor wanted the gossamer to help dress his wound. He decided that as the owner was gone, horrid as it might be, he might as well get all he needed from the web before he climbed down. He stripped away more from the beam, and as he did he saw what the spider had been feeding on. It was no fly. It was a sparrow.

"Poor wee bird," she said, "and poor

Connor. I know I told you Connor Mac-Taggart wasn't afraid of anything, but the sight of that half-eaten sparrow in his rafters . . . well, let's just say he was shaky on his feet as he stood on that chair. But he still had to dress his wound so he clambered down and got on with the job.

"He carefully spread the spiderweb gossamer along the length of the cut in his palm . . ."

"Would that not make it suppurate?" Billy Cadogan asked.

"I asked Himself, Doctor O'Reilly, the very question, and he said no. He said it's an old country cure that works well. The gossamer makes a framework for the blood to clot on, and it's from the clot that healing starts, so."

"And did they start you off with gossamer, Colin Brown?" Hazel asked sweetly.

"Why'd you think that?" he asked.

"Because," she said with more hardness in her tones, "you're the biggest clot in Ballybucklebo, so you are."

Kinky had to join in the laughter. Nice one, Hazel, after Colin's dig at you earlier, she thought. "Now settle down," she said, "or I'll never get this story finished. And I must because"—she looked at her watch—"in fifty-four minutes I've things to do in my kitchen, so. Now, hadn't we left Connor in his kitchen?"

"Aye. Wi'a spider's web in his cut," Micky Corry said.

She nodded. "So Connor looks at the cut. The gossamer's dark now, but there's no more blood seeping through, so he bandages it with the gauze. 'It'll be well on the mend by tomorrow,' he says, 'and just as well for I'll have to go to the high pasture.'

"Then he went out into the gale, latched the shutter, came back in, and made himself a cup of tea, extra sweet with three spoonfuls of sugar in it. 'There'll be no pipe practice tonight,' says he, 'with my hand cut, so. Aye, and no football either on the morrow.'

"Still, he comforted himself while sipping his tea, 'While I'll miss playing in the match, with a bit of luck Fidelma will be home. That bears thinking about, and the wee half-un I'd promised myself would help with the thinking.'

"He got up to fetch the bottle, still talking to himself, a habit which I hear comes easy to bachelor men. 'So,' says he, 'if I did truly hear an ould woman's voice, it told me to beware of the raven, the fox, and the spider.' He poured a measure of *poitín* and put the bottle back where it belonged in the rear of the cupboard. 'Well, I've had all three today and they've done me no harm—unless it's this scratch from the bird.' He glanced at his forearm. 'So if that's the worst the Shee can do—if it *is* the faeries—I don't think I'll worry too much even if it *does* snow tonight.' He took a hefty swallow as he remembered the warning from the voice beneath the blackthorn tree, then threw another of the logs on the fire.

"Connor didn't see the spider staring at him from the mousehole. And he hardly heard the weeping of the blackthorn log over the gale outside that racketed and shrieked and banged and tried to rip the thatch off his cottage."

7

"And it is what it was. When Connor arose early the next morning, the gale had nearly blown itself out. He washed his face, but didn't bother shaving, didn't even glance in the mirror. He wanted to get up to the high pasture as soon as he could, see to his flock, and then head on to let the O'Hanlons know why he'd not be joining Art for the football match against Dunmanway.

"He had a quick breakfast; pulled on his heavy boots, his coat, and his caubeen; grabbed his crook; and whistled up Tess.

As he was shutting the door he noticed the clock on the mantel said eight o'clock.

"The wind of the dying storm was sharp against his cheek. There was a heavy rime of frost, but he grinned to himself when he saw there was no snow. So, he thought, I needn't beware of snow today, and a backward glance reassured him that his thatch was intact despite the efforts of the wind the night before.

"It wasn't until they'd crossed the wall that he noticed the vixen. Had it waited all night? Connor wondered. Or with that great rock in the mouth of the hole under the felled blackthorn, had it gone to find another lair? No matter. She was there. A persistent animal to be sure.

"He scanned the heavy grey skies. At least there was no sign of a raven, and even if the spider in the web at home was big enough to eat birds, it wasn't big enough to climb outside and chase him.

"And it is what he said: 'Good luck to you, fox. It's a hard climb to the upper pasture. I hope you do get tired soon, so.' And on he strode.

"Now," Kinky said, "I'm not trying to tell

you that part of County Cork has mountains like the Sperrins or the Mournes, for
it has not. It's mostly good farmland, but
the first MacTaggarts had settled on acres
fit only for sheep.

"Connor did not know how many gener-
ations of his family had lived there. He
only knew that MacTaggart was the English version of the Irish *Mac an tSagairt,*
and it meant 'son of the priest.'"

Jeannie frowned as she said, "Maybe
the Irish king was angry when he gave the
land to Connor's great, great, I don't know
how many greats, grampa, because
priests aren't allowed to get married.
Father O'Toole's not anyway."

Kinky smiled at the mention of the
parish priest. He was a Corkman. "You
could be right, Jeannie," Kinky said, "but
let's get on with our story." She shifted in
her chair. "To get to the upper pasture,
Connor and Tess had a brave ways to
travel.

"It wouldn't be the first time Connor had
wished his family lands were down in the
valley. His fields were in a barren place,
treeless and exposed on the very summit
of the hills. Even in the summer it could

be cold, particularly when the mists crept in. In the winter frigid winds swept the hill-tops, often bringing snow even if there was none on the lower lands.

"Connor shrugged. He could wish, but that would not alter the fact that it was where his best pastures were and he had a living to make. The sooner he got going the better.

"He and Tess could have walked the mile along the main road toward Clon-akilty to reach the gate of the lane down to the O'Hanlon farm, then another two miles past that to a mile-long side road that climbed higher up the hill. It skirted his peat bog and a wide outcropping of flat bare rocks. That was the way he took when he moved the flock up to their graz-ing, but going that way took at least an hour and a half.

"There was a back route in, impassable to sheep and uphill all the way, that he and Tess would use. They'd be in the pasture in thirty minutes, and when he'd finished with the flock he could nip back down the shortcut and take the Clonakilty Road. He'd be at the O'Hanlons' farm before ten.

"He crossed the field where the chopped-down blackthorn lay and made a short detour to stand beside it. On the ground the trunks and bare branches lay mute. Skeletal. Cold. Perhaps he had been a bit impatient in cutting them down.

"The day before, it had been a living thing. Now it was dead. He'd miss the sloe berries he gathered here every autumn. In spring the branches had been nesting perches for the birds, the leaves food for caterpillars; the white flowers held nectar for the bees. Three years ago an owl had used the uppermost branch as a daytime roost before it went hunting at night for small animals like the shrews, voles, and field mice that had their burrows among the roots.

"Connor pulled some branches aside, taking care to avoid the thorns, and sure enough, when he peered down, there was his boulder jammed in the tunnel's mouth. But he also saw that fresh earth had been thrown aside and a new entrance gaped beside the boulder. In the damp soil, he saw tracks—bird and fox tracks. And he smelled the scent no doubt of the same fox that lay just outside a stone's throw, waiting for Connor and Tess. So she hadn't gone searching for a new lair. Instead she had repaired the old one.

"Connor bent down and cupped his hands to his mouth. 'Whoever's down there,' he yelled, 'I'm sorry. I should have left your tree alone, so. But what is done is done.'

"He laughed a bit at himself. Who was he apologizing to? He shrugged. No matter how much a man had learned or seen, beliefs of childhood died hard. He cocked his head. It was probably just the bit of a breeze that had sprung up rattling the dead branches, but the sound he thought he could hear was laughter. Dry, mocking laughter.

"Connor frowned. 'Take a grip on yourself, Connor MacTaggart,' he said. 'There's no need to be imagining you're hearing things two days in a row.' He straightened up. 'Come on, Tess.' And away they went.

"The top end of the field was bordered by a wall. Two leafless elms grew by it. The shadows of their branches were etched, immobile and bony, on the coarse grass below. As he neared, a wood pigeon with grey-blue plumage, white collar, and wings marked with white bars dived from a tree. The clattering of its wing tips meeting with each frantic beat sounded to Connor like a burst of machine-gun fire. The Lord knew he'd heard plenty of that as an eighteen-year-old in the Dublin Fusiliers at Passchendaele in 1917. Weeks he would rather forget.

"He looked over at the vixen and shook his head. Stupid creature if it thought that someone who could survive unscathed for eighteen months on the Western Front was going to worry about the Doov Shee. He'd seen London and Paris. He'd given the little people the benefit of the doubt right up to when he'd said he was sorry down the burrow, but stories about faeries and ghosts were nothing but a load of superstitious, rustic blether to scare the kiddies, and he wasn't going to let it bother him anymore. And that was that."

"It's not blether," Hazel Arbuthnot said. "I'm scared of ghosts. More scared than Jeannie is of spiders."

Kinky saw every head, girls' *and* boys', nod in solemn agreement. "I think," she said very seriously, "you're right to be. I think Connor was wrong.

"He made his way down the side of a bramble- and fern-choked gully and walked along a narrow path at its bottom. The path angled upward and was little more than a rabbit track, just wide enough for him and Tess at his heels. From time to time, he had to stop and pull thorns from his coat, and once when he did this a briar snatched at him as if trying to bar his way.

" 'Begob,' he muttered, dragging a tough stem aside, 'it's even more overgrown than it was the last time I was up this way.'

"After only a few more strides he had to pause and untangle himself again. The moment he was free he heard rustling. Something was forcing its way through the undergrowth. 'Och, well'—he shouted, so that whatever it was could hear him—'the last wolf in Ireland died about 1773, and heaven knows when the last bear or boar lived here, so I'll not be worried whatever you are.'

"Probably rabbits, he thought, or perish the thought, that bl—" Kinky checked herself. Her listeners were children. "That blooming fox. And when finally, a little short of breath and tutting over the plucks in the tweed of his jacket, he came to the field at the end of the gully, he saw he'd been right about the rustling. But what he saw made Connor frown.

"Six rabbits, plump and healthy-looking, were nibbling calmly on the short grass. He glanced at Tess and saw her looking up at him. 'Good dog. Stay.' She'd not hunt unless he told her to, and they'd no time to waste chasing coneys today.

"Beside the rabbits lay the vixen, staring at where the gully opened onto the field. It was as if the rabbits, the fox's natural prey, understood that she wasn't interested in them. She had more important matters on her mind.

"That fox must have something wrong with it, Connor thought. Foxes were shy animals and usually hid from men and dogs. But this one? It had been pursuing him as if she were a man-eating lion, and Connor, who liked his books, had read that man-eaters would ignore antelopes if they were hunting a human.

"He remembered a conversation he'd had during the war. He'd been in a trench at a dressing station with a medical orderly, a Dubliner who was bemoaning the number of cases of lockjaw he was seeing. And he mentioned a rare case of rabies; an infected dog had bitten a soldier. The orderly had laughed and said maybe the generals should try infecting some of the more timid recruits with rabies because when even the mildest animals got it, they'd attack anything.

"Connor knew there was rabies in Europe, but none in Ireland—thank the Lord for the Irish Sea—but maybe this fox had something akin. There had to be an explanation for how it was behaving."

"There was," Micky said. "The fox was the queen of the Doov Shee, and Connor was an eejit not to believe that. He should have heeded your Ma, Mrs. Kincaid."

"Aye, so," she said. "But if he had, I'd not have a story to tell you now, would I?

"Connor kept tramping. He soon reached and skirted the shorter side of the bog where he cut his turf. The brown grasses, where patches of purple heather bloomed despite the lateness of the year, were marked by shallow trenches. They were wide and black-walled where his slane had sliced off slabs of the dark, damp, compressed grass. The line of spade cuts shone wetly in the sunlight.

"The bog squelched under his feet as he strode along. At one end of the nearest trench, sods were stacked in piles drying, waiting to be picked up and transported to the turf heap beside his cottage. 'Never mind using baskets. I'll bring up the cart tomorrow,' he said, looking across to where the fox stood watching. 'If I can take down a decent load, it'll maybe spare me the trouble of cutting up any more black-thorn.'"

Micky Corry interrupted again. "I don't want to hold you up, Mrs. Kincaid, but was Connor being smart because turf burns slower than wood? Or was he maybe . . . maybe, for all his belief in science, starting to worry a wee bit about the faerie tree and wanting to leave the rest of it alone?"

"What do you think, Micky?"

Micky frowned, took a breath, blew it out down his nose, and said, "A bit of both, like?"

"Indeed you could well be right, so," she

said, "but whatever the reason, Connor, having decided, walked on. He wasn't a man to hang about worrying once he'd made up his mind.

"It didn't take him long to come to the end of the bog. Its far edge was marked by outcroppings of great, flat, moss-encrusted slabs of rock. He made his way by leaping from slab to slab, using his crook as a vaulting pole. The hobnails in the soles of his boots gave him purchase on the slippery moss, although once he did feel his foot start to slide and only saved himself from taking a tumble by jamming the butt end of his crook into the ground and leaning heavily on the staff. He paused to get his balance and catch his breath. 'There's times,' says he, 'I could use four legs like you, Tess. I'd not like to take a purler up here. A man could lie for days. Few folks but us come up here.'

"Tess, who was springing from one slab to the next, stopped at the sound of her name, turned, and looked at him. 'Go on,' says he, walking ahead. 'We haven't all day.'

"Off goes Tess, agile as a mountain

goat. The only thing moving through the rocks more nimbly than Tess was . . . the fox.

"The edge of the rocky plateau bordered the upper pasture, which was divided into two sections by a drystone wall. Irregularly shaped tree branches cut to four-foot lengths and trimmed had been driven into the ground at uneven intervals as fence posts. Many leaned to one side or another, creating a haphazard fence on three sides of a two-acre pasture. Rusting barbed wire—in places four strands, at others three—ran from post to post. Dirty tufts of wool hung from the wire where sheep had tried to push through.

"There was not a tree in sight, and the wind tugged at his jacket. The only possibility of shelter was the low stone wall ahead. Connor turned up his collar.

"Past the wall more fields sloped upward and over the crest of the hill. There the grass was greener and longer. Russet clumps of dry benweed stood bowing and rustling.

"His animals were scattered through the nearer, lower enclosure where the grass was cropped short. He was going to move them to the lusher grazing in the higher upper pasture.

"Connor was proud of his flock of black-faced mountain sheep, a breed more common in Mayo, Kerry, and Donegal. Their wool was coarse, and the meat of the lambs sweet. They were hardy animals and could live out of doors year-round on the grass of the pasture and the occasional load of silage in hard weather. He'd been lucky so far this winter. He'd not had to bring in extra feed—not yet.

"The nearest animal wandered in Connor's direction, and he admired its black face with white markings, its short horns, and its squat, compact stature; it was less than two feet high at the withers, weighing no more than forty pounds. If he had to, he could sling one over his shoulders and carry it to his cottage. He laughed when he remembered how, when he'd been a corporal in the British army, his pack, rifle, and equipment had weighed sixty pounds.

"Connor held an upper strand of barbed wire down with one hand and swung his legs over. Tess wriggled under the bottom strand. The fox, as if she knew he'd return this way, didn't bother to come into the pasture. She sat patiently. Watching. Waiting.

"She could wait, he reckoned.

"As Connor crossed the pasture with Tess close to his heels, the sheep clumped together and ran away from him. No matter, the dog would soon round them up. Connor reached the wall and opened a gate. The drystone walls of these fields served less as enclosures and more as depositories for the stones as the land had been cleared.

"From where he stood he could see over the crest. In the distance, twenty miles ahead and a bit to his right, the church spires of Cork City stood proudly above the houses beneath.

"Farther still to his left, from horizon to horizon he could see the ridges and peaks of the Caha and Shehy Mountains separating Cork from neighbouring County Kerry. Closer lay Macroom. Connor grinned. There was a good pub there. He hunched his shoulders and shuddered. He'd not mind being in there now with a glass of hot whiskey in his hand, even if it was only morning, so.

"But Connor knew he had to stop daydreaming and get on with his work. He bent and spoke to Tess, who raced after the sheep, ran past them, and started chivvying the flock back toward the gate. The panicked animals, bumping into each other in their haste to escape, rushed to avoid her, but she kept them hard against the wall and heading toward Connor.

"Connor stood, arms outstretched. With a man threatening ahead and a dog nipping at their heels, the animals had no choice but to run into the next field. As soon as the last one was through, Connor closed the gate. 'Good dog, Tess.' He fondled her head. 'Come on.'

"He walked quickly across the pasture and soon reached the field of flat slabs where he had last seen the vixen. She'd gone. Good.

"Connor started picking his way back down the hillside. Not only was the moss slippery now. A mist had rolled in from nowhere, just as the sudden gale had sprung up yesterday, and even the stones themselves were slick from the moisture in the air.

"It was as cold and clammy as the face of a corpse, and damp to chill a man to the marrow of his bones. He couldn't see more than a few yards, but Connor knew this hill as well as he knew his own kitchen. 'And I'll not be sorry to see the kitchen, Tess,' Connor said, tensing to jump from one slab to the next. As he leapt, out from a billow of fog darted the vixen"—Kinky heard several children gasp and saw that Colin Brown was holding his breath—"right under Connor's feet. He tried not to step on her, felt his boot hit, then slither.

"The next thing Connor knew he was lying on his back on one of the stone slabs. The mist had lifted. He had a ferocious pounding in his head. He'd no idea how long he'd lain there. He pulled out a fob watch. It said two o'clock. Connor started to shake his head in disbelief, but the sharp pain made him stop at once."

She heard Colin exhale. "Jesus," he said, "I thought your man was dead."

"Not big Connor MacTaggart," Kinky said. "It would take more than a rap on the head to kill him dead." She waited a moment to let that thought sink in before she continued. "Tess lay beside him and licked his face. He pushed her off, sat up, and cradled his aching head. When he took his hands away, the bandaged one was covered in fresh blood, and he knew he must have gashed his scalp. He struggled to his feet and supported himself on his crook. Connor looked all around. There was no sign of that cursed fox.

"But then he heard a *toc-toc-toc* from overhead. And when he looked up, he saw through a hole in the fog a black cross against the pale afternoon sky where a raven hovered, stared down, and mocked the man and dog below."

8

"It was too late in the day now to go to the O'Hanlons' farm, and Connor hoped Art had had enough wit to go on to the game without him. Kickoff was at two thirty. Connor'd need to go over there tomorrow, though; if he didn't show up for a couple of days, they'd start to worry about their neighbour and come looking for him.

"But now his clothes were damp, he was cold, his head ached, and he wanted to go home.

"He looked up at the bird. Hadn't he said he wasn't going to let a lot of blether bother him? He yelled at it. 'Some say you're Satan's own bird, some say you're a familiar of the Shee, but I say you're nothing but a raven, and I hope all your "tocking" does give you a sore throat, so.' And with that he started on the long walk home, not bothering once to look up to see if the bird was still there.

"But it was," said Kinky. "Oh, yes. It was.

"When he got home, Connor put Tess in her kennel and let himself into the cottage. He shivered, shrugged out of his damp coat, hung it up, and blew on his hands. He'd been away for so long the fire had gone out and the ashes were cold. But the fire would have to wait. He'd see to it later. He had a headache to beat Banagher.

"He got down the Queen Victoria tin and rummaged through the contents: surgical lint, cotton wool, a jar of Vaseline, some stomach powders, a little bottle of castor oil, a few sticking plasters, and what he was looking for, a box of aspirin. He took two tablets, and without even bothering with a drink of water he swallowed them whole.

"Then he had a look at himself in the

mirror he used on those few days when he actually shaved. Blood was matted in the hair on the right side of his head. He'd see to that after he'd lit a fire. He peered more closely at himself; the daylight was starting to fade, but in the half-light he could see red stuff sticking to the left side of his face. It looked like some of the sap that had come out of the blackthorn.

"He inspected it more closely. It wasn't an irregular blob, but had a definite shape. It couldn't be, could it? It could not. Not at all. Not . . . at . . . all, he thought. He was imagining things. If he could just put this newfound imagination to work, maybe he could write a book and get rich. And yet . . . He peered at his reflection, shook his head, then glanced up to where he'd got the cobweb gossamer yesterday. There was no sign of the creature.

"He looked back at the mirror. In this light, he could persuade himself, just barely persuade himself, that he was seeing the shape of a spider. There was its fat belly, its legs, the claws at their ends, and two curved, jagged mandibles."

"Mandiwhats?" Irene asked.

"It's a big word; I'm sorry, Irene. It means jaws."

"I don't like the sound of that one bit, so I don't," Jeannie said.

"Nor did Connor. He touched it. The surface was hard and not a piece came away on his fingertips. It must have been there since he'd cut down the tree. He knew the juices of plants could be like that. If you were silly enough to pull dandelions and get the white sap from inside the stems on your hands, they'd be black for days. Blackthorn sap must be like that too, he told himself."

"You'd have to be the right buck eejit to pull a bunch of dandelions, so you would," said Micky seriously. "*Everybody* knows if you do you'll wet the bed that night."

Kinky thought it was interesting how different parts of the country had their own lore. Where she came from, some people believed that if a man didn't shave on a Sunday he'd never get a toothache, but if you had a toothache or a gumboil, then carrying the two jawbones of a haddock in your pocket was a sure cure. Out on the west coast, they swore you should never ask a question of a dog, for if it gives you an answer you will surely die.

"Never mind that about dandelions, Micky," Irene said. "What did Connor do?"

"He grabbed a towel, moistened it, and dabbed at the stain. Divil the bit came off on the towel. He scrubbed harder, harder, but not a bit of it would budge. He gave up. 'What can't be cured,' says he, 'must be endured. Getting the sap off won't warm me up, and I'm frozen to the marrow.'

"So he got some kindling and more branches and lit the fire, and as it was taking, he set to cleaning the blood out of his hair. There was a bump and a small cut, but a few days should see it healed.

"The aspirin was starting to take effect and the fire was burning well, but he'd soon be out of peat again. Tomorrow he'd get the cart, drop by the O'Hanlons', then go up to the bog. And sure if he needed more wood, wasn't there still the black- thorn up in the field?

"He warmed himself in front of the fire. All in all, as the chill left him and his pants started to steam and dry out, Connor reck- oned things were improving, but now he'd stopped shivering he was hungry. He didn't feel like cooking his supper tonight. He'd make a cup of tea and in his pantry he had a couple of crubeens, boiled pigs' feet, to be eaten cold with vinegar."

"Pigs' what? Trotters?" Colin screwed up his face. "I'd rather have skate and chips." He looked at her. "Are you making that up to make us feel yucky, Mrs. Kincaid?"

"Not at all, Colin Brown. They are delicious, so. You should try them." She let her gaze sweep over the other young faces. "Do any of you know why a pig is such a valuable animal?"

There was nothing but the shaking of heads.

"Well, I'll tell you," she said. "You can eat every part of it except . . . except its grunt."

She had to wait for the giggling to stop before she could get back to the story. "Now," said Kinky, "by the time Connor had finished his supper, this is what it was: it was dark outside, for the sun had gone down, so, and the fog had rolled in. When he went to draw the curtains, he could see it through the window, thick and wet and chilling.

"He put his plates in the sink and pulled a book from a shelf, an old friend, *The Hound of the Baskervilles.* He moved the paraffin lamp and his rocking chair closer to the fire. Sure with the fog out there and he cosy in here, and content now he'd made up his mind not to be even remotely scared of faeries that didn't exist anyway, wasn't it just the night for a story about foggy moors and Sherlock Holmes and a great big, ghostly dog?

"He sat and started to read. That Doctor Watson was an awful plodder of a man. Connor smiled. The fire warmed him. He thought he might just have a drop of the pure later. The cottage was cosy and safe . . . until he heard a clicking coming from—"

Kinky was interrupted by the sound of ringing from the hall telephone. She flinched. "Hang on," she said. "I'll have to answer that. It could be a patient. People don't stop getting sick just because it's Christmas Day." She left the lounge and headed downstairs, hearing the children's chatter start quietly then begin to rise in volume.

It wasn't a patient; it was Jeannie Jingles on the phone. She'd met Maggie MacCorkle on the street, who'd told her she'd seen the children being brought in to Number 1. Jeannie was annoyed that Eddie, who was still recovering from pneumonia, was with them. He'd been told to come home when he'd been out for an hour.

Kinky reassured Jeannie that Eddie was inside, warm and well, and she'd send him home very soon.

Jeannie thanked Kinky, said she wanted him home by one, and because he'd been sick could someone walk him home?

Kinky reassured Jeannie, then went back up to the lounge.

The children had divided themselves into two factions. There was the "It's all right, Connor's going to be fine" group, headed by Hazel, and the "Connor's in deep trouble, the Shee are going to get him" party, headed by Colin Brown. Ireland in a nutshell, Kinky thought, the people ready to argue over anything.

"Settle down now," she said. "Settle down. That was your mammy on the phone, Eddie Jingles. She says you're not to stay too late.

"Have I to go home right now? Before you finish?" Eddie's lower lip trembled.

"No," said Kinky. "It's twelve fifteen now so you've another three quarters of an hour, if Hazel will walk you home, your mammy said. She doesn't want you out by yourself."

"I will. Sure I only live two doors away from Eddie," Hazel said.

Kinky thought the look Eddie gave Hazel would have served well on the face of a recently rescued shipwrecked sailor. She looked at her watch. "Settle down. Time is moving on, so."

She sat. "And this is what it was. Connor had heard a clicking. He looked around, but he couldn't see the spider." She lowered her voice to a whisper. "He listened, listened. There. The noise was coming from the cupboard over the sink.

"Connor rose very quietly and took a firm grip on his book. One good clout with it would make short shrift of the spider. He opened the cupboard door sloooowly, slooowly . . ."—she let her voice rise— "and jumped back!

"The *poitín* bottle tumbled out and

smashed in the sink, the fumes of the spirits stinging his nose. And the spider, pausing only to fix Connor with its hard eyes for a moment, hissed and scuttled out of the cupboard, leapt onto Connor's shoulder, and bit his ear."

"Jesus, Mary, and Joseph," Jeannie Kennedy whispered and crossed herself.

"Connor hit himself an awful rap on the shoulder with his book, but the spider was too quick. It had already hurled itself onto the floor and skittered into the mousehole before he could stamp his foot on it."

"You see, Hazel?" Colin sounded smug. "The Shee *are* out to get him, so they are."

Kinky ignored Colin. "Certainly Connor, who had been so sure that even if they did exist, the faeries were no threat, was having second thoughts now. He knew, he absolutely knew, that last night he'd put the bottle at the back of the cupboard. *Something* had pushed it to the front. And while he knew spiders would bite if you picked one up or tried to break its web with your finger, he'd never heard of one deliberately attacking.

"At least there was one good thing, he

thought, as he rubbed his ear. As far as he knew, there were no poisonous spiders in Ireland."

"Nor no thnakes, neither," said Billy Cadogan. "Thaint Patrick drove them out, tho he did."

"He did," said Kinky. "At least that's what the legend says. But maybe it was the Druids he drove out of Ireland. The snake was one of the Druids' chief symbols. Snakes shed their skin every year, and the Druids thought snakes died and came back to life, that they had eternal life and had to be worshipped."

"Never mind Saint Patrick. I think the Shee are trying to drive Connor out." Eddie Jingles looked very serious.

"And do you know, Eddie? Connor wasn't sure. He was willing to accept that there were things science could not explain; he was even able to grant that there might be such creatures as faeries. After all, sensible people believe there is a monster in Loch Ness in Scotland."

"Aye," said Eddie, "and I've seen a photo taken of it a wheen of years ago. There is one, right enough."

"Connor couldn't have seen that picture,

Eddie. It was taken after his time, but he did know that in August of the year 565, Saint Columba had rescued a man from the creature by ordering it to return to the depths of the loch. So, if there was a monster, there *might* be faeries. He reckoned he might have annoyed them by cutting down their tree. He rubbed his ear and felt the aches from his head and his hand, and the tingling in his forearm from the raven's peck.

"He glowered at the mess of broken glass in the sink. There would be no *poitín* tonight for a drop of comfort, he thought. And how in the name of the wee man could a spider, even one as big as that brute, be strong enough to shift a bottle?

"Connor shook his head. All right. *All right*. Perhaps the faeries *were* trying to annoy him, but to believe they could do him serious hurt when the whole German army couldn't was a hard lump to swallow. Wasn't it? he asked himself. Wasn't it?

"He was puzzling on this when he heard a new noise from outside, a scrabbling on the door, a *scritch-scritch-scratch.* It sounded like an animal's claws."

"The Hound of the Baskervilles," Micky said, with an evil grin.

"More like a fox," a wide-eyed Dermot Fogarty gasped.

"That's what Connor thought," Kinky said. "Or something in the shape of a fox. He could hear his pulse hammering in his ears. His mouth was dry. His palms were sweaty.

"*Scritch-scritch-scratch.* And now he could hear a low-pitched whining. He went to the corner, lifted his double-breasted shotgun, loaded it, and went to the door.

"He cocked both hammers, threw the door wide, and stepped swiftly back. He jammed the butt of the gun into his shoulder, but as he aimed and tightened his finger on the trigger, he saw what had been scratching.

"'Tess . . . Tessie.' Connor lowered the gun and uncocked it. 'Och, Tessie, I could have killed you.' He knelt and put his arms round the dog's neck. He could smell her, feel her hot breath and wet rough tongue on his cheek. 'So you didn't like being out there all alone in the fog? I don't blame you.

"'Tonight,' he said, as he closed and

bolted the door, 'you're sleeping in here.' And he wasn't sure if it was because the dog hated the fog or because he wouldn't object to having her company. He led her to the fire. 'Down.' She settled, put her head on her front paws, and stared at him.

"Connor sat back into his chair. The bump on his head throbbed, his forearm itched, his ear smarted, the cut on his palm stung. And he knew that he'd been rattled just before he'd opened the door, not knowing what might be on the other side.

"He'd go to the O'Hanlons' tomorrow all right on his way to the peat bog. He'd ask Mrs. O'Hanlon's opinion—everyone knew she was a wise woman. He didn't have to take her advice if he didn't want to.

"But she might have some ideas about why he thought he'd heard a voice telling him to beware the fox, the raven, and the spider.

"Maybe he'd just ask her about that— before the snow flew."

9

"Next morning, a Monday it was, Connor put the donkey between the shafts of the cart, called for Tess, and set off for our farm and his peat bog. There were no snow clouds and the fog had gone. It was one of those November days when the sky is blue as a forget-me-not, the air crisp in your lungs, and the light so bright the edges of everything look as if they'd been etched with a sharp chisel. All the colours—the yellows, the russets, the greens, the reds—were bright enamels, not the usual pale pastels and charcoals of winter.

"His nose was full of the scents of whin flowers and peat smoke and ploughed earth.

"The sounds of the countryside were crisp, of hooves and iron-rimmed wheels on tarmac, jackdaws and rooks cawing across the sky, sheep bleating, and over the next hill, from down in the valley, the barking of a dog.

"And there was not a fox nor a raven to be seen.

"Connor strode along, whistling to himself 'The Wearing of the Green,' 'Planxty Gordon,' 'The Wind That Shakes the Barley.' Maybe, he thought, now the night was over, he was making a fuss about nothing. Maybe, after he'd apologized for not showing up yesterday, he'd say nothing to Mrs. O'Hanlon. If he did, he knew she'd take him seriously, but Fidelma might laugh at him. And he'd not like her to think him a foolish, ill-educated, superstitious man.

"Of course, he remembered, on a Monday she'd be at her work at the linen mill in Clonakilty, so he'd no need to worry about her overhearing. But he decided he'd think on it later, for the sun was warming the air. It was a day to lift his spirits and banish his concerns."

"Sounds lovely, Mrs. Kincaid," Dorothy said.

Kinky smiled. "It was, and wasn't I stuck at home with the bronchitis?"

"Bet you got off school for a clatter of days. That's wheeker, so it is." Colin was clearly envious.

"I liked school, and I'd rather have been there than bundled up in a blanket, sitting in the kitchen, coughing and keeping Ma company while she washed pots in the sink. Mind you, if I hadn't been at home, I'd not have heard the things I'm going to tell you next.

"There was a knock on the door and in comes Connor. I thought it strange the way he had his scarf wrapped round his face.

"'Good morning, O'Hanlons,' says he. 'Can I come in?'

"'Come right ahead,' says Ma. 'I'm glad to see you looking fit and well. We were worried about you yesterday. Art had to go on to the match by himself. We won, by the way.'

"'Grand, so,' he said. 'Something came

up. I couldn't make it so I popped in today to let you know I'm fine.' Then he noticed me sitting by the stove. 'Are you not at yourself, Maureen?' he enquired.

"I shook my head and coughed.

" 'Well, I hope you'll soon be better,' says he, and with such a smile in his eyes didn't I feel the healing in it? 'I'm sorry I've no sweeties today.'

" 'Thanks, but never worry,' I said. 'My throat's too scratchy to eat them.'

" 'And how are you, Connor?' Ma asked. 'I see by the bandage on your hand you've been in the wars.'

" 'Och, sure I was clumsy. I cut myself. It's nothing. Nothing at all.' And yet by the tone of his voice it didn't sound like nothing. As he spoke, his scarf slipped and I saw a red stain on his face.

"Ma frowned as she looked at it; then she dried her hands on her apron, went to the kitchen table, sat, and said, 'Connor MacTaggart, it is none of my business, so, but if you'd care to, have a seat and tell me about what it is that does be troubling you.'

"I watched him hesitate, start to shake his head, and then make as if to speak.

Suddenly, he tore off his caubeen, held it in one hand, jerked out a chair, and sat at the table. I think they both forgot about me, so I just held my wheest and sat there listening like a fly on the wall.

"'Mrs. O'Hanlon,' he said, 'I'm not sure how to start, but . . .' He grinned. 'Mrs. O'Hanlon, I feel an awful buck eejit . . .'

"'There's no need, Connor,' Ma said. 'A lot of folks get embarrassed when they want to talk about the Shee.'

"Connor started back in his chair. 'How did you know what I wanted?'

"It was Ma's turn to smile. 'Do you think it's because I have the sight?'

"Connor swallowed. 'The people in these parts do say so.'

"Now she laughed. 'It's not that, Connor. It's not magic. You were bound and determined to cut down a blackthorn on Saturday, were you not?'

"He hung his head.

"'Since then you've been having bad luck. You cut your hand . . .'

"His eyes widened and he glanced at his bandage. 'I hit my head a ferocious dunder, too,' he said in a low voice.

"Ma leant forward, took his chin in one

hand, and turned his head. She peered, then took a short, sudden breath. 'And the Shee have marked you, so,' she said.

"Connor's hand stroked his cheek. 'I thought it was only sap.'

"Ma said nothing. She just looked at him and for a moment her black eyes were soft as if she were gazing on a sick child. Then her eyelids narrowed and she said with an edge in her voice, 'Connor MacTaggart, you do know fine it's *not* sap.'

"I'd only ever heard her sound like that if one of us children was for getting their head in their hands. I stared at Connor and I wondered if he was for it.

"Connor looked down at the floor, fiddled with his caubeen, sighed, then said quietly, 'I'm not saying I'm asking for help now, but supposing . . . just supposing a fellah *thought* the Shee were after him . . . is there any way at all to get them to go away? Put out milk at night or leave the fire burning so they can warm themselves while we're asleep?'

"Ma sighed. 'They do like those things, or even a drop of *poitín* left in the glass, but they won't be put off by a drink or a bit of warm if they're cross and are torment-ing a body.' Ma leant back and folded her arms across her bosom. 'For an animal being plagued by the faeries you take a hot coal and you sweep it all round the beast and above and below . . . but I don't think it would work for a man. Not if they're really angry—' "

"And they can get fit to be tied," Micky Corry broke in. "My mammy told me one night when I wouldn't go to sleep that the faeries would get cross as two sticks with me and they'd come and take me away and leave an old creature with a narrow face and bony fingers in my place . . ."

Kinky saw Colin Brown on the verge of making a comment, probably a sarcastic one, then obviously thinking better of it and staying silent.

"And she said if they did, she'd have to pass the . . . she called it a changeling . . . she'd have to pass it through a black-smith's fire to get it to go and me to come back."

"Honest to God?" Dorothy asked, wide-eyed.

"Cross my heart," Micky said and did.

"And she said there's worser things too, isn't that right, Mrs. Kincaid?"

"It is. I heard of one that very November morning from my Ma. 'Connor,' says she, 'it was a blackthorn and it was the eleventh of this month. 'Twas a terrible thing you did, so.'

"Connor blushed and hung his head.

" 'There's only one thing that I know that *might* work.'

" 'I'm listening,' says Connor.

" 'Tell me, Connor, have you seen any strange animals?'

"He stiffened. His face paled. 'There's a vixen and a raven hanging around at my place.'

"Ma pursed her lips and blew out a very long breath. 'And the fox has her lair under where the blackthorn stood, for there is a tunnel there?'

" 'There is.' And from Connor's voice I could tell he wondered how she knew that.

" 'Then go to it at the next full moon and speak into it, and tell them you want forgiveness, and to prove it say you're willing to undergo a "clearing." ' "

"Connor frowned. 'I've heard of a thing like that,' he said. 'Wasn't it a way a man could prove his innocence?'

" 'It was,' Ma said, 'but you don't want that. You're guilty. You cut down their tree. It's forgiveness *you* want.'

" 'I've told them I'm sorry.'

" 'And did you hit your head before or after you told them?'

" 'After. The vixen tripped me up.'

" 'A vixen? Aye, so. And have you seen that raven that's been around your farm since the fox did trip you?'

" 'I have.'

" 'Then they don't believe you and you'll have to convince them.'

" 'But how?' I could hear worry in Connor's voice.

" 'You must get a skull from a churchyard . . . '"

For a moment, Kinky hesitated to tell them any more, but she'd seen these kiddies at Halloween. Talk of skulls would not bother them. Not one jot or tittle.

Kinky continued. " 'You take it by a full moon to the burrow, and you kiss the skull—'"

"Yeuch," Irene said. "That would be nearly as bad as kissing Dermot Fogarty."

All the girls giggled. Dermot blushed. Kinky smiled and carried on.

"'—and you get down on your knees, and you swear the curse of the Druids, and if you don't know it, I'll teach it to you,' said Ma. 'It is so terrible it is not in the English language at all. You swear by it you are telling the truth, and you tell the Shee that if you tell a lie then all the sins of the skull when it was alive will become your sins for eternity—'"

"Oooh." Jeannie Kennedy crossed herself.

"'Then you tell them in all truth you know you were wrong to cut down their tree, and in truth you are very, very sorry, and you beg their forgiveness.'

"'I find it hard to ask that from any man,' Connor said quietly.

"'Do it this time, Connor MacTaggart,' Ma said, and there was a hardness in her voice. 'Do it this time and then wait.'

"'For what?' Connor asked.

"'For the faerie music on pipes and harps, and if they play to you, they believe you and you are forgiven.' She smiled. 'And you'll have learnt new music for your pipes. All the great Irish pipers, and harpists like blind Turlough O'Carolan, were taught by the faeries.'

" 'But if they do not play?'

"I'd never seen Ma look so sad. 'Connor MacTaggart, pray that they do, for if they do not, no mortal man nor mortal woman can help you.'

"And Connor took a very deep breath.

"Before he could say more, the back door opened and in came my seventeen-year-old sister, Fidelma. 'They sent us home early today. One of the looms broke down and—' She saw Connor. 'Mr. MacTaggart,' says she, 'I *thought* that was your donkey and cart in the yard. What brings you here today?'

"He leapt to his feet. 'I came to have a word with your Ma.'

"I thought he was going to swallow his pride and tell Fidelma why, but divil the bit. 'To seek her permission to ask you to come to the pictures with me in Clonakilty on Saturday.' He turned and looked at Ma.

" 'I probably should say no. You're young yet, Fidelma,' she said. 'But go ahead, Mr. MacTaggart.' She explained to me later that she hoped if Connor had somebody else to worry about instead of just himself, he might unbend and go and tell the wee folk he was sorry.

" 'Well?' he said.

" 'I'd love to.'

"Connor grinned like a hyena. 'I'll collect you at five then, and I'll have her back in good time,' he told Ma. 'But now'—he crammed his caubeen back on his head—'I've peat to collect from the bog, and standing here with both legs the same length won't get the baby a new coat.'

"He headed for the door, then stopped. 'I do thank you very much for your advice, Mrs. O'Hanlon. I may well follow it, but it's a couple of weeks till the moon is at the full so I'll have time to think on it. I'll get the teaching from you if I'm going to use it.'

" 'You think hard, Connor,' Ma said, 'and the teaching's yours for the asking, but I'll say no more for now, and nor will Maureen.'

"And I knew by the look she gave me I'd been told to keep my own counsel.

" 'Look after yourself, young Maureen,'

says he to me. 'Saturday it is, Fidelma.' And before he was out of the door, he had started to sing 'The Star of the County Down,' and I wondered if he was, in his mind, thinking of Fidelma instead of the girl Rosie McCann in the song.

"And if he was, I wondered, would he ever be able to make the last lines come true?

Though with rust my plough turns brown
Till a smiling bride by my own fireside,
Sits the Star of the County Down.

"I looked over at Ma. Her head was half turned from me, but I could see a single tear on her cheek. And my heart ached for Connor and my sister."

10

"And that tear was the last time Ma let her true feelings about Connor and the faeries show, at least until Saint Stephen's Day. Nor did she ever ask him to his face if he'd taken her advice, even though she'd plenty of opportunities over the weeks up to Christmas. Because he didn't ask her to teach him the Druid curse, she was quite able to draw her own conclusions—that and by the odd things that happened to him, and I'm going to tell you about them.

"This is what it was. We saw a lot more of Connor after he'd taken Fidelma to the pictures. When they came back she was glowing, and within two weeks everybody in the townland—aye, and many in Clonakilty—knew Connor MacTaggart and Fidelma O'Hanlon were walking out. I think she'd driven any of his worries about the Shee right out of his head. He was smitten. You could tell by the way he couldn't keep his eyes off her, kept trying to hold her hand when he thought no one was watching. He was always looking for an excuse just to pop by.

"I heard Da wonder aloud one day did Connor not have a home of his own to go to; he seemed to be spending so much time at our place, so.

"And every time he came over it seemed some fresh difficulty had arisen. His donkey had thrown a shoe. Two shutters had blown off in a gale. His thatch was leaking. His pipes had clogged up and he'd had to go back to using his pump.

"Ma didn't say much, but I saw her shake her head each time Connor mentioned a new misfortune, even though he always told the story with a laugh at himself and a great shrugging of his shoulders as if it was of no matter.

"Fidelma paid no attention to those things. 'Sure,' she told me one Saturday when I was feeding the chickens and she was hanging out the washing to dry, 'anybody can have a bit of bad luck.' I know she thought he was the most wonderful man in the world and, as far as she was concerned, could do no wrong. If you could have seen the eyes of her, the way they sparkled when she spoke of him.

"'Och, sure,' I told her, as I scattered corn from my pail. 'You think he walks on water. He's only just a shepherd man, so, and poor as a church mouse at that.'

"'And you,' she told me, 'are too young to be jealous . . . so hould your wheest.'"

Kinky smiled and said, almost to herself, "Any of you with older sisters know what it's like when you're young." She saw several heads nodding.

"Then I said, 'I think he cares a lot more for his sheep than he does for you,' and I had to drop my pail and run off because Fidelma dumped her laundry basket and took a charge at me, yelling, 'I'll kill you dead, Maureen O'Hanlon, you wee hussy!'

"And his flock did matter, maybe not as much as I'd told Fidelma, but the only time I saw Connor really upset was when three of his sheep sickened with the foot rot. I told you that, before Fidelma, he only really cared for three things: hurling, football, and his sheep. To have his animals sick pained him sore. He neglected Fidelma for days to watch over the rest of his flock, for if you don't isolate the animals with the rot, it can spread fast. He always put his animals before himself, and it was so bitter and damp on the high pastures that he came down with an awful cold and a chest cough.

"Ma made up a cure with wild cherry bark, aniseed, and dried wild lettuce mixed with honey and nine hairs from the tail of a black cat chopped up fine and sprinkled on it. She handed it to him and stood over him with her arms akimbo, a frown on her face. 'And you'll get that down you now, Connor MacTaggart. All of it. Every last drop.'

"'Yes, sergeant,' Connor said meekly, then grinned at me. 'It's like being back in the army when your Ma's in that mood.'

"And he was right. Our Ma loved us all, but she was no softie, and heaven help any one of us who'd left a chore undone.

"After Connor'd drunk it all down and pulled a funny face, Ma asked him, 'And do you still see foxes and ravens, Connor?'

"As I remember, it was one day in the middle of December, when the full moon had come and gone, and maybe that's why she asked him then.

"And his answer was not a lie, for I've told you Connor never told lies. He said, 'Och sure, isn't Ireland full of foxes and ravens?'

" 'Indeed it is, Connor,' was what Ma said. 'Indeed it is.' And her voice was sad. I think she wanted to change the subject so she coughed and said, with a smile, 'And will you be spending Christmas with us, Connor?'

"Connor's grin was as wide as Galway Bay. He said, 'I'd love that, Mrs. O'Hanlon, for I've no family of my own nearby.'

" 'Well,' says she, 'come on Christmas morning and bring your toothbrush; you'll likely want to stay until Saint Stephen's Day.' "

"Oooh, and is that when Connor meets the Saint Stephen's Day ghost?" Micky asked.

"Just you bide, Micky, and you'll find out very soon. There's a little more I need to tell you first.

"It was maybe a more subdued Christmas season that year. You're all too young to remember it the way I do, but there was a civil war going on in Ireland. It was in August 1922, at Beal na mBláth, that a very important man in the brand-new Irish government, a man called Michael Collins, was ambushed and shot dead.

"He wasn't shot on *our* farm, and anyway, long before that my Da had said that the O'Hanlons were having no part of the Troubles. Us O'Hanlons kept ourselves to ourselves and let the outside world go about its business. Most of our close neighbours were of the same mind, although many people in West Cork did take sides, mostly Republican.

"Ma and Da had both said that never mind the earlier shenanigans near where we lived; this Christmas would be no different from any other and we'd enjoy it to the full.

"Da, God rest him, and my big brothers Art and Tiernan had walked four miles to cut the Yule log and drag it home.

"We'd to light it from last year's log and it had to burn for twelve hours with enough left to start next year's. Some folks today talk about Yule being celebrated years before Christmas ever came about. Way back, what we call Christmas now, what the European Celts called Yule, was *Alban Arthuan* to us Irish.

"We went to church in the morning. We'd all got our presents before. Soon after we came back, the house was full. All the family was there and most of the guests who'd be staying for dinner. There was Malachy Aherne, the fellah my sister Sinead—she was the oldest girl at twenty-two—was walking out with. And Emer Mullan, the lass my big brother Art was going to marry the following April. They'd both come for the day and for dinner and to stay that night.

"It's a good thing ours was a big farmhouse.

"The kitchen was a grand room that opened onto the barnyard through an inside door, a porch, and an outside half door. You could open the top and leave the bottom shut to keep the hens out or open it all so people could come and go.

"And come and go they did that day. Neighbours kept dropping in for a wee jar . . . or two.

"A big porcelain sink stood in the middle of a counter. Da had bottles and glasses on that counter, and us girls took turns washing and drying the dirty glasses.

"Ma was always near, working at the big black cast-iron range at the end of the room opposite the porch door. It burnt turf and was never allowed to go out, for it was stove top, oven, water heater, and heater of the kitchen. The range and Ma together were the hearts of the O'Hanlon family and the kitchen was her domain.

"There were always half a dozen smoked hams hanging in nets from the thick black-painted beam that crossed the centre of the ceiling.

"Beneath the beam, half the room was taken up by a solid bog-oak dining table that, with its leaves in, could seat twelve.

"With family there and folks arriving, even our big kitchen kept getting crowded, and Connor was the last of those staying to come.

"I'd got a spinning wheel from Ma and Da. I was in the living room sitting on the stool behind it, trying out the treadle and the spindle. Sinead was in the kitchen taking her turn washing glasses, and Fidelma was supposed to be helping me, but her heart wasn't in it. She kept glancing at the door.

" 'Look, Fidelma,' I said, perhaps a bit tersely, 'if you don't really want to help . . . go away.'

" 'And a Merry Christmas to you too, Shrimp.' That's what she always called me if she was annoyed with me.

" 'We all know you're soft in the head for Connor. Soft in the he-ead. Soft in the he-ead.' I remember sticking my tongue out at her."

"Did you not get on with your sister?" Carolyn Kyle asked, looking pointedly at her twin, Dorothy.

Kinky laughed. "You two should know better than most. I've always *loved* Fidelma . . . but when I was fourteen I didn't always *like* her very much."

The Kyle twins nodded sagely.

"Anyhow, Fidelma scowled at me. 'Grow up, Shrimp, or I'll—'

" 'I'm growing as fast as I—' It was as far as I got. I heard noises in the kitchen.

"Fidelma leapt to her feet and ran.

"I followed her. The smells . . . well, just remembering them now they make my mouth water, and you could hardly hear yourself think for the clattering of pots on the range top and the chattering of lids letting steam escape.

" 'Merry Christmas, Connor MacTaggart,' says Fidelma.

"Connor carried a case that he set on the floor. 'My pipes,' he said. He wore a duncher and had a scarf wrapped round the lower part of his face. He offs with the flat cap and unwinds his scarf. By now we'd all got used to the red mark on his face.

" 'Merry Christmas to this house,' says Connor, blowing on his hands and starting to shrug out of his coat. 'It's grand to be inside, so. There's a cold wind out there that would scythe corn. It'll snow before morning.'

" 'You're right,' says Ma, 'and it will be a big blizzard, so.'

" 'If it is,' says Connor, 'I'm for a trip up to the high pasture. I'll need to bring feed up to the flock. They've had enough trouble this winter without having to go hungry too.'

"'It will snow,' says Ma, 'and your sheep can manage well enough without you. You might be better to let them be, Connor MacTaggart.'

"There was something in the tone of her voice, a tone I'd only ever heard when she'd suggest something important to others. She never made it sound like advice, but folks who ignored her could rue the day.

"Connor laughed, grabbed Fidelma by the hand, and she giggling the while, pulled her over to the hall doorway. He stopped. 'Would you look at that?' says he. 'Mistletoe. I want my Christmas kiss.'

"But she pulled away. 'There's an awful-looking spider sitting on the berries,' she said, and shivered.

"I looked straight at Ma. Her gaze was fixed on Connor. There was grief in it.

"I shivered when I looked back at Connor.

"'Funny,' says he, peering up. 'I've one just like it at my place. Pay no heed to it.' And he scratched his ear.

"He led Fidelma into the hall and I heard him say, 'I'm still going to get my Christmas kiss.' And he did. And more than one.

"I'd never seen Connor so gay, so full of life, as if he didn't have a care in the world, and if he did he'd clearly resolved to ignore it. He never seemed to sit still. He helped Ma set the table. He carried turf in for the fire. He greeted visitors. By halfway through the afternoon, he was helping them to brush snow off their coats. You could hear the wind when the doors were open.

"That evening he ate a Christmas dinner that would have satisfied Finn Mac-Cool, the Irish giant, and later on Connor played his pipes. I'll never forget that.

"We'd retired to the sitting room after the meal. You could hear the gale whistling outside, but in the room it was cosy warm, with turf sizzling in the grate and the scent of it mingled with the piney smell of the Christmas tree.

"Da, who was a famous *seanachie,* a storyteller, told us a story. I can see him sitting there with that twinkle in his grey eyes. He was taller than Ma, wide-shouldered, slim-hipped. He had a wind-weathered face and a scar under his left eye where a piece of shrapnel had wounded him in 1918. He'd been a soldier man like Connor—a sergeant. Da was bald as a coot and I think it embarrassed him, for I never saw him but he was wearing a tweed duncher. Ma said he even wore it to bed.

"He was down to a collarless shirt, sleeves rolled up, his green braces running over the front of it to hold up tweed trousers, and he'd one booted foot resting on his thigh. Da and all the fellahs had hot Irish whiskeys in their hands. I was allowed one toty-wee glass of eggnog just like the bigger ones—Ma, my sisters, and Emer, Art's fiancée—were drinking. To tell you the truth, I wasn't all that sure I liked the nutmeggy taste of it, but drinking it made me feel grown up."

"Did youth not wath TV?" Billy Cadogan asked. "We alwayth do. There's thome cracker programmth on Chrithmath night, tho there is."

Kinky smiled. "Billy, *Radio Éireann* didn't

start broadcasting until 1926, and *Radio Telefís Éireann*, that's the TV company, not until 1961. We had to amuse ourselves."

"Sounds like fun," said Micky Corry.

"It was," Kinky said, "and it wasn't just stories. When Da had finished, Connor said, 'I'll get my pipes. I'll be a minute tuning them.' And off he goes to the kitchen. In a moment, it sounded as if someone was strangling a cat out there.

"When he came back, he sat down, put the bag under one arm and the bellows under his right elbow. They're called *uillinn* pipes because *uillinn* means elbow, and you use your elbow on the bellows to blow up the bag. He gave us all a great grin and said, 'I suppose when I was tuning up you thought maybe I had the banshee in the kitchen with me,' and with that he lets go that great laugh of his and starts to play. His fingers flew over the chanter and the drones. I never heard pipe notes so sweet nor a hornpipe, 'Gusty's Frolics,' so happy.

"When he finished, Fidelma said, '*That* wasn't like a banshee.'

"I could just make out Ma saying to herself, very quietly, 'Don't mock the *Bean Sidhe*. Do not mock her.'

"And later that evening when it was my bedtime and I took my candle and went upstairs to my bed, I had cause to remember Ma's words."

11

"Candle?" Eddie asked. "Candle?"

"Bless you, Eddie. Back then, long before you were born, there was no electricity in County Cork except in Cork City, and even in the earlier days of gas lighting, the gas supply never came closer to our farm than to Lissavard, a few miles away.

"The downstairs at my house was lit by oil lamps, great shiny brass things. We had to polish them once a week. They had glass chimneys with a bulge in the middle and the chimneys were surrounded by beautifully etched glass globes. If I close my eyes, I can see the smoke if the wick wasn't properly trimmed and get the smell of the paraffin yet." And she could. It seemed sharp and pungent in her nostrils.

"So, with the candle all aflicker making shadows on the whitewashed walls, off I went.

"I'd a ways to go. The staircase from the hall went up to a landing. There were four bedrooms on that floor, for Ma and Da, Siobhan, Art, and Tiernan. The next flight went up to a space under the roof. Fidelma and I had an attic room each. We were a lucky family. For many less fortunate souls in County Cork, a bedroom of your own was unheard of, so.

"I chuckled to myself thinking tonight there'd be a lot of doubling up among the family to make room for the three guests. Art and Tiernan would be together so Malachy could have a bed. Fidelma was giving up her room to Emer and moving in with Sinead.

"At least I'd not be sharing my wee garret with lovesick Fidelma and having to listen to how wonderful Connor was. As if I didn't know. As if I hadn't heard it all before. As if I wasn't a wee bit jealous. Poor man, he'd be sleeping under a blanket on the sofa in the living room tonight.

"When I got to my room I put the candleholder on a wee table by my bed, got into my nightgown, and hopped in under the covers. I would gladly have given Connor my little attic, but Ma said no.

"It was a darlin' room. My bed was tucked in the low bit under the sloped roof and beside a mullioned window.

"I didn't draw the curtains for there was nobody for miles to see in. The light from the candle shone only a few feet into the pitch-black night, and for a little while I watched the snowflakes hurry by. The window frame fitted so snugly that not a breath of air could slip into the room. I could hardly hear the noise of the wind in the eaves. I was snug—"

"As a bug in a rug," Dermot Fogarty said, and sniggered.

"I was so, Dermot. I'd had a lovely day. Maybe the eggnog was making me drowsy, but I picked up my new Christmas book. Ma got me one every year. It was *Child Whispers*, poems by an Englishwoman, Enid Blyton. It had just come out that year.

"I'm not sure how long I'd read or whether I'd nodded off, but suddenly there did come a bitter draft into the room. I looked up and shivered, then pulled the eiderdown up round my shoulders. Another draft came more strongly than the first.

"The candle flickered, guttered, and cast horrible shadows on the wall, shapes of bats and bones and wolves." She paused. "The flame flared, almost died, burnt brightly again, and went out. The dark was so thick you'd have needed a drill to get through it, so."

Kinky heard a succession of small, startled "ooohs" from her audience.

"Outside, coming from the glass of the window, I heard an awful noise, one to set your teeth on edge, a racket as harsh as a blunt knife on a spinning grindstone.

"It started like the sound of a mouse behind a wainscoting, or boots through dry leaves. It was a shrivelled-up, whiskery kind of a noise. 'Ah, sure,' says I to comfort myself, 'it's only bare branches rubbing on the glass, even if they do usually make a rat-a-tat noise when they do.' A row of sycamores stood outside that wall of the house to make a windbreak. 'It's only the branches,' says I, but I snuggled further down the bed.

"I didn't want to get out of bed to relight the candle. And I didn't want whatever was out there to come into the room. I just pulled the bedclothes as close under my chin as I could without covering my face; then I pulled the blankets right over my head, but I couldn't stay there for long. The heat of my own breath soon made the little safe cave under the bedclothes hot as an oven, and so I had to come up for air.

"My first thought was that someone had brought a lantern, the room was so brightly lit. But it was a strange, liquid kind of a light, the sort you might see if you dived under the sea on a sunny day and looked up at the surface overhead. There was a silver to it the like of which I'd never seen. And there was no one in the room." Kinky paused.

"No one? No one at all?" Colin was trying to control his voice, but she heard a little quaver.

"Not *inside* the room."

"Outside? On the landing, like?" Micky held his hands clasped together.

"It was outside the window, and do you know what I saw when I looked out?"

No one spoke. Every head shook.

Kinky took a very deep breath. "And this is what it was. I saw—as plain as I see the nose on your face, Billy Cadogan—I saw a woman.

"The brass neck of her. For a minute I leant forward. I was very cross. She'd no right to be in *our* tree, so. Who did she think she was, shining her light and waking me up? The cheek of her. I was going to tell her to go away when I heard . . ."

"Heard what?" Billy asked.

"I heard . . ." Kinky deliberately pulled in a short breath and stopped it in her throat, then said, "a high-pitched sound. It was a keening like you might have heard at a funeral, but it was twice as loud as any noise made by mortal woman."

"The banshee," Jeannie whispered. "Jesus, Mary, and Joseph."

"I'm not saying it was the *Bean Sidhe*, and I'm not saying it wasn't, but she was old and thin and had on a long white dress under a wide, white cloak, and her silver hair flowed down to her bare feet. And no, she wasn't floating in midair. She was perched in the branches of the sycamore."

"So it could have been a real woman," Colin said. The quaver had gone.

"It could, so. Indeed, so. And maybe she was. She certainly could keen like a real keener, and I could hear the sounds of hands clapping, except her hands, so bony they looked like the hands of a skeleton, were held out to me.

"And I wasn't angry anymore. I was trembling. I shrank away from them and closed my eyes. I was just going to clamp my hands over my ears to shut out the awful noise when I heard her call one name, clearly and distinctly like a real woman would. I know, for I heard her, and the name she said was—"

Colin and Hazel were mouthing silently together, "Connor."

"Connor MacTaggart." Kinky charged ahead. "Behind me I heard a clattering and didn't know where to hide. By now, I was crying. Remember, I was only fourteen."

"It's all right, Mrs. Kincaid," Hazel said. "If it had happened to any of us, we'd all have been bawling for our mammies too."

"I needn't have, for I saw Sinead in the doorway. The beams thrown by her paraffin light had banished the silver luminance.

"'Are you all right, wee one?' she asked, moving to my bedside and holding the lamp high so I was bathed in its warm yellow glow.

"'I'm grand, so, but . . . but, Sinead, just give me a hug for I'm all atremble. I think . . . I think I just heard the banshee; indeed I saw her. And you know that when she keens, someone is going to die the very next day.' I shuddered. The old ones here were Da and Ma, and I loved them both dearly. I didn't want anything to happen to them. Except she hadn't called their names. She'd called for Connor.

"I spun back to the window, but there was nothing to be seen but the deep, deep dark—and the snowflakes. Nothing to hear but the rising of the wind of the blizzard outside. And I wondered, for it does snow only rarely in Cork, and I wonder still to this day, did the banshee come because there was a storm or did she start the gale herself? They can do that, you know. So can the Shee.

"Sinead set the lamp on the table and held me close to her. 'I'll not pretend you're imagining things, for didn't we all hear her too?'

" 'What does it mean?' I asked.

"She had let go her hold a bit and looked at my face. 'Here,' she said, and she handed me one of the new Irish linen handkerchiefs embroidered with an *S* that Malachy, her fellah, had given her. 'Blow your nose.'

"I did.

" 'Ma knew you'd be scared so she sent me up to comfort you and to tell you not to worry about our family. She knows the keening's not for any of us. She's seen something but won't tell the details. You know what she's like, how she'll keep her mouth closed when she knows a thing *must* be and nothing can be done.'

" 'Aye, so. We've all seen her when the sight's on her. It must be an awful curse to look into the future.' " I didn't know then what I know now, Kinky thought.

"It would be wheeker," Colin said. "If I could, I'd tell my Da, like, and he could win thousands of pounds on the football pools."

"It doesn't work that way," Kinky said. "It's not given so people can profit by it. It's there for the helping of others. Ma had understood what the banshee wanted, had seen what must be, and without telling anyone exactly what it was, had sent Sinead to comfort me.

"'You know very well, Maureen,' Sinead said, 'that the banshee doesn't usually pick on ordinary folks like us. The stories about her are all to do with special families, like the McCarthys of Tipperary and the O'Neills of Ulster, rich people with their own family vault in the churchyard and descendants of ancient kings, so. But aren't we just the O'Hanlons of Beal na mBláth? So we've nothing to worry about.'

"I took a few really deep breaths, then smiled at her. It was true what she said.

"'That's better,' she said, and she tucked the sheets more tightly round me. 'Good night, *muirnín*,' says she. 'I'll see you in the morning.'

"I smiled at the poetry of the two words; 'moornyeen,' for darling, and 'morning.' Then I put my head on my pillow and tried to sleep. But for all her reassurances Sinead hadn't told me something I needed to know, and it nagged at me now. Never mind O'Neills and McCarthys. I'd heard the name the banshee, the woman faerie, had called. Were the MacTaggarts of County Cork a special family, or was *this* spirit sent by the Doov Shee especially for Connor, no matter who his family was?"

12

"Sinead had lit my candle for me before she left. I lay awake, staring out the window. There was no sign of the old woman back in the tree, and the snow had stopped. I could see stars above and moon glow from behind a low cloud bank.

"The storm was over.

"I blew out the candle, but I didn't think I'd sleep a wink that night. Yet it seemed scarcely had my head touched the pillow when wasn't the morning sun streaming into the room? I rubbed my eyes and sat up.

"I leant across the bed so I could look

out the window. The sky was as blue as blue. The snow had stopped. The last sycamore in the row outside my side of the house lay on the ground. The wind and the weight of the snow must have brought it tumbling down.

"The branches of the tree where the banshee had perched were blanketed, and at its foot a drift was piled smooth and unbroken . . . with nary a sign of footprints either beneath the tree or across the field beside the house."

Kinky paused. She saw how Billy frowned for a moment; then his eyes widened and he shuddered as he worked out for himself what no footprints might mean.

"It gave me the goose bumps and I didn't want to be alone, so I washed and dressed as fast as I could and ran down the two flights of stairs.

"Ma was at the range cooking. 'Good morning, sleepyhead,' she said. 'Come and get some porridge. There's buttermilk on the table.'

"I bade her good morning and to Connor, who was tucking into his breakfast: a plate of eggs, slices of yesterday's ham fried just so and tasty, potato bread, and *drúishin,* good Cork blood pudding that would make your mouth water. Ma made her own, you know. I can smell it yet."

"My Da says drisheen smells like oul' socks and it tastes like boke," Colin said and pinched his nose.

The other children giggled

"Your father is entitled to his opinion . . . and I to mine, Colin Brown. I'll thank you to remember that, so."

"Yes, Mrs. Kincaid." Colin sounded suitably contrite.

"Grand. Now, children, you may be wondering where everyone else was."

"Yes, Mrs. Kincaid," came the voices in unison.

"Art and Malachy had gone with Emer and Sinead to Clonakilty. Fidelma was tending to the ducks and chickens. Da and Tiernan were seeing to the beasts. The work doesn't stop for farmers just because it's Saint Stephen's Day. Not for shepherds either.

"Says Connor, 'I'll be on my way as soon as I finish. After the snow last night the sheep in the upper pasture will need feed taken in to them, even if it's only a bale or two of straw, but'—he smiled at Ma—'I'll not rush such a grand breakfast.'

"Ma's voice was very solemn. She ignored the compliment and said, 'Connor MacTaggart, the people in these parts do say I am a wise woman, so. You yourself have said I am.'

"'True,' he said, a forkful of *drúishin* stopped halfway to his mouth. 'They do.'

"I watched the pair of them, the interest in Connor's eyes, the pity in Ma's, as she said, 'I've no doubt the faeries are still very, very cross. I've no doubt they haven't finished by a long chalk—'

"'Och, sure,' Connor said, 'I don't want to cause you offence, Mrs. O'Hanlon, but I honestly don't think the wee folk could hurt anybody.'

"I saw him swallow, fill his mouth, and chew faster, as if he was suddenly in a hurry to finish his meal.

"Ma shook her head. 'You haven't asked my advice, Connor, and if you tell me to keep it to myself I will, but if you'll listen for the sake of Fidelma—'

"'Mrs. O'Hanlon, I'll listen . . . for the sake of Fidelma, for I'd do nothing to harm that girl or cause her hurt.' He mopped up egg yolk with potato bread and hardly chewed it at all before it went down his gullet.

"'All right.' Ma spoke very softly. 'On today of all days, the feast of Stephen, before noon hour, before the snow flies again—'

"'Come on now, Mrs. O'Hanlon,' Connor said, glancing up at the clock. 'There's not a cloud in the sky from here to Cork City, nor enough wind to make a spider's web flutter.'

"I saw in my mind's eye the spider in the mistletoe that had frightened Fidelma yesterday. I took a long swallow of my warm buttermilk, and somehow that morning it tasted more bitter than usual.

"As if Connor hadn't spoken, Ma continued. 'I'd want you safe and warm inside with a good fire roaring . . .' She put a hand to her temple, and her eyes went glassy, her voice deeper somehow. 'For I see gales, and snowbanks, and smothered sheep, and a vixen running on top of the snow, and a raven soaring on the wind.'

"She stopped speaking.

"I shivered. I'd never seen Ma like that before. I didn't know what to do. I just sat there staring at her, and my mouth wide enough to catch flies. Connor didn't open his cheep either for quite the while; then he rose.

"Says he, 'Thank you for my dinner yesterday, my bed last night, and my breakfast this morning, Mrs. O'Hanlon.' He set his knife and fork on his empty plate and finished his tea in one gulp. 'And thank you for the advice. I will think on it. But I'll not let my animals go hungry'—he grinned—'faeries or no faeries. So thank you very much. *Go raibh míle maith agat.*' He stood, his chair legs scraping quickly over the tiles.

"'*Tá fáilte romhat;* you're welcome,' says Ma. 'And I know you're no Cinderella who'd to be home before midnight, but heed my words, Connor MacTaggart. Noon. For you heard what we all heard last night.'

"I shivered just to think of that awful screeching, but Connor smiled.

"'I heard a noise all right,' he said, 'but I know what it was . . .' He was speaking over his shoulder as he went to the door to grab his duncher and overcoat.

"'The banshee,' whispers I.

"'Divil the bit, Maureen,' says he, putting on his coat and cap and leaving his coat unbuttoned. 'When I went out to feed Tessie in your byre this morning, I noticed one of your sycamores was down. The falling of it must have been what caused the caterwauling last night. I've heard the likes of it before when I felled a tree.'

"'Aye,' says Ma very softly, 'a blackthorn.' She looked him straight in the eye and the edge came into her voice, the way it sounded when she'd told him the stain on his face was not sap. 'If it's bound and determined you are, so am I. You'll take two bales of feed from our barn, Connor MacTaggart, and a barrow. You'll not gainsay me. You can bring the barrow and replacements back the next time you're out this way. If you're going to your sheep, go straight from here to the hill road. Even if the road is clear, your gully will be half choked. It'll take you forever to go home and collect your own barrow and feed, and you can't push a barrow up your gully. Start from here instead and you'll be home by noon.' She lowered her voice. 'You have to be.'

"I expected him to refuse, like he had

turned down Ma's offer of peat, but instead, glancing at the clock again, he said, 'I will, so. Thank you.' He grinned at Ma with his head tipped to one side. 'After the seeing to of the sheep, I'll leave your barrow in the pasture and go back down to my place by the gully. Even if there's snow in it, it'll not be too hard going down, and I *will* be home before noon. Not, mind you, that a skiff or two of snow, if it comes at all, would trouble the likes of a man like me. I'm strong as an ox and stubborn as my own donkey, so.'

"He crossed the floor, bent down and pecked my cheek, turned, and was in such a hurry to get to the door he knocked over a chair, and the falling of it made a ferocious clatter. 'Sorry,' says he, as he picked it up. He blushed and that funny red thing on his face seemed redder still.

"On his way to the door he grabbed his pipes and crook.

"I think I'd stopped blushing by the time he'd opened the door. I hesitated for a wee while, but then I ran after him to say one more good-bye. And didn't I see him coming out of our shed pushing a barrow of bales of straw. He stopped and kissed Fidelma, then waved good-bye as he strode out along our lane, Tess at his heels and 'The Star of the County Down' on his lips.

"And it bothered me not at all that a raven flew overhead—sure, ravens are ten a penny in Cork—but I thought it strange that running lightly over the snow, its coat a bright contrast to the unbroken white, was a single vixen."

13

"I didn't have any time to spend thinking about foxes, for Ma believed the devil would find work for idle hands. There was a lot of tidying up to do after Christmas Day, and if that wasn't enough, she was a great one for children writing thank-you letters on Saint Stephen's Day."

Kinky heard a communal muttering among the children. Even in 1964, the thank-you letter was not dead, and Kinky could imagine any one of her audience being just as unthrilled as she had been to pen: "Dear Aunty Bridget, thank you for the lovely string vest. It was just what I wanted."

Although the warmth of a string vest would have been very useful that year.

"I'd just finished writing 'Yours truly, Maureen' on the fifth 'Dear Aunty' letter when a shadow fell over the table. It was twelve noon by the kitchen clock. The whole room, which had been as bright as it would have been on a day in July, suddenly was as dark as if a switch had been clicked.

"The north wind came shrieking in. The window frames rattled, and I knew by crashes from outside that slates had been blown off the roof.

"On the other side of the window, the flakes tossed and fell, soared and danced. I couldn't see the wall of the farmyard.

"Fidelma ran into the kitchen and slammed the door behind her.

"'Mother of God,' says Ma. 'I hope Art and Sinead and their ones have enough wit to stay in Clonakilty. Da and Tiernan'll be all right if they stop in the barn until the wind drops.'

"Ma lit two oil lamps, and in their glow

the room seemed a safe place. The three of us sat round the table warmed by the heat from the range and the steam from the pots where Ma was boiling yesterday's ham bone and the turkey carcass to make stock. We were warm, but outside it must have been like . . . like . . ." Kinky struggled for an analogy the children would understand.

"Antarctica," Micky Corry suggested. "Our teacher, Miss Nolan, took us to see a film about Captain Scott."

Kinky saw heads nodding.

"You never saw nothing like the wind there, you know, and the way it blew the snow across the ice. And poor oul' Scott, you know, and all his men got froze dead, so they did. But they were very brave," Micky said. Then he shuddered.

"It *was* like Antarctica. You're quite right, Micky. Just like Antarctica."

He grinned.

"I wish," she said, "we'd been able to smile like you, Micky, but my sister Fidelma, bless her, started to cry."

"Ahhhh," went three of the girls.

Kinky waited for quiet before saying, "Ma leaned over to us and put a hand on

Fidelma's. 'There, there,' she said, all soft and comforting.

"Fidelma collected herself a bit and sniffed. 'Connor's out in that.' She swallowed hard and I could tell she was trying to stop the tears. 'Him and his stupid sheep.'

"I was going to say, 'And sure wasn't he every bit as thick as his sheep?' but I bit my tongue.

"'I know,' said Ma. She looked straight at me, and I must have been wiser than my years for I said not a word about the warning she'd given Connor before he left. I could only hope he'd taken Ma's advice about getting home.

"I swear, by then I'd thought that the storm could not get any worse, but it did. It wasn't the windows rattling. It was the whole place. I felt like a pig in the house of straw with the wolf outside, huffing and puffing.

"Nobody spoke, and we huddled there listening to the wind batter at our doors and windows, trying to get in and blow us all away, or whirl the whole house into the sky like Dorothy's in *The Wonderful Wizard of Oz*.

"All we could do was sit there and wait for the blizzard to blow itself out.

"Fidelma and I looked at each other every time a gust of icy snow rattled the panes. I could imagine what she was thinking because I was thinking it too. We knew the time when Connor left our house. We knew how long it would have taken him to get to the upper pasture. We didn't know how much time he might have spent with his blessèd animals, but by my reckoning he must have still been outside either in the pasture or halfway down the shortcut home.

"If he was in the pasture, he'd be trying to shelter. I could see him, as if I was on the hillside with him, gathering his solid woolly little sheep around him, and Tess in the lee of the drystone walls on the far side of the hill. That was all there was up there to stop the storm screaming across the open meadow, piling snow in man-deep drifts, cutting through clothes until Connor would think he was naked before it. The same wind that was battering itself against our doors and windows would be slicing at him and chilling him to the marrow of his bones, whirling his cap away to vanish in the white walls of blown snow.

"Would the vixen be out, I wondered, the wind blowing her fur against the grain, lifting the coarse hairs straight up? Would she be sitting on a snowbank, eyes slitted against the cold and the sheer brute force of the wind, silently surveying Connor?

"And would Connor plead with the creature, would he ask forgiveness of the Shee then? Would he try to bargain? Connor MacTaggart plead? I thought he would not. For he was a proud man. Perhaps he was thinking that sitting there surrounded by his sheep, dug in against the snow and the wind, wasn't all that different from being in a trench in France, facing the enemy's onslaught. Facing it without flinching, for that's the kind of man Connor was, so.

"If he was in the gully he'd be hunched against the wind, struggling one step at a time to force his way home to the sanctuary of his cottage.

"The back door banged open, and the sound of it brought me back into the kitchen, safe, warm, and dry. Fidelma was silently weeping. I glanced outside. The sun was beaming in through the windows when Da and Tiernan came clumping into the kitchen, leaving puddles of melting snow on the tiles.

"I glanced at the clock. Half past one, and I realized the storm had lasted for an hour and a half. It had vanished as quickly as it had come, but the snow dumped on top of what had already fallen would make deep drifts up in the pastures.

"Da and Tiernan went straight to the range and turned their backs to it. I could see wisps of steam rising. Da's cheeks were grey, and both men had snow clinging to their pants. 'Dear God, but that heat's grand,' Da said.

"But poor Connor had no friendly range to warm him unless he'd heeded Ma and left in time to get to his cottage. Had he? I didn't know, and if the not-knowing tormented me, what was it doing to Fidelma?

"'Da. Connor's—' Fidelma started, but she had enough sense to close her trap. Da would have been far too chilled to worry about anything other than getting warm.

"'For the love of God, Roísin,' says he

to Ma, and his teeth chattering faster than a spoon player's instruments, 'get us both cups of tea, lots of sugar, and I'll not complain if you put stiffeners in them. I'll not complain at all.'

"Ma got the bottle of whiskey and poured from it into the cups. "'Here. Tea with whiskey,' says she solemnly, 'keeps away the dew.'

"By the time Da and Tiernan had warmed up, Fidelma tried again. 'Daddy,' says she, and she only ever called him Daddy when she was trying to wheedle something out of him. 'Daddy, I know it's awful cold outside, but the sun's shining now. Connor's gone to the high pasture—'

"'Wheest, wee one,' says Da in his gentlest voice. 'Wheest now, for the answer's no. No man could get through the drifts. It was as much as Tiernan and me could do to get back here from the barn. It'll be up to your oxters on the hill.'

"Fidelma whimpered.

"'Please, God,' I prayed silently, 'please, God, let him have taken Ma's advice and got home in time.' That's what I wanted, but the picture in my mind would not go away: Connor and the great muscles of him, leaning his shoulders into the wind, straining with every step, the snow in his hair, snow caked on his eyebrows, his cheeks slatey blue, his great, grasping breaths steaming and being torn away by the gale. Refusing to give up to the faeries or to nature itself until all the strength of him was drained entirely.

"Da must have been having the same thoughts. 'If the blizzard hit before he left the upper pasture we'll just have to pray that Connor found shelter behind a wall or in a sheep cot and he got warmth from the sheep themselves,' Da said, 'for it'll be a day or more before any man can get up into the hills.'

"He didn't say what might have happened if Connor had been caught on his way down.

"Fidelma gave a great shuddering sob, and Da put his arms round her. 'I tell you what, girl. The minute I can get out of the yard here, Tiernan and Art, if he gets home in time, and me will round up every man in the townland and we'll search every glen and every gully where Connor might be.'

"'Thank you, Daddy,' says Fidelma.

"'But all we can do now is hope and pray.'

"At his words I heard Ma start, 'Our Father, which art in heaven . . .'

"And we all bowed our heads and joined in until the final amen."

14

"And it is what it was. Da was right. Two days and two nights passed before the O'Hanlon men could go out anywhere with search parties, and in a very few hours Da came home alone, cold, tired, and defeated-looking."

Jeannie Kennedy looked as if she might start to cry. "But what about Connor, Mrs. Kincaid?" the girl said in a small voice.

Kinky shook her head and ploughed on. "Da called the whole family together around the kitchen table. Ma held Fidelma.

'I'll not pussyfoot,' Da said. 'We found neither hide nor hair of him on the hill.'

"Big tears coursed down Fidelma's cheeks. I wanted to hold her, but that was Ma's job.

" 'I'll tell you what we did find,' Da said. 'The sheep were all dead, every last one huddled against a wall and each other. His pipes were there too, and our barrow.

" 'No footprints, man's or dog's, led into the gully Connor used as a shortcut. The new snow would have covered them if they'd been made before the snow flew. Art, Tiernan, and I scoured the track anyway. Tess was lying frozen-stiff halfway down, and we found Connor's crook about ten yards from the bottom. From there were a man's faint footsteps, made after the snow started, with not enough fallen to cover them by the time the blizzard stopped. Connor *was* caught away from any shelter. Those prints led us right on to the felled blackthorn.' Da lifted his cap and and scratched his pate. 'What persuaded Connor to make a detour the Lord only knows.' He shook his head and blew out his cheeks.

" 'What is it?' asked Ma. 'Finbar, what did you find?'

" 'I can hardly believe what I saw. The blackthorn trunks and branches were half covered in snow, the wood still in a great pile, right where Connor had left them when he chopped the thing down.' Da looked deep into Ma's eyes and said very quietly, 'Alongside the dead wood were new green shoots, as if the tree thought it was alive and spring had come.'

" 'No Connor?' Fidelma asked. Her voice quavered. 'Where was he? He must have been in his cottage. Mustn't he?'

"The pleading in her voice nearly brought the tears to my own eyes.

"My father shook his head again. 'The footsteps stopped at the tree and we found no others, so my hopes rose when we started for Connor's cottage. Where else could he be? Even before we got there we could see there was no smoke coming out of the chimney.' "

Kinky looked quickly at each of the children in turn. "And I remembered who the banshee had called for on Christmas night. One name: Connor MacTaggart.

"Da said, 'When me and the boys got

to the cottage, I opened the door quickly. It looked as if it hadn't been lived in for years. Cobwebs like sheets of butter muslin were strung from the rafters to the mantel to the kitchen table. Through that shroud I thought I saw him'"—a sharp collective intake of breath came from Kinky's audience—"'lying in front of the hearth, an arm stretched out to the fireplace. I tore the gossamer apart,' said Da, 'but when I knelt to touch him, it was just Connor's greatcoat, dry and warm even though the cottage was as cold as a tomb.' Da shifted in his chair, and it creaked. It was then I realized Da was sitting in the one Connor had knocked over in his haste to leave our kitchen two days before.

"'But it wasn't the cold that made me shiver,' Da went on. 'It was the sight of a huge spider sitting on the coat's collar. It hissed at me. I tried to stamp on the creature, but it was too quick for me.

"'The sight of that empty coat made my heart heavy, but our job wasn't done until we'd searched everywhere, so I looked in the bedrooms. The boys went outside to search the outbuildings. They found nothing either.'

"Fidelma sat rigidly, staring at Da, biting her knuckles. I think it would have been easier on her if she had cried.

"Da said, 'I'm sorry, Fidelma. I . . . I cannot say where Connor is. I only know that we've searched every inch of the townland and found nothing. The Shee have taken Connor, God bless him. May his soul find peace. Your brothers are seeing to his cottage . . . and to Tess,' said Da. 'They'll be home presently. I came back at once to bring what news we had.' He looked at Ma and said, 'It was strange, but as I was leaving, outside his cottage didn't I see a vixen crouched on the wall, grinning at me, and from overhead, high, high against the blue was a black speck, and it laughing, *toc-toc-toc*.'

"We all sat silently, the only sound Fildelma's catchy breathing. Then the crash of the back door as it banged on its hinges. It was Tiernan who opened the inner door.

" 'We found him, Da. Under the blackthorn—'

" 'But how?' Da half rose.

"Tiernan shook his head. 'We were in the cottage and Eamon MacVeigh our neighbour heard pipes outside, so he followed the sound of them and it led us to the tree. We found no piper, but when we shifted some of the piled branches, I found Connor. He'd no coat, no boots.' Tiernan, with softness in his eyes and gentleness in his lowered voice, said, 'I'm sorry, Fidelma, but he was dead.'

"Fidelma made a high, mournful keening sound, like the banshee had made on Christmas night. Then in her grief she spoke only one name, over and over. 'Connor . . . Connor.'"

Kinky let her words hang until at last Hazel said, "Aaah, that's awfully sad, so it is. Poor Connor. I think he'd have been all right if he hadn't been so worried about his sheep."

"Or mebbe," Jeannie added, "if he'd listened to your Ma and said he was sorry to the faeries. My mammy says you should always apologize, like."

"I'm sure you're both right," said Colin, "but I want to hear more about the ghost."

"And so you shall," Kinky said. "So you shall.

"It wasn't long after that people stopped pasturing their sheep on the hill, for if they did, within two days a vixen would appear on the slopes. Even in the sunniest of weather here below, strange beasts would appear out of a hilltop fog with bluey-grey paint blobs over one hip.

"People would find man-tracks and sheepdog tracks where no man and no dog had been. The blackthorn lay where it had been felled. The fresh crop of new green leaves had turned dry and brown, but the trunks Connor had chopped looked fresh as the day he cut them. Everyone knew they would not decay until Connor's spirit had found its peace.

"Eamon MacVeigh, from the farm over fornenst ours, went up there to his bog beside Connor's on the next Saint Stephen's Day. He swore on the holy Bible he had heard the *uillinn* pipes played sweetly, like he had when they'd found Connor. And the tunes the piper played were 'The Wearing of the Green,' 'Planxty Gordon,' 'The Wind That Shakes the Barley,' and, soft and low, 'The Star of the County Down.' His two brothers who'd been with him hadn't heard a thing, and I thought that strange, but Ma explained that not every human was sensitive enough to hear ghostly music. And she was certain that Eamon had twice heard Connor playing.

"For a ghost that has left some earthly duty undone, some ill deed not atoned for, must haunt this earth and will not find its rest until it has made amends or done some act of great kindness to a stranger."

"Ooh," said Colin, "that is dead spooky, so it is."

"And *that*," she said, "*that* is the story of how Connor MacTaggart cut down a faerie tree, was tormented by the Shee, was summoned by the banshee, and became the Saint Stephen's Day ghost—the Thevshee of Beal na mBláth, in thrall to the Doov Shee for as long as they wished."

There was a very long silence. Then Colin said, "That's a cracker story, Mrs. Kincaid, so it is." He was obviously impressed. "Thank you very much."

"I think it's terrible sad, so I do." Jeannie Kennedy's lip trembled. "Poor Connor. Poor Fidelma." She looked up at Kinky. "I like stories with happy endings, so I do." Then she smiled. "Mebbe the second part of the story'll have a happy ending? Mebbe you'll tell us if Connor's ghost got away from the Shee."

Kinky shook her head. "Not now, Jeannie. I'm sorry, we've run out of time. It's not just Eddie's mammy'll be after me if I don't get you home now. It's nearly quarter to one."

She was fully prepared for a chorus of "boo-hiss" and "not fair."

She held up her hands. "There'll be another time, and I don't want to spoil the story by telling you the ending, so now I want you all to get on your hats and coats."

It was crowded and noisy in the hall as the little mob got dressed. When they were ready to leave, Hazel stepped forward. "Mrs. Kincaid, I—that is, we—want to thank you very much for the pies, and the Ribena, and the lovely story, like. And we hope you have a very merry Christmas, a happy new year . . ." Then the words tumbled out: "And we hope you'll have no ghosts this Saint Stephen's Day."

Kinky was still laughing as she shut the door behind the last child. She shook her head. If only Hazel knew how appreciated her wishes were. Kinky certainly wanted no more ghosts, no more doings with the supernatural.

She stood looking at the closed door.

Children, she thought, they'd all really enjoyed the story. Even Colin Brown, she'd recognised, after his initial skepticism, had believed every word. Perhaps it was because she'd told the tale convincingly. And why shouldn't she? Hadn't she lived it and wasn't it true?

When she'd been telling it, hadn't she been transported back to her own childhood, to the sights, the sounds, the smells, and all the feelings of her home in County Cork?

When the children wriggled at the talk of spiders, she'd been uncomfortable herself. To this day she couldn't stand the creatures. The kiddies might not have been feeling the chill of the blizzard when she described it, but when she'd been speaking, the sights and bitter cold of it had been as vivid to her as they had been forty-odd years ago.

As had other things in her childhood that hadn't been part of the story, so she'd not mentioned to them.

She'd been lucky growing up there when she did, she told herself, when life was simple, her world was small, and her family was all she'd really needed.

Kinky sighed. Over the years she had learned that life is always moving on, and it was from that year and its terrible ending that her own life had changed at a terrifying speed.

Seeing and hearing the banshee on Christmas night and the death of Connor on Saint Stephen's Day were bad enough if they had been all that had happened. They weren't. Not by a long chalk.

In the next four years she'd grown from a girl to a woman, had seen more, much more of the Shee, had fallen in love, and had started down the road that brought her here to Ballybucklebo, where, if she didn't get into her kitchen, this year's Christmas dinner would spoil for lack of her attention.

Da had been fond of sayings like "Eating time is eating time, and talking time is talking time, so eat up . . . and shut up."

Now was "start seeing to the dinner" time. More reminiscing could come later.

15

Kinky lifted two ceramic bowls with aluminium foil lids tied on with string. She placed them in a huge pot full of water and put it on the stove top. Christmas puddings took the longest time to cook of all the dishes she was going to prepare. She lit the gas. They'd be boiling soon.

Potatoes needed peeling and she concentrated on her task, putting the white tubers in another water-filled pan ready to be parboiled prior to roasting in the turkey fat.

It was her pride and joy to cook for her doctor and his friends, but her inner woman needed attention too. It was a bit past her usual lunchtime.

She put the kettle on, slipped three potato-apple fadges under the grill, and sat on a stool to wait for them to toast. She'd be having her Christmas dinner with Cissie Sloan and her family later, so now she wanted only a shmall little snack to tide her over.

She smiled when she thought about Cissie Sloan, who was one of Kinky's best friends. Cissie, it was whispered, had her dresses made by Omar the tentmaker she was so large. The only other woman of comparable girth in the townland was Flo Bishop, wife of Councillor Bertie Bishop, the richest and meanest man in Bally-bucklebo.

Doctor O'Reilly would have more time for the medicine, so, if he wasn't forever locking horns with that Bishop over one or another of the man's get-rich-quick schemes. Like the time he'd tried to take possession of Sonny Houston's empty house while Sonny was in hospital. Kinky snorted at the very thought. The cheek of that man Bishop. As they'd say up here, "He'd wrestle a bear for a ha'penny." Be that as it may, despite all the conniving of Bertie Bishop, Sonny was living in his own home now married to Maggie Mac-Corkle, her that had told Eddie Jingles's Ma that her son was here today.

Maggie was one of Kinky's and Cissie's friends too.

Cissie Sloan. Kinky chuckled. The woman could talk on the intake of breath, but she had a heart of corn, one of the kindest souls in the place. She was a patient of the practice, but then weren't most of the inhabitants of Ballybucklebo? And didn't Kinky Kincaid know as much about every one of them as her employer, Doctor Fingal Flahertie O'Reilly, did? And wouldn't that knowledge stay with Kinky to the grave even if they tried to drag it out of her with teams of wild horses, so?

One thing about living in the village and her position here, both of which she loved, was she had to have the trust of everyone. And in a community as wedded to gossip as this one, the fastest way for Kinky to lose that trust would be to let something slip.

All of Doctor O'Reilly's patients had their weaknesses. Kinky knew many of them. Even her doctor was not faultless. It wasn't often the big man made a mistake, but he could. The last time one was pointed out to him, had he got angry? He had not. Not at all. Doctor O'Reilly was a big man in more ways than one. He'd thanked his assistant, Doctor Barry Laverty, for noticing.

He was a smart one that Barry Laverty, even if he was a bit unsure of himself. He was going to make a great partner next year. If he stayed. That lady friend of his, Patricia Spence, was a beautiful girl and a Cambridge student of civil engineering. Sometimes Kinky wondered if the demands of her profession and of his might come between the youngsters. Och, well. Time would tell.

No matter what happened to his love life, Barry could do a lot worse than live his days in Ballybucklebo. Granted, it was a bit bigger than her corner of County Cork, but it was the kind of place Kinky loved best. Small enough that everybody knew everybody else. Were the people inquisitive about each other? Certainly, but if one villager needed help they'd not have far to go for it here. In the years she'd lived at

Number 1 Main Street she'd seen more Good Samaritans than the travellers on the road from Jerusalem to Jericho.

A grand spot with grand people.

Kinky heard the kettle whistling and went to make her tea.

She put the tea things and the hot buttered fadge on a tray and carried it along with still vivid memories of her girlhood to the upstairs lounge. She set the tray on the coffee table and plumped herself down in the comfortable overstuffed armchair by the fire.

Now that the children were gone, Arthur Guinness had reclaimed his rightful place close to the hearth. He lifted his head, half opened one eye, yawned mightily, and went back to dozing. Lady Macbeth lay curled in a ball against Arthur's tummy. Her breathing was shallow, her eyes tightly closed, and the tip of her pink tongue stuck out from the centre of her small mouth.

Kinky poured tea through the strainer, then guiltily put in two spoonfuls of sugar. She was on the heavy side—fat, if she told the truth. And what was the point of telling lies? Och, but sure, and hadn't her

Da always liked his tea sweet, so? All the O'Hanlons had.

She gazed through the window. The steeple of the Presbyterian church opposite was limned against a sky of smoky indigo. Wind lifted flakes past the icing sugar–trimmed spire, then dropped them onto already laden yews that bowed over dark tombstones. Each grave marker wore an ermine stole.

It was pleasantly dim inside the room, and the glow from the fire made a cosy half circle around Kinky and the animals. Just the spot for a nice cup of tea, a bite, and a think. She added milk to her tea, sipped, and remembered.

Was it really forty-two years ago tomorrow that poor Connor MacTaggart had been lost in the blizzard? She shook her head. Forty-two years.

It was then that Kinky, a girl still answering to the name of Maureen, had started becoming a woman. In those early years after his death, Maureen O'Hanlon, who had heard and seen the banshee on Christmas night, had more glimpses of the other world. And had understood how the sight, Ma's gift, could come to a body.

But forty-two years? She bit into a cake, savouring the contrasting tastes of the potato and apple. My Lord. So long ago, and yet the story she'd told the children and what had followed had stayed with Kinky as clearly as yesterday.

She smiled and looked outside to where the flakes whirled and tossed. It was a pretty sight, the gently falling snow. Looking through the window was like peering into one of those fluid-filled glass globes with a miniature church or winter scene in it. When you shook the ball, tiny flakes were stirred up, and as they settled it looked as if it were snowing.

She wondered if God liked to watch snowfalls and so shook up the earth's globe from time to time.

The thought made her smile, but whether it had been the Almighty, the banshee, or the faeries who'd caused the Saint Stephen's Day blizzard of 1922, that had been no matter for humour when poor Connor froze to death out in it. The storm had rocked the lives of everyone involved.

Despite the warmth in the room, she shuddered.

Since Connor's passing, life on the O'Hanlons' farm had followed its cycle of the seasons; the work of a farm never ceases, but there had been a subdued air about the place. A sadness. Everyone grieved for Connor in their own way.

Fidelma, the saddest, grieved most of all. For more than a year after Connor's death, she'd barely spoken, couldn't be bothered to bicker with her younger sister, stopped going to dances, kept away from boys. Fidelma was eighteen and strikingly lovely. She had Ma's black eyes set under heavy lids that gave her a mysterious look. Her dark hair hung to her waist, and when she walked it swayed to the thrust of her hips.

Fidelma went to her work as a shifter at the linen mill in Clonakilty and did her share on the farm, but mostly she kept to herself. If she was free and the weather fine, she would take long, solitary walks. Where she went, nobody knew, but Maureen sensed that always her sister took memories of Connor with her.

Maureen too felt for Connor, but in her own way. She certainly missed him, his cheerfulness, his music, his love for her sister, but she didn't have time to brood over his loss at a time when she was leaving girlhood behind, becoming a young woman. Schoolwork was getting more difficult, but she loved it. She had also discovered camogie, the women's version of hurling, a team sport that was reckoned to be the fastest stick and ball game on earth. And it was great *craic* after the schoolday was over, and on weekends.

When Miss Murphy who taught Latin droned on about *mens sana in corpore sano*—a healthy mind in a healthy body—she had a point. You felt so alive after an hour of galloping about a field with twenty-nine other girls all carrying curved sticks, chasing a hard ball, and trying to whack it past the goalposts. You felt even more alive when your team won.

She'd been so busy with her schoolwork, her camogie, and her chores that next Christmas was on her almost before she knew it. She'd tried on that next Saint Stephen's Day to comfort her sister but had been politely kept at arm's length.

A couple of days later Fidelma had burst into tears and run off to her room when someone told her that Eamon

MacVeigh had heard pipes in the high pasture on Stephen's Day.

She would take no comfort and for months became even more withdrawn—until one Sunday in May, after church service and a family lunch, she rose from the table and said, "I'm going for a walk. Would you like to come, Maureen?"

Maureen blinked. She and Fidelma hadn't gone walking together since Connor's passing. Why was she asking her now? She looked at Fidelma and knew her sister well enough to recognise that something had changed. She hoped it was something good. Maureen glanced at Ma.

"Go on with the pair of you," Ma said. "The fresh air will do you both a power of good, so."

Maureen smiled as she rose. "Hang on. I'll get my cardigan." She rushed up and down the stairs, nearly tripping on the bottom step.

She followed her sister across the farmyard and onto the lane.

Puffball clouds drifted drowsily across a soft blue sky, and through the fields their sleepwalking shadows trailed after. Bees hummed in soft airs that were heavy with the scents of gorse, broom, heather—and cow clap.

Fidelma strode along and Maureen walked at her shoulder, glancing at her sister, willing her to speak.

As they turned onto the main road, Maureen asked, "Where are we going?"

"You'll see." Fidelma walked away from Clonakilty in the direction of Beal na mBláth. The road curved to the west, and the sun, shining now in Maureen's eyes, forced her to hold a hand to her forehead to cut the glare. Drystone walls shimmered in the heat.

The road was dry, and tiny puffs of dust rose from their steps. Ahead of them a pair of brimstone butterflies fluttered, partners in an aerial slip jig.

The hedges were ripe with fuchsia, flowers purple and scarlet like gypsies' petticoats, and hawthorn blooms, white as bridal dresses. Maureen took off her cardigan and knotted the sleeves around her waist.

They rounded another bend, and Fidelma stopped.

"Fiddles . . ." It was the pet name Maureen had used in babyhood when she couldn't say Fidelma. She only used it if she was trying to get closer to her sister. "Fiddles, that's Connor's place." Another deserted and decayed cottage, she thought, just like the hundreds of abandoned cottages that have littered Ireland ever since their occupants were evicted during *An Gorta Mór*—the Great Hunger—the potato famine of 1845 to 1849.

Fidelma turned and looked at Maureen. "I know," she said. "I come here a lot." She took Maureen's hand and squeezed it. "Don't think I'm crazy, but . . . but, Maureen, I did love him so very much."

She tried to understand exactly how Fidelma felt, but Maureen was fifteen. She loved her family but she'd never been in love, although she'd had a very soft spot for Connor. She tried to put herself in her sister's place. "I know that," she said, still not fully comprehending. "We all do."

"When I come out here, I feel him somehow . . . somehow close."

Maureen thought of Eamon, who'd been guided by pipe music to Connor's corpse and who'd sworn he'd heard the *uillinn* pipes in the high pasture five months ago on Saint Stephen's Day, the anniversary of Connor's disappearance. "Have you ever actually . . . actually seen him, or maybe heard his pipes?"

"I have not." Fidelma shook her head and sighed. "I've not been as lucky as Eamon MacVeigh." Fidelma looked hard at Maureen. "It's just . . . just a feeling. It's silly, I know that." Her look was so wistful it tugged at Maureen's heart.

For a moment she didn't know what to say; then she ventured, "Should you not . . ." She looked down, scuffed one foot, looked up, and cocked her head to the side. "Should you not, maybe, be trying to get over him?"

Fidelma nodded. "I know I should, but it comforts me to think he's near. Can you understand, Maureen? I did love him. I still do, so."

And that love could well be keeping Connor nearer than Fidelma knew. Maureen hesitated. What she was going to say would hurt Fidelma, but Ma had taught her that sometimes hard things had to be said when you loved someone if you thought it would help. "I think, Fidelma . . . I think you have to let his memory fade.

You must. For *his* sake as well as your own."

Fidelma took a step back. "Maureen, that's cruel." Her voice was harsh. "I know you used to tease me about him when he was alive, but I don't need you having a go at me now. It's cruel."

"It's not meant to be, Fiddles. Honestly. I know you're hurting, just like I did two years back . . . you remember, when Snooks died?"

"For goodness' sake." Fidelma tutted and shrugged her shoulders up. "Snooks was only a mangy old cat. Connor was a young man."

Maureen swallowed. She sensed that her sister was lashing out like a wounded animal. She wasn't going to let Fidelma hurt her, but she wasn't going to swallow the hurtful remark either. Her voice was cool. "I was only little. I loved Snooks. He'd been there since I was born. I loved him. He was *my* cat."

Fidelma's shoulders sagged. "I know. I'm sorry. I shouldn't have snapped."

"No. You shouldn't, but I understand. It's all right." Maureen hugged her sister. "You did try to comfort me then, Fiddles. I'm only trying to help you now."

"I know, wee one. I'm sorry I shouted."

"It's all right."

"And you're right about me letting go for Connor's sake. Everyone knows that if someone loves a ghost too much, its spirit can't get away and find peace. If he's still here on earth and it's me that's holding him, I'm sorry." Her voice cracked. "But I can't let go. Not just yet. I can't."

Maureen held her sister until her shoulders stopped shaking and she stepped back. "I miss him so," Fidelma said, wiping her eyes with the back of her hand. Fidelma sniffed in a great breath, exhaled slowly, and said, "It's all right." She swallowed. "And I'll be better after I've shown you something. It's why I brought you here." She started to walk along the short lane to the cottage.

Maureen followed. Was Fidelma going to go inside? Just before the red door, Maureen stopped and tugged at Fidelma's hand. "I don't want to go in," she said.

"Why not?"

"Because Da said the place was full of

spiders' webs. I hate spiders." She thought of the room where a Charles Dickens character, Miss Haversham, kept her memories alive. The place had been all dust and cobwebs. Maureen screwed up her eyes and squeezed her elbows against her sides.

"You needn't worry." Fidelma opened the door. "Look."

The sun's rays spilled into the room. A few dust motes sparkled in the doorway. Maureen hesitated, then leant forward to peer inside. There wasn't a web in sight in the kitchen, and the floor had been swept. The place smelt clean and fresh.

"Will you come in?" Fidelma asked, smiling widely before she crossed the threshold.

Maureen could see inside the whole room. The plates on a Welsh dresser were shining clean. There was no dust on a calico tablecloth covering the table. A white delft vase, the centrepiece, held a bunch of drooping bluebells.

Places were set for two.

"Are we going to have tea?" Maureen asked. "Or . . . ?" Ma had explained about the ancient custom of keeping a place for the departed. It was akin to setting an extra one for Christmas dinner in case Christ returned.

"We'll not be having tea," Fidelma said and looked Maureen straight in the eye. Fidelma crossed the tiled floor to open the curtains, then took the vase to the sink. As she removed the dead flowers and poured the discoloured water down the drain, she said, "I put these here last Sunday. It's time I got some new ones. Connor always likes bluebells."

Maureen took three steps into the room. It was cool inside after the heat of the day. She gazed at Fidelma washing and drying the vase, as if—as if this were her home and she was house proud. And Fidelma had said, "likes." She should have said Connor "liked."

"Have a seat," Fidelma said.

Maureen moved to the table and pulled back a chair, avoiding the set places.

Fidelma smiled and took the set place opposite. "I think," she said, "that it's such a tidy wee place it would be a shame to let it go to wrack and ruin, so I do a bit of housekeeping now and then." She glanced at the empty chair.

Maureen half turned—and stared. She felt the hairs of her forearms rise.

It couldn't be. She blinked, rubbed both eyes, and stared hard. The chair was occupied by the shape of a big man. But it was only the suggestion of a man, formed as it was by something no more substantial than the palest mist on a still, calm day.

She stretched out one hand and immediately pulled it back to massage it with the other. It was as if she had touched a block of ice.

Her mouth gaped. Her eyes widened. She pushed her chair away so forcibly it tumbled backward as she stood. It crashed to the floor. In her haste she tugged at the cloth, dislodging a plate and fork. The cutlery landed on the seat beside her, but the plate stopped a foot above the floor, grasped by a tenuous tendril. It hovered, then was gently lowered to land on the tiles.

Maureen gasped, covered her face with her hands, and took two steps back. She turned to her sister. "Fidelma?" Her voice was shrill.

Fidelma was already coming round the

table. "Whatever's come over you, Maureen? Did you see a spider?" She looked at the fork on the chair's seat and without hesitating bent over and picked it up.

Maureen saw Fidelma's arm pass through the smoky, icy thing. She didn't flinch. She didn't draw back. She simply put the utensil back on the table and said, "Pick up the plate, will you? It's lucky it didn't break."

Dear Lord, Maureen thought, as she did as she was told. Fidelma doesn't see anything strange. Feel anything. Maureen set the fallen chair back on its legs. "Sorry," she said. "Clumsy of me." What am I seeing? she wondered, as she started to edge toward the door. "I really think we should be getting home, Fiddles. I think it's . . . it's spooky in here." She tried with all her might to keep her voice from quavering. One glance confirmed that the mist had not left the chair. "I'm going outside."

"You go on then," Fidelma said. "I'll just be a little minute, so." She sounded more like the old Fidelma. Perhaps, even if she wasn't aware that she had company other than Maureen, it had been good for her to come here today and bring her sister. Perhaps, she thought, finally letting someone into the secret of her mysterious walks meant that Fidelma was starting to get better. That must be the change Maureen had sensed when Fidelma had suggested a walk together. Maureen hoped so.

She stepped out into the bright, warm day. That had been scary a moment ago. She'd heard enough stories of the Shee and the Thevshee from Da to be convinced that Connor's spirit had been taken by the faeries and forced to haunt his familiar places. It had to be him and Tess that left tracks on the upper pasture, *his* sheep that appeared on the hill from out of the mists, *his* pipes that Eamon MacVeigh had heard.

That must have been him in the chair.

But why could she, Maureen, see and feel him when Fidelma could not, even though she said she felt closer to Connor in his cottage? It must be, Maureen thought, she herself was more sensitive, the way Eamon was. Ma had said only some people could be aware of such things.

She heard the door close and turned to see Fidelma leaving. Her sister took Maureen's hand. "You're right. It is time we headed home."

Should she ask Fidelma if she too had been aware of something?

Fidelma stopped and Maureen turned to face her sister. "Thank you for coming, Maureen, and thank you for being honest. You're right. I should try to let him go."

Maureen squeezed her sister's hand.

Fidelma's fingers tightened in return. "I know it's silly, because . . ." She sniffed. "Because I know Connor is never coming back. I know it for certain, but I told you, I feel closer to him in there."

Maureen took a deep breath, held it for a second, then asked very quietly, "Have you ever actually seen him, Fiddles?"

"Sure, I told you, I have not. More's the pity. I'd like to see him . . . just once more."

Maureen thought, you'll never hear it from me, Fidelma, but I just did.

"It was the faeries took him," Fidelma said. "Eamon's heard Connor piping in the high pasture. He must be near. If Eamon can hear him, why can't I?"

"Didn't Ma explain that some folks"—like me, she thought—"can see or hear things others cannot?"

"I suppose so," said Fidelma. She turned, looked long and hard at the cottage, then turned away.

Maureen saw the brightness in the corners of her sister's eyes, heard the quaver in her voice when Fidelma said, "Come on. Home." She started to walk, and Maureen, still holding her hand, hurried to keep up. She wanted to get home. She knew what she'd seen. She wanted to know why she'd seen it. Was she a bit like Eamon? Ma would know.

As the two girls trudged back along the hot dusty road, Maureen heard a familiar sound rise out of the summer music of bees and birdsong. At first it was discordant, as the musician warmed up his instrument. Then sweetly, tunefully, sadly played, Maureen heard the sounds of *uillinn* pipes coming from the cottage. And the tune the piper played was "The Star of the County Down."

16

Fidelma was silent and she became more withdrawn the farther they walked from Connor's cottage. Maureen knew she should be trying to lift her sister's spirits, but she needed time to collect herself. She wanted to remember exactly what she'd seen and heard so she could tell Ma and have her explain what it meant.

Her mental picture of the smoky shape in the chair was torn to tatters by a harsh, rapid chattering. A single large bird swooped past. Its head was glossy black with a metallic green sheen, its shoulders pure white at the bases of stubby wings, and its long tail feathers trailed behind.

Fidelma ignored the bird. Although seeing a single magpie foretold coming sorrow, Fidelma must have been too preoccupied to have noticed, Maureen thought, as she whispered, "One for sorrow, two for joy, three for a girl, four for a boy, five for silver, six for gold, seven for a secret never to be told." When she was five she'd learnt the rhyme—and that a salute would ward off the sadness. She saluted. Everyone knew to do it.

Like all Irish children, she'd grown up surrounded by stories of the supernatural; the Shee, the banshee, and the Thevshee. Then there was the Phouka, a friendly being who might help a farmer at his work.

But there was also the evil eye, which was far from benign.

When Maureen was seven, Ma had taught her about how the giant Balor, a Fomorian, the first race of people to live in Ireland, could turn his enemies to stone with a single glance.

Even today, long after the Fomorians had faded into the Celtic mists, if someone possessed of the eye muttered a verse over a sleeping baby, that infant would die, for the verse was the curse of the devil and no charm could resist it or remove it. If the evil-eyed one stared at a cow, the beast was doomed.

You must always observe certain rituals to prevent folks thinking you have the eye, Ma had said, and she herself had to be particularly careful because people knew she was a wise woman. To avoid suspicion you must never, never stare through nine fingers at anybody or any animal. You should immediately say, "God bless the child," when you looked on a baby. And when you passed a herd of cattle, it was customary to intone, "The blessing of God on you and all your labours." That was because the word "God" could not pass the lips of the afflicted, but the saying of it gave proof of your innocence.

When she was little, Maureen had always paid close attention to Ma's teachings and had followed her instructions.

As she grew she'd begun to doubt some of the old beliefs but hadn't discarded them altogether. And she had put away other childish things as well—the games she'd played with dollies, her skipping rope. She was experiencing so many changes. Hair on her body, budding breasts—she liked those—her monthlies—she definitely didn't like those—and their cramps. But she was growing up, and as she did, she questioned the things she had been taught.

She no longer always muttered "God bless the child" over a baby and had even toyed with the idea of no longer saluting birds, even though she found the ritual comforting. After what had happened earlier, she was certainly taking no chances with a single magpie today. The Lord alone knew what they might see next. The sooner they got home the better.

"Let's take the shortcut," she said, as they came to a tumbled-down old wall.

"All right."

Maureen led the way, scrambling over the moss-grown jumble of grey stones, then striding along a well-worn track down a gentle grassy slope where tufts of short rushes grew.

She jumped when a loud rustling came from a clump of rushes not five paces away and a hare burst out to race off with huge bounds before vanishing into the glen ahead.

She took a very deep breath and tried to control her trembling hands.

"You're jumpy today," Fidelma said.

"Och, sure the hare and the noise of it only startled me, so." She forced a smile. Liar, she thought; you nearly wet yourself, girl. She lengthened her stride.

They rounded a corner to where trees flanked the path. Their buds were ripe and bursting. The many-fingered leaves of a solitary horse-chestnut tree were in their first spring freshness, the old tree's branches heavy with white candle-shaped blossoms.

The ground beneath looked like a green lake where islands of flowers—primroses, wood anemones, sorrel—were painted in bold tones by the sunlight that made its way past the branches. In the shadows of the boughs, the blooms were drawn in muted pastels.

Everywhere bluebells dozed under their neat bonnets, their heads bent in the warm afternoon. This must be where Fidelma had picked her bunch last Sunday.

"Aren't the bluebells lovely?" Fidelma said.

"They are."

"I love this time of the year," she said. "Everything's so new. So clean. Everything's getting a fresh start." She sighed. "I wish I could get a fresh start." She stopped walking and turned and faced Maureen. "Don't you make the same mistakes I have, girl."

"I've no intention of—" Maureen started to say, but realised she really had no idea what mistakes Fidelma was talking about. She had meant to say she had no intention of falling in love, and it was the truth. She had big plans for her life, but perhaps this wasn't the time to tell Fidelma about them.

Fidelma shook her head, said nothing, stooped, and plucked a wood anemone. She tore off one small white petal, then another. "I wish I'd never gone to work at that stupid mill. I hate it."

"You never said so before. I thought you liked it."

"I do not, but it wasn't worth the talking about." Fidelma curled her lip. "It's a job," she said, "that's all. It's tiring, stupid, boring work. The mill's dirty, smelly, and ferociously noisy. The looms clatter and thunder all day. They're always breaking down. The building's ancient. It was put up in 1820 by Doctor John Elmore, and because it's so old it's far too hot in the summer and icy cold in the winter."

Fidelma pulled at another petal. "I shouldn't have gone there in the first place, but sure wasn't I sixteen, and wasn't I sick of school? I'm not like you, Maureen. I didn't like the studying. And hadn't half the other girls left as soon as they turned fourteen, so? We all thought a job like the mill or domestic service would do for a couple of years until we found a man. It was only Ma kept me at my books longer. But I'd had enough."

Maureen hesitated. "Fidelma, you'll remember Miss Toner, the teacher from the north?"

Fidelma shrugged. "The wee, mousy woman? Her with the thick 'so I do' accent? What about her?"

"She says women should be able to do more than any old job and then just get married."

"And end up as one of nature's unclaimed treasures? Would you like that?"

"Being a spinster? No. But, Fidelma, I think she's right. I don't see why a woman couldn't have an interesting job and a husband too."

Fidelma remained silent for a moment, then said, "Aye, I suppose so. Some of the mill girls do go on working after, although a job there is far from interesting. I don't doubt the extra money would help at the beginning of a marriage. But they all quit once the family starts."

"I think that's the right thing to do. Babbies need their mammies . . . but I don't see why you couldn't go back to work once the kiddies are all in school."

"Not me. Unless the man I marry is nearly penniless, even before I say, 'I do,' I'll give that mill the back of my hand, so, and good riddance to bad rubbish."

Maureen smiled at her sister. "And I think you'd make some lucky man a grand wife, so."

"Are you being sarcastic?" Fidelma frowned.

"I am not. Not at all."

"All right. Thank you." Fidelma smiled weakly. "I would have for Connor. I wish . . ." She pursed her lips, then swallowed. She shook her head. "Ah sure, if wishes were horses, beggars would ride."

Maureen touched her sister's arm, but said nothing.

Fidelma kept her voice level. "So, I've no Connor. I've a horrible job because I didn't even sit for my Junior Certificate. Don't you make the same mistake and leave school too early."

Maureen cocked her head and looked at Fidelma. "I'll not. I'll do what Miss Toner says. She says the first step to having good employment is getting an education."

"Don't I know it now?"

"And she thinks women should be able to get good jobs too. Maybe even be doctors or lawyers."

"She's some brave ideas, your Miss Toner." Fidelma said. "So are you for being a doctor? First woman head of the new parliament, the *Dáil Eireann*? We'd all have to curtsey to you, Lady Muck." Fidelma's lip curled ever so.

Eighteen months ago Maureen would have gone for her sister. Now she was willing to let the slight go by. Fidelma's sarcasm was better than the horrible silences. Maureen shook her head. "Not at all. I'm not that smart." Her a doctor? She laughed at the thought. "But I am going to stay on until I pass my School Leaver's Certificate exam. And you know, Fiddles, women *can* rise in the world."

"Like who?" There was still a bit of an edge to the voice.

Maureen kept on turning the other cheek. "Miss Toner's been telling us about Countess Constance Markiewicz. Mister Yeats wrote a poem about her and her sister. Called her a gazelle."

"And who's she when she's at home, then? Some foreign highheejin?"

"She is not. She's as Irish as you and me, even if she was born in England. She grew up in Lissadell in Sligo. She married a Polish count from the Ukraine, but she was born Gore-Booth."

"With a double-breasted English name like that, she must be upper crust."

"Yes, she is, and Miss Toner says that does give those folks an advantage, but they have to use it. The countess did. She was an officer in Dublin in the 1916 Easter Rising, the first woman elected to the Westminster parliament when Ireland was still part of Britain, and she became a cabinet minister—minister of labour—in the new Irish parliament."

Fidelma's eyes had widened. "She must be a powerful woman, so."

"Miss Toner says—"

"You think a lot of her, don't you?" Her voice was softer now.

Maureen nodded. "I do."

"I never paid much heed to the woman. Maybe I should have." Fidelma's eyes shone, and a tear ran down her cheek. "I couldn't be bothered with classwork. I thought exams didn't matter. I didn't think anything mattered except falling in love." Her shoulders shook.

Maureen put her arms around her older sister and hugged her close. She made soothing noises, then hunted in her pocket for a clean hanky.

Fidelma threw away the tattered flower, accepted the hanky, dried her eyes, and blew her nose. "I'll be all right," she said, "in just a shmall little minute, so."

Maureen waited.

Fidelma returned the hanky.

"Fiddles," Maureen said, "maybe you *could* get a new start?"

"How? I've no real education. I can

read and write and number; that's about it." She gulped in a breath. "And do you think Connor's going to come back? It's him I want."

"I know," Maureen said, as gently as she could, "but maybe you'll meet someone else. Get married." She knew her sister was right about not being educated. Marriage was about the only choice left to her now. "And like you said, when you do, you'll not have to work at the mill anymore."

"Married? I don't want to get married just to get out of the mill. I want to get married because I'm in love. I'll never find another Connor. It was pure luck that he lived just up the road a ways. It's not easy meeting boys. There does not be that many dances. I see some lads on the bus going to work, farm labourers going to a hiring fair, fellahs that work at the mill, road menders, peat cutters." She gave a snorty little laugh. "I don't think a Ukrainian count is going to sweep *me* off my feet."

"That's another thing Miss Toner's hot about. She says Ireland's no better than England for maintaining the class system." She mimicked her teacher's northern accent. "'Youse peasants had better know your place, so youse had,' Miss Toner says. Why can't a farm girl like me better herself . . . and not just by getting wed to Doctor O'Lunney's son? I'm in no rush to get married for a while anyways. Not until the right fellah comes along."

"Nor me," Fidelma said. "But I don't want to work at the mill either."

"Could you not just quit?"

"I suppose . . . I suppose I could, but with Tiernan and you and me still at home, my wages help."

Maureen swallowed. "If it would do any good, Fiddles, I could give up the weekend camogie games. Get some part-time work then. I'm a good seamstress. I can clean a house. I can cook. You could have a wee break from the mill. Look for something better. I hear Mrs. Thompson, the major's wife in the big house, needs a cleaner."

Fidelma shook her head. "Thank you for suggesting you'd do that. You're a generous girl, Maureen O'Hanlon, but me a cleaner is it? A skivvy?" There was a bite in her voice. "I'll do no such thing and nor will you. You go on and get good enough to play camogie for County Cork. Da will be so proud."

"Are you sure you won't let me help?"

"I am, and I'm sure of something else. I've had a bit of time to think since Connor died. I would have had more choices if I'd stayed at my studies. Sometimes I wish I had, but I never made a great fist of it. Your Miss Toner's right about the learning, so don't you leave school early. You get your Leaver's."

"I'm going to."

"Good girl." Fidelma held Maureen's chin in her hand and looked into her sister's eyes. "I've made my bed. I'll lie in it, but the mill's not for you, Maureen, nor the cleaning. You've got to have more to look forward to in your life. Promise me you'll keep at your studies, now. You were top of your class last year. Do better than the farm, the mill, boys. Promise me."

"I promise, Fidelma. Cross my heart."

And it wasn't a hard promise for Maureen to make. She loved her books, particularly Irish history, and boys didn't interest her. There was a Donovan Flynn who she sometimes bumped into at weekends after his hurling practice on a pitch next door to the camogie field. He was a year older, and when she saw him she felt—well, she wasn't sure how she felt. She'd let him hold her hand, but she'd drawn the line when he'd tried to kiss her behind the GAA sports pavilion last Saturday. "You know I'm going to sit the Junior Certificate examination next year."

"Pass it and go on for your School Leaver's Certificate two years after with good marks so you can get a job as a bank teller or with a bit more training, a secretary. Good jobs. Clean jobs."

She hesitated. Maureen had not even mentioned to Ma what she was going to tell Fidelma. Maureen felt deep inside that she could trust her big sister. "Fidelma," she said very quietly, "I don't want to be a secretary."

"All right. Bank teller? Nurse maybe?"

Maureen shook her head. "Miss Toner said with the certificate I could be a teacher."

Fidelama whistled. "A teacher, is it?"

"Aye, so."

"In a country where most girls leave school by fourteen or, like me, by sixteen at the latest, you'd be a marvel in the townland, Maureen O'Hanlon, so." Fidelma folded her arms and stroked her chin with her left hand, frowned, and then grinned and said, "Good for you, Maureen. You're right, and if you have a dream, you follow it, and I'll . . . and I'll help you, so."

Maureen kissed her sister's cheek. "You're sweet, Fiddles, mavourneen. Now keep it to yourself. I don't want people laughing at me. Calling me a farm girl with ideas above her station."

"I'll say not a word, but I think it's grand, so. There'll be nobody laughing if you pull it off, and why shouldn't you succeed? You're a smart girl, Maureen. If you keep at it and go on to something better, the world'll be your oyster."

Maureen chuckled. "I don't like oysters, but I would like to see a bit of the world one day."

Fidelma said. "So keep as many choices open as possible."

"I will." Maureen looked at her big sister. She hesitated. Fidelma was as proud as Connor had been. "And maybe I could help you?"

"How?"

"Would you think of taking a correspondence course?"

"Are you taking the mickey?" Fidelma's eyes narrowed.

Maureen realised her sister was starting to bridle again. She rushed to say, "I am not, so. Not one bit. You *could* take one. I *will* help you with it."

Fidelma shrugged. "Divil the bit. I'm no hand at the studying. I'll stay on at the mill for a while." She managed a weak smile. "I'll be grand. Don't you worry. Do you know?" she said, "nobody can tell what their future might hold, so you be sure you're well prepared for anything that comes along."

"I will." Maureen hesitated, then said, "Wouldn't it be lovely if Ma could tell our fortunes? Then we'd know."

"Like a gypsy?" Fidelma shook her head. "It doesn't work like that for her. She never seems to know when it's going to come on her, or sometimes what she's seen confuses her."

"Och, sure I know." The talk about foretelling things gave Maureen an idea that might bring a smile to Fidelma's lips.

"But," she said, "I'm . . . I'm seeing the future right now." She held her head in both hands. Her voice was quavery.

Fidelma, eyes wide, asked. "What . . . what are you seeing, Maureen?"

"I see that Ma has a ham on for tea . . . and if we're late she'll have our hides." She laughed.

Fidelma frowned. "Ma's got . . . ?" Then she smiled. "Maureen, you had me going there." A chuckle started, then Fidelma laughed. "You were having me on. I thought you meant you were getting the sight, like Ma, so."

Maureen thought that too, after what had happened at the cottage, but while she'd been happy to tell Fidelma about her secret plans, this other thing was one concern she'd keep to herself until she'd spoken to Ma. "Not at all," she said. "I said it for to make you laugh, Fiddles."

"You're an eejit, Maureen O'Hanlon. *An poc ar buile.*"

"A mad goat, is it?" Maureen grinned. It was the first time for months she'd seen her sister laugh at anything. She kissed Fidelma, then said, "Come on." She started to run. "Last one home washes the dishes after tea."

And as she tore along, easily outpacing her sister, Maureen thought about gypsies seeing the future. She very much doubted if they could.

But Ma did. Ma understood things not of this world, and much as Maureen might be laughing with her sister now, it didn't change what had happened at Connor's. After the meal, she would get Ma on her own, tell her about everything at the cottage, and ask Ma to explain.

17

After tea, as Fidelma washed the dishes, Maureen dried, and Ma set the table ready for tomorrow's breakfast. Maureen hung up her tea towel and whispered to Ma, "I need a wee word, Ma."

Ma nodded. "Go on up. I'll be along in a shmall little minute."

Maureen left the kitchen and climbed the uneven wooden stairs. The treads were worn concave, and as usual the third and seventh treads creaked underfoot. The banister of the second flight was wobbly.

It was warm in her room. When Maureen opened a window she heard a thrush making sweet, double-noted music, and a flock of starlings squabbling on the barn roof. The evening sunlight fell as softly as ducks' down on the new leaves of the sycamores outside.

"Can I come in?" Ma stood in the doorway.

"Of course." Maureen sat on the bed.

The springs creaked when Ma sat beside her. "Now . . . tell me all about it, Maureen O'Hanlon. What is it that does be troubling you?"

Maureen took a shallow breath. "I went with Fidelma to Connor's cottage today. She goes there a lot. She keeps the place clean, says she feels closer to Connor there." From the corner of her eye Maureen noticed her old teddy bear, patched and missing both ears. He was lying askew on her pillow. The sight distracted her for a second; then she looked at Ma and took a deeper breath. "I saw . . . I saw Connor sitting at his table. Later on I heard his pipes."

Ma pursed her lips and rubbed one reddened, knobbed hand with the other. "Did you, so?"

Maureen nodded. "I did." She hesitated,

expecting some exclamation, but Ma simply looked deeply into Maureen's eyes.

She told her mother exactly what had happened: the misty figure, the falling plate, the cold, and how she had seen what Fidelma clearly had not.

Ma didn't interrupt, but when Maureen finished, she asked, "And were you scared, *a chara*?" Ma always called her "dear" if she thought Maureen needed comfort.

"I was, but I remembered how Connor was always so nice. I didn't think he'd harm us."

"You're sure it was Connor? You said you couldn't make out its face."

"Who else could it be, and when we were leaving who but him would have been playing the pipes?"

"And you could sense him and Fidelma could not?"

Maureen nodded. "I could, so, and it wasn't sense, Ma. I saw the outline of a man, I felt the icy cold, and I heard the pipes."

Ma's question came rapidly. "You didn't say anything at all to Fidelma?"

"I asked her if she'd ever seen him or

heard him, and she said no, but she would like to . . . just one more time."

"But you didn't tell her what you'd seen?" There was an urgency as she spoke.

Maureen shook her head.

Ma blew out her breath. "I'm glad for that, so, for it is impetuous you can sometimes be, Maureen O'Hanlon."

Maureen shook her head. "I did not. I didn't think it was a very good idea."

"You were right, so." Ma held her own chin in the web of her left hand, index finger across the corner of her mouth, and stroked Maureen's hair with the other. "I'm sure, daughter," she said very seriously, "it *was* himself you saw."

"What does it mean, Ma? I'd have thought he'd have come to Fidelma, not me."

Ma went on stroking. "I think he probably was hoping she'd see him, but not everyone can, except in very special circumstances. Sometimes if there does be great danger and a Thevshee's trying to help, it can be noticed by folks who ordinarily would not be able to appreciate it. There was no danger today to Fidelma was there?"

"No, Ma."

"Aye, so." Ma sighed. "In this life, *muirnín*, there are those who can see and those who cannot, and don't ask me why. I think it's like the music."

"Connor's music that me and Eamon MacVeigh heard?"

"Not Connor's. The music live people make. There's a few folks have voices like angels, but most can't carry a tune in a bucket nor play for toffee apples. Some have the talent for melody. Most don't." She hugged Maureen. "I think you have a gift like the tuneful ones, only your gift is to see."

She felt her mother's strong arms and soft breast. She snuggled and looked into Ma's face.

"It does run in families. I got the sight passed on from your Granny Fogarty when I was still living at home in Bantry." Ma inhaled deeply. "I was about your age when it started. The first time something happened I was fourteen, helping with the harvest."

Maureen saw her mother's eyes. They were not entirely in focus.

"I was come over queerly," she said.

"The world about me slowed down. It looked as if the horses pulling the harvester were trying to wade through a sea of cold molasses. Men with scythes were frozen like statues—"

Maureen could picture the scene. Her words slipped out. "It must have been awful."

Ma's eyes came back into focus and she turned her gaze to Maureen. "Can you not hold your wheest, child? 'Twas not awful; it was what it was and that's all."

"Sorry, Ma."

"Aye. Well . . . it's rude for a child to interrupt an adult. Have I to tell you that until my face turns black?"

Maureen hung her head. "No, Ma. Sorry."

Ma smiled. "All right then, girl. We'll say no more about it. Now . . . where was I?"

"Everything had slowed down."

"That's right, and the edges of things got blurred, colours faded, sounds were muted. I couldn't hear the harvester blades, and you know what a clattery racket they make. Then I saw a brackeny place I'd never seen before and a lamb at the bottom of a pit. I heard it bleat; then I heard the harvester again, and the lamb faded away and the horses plodded on as if nothing had happened."

Maureen moved back a little. She didn't want to make Ma cross again, but when she hadn't spoken for a while Maureen's curiosity got the better of her. "A lamb?"

Ma nodded, her eyes now bright as ever. "When I got home, I described everything to Granny. She said she knew the place I'd seen and that a neighbour had been looking for a lamb for two days. She sent my brother, your uncle Seamus, to run over, and sure enough, didn't he come home with the wee craytur?" Ma blew out her breath. "I've had the sight since."

Maureen looked at the floor, then back up at her mother. "Could I get it from you?"

"I think," said Ma, "I think you already have, or anyway you're starting to get it."

Maureen swallowed and took hold of her mother's hand. "Starting to be getting it?"

"It never comes all at once. Your Granny Fogarty told me it always starts slow. 'Do you remember, Roisín,' says she, 'how when your monthlies began they weren't much at all and you never knew when they might happen?'

" 'I do,' says I. 'Then after a bit they were stronger and regular.' That's the way the sight comes on. Weak at the start, but one day, strong."

"It was only a smoky thing, but I didn't think seeing Connor was weak," Maureen said, still feeling flattered that Ma would be so honest about personal things in her own girlhood.

"I never said that it was. You saw his spirit all right."

"And will I see into the future like you, Ma?"

"I'm not sure."

"But you can sometimes tell what's going to happen?"

Ma shook her head slowly. "Sometimes," she said. "But usually when the sight comes to me, it's not like looking through a telescope. Things do come in blurs and fragments. It's like looking into a kaleidoscope with a mirror missing." She fixed her gaze on Maureen. "And it's not every time I'm able to understand, so I prefer not to say much except in vague terms. Like the advice I gave poor Connor." Ma wrung her hands without seeming to know she was doing it. "I knew there'd be a blizzard, for I saw the snow, and I saw dead sheep, but I didn't know it would be the death of him. I only suspected."

"But you warned him anyway."

Ma smiled at Maureen. "Of course. That's what the sight's for. For the good of others. Better for me to warn someone and be wrong than hold my wheest and let something awful happen. Always remember that, if you do find you can tell the future."

"I will, Ma."

Ma wagged a finger. "You'd better, girl. I know you like to act the lig, tease Fidelma, but the sight is not to be taken lightly."

Maureen nodded.

"Now, I'm not saying it will come so strong." Ma stroked Maureen's hair. "It is given to each one differently. I can't make out spirits the way you can. Sure didn't you see the banshee?"

"I did, so." Maureen shuddered. It had been nearly eighteen months ago, but she could still picture the eerie light in this room, the white-haired woman and the keening of her, and her own temerity at thinking for a moment she was going to chase the terrible faery away. Maureen smiled at the memory.

"It's no laughing matter, Maureen." Ma's voice was very serious.

Maureen's smile faded.

"Now," Ma continued, "you'll maybe see Connor again or the Shee, and when you do, it will be more clearly each time, but only if they want you to see them."

"So Connor wanted me to see him to-day?"

"He did. He may sometimes be near and not want anyone to know, and why that might be I'd have no idea, but I know it to be true, so."

Maureen thought about that. "Only if *they* want to," she said. "I understand."

"Good," said Ma. "For seeing the others may be all you ever do, so don't you fret about seeing the future. That may never happen at all."

Maureen swallowed. "I'll tell you, Ma, if anything does come on me."

"Aye, so, and nobody else. Not a soul.

Not everyone understands. If you do find out something that might help somebody, come to me and I'll tell them in your stead, at least until you are full grown and on your own."

Maureen remembered Ma's advice about how to stop people thinking she had the evil eye. From now on she'd not neglect to say, "God bless the child," when it was needed.

"I'm not saying you will and I'm not saying you won't," Ma said slowly, "but it's best to be prepared."

Maureen thought of the other advice she had received that afternoon from Fidelma. This was the second time she was being told to be prepared for what the future might hold.

"You might very well get the sight clearer than I. You're already seeing the spirits, and most folks I've heard tell of who have that gift often go on to see the future."

Maureen shuddered as Ma continued. "I think for a while it'll not be clear to you at all, but one day something, and I don't know what, something enormous will happen in your life—"

"The way it did to Saint Paul on the road to Damascus?"

"Exactly. And from that day on, things will come to you as clear as day."

"And it'll be all right? I've no need to worry? It won't hurt me?"

"Lord bless and keep you, daughter dear, not at all. Haven't I just told you it's for the good of others?"

"You have."

Ma kissed her. "No more concerns, accept what you are given, and don't let it trouble you. A lot of things come with growing up."

Maureen glanced back at her tattered teddy. Poor old thing. "I know. And I'll not worry." She smiled.

"Good girl. Growing up's a voyage. And may the strength of three be in the journey for you."

"Thank you, Ma," Maureen said.

"So you've understood what I've told you?"

"Yes, Ma."

"See you do. Now . . ." Ma rose. "I've to be getting on. I've pies in the oven."

"Would you have one more wee minute before you go?"

"Only a minute now."

"You've always encouraged us to stay in school, so if I go on getting good enough marks there . . ." The words tumbled out. "I want to be a teacher."

Ma frowned. Inhaled. Breathed out. "Teacher? Teacher, is it? There's a thing." She steepled her fingers under her lips, then cocked her head to one side. "Would that mean university?"

Maureen shook her head. "All I'd need is my Leaver's. Then I'd start as a monitor—that's a kind of junior teacher— and after a year or two they'd promote me to teacher proper, Ma. Miss Toner explained that to me."

"I see." Ma looked very thoughtful for a moment. "I'm not sure we'd have the money to send you to the University College in Cork City."

"Miss Toner says there's no need."

"Your Miss Toner's an unmarried lady, I believe."

"She is."

"And have you no notion of getting married? Having a family of your own? Your Da and I want lots of grandchildren."

"Of course I'll get married one day and

have a family. I love kiddies. But it'll not be for a while . . . I'm young yet. I'm only fifteen."

"True on you."

"And it would have to be the right fellah. And I'll know him when he comes along."

"You make sure of that now, so. Marry in haste, regret at your leisure." Ma frowned. She slipped her right hand behind her head and stroked her neck. "A teacher? Huh."

Maureen knew her mother always did that when she was deep in thought. She waited, wondering what Ma might say.

"Going on would make you happy, *a chara*?"

"It would, Ma. It really would. I've have a career, a good wage, a *really* interesting life."

Ma bridled. "And do you not think being a farmer's wife is interesting, Miss High and Mighty?"

"Ma, come on. I didn't mean that at all."

"Well, it sounded like it. Maureen O'Hanlon, *think* before you speak."

"I will, Ma. I promise." Maureen remained as silent as her mother, willing her to say yes.

Finally Ma said, "So you'd be happy and the O'Hanlons would have a scholar in the family?" She made a low whistling noise. "A teacher, by the hokey."

Maureen smiled and nodded.

"All right. I'll think it over." Ma frowned again.

Maureen jumped off the bed and hugged her mother. "Thank you, Ma. Thank you."

"Now slow down. I haven't agreed yet. I will need to give this a lot of thought. It's a big step for a girl. And your Da can be a bit old-fashioned. He's like a lot of men. He thinks girls should make good marriages. He was happy as a clown when Sinead wed Malachy."

Maureen's grin faded. "But, Ma, I'm not going to get wed straight out of school. I have to do something. Why not teach? And it's the kind of job you could maybe go back to when your family's grown a bit."

Ma pursed her lips. "Lord, Maureen, you're at it again. You already have me half persuaded. You don't need to keep worrying at me like a terrier at a rat. I said I'll think about it, and I will, so. It's your Da I need to talk it over with," Ma said. "He's head of this family."

"Would you, Ma? Would you? I really want to do it. I don't want to get married yet. I do so want to be . . . to be educated."

Ma hugged Maureen. "Do you, now? Well, you could want worse. So, I'll tell you what we'll do. Get your Junior next year; then it's two years away yet to your Leaver's, but you go on getting the marks. If I still think it's a good idea by then, I'll see to your Da."

Maureen wondered, was Ma testing her? It didn't matter. Deep inside, Maureen knew Ma would agree when the time was right. And if she needed more persuading, wouldn't Fidelma be an ally?

Maureen had been aware for quite some time who the real head of the O'Hanlon family was. Ma would twist Da around her finger. Maureen hugged her mother. "Thanks, Ma. Thanks for explaining about the sight." She kissed Ma. "And thanks for saying I can go on at school and that you will think about what I want. Thank you, Ma. Thank you."

"Och, sure, isn't that what Ma's are for? Now you do your best, enjoy your life, and I'm sure good things will happen one day."

18

Kinky told herself she'd been idle long enough up here in the warmth of the up-stairs sitting room. The apple-potato fadges had been lovely. Just the right mix of Bramleys and potato. She wiped the crumbs from her lips with a linen napkin. Ma had been right. Good things *had* happened back then, but they'd not be happening here if she didn't go and see to her cooking. As Ma often said about a lazybones, it was a bad hen that wouldn't scratch itself.

Kinky headed for the kitchen, her mind still half in the past.

They *had* been some marvellous years. In June of 1925 she'd sat for and passed her Junior Certificate with honours. Ma was jubilant. Even Da was impressed. He'd had Ma help him pick out and buy Maureen a garnet necklace. Kinky's hand went to her throat. She wore the red pendant to this day. It was then Ma had told Maureen that if it was teaching she wanted, teaching she could have, and a Da who bought necklaces wouldn't be hard to persuade. He hadn't been.

In September, one week after her sixteenth birthday, she had been selected as substitute for the Cork junior camogie team. Everyone said unless the unexpected happened, she'd be a full team member by next season and on the senior team soon after.

On New Year's Eve in 1925 she'd finally let Donovan Flynn kiss her a few times and found she enjoyed it. But when he tried to put his hand under her blouse, she'd pushed him away, called him a dirty wee gurrier, and slapped his face so hard her hand stung. Keep away from boys, Fidelma had said. By all the saints, she would.

Another Christmas came and went. That was the Christmas Ma had taught her to make chestnut stuffing.

It was funny how she remembered those little things, she thought, as she opened the oven. That was Ma's stuffing cooking in the neck end of the turkey. She basted the bird, listening to the hot fat sizzle and spit. It was coming on a treat. About an hour before she'd be ready to serve the meal, she'd put the ham in the oven to bake, and twenty minutes later she'd surround the bird with half-boiled potatoes to roast in its fat. The chipolata sausages would join the potatoes fifteen minutes before she took the bird and the ham out and let them rest before serving.

The front doorbell rang. Kinky closed the oven and went to answer the door. After the warmth of the upstairs lounge and the heat in the kitchen, she shivered as snowflakes swept by.

A skinny man with a bulbous red nose stood on the doorstep. He lifted his black trilby hat. "Merry Christmas, Mrs. Kincaid. Are the doctors in?"

"Merry Christmas, Mr. Coffin. Is it sick you are for they are both out?"

"Sick? Not at all. Hale and hearty, so I am." The brown paper bag the village undertaker thrust at her made a chinking noise. "That's a wee Merry Christmas from me to the doctors. A wee thanks for telling me to take Saint-John's-wort tea to keep me cheerful." He grinned. "I'll be seeing them at the marquis' party, but I didn't want to take the, ahem, gift there." He tipped his trilby. "Good-bye to you now."

"I'll tell them and I'll see they get these," she said. Kinky closed the door, put two bottles of Jameson's whiskey on the sideboard in the dining room along with serried ranks of Christmas cards, and went back to the kitchen.

All the pans of vegetables and potatoes were waiting on the stove top or on the shelf nearby.

The bread sauce wouldn't be ready to put on the stove until she'd stuck enough cloves in a whole, peeled onion, then cut it in half and put that in the pan with the rest of the ingredients she'd mixed before the children came. The sauce needn't go on yet, but she'd get the cloves for when she was ready to start on the onion.

She opened a cupboard and took down the bottle of cloves and, while she was at it, a jar of the crab-apple jelly she'd made that summer. Doctor O'Reilly was very fond of the crab-apple jelly, but then, she smiled, if there was anything a body could eat, himself would take a shine to it.

He'd have liked her bilberry jelly, but bilberry shrubs didn't grow here in north County Down. Bilberries, called *fraochán* or frockon in County Cork, were everywhere in the peat bogs near the O'Hanlon farm. They ripened in late July and early August.

It was customary for unmarried girls to pluck them on *Lughnasa,* the festival held on the Sunday closest to August the first. It marked the end of what were known as "the hungry months" because it was when the harvest started. People could stop eating preserved foods like salted beef and pickled beetroot. There'd be no need to cook old potatoes because now it was time to harvest the new ones.

It was the same every year, with Da saying, "There's two things too serious to be joked about: matrimony and potatoes, so." There was a ceremony for the first pulling of the praties, and as part of the tradition Ma had to wear a clean white apron.

Come to that, Kinky reckoned, she'd better change her own apron. This one had been splattered while she was basting the turkey.

Once she'd changed and had satisfied herself that the meal was coming along as it should and could be left on its own for a while, Kinky pulled out a stool and sat. She remembered Ma in her clean pinafore on *Lughnasa* in 1926.

That year the first of August had fallen on a Sunday.

All Kinky had to do was close her eyes and there she was, after lunch, tramping with Fidelma along the road toward the peat bog where the frockon grew. As the girls walked they were accompanied by the lilting of wood pigeons in the sycamores and the steady distant thumping of a threshing machine being driven by a broad leather belt round the flywheel of a steam traction engine. She could see the smoke from the engine's funnel and a cloud of dust rising from the thresher. It was dirty, dry work feeding the sheaves of cut grain into it.

The air was heavy, but not with the scent of flowers. This was the time of year farmers had their muck spreaders in action, fertilizing the fields for this year's planting. Pig manure was pungent and smelt like ammonia. Maureen wrinkled her nose.

Somewhere a dog barked and from a large patch of nettles came the harsh kerrx-*kerrx* of a corncrake. The sound the slender, rail-like brown bird made was like that of two cheese graters being rubbed together.

Maureen heard a motor put-putting behind them, turned, and saw the MacVeighs' lorry trundling along the road. It pulled alongside and stopped. Eamon leaned out of the windowless cab, his carroty hair jutting out from under the peak of his tweed duncher. "Afternoon, girls. Grand day for the time of year that it's in, so."

"'Tis marvellous altogether, Eamon," Fidelma said. She smiled.

"Can I lift you two? I'm going to Clonakilty. We're setting up the bandstand for the dance tonight."

"We're only going to the frockon bog," Maureen said.

"Hop in anyway. I'll take you as far as the road up."

Maureen followed Fidelma round the vehicle and climbed in after her sister. It was a tight fit, three of them on the bench. Eamon was rather tall around. He started off with a great grinding of gears. "How do you like the lorry?"

It's noisy, smells of pigs, and on its solid tyres it bounces like a jelly, Maureen thought. But she said, "It's wonderful. What kind is it?" Boys, she'd discovered, liked being asked that kind of question.

"It's a Thorneycroft J Type, 1916, British army," he said proudly. "My Da got it cheap when the English sodgers sold off a bunch of stuff before their army left Ireland a couple of years back."

"It's wonderful, and you're very clever to be able to drive it so nicely," Fidelma said in her most sincere voice.

Eamon grinned and accelerated. The lorry backfired.

Fidelma laughed.

Maureen held tight, looked at her sister, and smiled. In the nearly four years since Connor's death, Fidelma, now twenty-one, had mellowed and was coming out of her shell. She'd stopped visiting Connor's place a year ago, and about the same time she'd started going to the occasional dance. She still was not walking out with anyone, but she could laugh again, enjoy boys' company. Here she was teasing Eamon, and by the way he was blushing, he must have thought she'd meant her praise. "Are the pair of you going to the *céili* tonight?" he asked.

Maureen tingled. It would be her first grown-up dance. Ma had said she was old enough to go with Fidelma as her chaperone.

"We are," Fidelma said. "Malachy's taking us in the jaunting car. We'll maybe see you there?"

A chaperone. Maureen didn't think she'd need much watching over. She'd got over Donovan Flynn's clumsy fumbling, had been to several birthday parties, and had been kissed by more than one boy, but not by anybody who made Maureen feel the way she knew Fidelma had felt about Connor.

"Aye, so." Eamon slowed and braked.

"There's your road. May it rise up to meet you."

"Thanks, Eamon." Maureen got out and waited for Fidelma. She heard Eamon say to her sister, "M . . . maybe you'll give me a d . . . dance tonight, Miss O'Hanlon? A h . . . hornpipe?"

Poor Eamon stuttered when he was embarrassed.

"Maybe I will," Fidelma said, hopping down, "and maybe I won't, but thanks for the ride." And she laughed.

Her laugh gladdened Maureen's heart. That Eamon hadn't asked *her* bothered her not one whit.

"Come on, Maureen," Fidelma said. "The sooner we get the berries picked, the better." She strode off.

Maureen followed. "And maybe the mile walk up to the bog'll help work off Ma's *Lughnasa* lunch," she said. "That colcannon was lovely, all those new potatoes and cabbage, green onions and bacon. But I shouldn't have had a second slice of gooseberry pie, even if I did make it myself."

"Och, aye, you're so fat, Maureen, you'll

be breaking the scales Da uses to weigh the piglets." Fidelma laughed. "You're no shrimp now."

"Less of your slagging, Fidelma O'Hanlon," Maureen said. "I can run the legs off you any day, you snail." She was pleased that the teasing, which had always had an edge when they were younger, was good-natured now. They had started to grow closer ever since the day two years ago when Maureen had gone for a walk with her sister and seen Connor's ghost.

"True," said Fidelma, and shook her head. "Honest to goodness, girl, you've nothing to worry about. You're the best-looking seventeen-year-old in all of the province of Munster, you with that chestnut hair, those dimples, shining dark eyes—"

"Go away on out with you, Fiddles," said Maureen, interrupting her sister. "You can flatter Eamon all you like, but you'll not get away with it with me. Soft words butter no parsnips, so."

"It's not flattery. It's true, Maureen. It's all that galloping about, playing camogie, keeps you trim. You've a figure like Clara Bow." Fidelma scrutinized her sister's bust. "Maybe a bit better padded." She chuckled.

Maureen glanced down at herself. "I'm not so sure I am. I like Clara Bow," she said. "She was wonderful when you took me to Dunmanway to see *My Lady's Lips.* And I liked William Powell too."

Fidelma sighed. "Eamon MacVeigh's no William Powell," she said, "but I will let him dance with me tonight." She pulled up a stem of grass and nibbled the end of it. "Working at the mill's still a terrible drudge. I'd love to get away from the scruffy old place." She sighed again. "Eamon's the oldest MacVeigh boy. He'll get the farm when his Da passes. I suppose I could do worse than a *garsún* like him."

"Gossoon? Eamon's more like a bassoon if you ask me . . . the size of him. If he's what you want . . . but you could do better, Fidelma. Far better."

"Maybe, but we're farmers, Eamon's a farmer. He'd be more of a catch than a labourer, a bricklayer, a road sweeper"— she laughed—"or a tinker, and as you said, neither one of us is going to land Doctor O'Lunney's son." She hesitated, then said, "Maybe *you* will, once you're a teacher, a professional lady. More of his station."

"Huh. I'm in no rush for Dennis O'Lunney," Maureen said. "Have you seen the lad? He's like a long drink of water with buckteeth."

Fidelma laughed. "And Eamon's a bit on the chubby side, but he has a heart of corn. I could do worse."

"You are a bit strapped for choice, I grant you, but there's bound to be other lads at the dance." Maureen widened her eyes, held the back of her wrist against her forehead, and said huskily, "Maybe himself, Rudolph Valentino, will be there and whisk you off to his tent."

"You can laugh. I think he's the berries."

"And so are these." Maureen pointed. "There's frockon everywhere. We'd better start picking."

They were on the edge of what had been Connor's turf bog, for bilberries favoured damp acidy soils, and judging by the squelching underfoot it was damp enough to please any shrub that liked growing in a sheugh.

Maureen stooped to pluck the dusty, blue berries as they grew two by two from their low shrubs. A caterpillar, brown with black markings, was feeding on a leaf. She'd found the story of insect metamorphosis fascinating when she'd read about it in nature-study class. Soon the wriggling thing would become a pupa growing inside its shell, waiting to hatch. Then a moth, a delicate little feathery creature, would flutter in the August dusk in search of love with one of its own kind or, she reflected with a sigh, a fiery death against a light. It was, she thought, a beautiful sad story.

She worked away, filling her basket. *Am I a pupa still?* She certainly wasn't the awkward schoolgirl who hadn't wanted Donovan Flynn to fondle her. She hoped she wasn't being vain, but Fidelma hadn't been flattering. Maureen knew she was a pretty girl.

When will I become a woman? When will I fall in love? When I do, will it have to be with a local? Maybe once I've got to be a real teacher with a decent wage, I'll get a job at a school in Cork City, even if it is a good twenty miles as the crow flies, or, the thought staggered her imagination, in Dublin. And if I did, who would I meet there? Who knows? They'd not be farm labourers, that's for sure. And anyway it wouldn't be for a while yet, if she went at all. Still, Miss Toner had said at the end of term that if Maureen could keep her marks up next year she'd certainly get her Leaver's, and with distinction too. It was only the first step. Then a couple of years as a monitor and maybe, maybe—Maureen smiled at the thought of her future—a clean page for her to write on as she saw fit.

She ate a handful of berries, the juice red on her hands and tart on her lips. She was reaching for another when a sound made her freeze, her hand halfway to the bush. The notes of "Planxty Gordon" were faint in her ears. The sound of the pipes came from the high pasture.

Maureen looked at her sister, but Fidelma must have been unaware. She was plucking away, filling her basket.

As hard as Maureen strained to make out who was playing, she could see nothing further up the hill except the haze of summer heat above the sere grass and purple heather. Yet she knew who was playing. Poor Connor. Poor man. Will you never find peace?

She wanted to leave, to go down home to where she'd not be hearing ghostly music. To be where she could run to Ma for comfort.

"We've enough, Fiddles," she said.

"Just a few more." Fidelma picked more quickly.

"Then let's head home. We'll need time to get ready."

"Soon," Fidelma said, "and sure who knows what might happen at the hooley? Maybe a really good fellah will take a shine to me." She laughed. "Maybe even your man Valentino."

"I hope it's a real man, Fidelma. I really do."

"Thank you," Fidelma said. "Who knows? Perhaps you'll find a sweetheart yourself."

Minutes ago, Maureen'd been wondering about the lads in Cork City, but going there was years away. She'd got over her shyness with boys, and she did enjoyed being kissed. And she reckoned local lads were probably just as good at that as city fellahs. A sweetheart, but not a serious one, would be nice.

She found she had embarrassed herself by the thought. Maureen felt the heat in her cheeks, but didn't care if she was blushing. There was no one to see her except Fidelma. She looked over to her sister, bent over a bush, intent on her picking.

A sudden movement off to one side made Maureen turn her head. A red vixen was sitting on a hillock, her brush twitching. As Maureen watched, the pointy muzzle and dark brown eyes were transformed into the face of a beautiful woman. Her gaze bored into Maureen's eyes.

The summer hillside's constant music of birdsong and breeze fell silent, and the haze blurred everything—except the foxwoman. Maureen felt her basket slipping from her grasp. Her arms were powerless. The woman winked slowly once, as the basket tumbled to the ground.

She heard Fidelma call, "Maureen O'Hanlon, have you lost your senses? Sometimes you're as loose and careless as the leg of a pot, so."

Maureen blinked and saw Fidelma

scooping up the berries and putting them in the basket. But on the hillside there was nothing else in sight. Only the peat bog, brown and grassy, and the heather, blue and purple under the August sun.

19

"So you heard the pipes up on the hillside and then saw the fox with a woman's face?" Ma asked, as she brushed Maureen's chestnut hair.

"I did, Ma, and the fox winked at me."

"Were you scared?"

"I was not. Not of the pipes. I . . . I sort of got used to the notion of Connor after the first time I saw him and you explained to me about my gift, but I was so startled by the vixen I dropped my basket. I think Fidelma thought I'd taken leave of my senses."

"You didn't see Connor at all?" Ma kept brushing.

"Not this time. You've told me I'd only see Connor if he wanted me to see him. But I did hear his pipes very clearly and I'm sure it was him playing." She forced a weak smile. "Foxes don't have enough fingers for the *uillinn* pipes."

Ma smiled.

"Ma, what does seeing the fox-woman mean? Did *she* want me to see her?" Maureen half turned.

"I reckon there's not much doubt, but—"

"Ouch." Maureen's hand flew to her head. The brush had caught in her hair.

"If you'd stay still that wouldn't happen," Ma said levelly. "But not you. Even when you were a little girl you always had ants in your pants." She brushed firmly. "Now sit you still 'til I'm done."

"Yes, Ma."

"I'm sure that vixen's the queen of the Doov Shee," Ma said. "It is her that holds Connor's soul. You heard him piping before you saw her. The Shee love music. I think she was making him play for her."

"But why would she show herself to me?"

"I'm not sure altogether. To almost anybody else she'd have seemed to be a fox. Maybe she understood you had the gift, knew you could see past her disguise if she let you, and she acknowledged that by letting you see her face and winking at you. I think in a way she was saying that because you have the gift, the Doov Shee will be your friends."

"My friends?"

"I think so."

"So she won't hurt me, will she, Ma?"

"Not unless you hurt her first."

"I won't. Sure why would I?"

"Good girl. You treat the Shee right and they'll do you no harm. They'll keep an eye to you and yours." Ma put the brush on the dressing table. "It's a comfort," she said, "not granted to many."

Maureen swallowed. "And you think I'm lucky about that?"

"I do, so," Ma said. She smiled at her youngest daughter.

Maureen smiled back. "Thanks, Ma."

"Now, stand up," she said, "and let's be looking at you."

Maureen saw herself in the mirror. In the rays of the afternoon sun her hair shone like polished copper.

She admired the dress Ma had bought two weeks ago in Clonakilty. It was patterned with red tea roses scattered at random over its white linen fabric. The sleeves ended just above her elbows, and the neck was demurely closed with a Peter Pan collar. The wide satin belt, tied in a bow in front, sat on the top of Maureen's hips; the hem was knee-length and covered white lisle stockings that disappeared into patent-leather half-heeled shoes.

It was a far cry from the demure ankle-length, blue serge dress covered with a white pinafore that she wore at home and to school, but then it wasn't school she was going to today. It was her first grown-up dance. Maureen tingled. She turned to leave, but Ma said, "Take your hurry in your hand. Pin this on." She handed Maureen a cameo.

"I couldn't, Ma. It's far too precious."

"Of course you can. Just bring it back to me. Your Da gave it to me when we'd been married ten years."

"I'll take very good care of it." Maureen

fastened the brooch high over her left breast. "Thank you."

"Now put on your hat."

She pulled on her new green-felt cloche hat and tilted it to the right. She'd always wanted one that colour.

Ma cocked her head, looked at Maureen from head to toe, and smiled. "You'll do, so. Now run along and enjoy the dance tonight."

"I will." Maureen didn't wait to pull on her white cotton gloves. She grabbed them and her handbag and clattered downstairs, but then she decided she hadn't thanked Ma properly for the loan of the cameo. She climbed back up.

Ma stood, hands clasped, crying quietly.

Maureen crossed the room. "What's wrong?"

Ma smiled through her tears. "My littlest girl's all grown up now."

Maureen kissed her mother. "No, I'm not. I'll always be your girl. I love you, Ma."

Ma patted the back of Maureen's hand. "Thank you, *muirnín*." She wiped her eyes with the back of her hand. "Now off with you. You can't keep the rest waiting, so."

As Maureen went downstairs, the walnut-cased grandfather clock whirred, then struck three. Its familiar brassy sound comforted her. She'd been listening to it all her life, and it moved something deep inside her. The clock always said, "This is your home, girl. You're safe here," even if there were strange things like vixens with women's faces out in the big world.

"Very smart," Tiernan said. "You're done up like the Queen of the May."

"Your majesty." Fidelma, who was also in her best dress and hat, dropped a curtsey. "Your most humble servant."

"Stop acting the *óinseach*, Fidelma," Ma said, from the first landing, but she was smiling broadly.

"I'm no eejit, Ma. If there's any own-shuk here, it's Tiernan."

"I'll let that pass," Tiernan said, grinning, "and anyway that's a girl eejit. I'd be an *amadán* . . . which I definitely am not, so."

"Here, Maureen. You were in such a rush, you forgot this." Her mother threw down a woollen cardigan. "It does get chilly, so, when the dew starts to fall."

"Thank you, Ma." She draped it round her shoulders.

"Don't forget your supper. It's in the hamper on the table. There's ham sandwiches, chicken sandwiches, tomatoes, hard-boiled eggs, apples, plum cake, and big bottles of my lemonade. Now, you've kept Malachy and Sinead waiting long enough. Go on with the lot of you, then," Ma said.

Tiernan grabbed the hamper.

Maureen's "*Slán agat*"—the good-bye of the one leaving—was echoed by Ma's "*Slán leat*," the good-bye of the one staying behind.

Out in the farmyard, Sinead, her husband Malachy, and their eighteenth-month-old son Finbar, named for Da, waited in their sidecar. The roan horse between the shafts turned its blinkered head and stared at Maureen with limpid brown eyes, dark and soft as molasses. She could smell the tang of a pile of horse apples.

Malachy sat in the driver's seat holding the reins in one hand, a whip in the other. His red braces crossed in the middle of the back of his white shirt; his black jacket lay on the seat beside him. It would be warm work driving today, but that hadn't stopped him wearing a tan bowler hat with a narrow curved-up brim. His lips were pursed and he was frowning at whatever Sinead was saying. He mustn't have heard the three O'Hanlons approaching.

Sinead, with her back to the cart bed, sat stiffly on one side bench, which ran the length of the vehicle. Her high-button boots rested on a footboard over the wheel. Behind her was the well of the cart where baby Finbar sat in his pram. Past the well, a second bench ran along the other side.

Maureen saw her eldest sister in profile. She was half turned to Malachy, pointing at him with one finger. She wore her black hair scraped back in a bun as befitted her matronly, married state. The style accentuated her high cheekbones, above which a pair of bog oak–brown, narrowed eyes flashed. "And you'll *not* wager any more money at the bowling, and you'll keep away from the hard stuff or I'll—"

"Good-day to you, Sinead," Maureen said loudly.

Sinead stared at her husband, then turned to Maureen and said coolly, "Hello, yourself. Grand to see you all and a grand day, so. Now let's get going. Get you up beside me now, Fidelma, and Maureen, you and Tiernan get on the other side and we'll be off."

Marriage hadn't changed Sinead, Maureen thought. Her eldest sister would have made a good sergeant major the way she was forever organizing things.

Maureen followed Tiernan round the car. She felt it sway as Fidelma clambered up beside Sinead. Maureen waited until Tiernan was aboard, put her own foot on the metal step, and accepted his hand to haul her up.

As soon as she was seated, Malachy asked, "Are we right now?"

"Right as rain, and hello, Malachy," said Maureen.

He was a heavy-set, dark-haired man with a hint of a squint and the scars of acne on his cheeks. He tended to be taciturn, but Malachy Aherne was reckoned to be the best farmer and finest judge of horseflesh in West Cork. Perhaps he had that skill because his name in Irish, *Ó'Echtigerna*, meant "grandson of the lord of the horses." It was widely believed that Sinead had made a great match, and fair play to her. But Maureen had meant what she'd told Ma a couple of years ago. She was still in no great rush to be wed, even if her sister had done what girls were supposed to do—found herself a good husband and produced a wee son to carry on his family's name. Maureen looked over at Finbar, who was kicking his little feet in the air.

Would she have expected anything less orderly from her well-organized, oldest sister? Not at all. Maureen smiled to herself. Following the beaten track was all very well for Sinead, but she, Maureen, didn't think she wanted such a conventional life. And beside, was life all that predictable when foxes turned into women and the sound of *uillinn* pipes seemed to come out of the very rocks and hedgerows?

Her thoughts were interrupted when she heard Sinead ask, "Is it today we're going, Malachy, or were you waiting for the horse to make up your mind for you?"

Maureen saw her brother-in-law's eyes turn up to heaven, but he clicked his tongue, cracked his whip, and away they bowled with a creaking and jangling of harness, the steady clopping of hooves, and squeaks from the springs. Maureen clung on as the jaunting car pitched and rolled. They were in for a bouncy ride. She let her body sway to the rhythm of the vehicle.

She'd noticed that Sinead's cheeks, normally rosy like Ma's, were discoloured by a dusky area in the shape of a butter-fly. The mask of pregnancy. Her second. Perhaps being pregnant made her bad-tempered with Malachy. It must be very uncomfortable to have a belly on you like the sidewall of a house, and on a hot day like this too.

If the pair of them were going to bicker, Maureen would not let it spoil her day. She looked away from her family and over the hedgerows to the little fields bordered haphazardly by mortarless stone walls built when the rocks had been cleared from the fields. The labour must have been backbreaking.

The pastures were busy with flocks of sheep, herds of cattle, horses. She took the cardigan off her shoulders, for the day was hotter than warm and the breeze had no cooling in it. She felt sorry for the sheep in their woolly overcoats, which were well grown back after the spring shearing. They must be boiling, particularly the black ones.

Some of the barley crop had already been reaped. In the fields that awaited harvest, waves of dark and waves of light yellow played tag as the wind blew gently across the bearded grain. And in her head she sang "The Wind That Shakes the Barley."

> I sat within the valley green,
> I sat me with my true love . . .

She thought back two years to hearing the music of it in Connor's cottage, thought again about the piping near the frockon patch earlier today.

Fidelma may have laid Connor's ghost

to rest; she certainly never mentioned him now. But Maureen never would forget him as long as she kept sensing reminders of his presence.

> My sad heart strove to choose between
> The old love and the new love . . .

She glanced across at Fidelma, whose old love was gone and who had no new love to replace him. Then she looked at Sinead, who was staring at the back of Malachy's head. That exchange in the farmyard wasn't the first time she'd heard Sinead carping at her husband. God love him, he was such a placid man he never yelled back. He must love her very much, and maybe Sinead still loved him. The sharp tongue was only a part of her nature.

Ma and Da? She'd never heard them have an angry word. She'd once heard Ma say, "For every old slipper, there's an old stocking to match it." They were the living proof.

Love, she decided, must be different for everybody, and sure hadn't she plenty of time before she found out for sure?

Maureen looked into the distance and sang gently to herself.

> I never will marry
> I'll be no man's wife
> I expect to stay single
> All the days of my life.

Perhaps not quite true, but she was in no rush. No rush at all. She chuckled.

"And what's so funny?" Tiernan asked.

"Nothing," she said. "I was just thinking about how much fun the *fleadh*'s going to be."

"Sure it'll be like any other flah, lots of *craic*, lots going on, dancing, and"—he rubbed his hands—"I can't wait for my go at the road bowling. There's some new competition, a man from Clonakilty or thereabouts, who I'd like to get a match with." He looked along the road. "I'll find out about that soon, for the place we're going's only about four miles more from that farmhouse with the red roof."

"Four more miles?" Maureen said, as the sidecar jounced over a pothole and forced her to cling on. "My bottom's going to be black-and-blue bouncing about like this."

"Ah, sure," said Tiernan with a grin, "aren't they grand colours anyhow? And four miles is nothing. We'll be at the hooley in no time, and then the fun'll begin."

20

Four more miles. Tiernan might think covering the distance would take no time, but Maureen willed the horse to move faster. She remembered something Da'd say when they'd go for a walk together. "Make short the road now for me, Maureen." He meant for her to chat with him and make the miles pass more quickly.

Tiernan wasn't always talkative, but in one way he was like most of the few men she knew. Ask about something that interested him and you'd get a sermon, the Law *and* the Prophets.

"Tiernan, I should know more about the road bowls, seeing you were last year's winner, but I don't. Tell me about it? Maybe I'll come and watch you."

Tiernan smiled and looked pleased. He leaned back on the wooden bench as if he were settling into a chair by the fire, hooked his thumbs around his braces, and said, "Well, now, Maureen girl. It's not like your camogie that's only been around a few years. Road bowling's a very ancient sport. Some say the Celts played it four thousand years ago, and it's got popular again in about the last two hundred years. Now it's played here in the Free State in County Cork, and up in County Armagh in the north. I do hear that some fellahs have got the bowls going in Boston."

"Which Boston? In Kildare or Galway?"

He laughed. "No. In America, lass. Massachusetts. Maybe one day we'll have an international match there."

She squeezed his arm. "You get on the Irish team and I'll definitely come and watch. I'd love to go to America." She knew, she just knew, that teaching wouldn't only give her a better wage; it would allow her to broaden her horizons, and why shouldn't she want to see the world?

"America, is it? I think it'll be a long year or two before we play the Yanks. But you could go and see Art and Emer in Philadelphia. You could stay with them."

"Maybe I will. I miss my big brother, but I've things to do here first." Her voice became serious. "Then maybe I *will* go after that, once I have the money." She smiled at him. "But that's to come. I still want to hear about the game. I like sports, you know that. Maybe if I fancy the sound of it, I'll take it up too."

He frowned. "There's no women at it yet."

"There will be. I could be the first, with a brother like you to teach me."

Tiernan smiled and shook his head.

"Tell me about it," she said. "Go on."

"Right you are. There's teams or single players, and they compete along a road course of two and a half miles."

"That's a fair stretch of the legs."

"It is on a hot day like today. You can work up a thirst." He winked.

"Tiernan." She shook her head at him.

"Don't you worry about me, Maureen. A fellah with a skinful can't get his lofts right."

"Lofts?"

"A loft is a throw. We bowl with a twenty-eight-ounce iron-and-steel cannonball called a bullet. The fellah with the least lofts over the distance wins. Or there's another game where whoever gets farthest in twenty throws wins."

"Sounds like fun to play, but I can't see myself watching it. Too slow. So I'll not come today."

"You can suit yourself, but it *is* great gas and . . ."—he glanced at Malachy and lowered his voice—"and it does be fun to bet on, so."

Maureen smiled. "I heard Sinead giving off to him about that. Maybe she'll not let him go with you at all."

Tiernan winked and, still speaking quietly, said, "Malachy has to come. He's my helper. I'd not play without him."

"Helper?"

"Aye. Each player has a wee team of his own. There's the road shower, a fellah who picks the best line for the shot, and there's a helper too. He goes ahead and stands in the road with his legs apart at the best spot to aim for with the next loft. There's always quite a crowd at a match, and you'd not want to hit someone with the bullet, so the helper yells, 'Faugh a ballagh!' Clear the way!"

"I think," she said, looking around, "we could use one of those fellahs right now roaring, 'Fawk a bollah!' here. There seems to be a lot more folks about all of a sudden."

The traffic was heavy and Malachy slowed the horse to a walk, stopping when his way was blocked by sidecars, ponies and traps, and even the occasional motor car, a nasty smelly thing that scared the horses.

Maureen saw one car that was made by the Austin Company over in England. And there was one of those funny-looking, open Morgan three-wheelers, driven by a young man wearing a cloth cap and sporting a Ronald Coleman moustache. He was a very flashy-looking lad, maybe from Cork City or even Dublin, she thought, and probably as a city fellah not to be trusted by a girl not yet eighteen. A spalpeen to be avoided at the *céili*. She might be thinking about teaching in a big city, but that was going to be later, when she was more able to deal with city folks and their ways.

A horse-drawn caravan carried part of a family of travelling people. One man guided the horse by pulling its lead rope. Others tramped beside the vehicle, and four skinny mongrel dogs ran alongside. Although they referred to themselves as "Pavees," not gypsies, in Irish they were called *Lucht siúil,* the walking people.

Maureen jingled some change in her pocket, a few coins Da had given her for spending money. The gypsy women would tell fortunes later in the day. She might go and see one of them. Just for fun.

Maureen inhaled. The warm air was redolent of horse sweat and flower perfume, car exhaust, and the tang of the nearby salt sea. Clonakilty was round a couple of corners and down in a valley. All she could see from here were the tops of two steeples. One, needle sharp, was the steeple of the Roman Catholic church; the other one, squat and square, was Anglican. Further out, the sun sparkled from the mudflats of Clonakilty's tidal harbour.

They weren't going as far as the town.

Everyone was converging on the fields near an ancient hill fort about a mile north, where the fair was already started, and the dance would be held later. There were folks on bicycles and tandems, women wheeling prams, and people on foot. A man smoking a dudeen led a chestnut gelding by a twisted rope halter. In Ireland wherever people congregated, there would be horse-trading.

Malachy dismounted, opened a gate, and led his horse through. "This field belongs to a friend of mine. He's letting me leave the car here. You ladies go back to the road and follow the crowd. It's only about a quarter of a mile to the fields around the hill fort of Lios na gCon. Enjoy yourselves at the fair. We'll be off to the bowling."

Sinead said, "We'll be at Lish na Gun alright. Mind *you* what I told you now, Malachy Aherne. Pay heed, and do not you be leading Tiernan astray. Now help me down; then give Tiernan a hand with Finbar's pram. Fidelma. Maureen. Off. Fidelma, take you the hamper."

Maureen, accepting Tiernan's hand as she dismounted, felt like saluting her sister, not as she would a magpie, but as an outranked soldier to a senior.

"Come on then," Malachy said, as he and Tiernan lowered the pram to the ground, "let's see to the horse." He turned to Sinead. "We'll be back by six in time for tea. We'll meet you all at the bandstand."

"Six. No later, hear now. And none of the hard stuff either one of you," she said. "Now, girls, let's head down to the fair."

Sinead, pushing the pram, followed by Fidelma and Maureen, set off for the *Lughnasa* festivities and the *céili* to come in the fields around the hill fort. Maureen felt like running ahead but, as befitted a young lady, kept steady pace with her older sisters.

While Fidelma helped Sinead find a shady spot for Finbar's pram under the trees near the bandstand, Maureen wandered over to examine Lios na gCon, the hill fort of the hound. She wanted to get a good look at it and paid little attention to the throng around her.

It was one of only three forts in this, the townland of Darrara. Forty-eight such structures surrounded Clonakilty.

The road they had come down ran

close to the back of the ancient structure. It was on the crest of a gentle hill and faced east. From where she stood on the north side, she could see how the little plain gradually became a slope that rolled down to two coppices separated by a gorse hedge at its foot. The bandstand was on this side of the earthworks.

She moved closer to the outer circular ditch. These hill forts were all of the same pattern. They had a central flat area where, in olden times, a farmhouse and pens for the animals stood. When the protective ditch surrounding the living quarters was dug, the earth was used to build the rampart.

Maureen had been taught that the forts and other constructions, like passage graves, dolmens, crannogs, and stone circles, could be found all over Ireland. The biggest passage grave was beside the River Boyne at Newgrange in County Meath.

Miss Toner had explained that hill forts, mounds, and graves had been for human habitation or burial, while stone circles had religious functions for the Neolithic people. Maureen knew that hill forts had other purposes too. The mounds and hill forts were called *sidthe* and the faeries who lived in them the *Sidhe*, or Shee, the people of the mounds. The hill forts, like blackthorn trees, were special places for them.

There'd be no sign of them today, but who knew what might happen tonight? Lugh of the Long Hand was one of their chief gods, and it was his festival, *Lughnasa,* that was being celebrated.

Maureen strolled round the circle of *Lios na gCon.* She guessed it was probably a hundred yards in diameter. All that was left were the outer works, and even there much of the ditch had been filled in. She was disappointed that there wasn't more to see.

She reached the other side of the grassy mound and looked out across another field to the wall that surrounded the high Celtic crosses in the graveyard of the Darrara church. The ground was flat and everywhere she looked, "There were multitudes assembled," just as she remembered from the song "The Galway Races." The fair was in full, exuberant swing.

People were on holiday, enjoying the

sunshine and the soft summer day. Not every man wore his Sunday suit; some were in shirtsleeves, but every woman had on her best dress and sported a cloche hat like Maureen's own. A few carried parasols.

Little boys in short pants chased each other hither and yon and yelled in their high-pitched voices. They darted erratically over the grass while the swallows above jinked through the sky.

Dogs barked. From the distance came the lowing of cattle. Maureen heard a donkey bray, harsh and grating, and looked across the road into the next field where a girl of about her own age was leading one of the little animals with a youngster on its back. She remembered being taken for a donkey ride herself when she was six or seven, and Ma telling her that every donkey had a cross on its back because one of its kind had brought Christ to his trial.

She wandered past stalls selling cold drinks, candy floss, *crúibins,* gingerbread, toffee apples, yellow-man toffee, carrageen moss. She'd not waste her money on food.

A group of kiddies sat on the grass in

front of a tall, narrow, red-and-white-striped canvas structure. A square opening above a narrow shelf acted as a simple stage. The children were watching a Punch-and-Judy show, an entertainment that hadn't changed in hundreds of years. The puppeteer was inside the small tent working the hand puppets and giving them their voices.

Maureen stopped to watch, thinking back to being held on her father's shoulders the first time she'd seen hunch-backed Punch in his jester's motley, him with his great, hooked, papier-maché nose almost meeting his chin. She'd giggled and laughed and banged her little fists on Da's head.

"So you liked that, did you, *muirnín*?" her father had said when the show was over. "Did you know Punch-and-Judy shows have been going for three hundred years? A learned fellah once told me they started in Italy."

Punch was now beating the baby Judy held in her arms. He thumped with his stick and squawked in his raspy voice, "That's the way to do it."

She'd loved the show when she was

little, and even today in her nearly eighteen years, she laughed when Toby the dog growled at Punch. Imagine her father knowing it had started in Italy. She wanted to know things like that. Be a learned woman. Italy must be a colourful, boisterous sort of a place to invent such fun. Perhaps she would get the chance to go there one day, as well as to America. Once she'd earned and saved the money.

She walked past musicians, pausing at each one to listen for a while—here two fiddlers, there a girl playing a melodeon, further on a man with a ceramic flute being accompanied by a girl playing the spoons and a bald-headed lad plunking a banjo. She didn't see or hear a piper and for that she was grateful.

She regretted she couldn't play an instrument. When Ma told her about the sight, she'd mentioned music to help Maureen understand how some people were talented and most were not. Maureen had learnt she was not when Ma arranged for a harper to instruct her daughter. Maureen could sing a song, but had plucked the harp strings like a girl with two left hands.

She threw a penny into the flautist's cap on the ground and moved on to where the gypsies had parked their caravan near the graveyard wall.

A man with grey hair to his shoulders, a single gold earring, and a face as wrinkled as a dry chamois leather sat at a table covered with small sheets of metal, hammers, pincers, solder, and an old soldering iron. He was a tinker waiting for folks to bring their pots and pans to be mended.

A younger man wearing a red spotted bandanna stood at an upended crate. She noticed that one of his eyes had a dark brown triangle at the bottom of its green iris, and for a moment he stared at her.

"God bless me," she whispered.

The travelling man put a pea under one of three walnut shells, then arranged and rearranged them, lifting a shell from time to time to reveal the pea. A knot of youths had gathered in front of him.

His hands flashed, shifting the shells. "Roight now, oim on for taking bets at two to wun. Truppence wins youse sixpence, a shilling gets yuh a florin. All youse've to do is find the pea. One of youse at a toime now."

She didn't recognise his accent. It certainly was *not* from County Cork. His hands stopped.

"Will your honour have a go, sor?" He looked at a strapping fellow with cheeks the colour of red poppies, and he dressed in a shirt and moleskin trousers tied at the knees with leather thongs called nicky tams. "Where's duh pea, do you tink?"

"I know, for I've been watching you like a hawk, boyo." The lad put down a silver thruppence and pointed at the middle shell. "It does be under that one there, so."

When it was lifted, there was no pea beneath. The youth groaned. His friends laughed at him, and the threepenny piece disappeared into the Pavee's hand. Thruppence was a fair sum to lose.

"Better luck next time, sor." The pea was replaced with great ceremony, and the hands flashed again. "There'll be no money paid if there's no wagers laid. Who's next? Step up now. Step up."

Maureen shook her head. A fool and

his money are soon parted, she said to herself, and moved on until she came to a tent and a sign that said: Madame Rosita. Palms Read. Fortunes Told.

Maureen shook her head and smiled. Why on earth would she waste money on someone who probably had no idea what the future held, but simply had a well-rehearsed line of patter? Da said some of the walking people would steal the cross off a donkey's back. She rummaged in her handbag for one of the silver thrup-pennies he'd given her.

She was seventeen, eighteen next month. She knew her own future stretched ahead to an invisible horizon. Ma had said not to worry about it, whatever was going to come would come, but Maureen was impatient to find out. She had her own clear ideas about what she wanted to happen. Would she get good enough marks next year to be the teacher she'd set her heart on being? Would she travel to America? The next question was more important for Fidelma, but Maureen was curious about herself too. Was love in her stars and, if so, when?

Maybe, just maybe, Madame Rosita

would be able to predict that Maureen's dreams would come true. And if she couldn't? Maureen chuckled and stepped forward.

She'd not be wasting money, not like the eeejit at the shell game, she told herself as she lifted the tent flap. It was her thruppence to spend as she saw fit, and nobody would be robbing her.

21

Maureen waited for her eyes to become accustomed to the dim light. Madame Rosita was seated behind a baize-topped card table where a glass sphere and a pack of well-thumbed cards lay. Her features were hard to make out, but Maureen thought the woman seemed to be dark-complexioned and probably middle-aged. Her hair was hidden under a head scarf. She smiled. One of her upper front teeth was missing.

Heavy rings hung from her earlobes, and bracelets encircling both wrists jangled as she moved one hand to indicate that Maureen should take the folding chair opposite. It was easier to see now. The woman wore a scarlet shawl and rings on every finger.

"You want your future told, pretty one?" The voice was soft, melodious.

"Yes, please."

"Hold out your hand."

Maureen extended her hand, palm up. She still clutched the silver thruppence in the other. So, she thought, the crystal ball and cards were simply props. She was going to have her palms read. The Pavee took Maureen's hand in her own. They were warm, dry, and rough. She leant forward and narrowed her hazel eyes. Wrinkles on her forehead deepened. When the woman moved closer, Maureen could smell foetid breath.

Maureen moved back, but the Pavee held tight, her gaze leaving Maureen's hands and moving to her eyes. It was as deeply penetrating as the fox-woman's had been.

The Pavee had a cast in her right eye. "So," she said, "it's your future you want?"

"I . . . I'm not sure." Maureen half rose but found she was held fast. "I think I'll . . ."

"Don't go, child. I have seen things I do not understand in your fate line, your heart line, but I see a cross on your Mount of Venus that says you will find true love."

"Love?" Maureen stopped trying to pull away. "Love?" Hadn't that been what she'd been wondering about at the oddest times for the last year or so, like after she'd seen the caterpillar earlier today, and moments ago as she lifted the flap of this tent? She lowered herself into the chair. In for a penny, or more likely sixpence, in for a pound, she thought. "Anybody can predict love." She half turned her head and looked sideways at the woman. "What don't you understand?" Maureen asked.

"I cannot tell without the tarot." She nodded at the cards.

Maureen allowed herself a small smile. This woman was as much a chancer as the man with the walnut shells, and yet— and yet why not? "How much?"

"I will set out ten cards in a Celtic cross. Card one will tell your present, card two your immediate challenge, card three your distant past. Each card has its own story to weave, right up to nine, which reveals your hopes and fears, and ten, which will speak of the final outcome. You must tell me whether you want a life reading, which is the telling of your whole span, or your future for a shorter time."

I'm the fly and she's the spider, Maureen thought. She looked down, first at her hand still held by the woman, then at the pack of cards, then back into the fortune-teller's eyes. "How much for a whole life? How much for . . . a year or maybe two years?"

"A shilling for a whole life and thruppence for a short time." She released Maureen's hands.

"And you're not sure from my palm?"

The Pavee shook her head. "I see something powerful about you. I *feel* something powerful about you, but only the tarot will tell."

She'd nearly been right about "in for sixpence." A shilling was far too expensive, but she could afford to pay for a two-year reading. Maureen hesitated, still clutching the small silver coin in her hand. Sure wasn't it only a bit of fun she was buying? She handed the thruppence to Madame Rosita. "Here. Tell me two years."

That would cover the all-important next summer, when her examination results, pass or fail, would be definite predictors of her future career. It would be a comfort to hear the gypsy woman's view today. Maybe Miss Toner's confidently expressed opinion would be more accurate than this woman's, but the teacher couldn't say if Maureen would fall in love. That was important too, and hadn't the Pavee already said Maureen would find true love? She'd just not said when.

"Two years it is." The gypsy took the money, let go of Maureen's other hand, then lifted the pack. "Can you shuffle cards, child?"

"You mean mix them before the deal? I've seen Malachy and Tiernan and their friends playing Spoil Five for halfpennies." The bowls wasn't the only thing Malachy liked to gamble on.

The teller smiled and handed Maureen the pack.

She shuffled, cut, and returned them.

"Now." The woman started to lay out the cards facedown.

Maureen watched until there were four parallel vertical rows. The first row of a single card, the second of three with a fourth card laid crosswise over the middle one, the third of a single card, and the fourth of four.

"Number one, the present." The gypsy pulled out the covered card from the second row and turned it face up.

Maureen saw a sword, hilt down, blade up, its point thrusting into a circle of rays of light.

The teller smiled. "That is one of the minor arcana, the Ace of Swords. Alone it foretells a long life."

Maureen leant forward, ignoring the smell of the Pavee's breath as she turned over card after card until nine were face up.

"Now, I can tell you that you will go on a journey within the next year. The Wheel of Fortune says so." She pointed to a wheel surmounted by a sphinx. "The Prince of Cups"—a man holding a cup aloft while a small naked figure knelt at his feet—"is a moody card, but whether those moods are of a man or woman, a man and a woman, or indeed even the sea, I cannot tell."

"It'll not be the sea. I live ten miles

inland. My sister Sinead more like. She's the moody one."

"And are you not?"

"I don't think so."

"But there is something . . . something special about you, girl. I felt it when I held your hands, yet the cards haven't told me what it is."

Nor will I, thought Maureen. My sight is my secret. Only Ma knows. "Go on with the cards, please."

"There at number six, which tells your immediate future, is the Two of Cups." Maureen saw two entwined fish spilling water into two goblets.

"It says love is coming. Romantic love. Romance. Perhaps a marriage."

Maureen frowned. "Within the next two years?"

"The card says so."

Maureen frowned. Well, she thought, she'd be nineteen next September, not too young for marriage—as long as the right fellah came along. And if he did he'd not have to mind her teaching. Lots of men thought it shameful if their wives worked, making it seem to others that they as husbands couldn't provide.

The woman peered more closely at the six position and the preceding five cards.

While the Pavee mumbled, Maureen told herself not to be taken in. If she didn't want to get married in the next two years, then it wasn't going to happen, no matter *what* the cards might say. It would have to be the right lad or bust.

"You *will* find love, or love will find you. The cards say so."

"Aye, maybe at the *céili* tonight." Maureen laughed. "My sister Fidelma reckons Rudolph Valentino may show up, sweep me off my feet, and have me up the aisle in two shakes of a lamb's tail, so."

"Do not mock the tarot." Her voice was flat. Chilling.

Maureen swallowed. "I'm sorry."

The Pavee did not smile as she turned over the tenth card. She jerked back, eyes wide, mouth agape. She crossed herself with her left hand and muttered something under her breath.

Maureen leant forward to see better. The picture was of a dancing skeleton carrying a scythe. "What is it?" she asked. "What is it?" She heard her own voice rise.

"It is the most feared of cards, and it is in position ten, the final outcome." The woman leant back from the table.

"What is it? Please." Maureen felt the hairs on her neck tingle. "Please tell me."

"The name of it is . . . Death."

"Death?" Maureen heard her voice rise higher in pitch. "Whose death? Mine? In two years?" She started to stand.

The Pavee shook her head. "I know not. This card, though called Death, is the most complicated of the tarot. It *can* foretell the death of the subject or of a loved one, but it is rarely so simple."

Maureen lowered herself back onto her chair. "Go on."

"It can mean the death of an old life and the beginning of a new one—"

"Like leaving school and getting the job you want?"

"It can."

Maureen managed a weak smile. "Then it's not quite so scary."

The Pavee woman shrugged. "It could mean being single and in love, then losing a lover."

"And you said I was going to find love." Maureen pointed at the Two of Cups.

The teller nodded. "You are. Maybe all this Death card says is that the change will be from a single girl to a girl in love."

"That's not so bad either. After all, there's not much point in predicting death. We all die one day."

"We do, but remember today we are asking the cards about only the next two years."

Maureen felt a chill. It was true, and as she thought about the implications, everything about her altered. The walls of the tent vanished. The woman opposite became a blur. She changed her shape. Her face was Maureen's own, her clothes mourning black. Then as suddenly as the gypsy had been transformed, she was once again Madame Rosita in her scarlet shawl sitting quietly in her fortune-telling tent.

Maureen's breath came in short gasps as she clasped her chest and felt the sharp edges of Ma's ivory cameo cold on her fingers. She had a sudden longing for her mother that brought a pricking behind her eyelids.

Madame Rosita pushed her chair back. "What have you seen, child?"

"Myself in mourning." The whispered words slipped out.

The Pavee woman stood. She thrust the thruppence back at Maureen. "Take it. I'll not ask money from one of us. I felt your power earlier, but I did not understand. I do now. The sight is on you, girl."

Maureen's breathing slowed. She shook her head. "Keep the money . . . and please . . . keep your mouth closed about this."

The walking woman crossed her heart. She stared at Maureen with her left eye, while the right one looked over Maureen's shoulder. "May I die if I utter a word, as God is my witness."

Maureen felt the comfort of those words, for those with the evil eye could not utter the word "God."

"Thank you," she said. "Thank you very much." She rose. "Good-bye, Madame Rosita."

"Good-bye, girl, and may the Lord always walk at your side."

Outside the tent the sun was blinding. Colours seemed sharper, the noises of the fair crisper. Ma had been right. The sight *had* come, but as for the meaning of what she had seen? It was she who had been wearing black, so it could not be her own death. Ma said it was hard to understand. Was she going to be in mourning? Who for, and when? Within two years?

Ma and Da were young yet. Healthy. Granny Fogarty was the only grandparent left.

She tried to understand what Madame Rosita had said about the Death card symbolizing the passing of an old life and the beginning of a new one. Did the sight work that way too? Were her widow's weeds an expression of how she felt about leaving childhood behind, becoming a woman, leaving school, moving on?

While the thought of getting on with her life was exciting, the prospects *were* a bit unnerving. Working for a living, falling in love, getting married—it would all be so new. She'd have to leave her home, her Ma and Da, her family, even the comforting grandfather clock.

On the day she'd first told Ma about seeing Connor, noticing her old, tattered teddy bear had helped her to acknowledge she was leaving childhood behind. Perhaps the vision, brought on by the shock of seeing the Death card, only meant that she would experience a transformation within the next two years.

The more she thought on it, the more she liked that explanation. She decided she'd not ask Ma to try to explain. Maureen was certain her mother would have no clearer answers than she herself had, and Ma would probably give her a tongue-lashing for listening to such foolishness.

She skirted the now empty Punch-and-Judy tent.

Ma had told her never to be frightened of the power, but Maureen had been afraid in the gypsy woman's tent. Terrified. Now her pulse had slowed; her breathing was steady. It was true, she told herself, she could do nothing about what she had seen. What could not be cured must be endured. She should try to stop worrying.

What concerns she had she'd keep to herself. She'd not spoil the day for everyone else with her brooding. She stood more stiffly and forced a smile. She'd not brood. She'd not.

She quickened her step round the fort

and waved to Sinead and Fidelma where they sat on the grass beside Finbar's pram.

From the single bell in Darrara church came the slow notes announcing the six-o'clock Angelus. Maureen smiled. Malachy and Tiernan were late for tea.

22

Maureen reached her family in the shade of an elm tree as the last solemn chime echoed over the fields. Fidelma held a gurgling Finbar and chucked him under the chin. She rolled her eyes to heaven and nodded her head sideways to where Sinead hauled the picnic hamper out from under his pram.

"At least you're *nearly* on time," Sinead snapped.

No wonder Fidelma was rolling her eyes. "Och, come on, Sinead," Maureen said, "sure it's only a cold tea we're having. It'll not spoil. The boys are having fun.

Let them. It's a holiday." She wished Sinead could be more easy about things. She wasn't usually this bad-tempered. It must be because she's pregnant, Maureen thought.

"Huh," Sinead said, "I'm for starting anyway. I've to eat for two. Fidelma, put Finbar back in his pram. Maureen, give me a hand to get things ready." Together they spread a chequered cloth on the grass, opened the picnic hamper, and began setting out the meal. Sinead, on all fours by the basket, flapped at a wasp snarling around a plate of chicken sandwiches. "And I'll not care if the wasps have it half eaten by the time the menfolk get here—"

"We are here," Malachy said and gave Sinead a solid pat on her upturned bottom.

Sinead jerked round. "Malachy Aherne, I'll thank you not to—"

Maureen, who had just handed Sinead a plate of sandwiches, watched her sour look turn to a smile, at least with her lips, when she saw that Tiernan, who stood beside Malachy, had his arm round a stranger's shoulders.

Maureen studied the man. He was as tall as Tiernan, younger, early twenties, well-built, broad-shouldered, narrow-hipped. He wore hobnailed boots and moleskin trousers held up by a broad leather belt with a brass buckle. The top three buttons of his red-and-white-striped, collarless shirt were undone. There were damp stains at his armpits.

"Sinead, this here's Paudeen Kincaid from Ring, just outside Clonakilty. He's a powerful bowler, so," Tiernan said. "Paudeen, my sister, Sinead Aherne."

Maureen hardly noticed her sister stand and say, "Pleased to meet you, Mr. Kincaid."

The dark hair of Paudeen Kincaid's head, which he parted to the left, was almost as long as her own. Unusual, she thought, for an Irishman. His forehead, broad and uncreased, glistened in the early evening sun. Bowling, she thought, must work up a powerful sweat. A snub nose separated two eyes of the deepest blue she had ever seen.

His forehead might be smooth, but there were deep crows'-feet at the corners of his eyes. Either he liked to laugh or he spent a lot of time outdoors squinting against the weather. His mouth was generous. He could use a shave, and his stubble, like his hair, was dark.

"And this here's Fidelma, and the young one's Maureen, so," Malachy said.

Kincaid bobbed his head at each in turn.

Maureen smiled and watched his eyes, well aware that the stranger was inspecting her. A year ago she would have blushed at his appraisal, but her confidence in herself had been growing. If he wanted to look he could. As Ma said, a cat can look at a king—as long as it doesn't think the king's a mouse.

"Did you win, Tiernan?" Fidelma asked.

"I did, so," he said and hiccupped.

Maureen sucked in her breath and looked at Sinead, who narrowed her eyes at Malachy, cocked her head, and said, "Have you been—?"

"It's all my fault, Mrs. Aherne," the newcomer said. "Tiernan only beat me by one loft, but a throw so sweet you've never seen the like, bye. I had to cheer at it myself even though I'd lost. I reckoned I should get to know a bowler like him better, and didn't I owe your man here and his road shower and helper the victory glass, bye?"

Maureen smiled. Not all Corkmen ended sentences with "so." Some used "boy," pronounced "bye," as well, regardless of whether they were addressing a man or a woman, a girl or—a boy.

"Generous of you," Sinead said.

"And we'd only the one," Malachy added, holding up a single finger. "One, and it a shmall little one at that."

"Only one?" Sinead seemed to be softening. Perhaps, Maureen thought, she was regretting her earlier snappishness. "You could have done worse, I suppose."

"I'd take no more, for haven't I to drive us all home, so?"

"And I've a tide to catch tonight," Paudeen said.

Tiernan said nothing.

"A tide?" Maureen asked. He really did have the deepest blue eyes.

"Aye. Clonakilty Harbour's got a one-fathom gut by Ring Harbour that's not passable at two hours before and two hours after slack ebb, and at low water all the harbour itself is just mudflats."

"And would you be a fisherman, Mr. Kincaid?"

"I would that, Miss O'Hanlon, bye."

She inclined her head as he spoke her name.

"I have my own long-liner boat in the harbour at Ring. I mostly fish for ling for the salting, but tonight I'm after lemon sole." His voice was a light tenor, and made musical by his thick Cork brogue.

Maureen was taken with the softness of his speech and—if she told herself the truth, and why should she lie?—with his eyes, blue like the calm summer sea. She'd ask him later what a long-liner was. A ling, she surmised, was some kind of fish.

Malachy moved closer to Sinead and said, "I knew you'd not mind, pet, but Tiernan and me asked Paudeen to come and have a wee bite with us before the dancing."

"It does be nice to have company," Sinead said, now smiling with her eyes and, Maureen thought, remembering her manners. "Mind? Not at all. It is very welcome you are, Mr. Kincaid."

"Thank you," he said.

"Grand, so," said Malachy. "Let's be having our tea. I could eat a back door buttered, and we'll all be needing our strength for the dancing after." He sat beside Sinead, leant across and pecked her cheek. "And I'm sorry we're late, love."

"Och, you're forgiven, seeing it's only a few minutes and you did have only the one," she said, then offered Paudeen a ham sandwich.

"Thank you, Mrs. Aherne," he said.

He's a polite man, Maureen thought, as she sat on the grass beside Fidelma. She helped herself to a chicken sandwich and a glass of lemonade. She was trying to think of a good question to ask him, the way she'd asked Eamon about his lorry. She'd ask about his long-liner, but Tiernan beat her to it.

"Go on, Paudeen," Tiernan said, "tell the womenfolk what the stationmaster at Clonakilty station told the Englishman who was fit to be tied because the train from Kildare was three hours late." Tiernan gave a wry grin at Sinead. "You'll like it, Sinead. Your man here's a grand one with the stories, Fidelma. A right *seanachie,* Maureen, just like Da."

Paudeen blushed and shook his head. "Och, no." He took a bite from his sandwich.

"Go on with you, Paudeen Kincaid," Malachy said. "Tell us. It's perfectly fit for mixed company to hear, and Tiernan's right. It'll suit Sinead."

Paudeen nodded, held up one hand, but finished chewing first.

When his mouth was empty, he wiped his lips with the back of his hand and said, "An Englishman, very snobby, does be waiting in Clonakilty for the train from Kildare, but it does be late. He keeps scowling at his timetable and getting very red in the face. Finally he storms into the stationmaster's office. The Englishman had a look on him like the scowl on a bulldog that had chewed a wasp."

Maureen was already chuckling. "A bulldog that had chewed a wasp" painted a wonderful mental picture. He was a *seanachie* all right, with a great turn of phrase. She liked that quality of storytelling in her Da, she always had, and she realized she admired it in this man too.

Paudeen continued. "'My man, the train's precisely three hours and four minutes late. What on earth is the use of this timetable?'

" 'Och, sir,' says the stationmaster . . .'" The corners of Paudeen's eyes crinkled as he spoke.

So those were laugh lines. He had a sense of humour all right. She liked that.

" 'We print them only so learned men like yourself, your honour, can know not just that the train is late, but *exactly* how late it is.'"

Paudeen had to wait until everyone's laughter died down before he delivered the final line: " 'And that does be her coming round the corner now, sir. So good day to you, my wee maneen.'"

There was a fresh round of laughter, and Maureen clapped, pleased to see Sinead laughing as heartily as everyone else.

It had been four years since the English left the twenty-six counties of the Irish Free State, but Maureen, like everyone else, still enjoyed a good joke at their expense. And this man Paudeen made her laugh, just the way Da did. She found herself looking straight at him—and him looking straight back.

She noticed her pulse was going as if

she'd just played half an hour of hard camogie.

"You're a gas man, Paudeen Kincaid," Tiernan said, wiping his eyes. "But you should stick to the stories and not get any better with the bullets. I'll not be wanting you to beat me next time out."

Maureen waited to see how Paudeen would respond.

"Tiernan," he said very seriously, "you're a sound man yourself, bye, but in singles I'll try to beat you every time. I don't play to lose."

Neither did Maureen when it came to her camogie.

"But I've a better notion."

"And what's that?" Tiernan asked.

"I think the pair of us would make a powerful two-man team."

Tiernan's eyes widened. "And Malachy here could still be our helper."

"True on you," Malachy said.

"And here we are, come all this way to go to a dance," said Fidelma, "and what do we get? Three men with nothing better to do than sit around blethering about playing marbles for grown-ups." She helped herself to another sandwich.

"I'm sorry, Miss O'Hanlon," Paudeen said. "Would you like some lemonade to go with your sandwich?"

"I would, so."

Paudeen leant over, filled her mug, and looked her right in the eye. "And now we've stopped blethering, can I ask you a question?" Those blue eyes twinkled.

"You may, so."

"Would you give me the pleasure of the first dance, bye?"

Fidelma blushed, then chuckled and said, "I will, so. When I've finished my tea. And the music starts."

"Don't bother asking me, Malachy," Sinead said. "I'm far too big to go lepping about. You'll stay and keep Finbar and me company."

"And you'll be my partner for the first one, Maureen," Tiernan said. "I'll not take no for an answer."

Maureen laughed. "My pleasure." She stole a glance at Paudeen Kincaid, at those amazingly blue eyes, and wished he'd asked her, not Fidelma. She really wished he had.

This fisherman from Ring had stirred something in her, something that she had never known before. And it felt good. She blushed. Was one of the Pavee's prophesies coming true already? Was Maureen O'Hanlon starting to fall in love? And if Paudeen asked her to dance with him—and she accepted as she knew she would—would the feeling grow stronger?

23

Tiernan had Maureen on her feet the moment the music started. He led her to the bandstand, where the musicians were at one end warming up. Melodeons, spoons, pennywhistles, *bodhrans,* a banjo, fiddles, and pipes tore into "The Wearing of the Green," while the dancers formed sets of four couples.

Fidelma and Paudeen, Maureen and Tiernan, and Eamon MacVeigh and Dolores Hennessy, a girl from Cappeen who attended Maureen's school, were joined by two smiling strangers. The young man had as many freckles as a queen bee has workers.

The music stopped and the leader of the band held up his hand. "Is it good and ready youse do be now?"

There were loud cries of assent.

"Right youse are. Three jigs for to start with," he said, tucking his fiddle under his chin. Then with the hand that held the bow he gave a four count, and the musicians let rip with "The Irish Washer-woman."

Away the dancers went, arms and upper bodies rigid, feet and legs flashing to the six-eighths time, their shoe leather pattering on the wooden floor. Maureen was so busy keeping step she could manage only the occasional glance at Fidelma and her partner. At first she'd been disappointed that Paudeen had asked Fidelma and not herself; by now, though, she'd had time to half hope her sister and this Paudeen would hit it off—for Fidelma's sake. But as he flashed past, dark hair tossing, blue eyes shining, smile as wide as MacGillicuddy's Reeks, she wondered if perhaps she wasn't being too generous. What was it that made this man so attractive? She missed a step. Concentrate, girl, she told herself.

Tiernan was light on his feet, a pleasure to have as a partner, but after the third jig, "My Darling Asleep," he gasped, "Have mercy on your big brother, Maureen. I need a drink." He led her off the bandstand.

"Lemonade?"

Tiernan grinned and lowered his voice. "Archie Bolan—he's another of the bowling crowd—has a bottle of *poitín*. He's round the back of the fort. I'm going to nip round for a minute or two."

"What'll Sinead say?"

He winked. "You won't tell and . . . what the eye doesn't see, the heart doesn't grieve over. Anyway, I don't have to drive . . ."—they saw Fidelma and Paudeen approaching—". . . or catch a tide like your man there."

"Reels next," the bandleader announced, "so get your partners, form your sets, and get ready to kick up your heels to 'The Bucks of Oranmore.'" Fidelma stood close to Maureen.

Eamon MacVeigh appeared. "And could I have this set, Fidelma? You p . . . promised."

"I thought this afternoon you asked me for a hornpipe," she said, but she was smiling.

"Well, I—. W-w-w-well, I—"

Poor stammering Eamon. The more he stuttered, the more embarrassed he became.

"Would I do instead, Eamon?" Maureen asked. It would only be for one set, and now with Tiernan leaving, she didn't want to be partnerless.

His face lit up. He took a deep breath. "Thank you, Maureen. I'd like that," he said clearly.

"You would not," Fidelma said. "A promise is a promise, even if it was supposed to be for a hornpipe. I'll dance with you, Eamon, and anyway"—Fidelma turned and winked at Maureen—"I think you'd fancy a turn with Mr. Kincaid here." She lowered her voice so only Maureen could hear. "I saw the looks you gave him up there. And each time you did, I thought you were going to trip over your own feet. Go on. He's not my kind anyway." She looked Paudeen right in the eye. "And he's already told me he was going to ask you, Maureen. Haven't you, boyo?"

Bless you, Fiddles, Maureen thought.

Paudeen half smiled. "I . . . that is . . . I . . ."

Lord, Maureen wondered, is every young man in County Cork tongue-tied by the O'Hanlon girls? "I'd be delighted," she said, dropping a small curtsey to Paudeen, but smiling her thanks to Fidelma. "Who else'll we get to make up the set?"

"Your man with the freckles," Paudeen said, "and there's an older couple there on their own. Come on. We'll ask them to join us."

By the time the third reel, "The Boy in the Gap," was finished, she'd seen what an excellent dancer Paudeen Kincaid was, but that was all she'd found out about him. Irish dancing was so strenuous it barely left time for thought, never mind conversation. Nor did the dancers ever touch anything but their hands. She wondered what it might be like to be held and waltzed by a man like Paudeen Kincaid.

As the sets began to reassemble for

the next dance, the evening fell quiet with little to be heard but the buzz of muffled conversations and the plinking of the bald banjo player retuning his instrument.

Maureen overheard the bandleader say to him, "Jasus, Cathal, if you don't stop picking at it, it'll *never* get better."

She and Paudeen both laughed then, and, wiping the back of one arm across his forehead, he said, "This dancing's the hot work, bye."

He'd taken hold of her hand and she didn't want him to let go. "Do you fancy another glass of lemonade, Mr. Kincaid?"

"Grand, so. And would you please call me Paudeen like everybody else does, bye?"

"I will if . . . if you'll stop calling me 'bye' and use my real name. It's Maureen."

"Maureen it is, bye." He shook his head and grinned. His laugh was deep and made her think of the taste of a cup of hot chocolate. "Och, dear," he said, when he finally stopped laughing. "I'm sorry. I will try to stop, I promise—"

"Bye," she said and stuck out the tip of her tongue.

They were still laughing when they found Sinead, Malachy, and Finbar.

Sinead was rocking Finbar's pram. "Hello, you two," she said. "Fidelma and Tiernan still at it?"

"Aye, so," Maureen said. It wasn't really a lie. Sinead hadn't specified what "it" was. She'd no wish to set Sinead off on another scold by telling tales on Tiernan. "Is there a taste of Ma's lemonade left?"

"There is." Sinead handed Maureen the bottle and two mugs. "Here."

Maureen gave a mug to Paudeen. "I'm glad you're not a bowsey," she said. Heading off with your bowling friends, she thought.

"Divil the bit. A jar now and then is plenty, and I've had one today, buh—" He bit off the "bye" he had been going to say.

His slip set them both off laughing so helplessly that not only Malachy but Sinead too joined in.

When he had calmed himself, Malachy asked, "And did you enjoy your dance with Paudeen, Maureen?"

"I did, so."

"And so you should. I knew when I met

him at the bowls I'd seen Paudeen somewhere before. It was last year at the *feis*,
the festival, in Cork City."

"Och, it was only a small faysh,
Malachy," Paudeen said, frowning. "Let
that hare sit now."

"I will not, Paudeen. There's no need to
hide your light under a bushel. Your man
here and his partner were Cork slip-jig
champions, so."

Paudeen shrugged and pursed his lips.

His partner. Maureen felt a twinge of
envy, but said, "Malachy's right. You
should take pride in it. *I'm* proud of you."
And she was, as much for his modesty as
for his achievement. She finished her
lemonade. "And if the Cork step-dance
champion thinks he's getting off with just
the one set . . ." She rose and Paudeen
followed.

The evening was three quarters gone
before she knew it. Moths and night in-
sects fluttered round the Japanese paper
lanterns strung around the bandstand. In
the distance, the lights of Clonakilty threw
a low aurora over the valley.

The fields were bright in the glow of the

newly risen moon. As she skipped and hopped, Maureen could see that it was waning, just past the half. It hung low over the hill fort, so low it looked within her grasp should she but reach out.

As if using sparkling hands just beneath its surface, the distant sea caught moonbeams, then held and polished them before releasing them to rise shimmering from the calm waters.

"So," Paudeen said breathlessly, after the last set, "would you like to sit the next one out, Maureen? I'm getting puffed."

"I would." Maureen hesitated, then the words came out in a rush. "Paudeen, would you . . . would you like to get a bit of quiet away from the music?"

She could see the lantern light reflected in his eyes as he looked into hers and said quietly, "I'd like that very much." He took her hand and they strolled away from the bandstand toward the hill fort.

She walked with him through the still night where the dew fell gently on the springy grass and the almond scent of the whins was as gentle as eiderdown. The squeaks of bats were muted descants to the trilling of a nightingale. And high overhead, the stars bored diamond holes in the anthracite sky.

"Tell me about yourself, Paudeen Kincaid," she said quietly. "I'd like to know."

"Would you now? There's not much to tell. I'm twenty-one. I was born in Clonakilty. I live in Ring now. I have five sisters, two older, three younger, and an older brother. I like to dance—"

"I know that. You are very good."

"Thank you. I like to bowl and I like reading."

"I love reading. My Da and Ma have been telling me Irish stories since I was a wee girl, and my teacher has a wonderful way of teaching Irish history. If I was a boy, I'd want to go to university and study it, but I don't think you'd get much of a job with a history degree."

"You're likely right," Paudeen said, "but you can read about it to your heart's content. It's not my cup of tea. I like adventure novels. I like P. C. Wren. He does great stuff about the French Foreign Legion."

"*Beau Geste*?"

"Right."

"I don't just read history, you know." She'd not want him to think her a dry stick. "I borrowed Tiernan's copy a couple of months ago. I thought it was very sad."

"Aye, sad, so, but your man, Beau, was someone who took his honour seriously . . . as a man should. He was quite the hero in my book."

"And mine. You like heroes?"

"I do."

"Have you read *King Solomon's Mines*?"

"By H. Rider Haggard, and his *She* and *Allan Quatermain,* and G. A. Henty does great stuff about the North-West Frontier, R. M. Ballantyne's *The Coral Island* and *The Gorilla Hunters.* I love them all."

So, she thought for a moment. Paudeen was a fisherman, probably left school at fourteen, but he liked to read. That was interesting. "Do you read on your boat?"

He shook his head. "No time for it at sea. I read onshore. I've always liked the reading and the learning well enough. I had my Junior Certificate, hoped maybe I could go on and eventually get to university. I'd a notion for studying the architecture."

She felt a kinship to a man who liked learning. He wasn't simply an unlettered fisherman, she thought, and wondered why he hadn't gone further at school.

She'd heard a wistfulness in his voice when he said, "I had a notion . . ." She waited for him to explain and wondered if she could trust him with her own dreams. Paudeen did not elaborate and she was not surprised. She had already understood that he was a private sort of a kind of a man, so she said, "I'm sure you had your good reasons."

"I had," he said.

She sensed the loom of the fort's old earth rampart, darker against the indigo sky.

She felt his hand tighten on hers. They stopped walking.

"I'm glad Ma let me come to the *Lughnasa céili*," she said.

"So am I." He moved closer to her, and in the moon's light she could see that he was smiling. "Very glad." With that he bent forward and she felt his lips on hers. His were soft as dandelion fluff, fine as a bee's wings, fluttering and making her tingle. Hers parted, and she tasted him, and her heart swelled.

"Paudeen," she said. "Paudeen."

He stepped back a pace. "Thank you, Maureen," he said. "Thank you for letting me kiss you."

She didn't know what to say and was happy when he kissed her again.

"I think," he said, leaning away, "we'd better be heading back. I'd not want your Sinead to think we've been handfasting."

"Handfasting? What's that?"

"It's a *Lughnasa* custom. Boys and girls would stand on either side of a gate with a hole in it. One would put their hand through the hole, and if the other clasped it they were married and they could live together for one year."

She gasped. "Just one year? I mean, was it like they were married properly?"

"Not at all. At the end of the year they might get married in church, but if they'd found they didn't like each other, all they had to do was stand back-to-back and walk away, and the handfasting marriage was over." His face was smooth when he said, "You needn't be worried, Maureen

O'Hanlon. I have no time for a half-baked marriage, nor will I want no easy way out neither. When I give my heart to a girl, I'll give it for good and all, and I'll be on one knee with a ring in my hand, so."

She leant forward and kissed him as softly as he'd kissed her. When they moved apart, she said, "That's a picture, you on one knee . . ." The imp in her spoke. "Bye."

Paudeen laughed. "Bye yourself, *bye*." He held her in his arms and kissed her again, then took her hand and started to walk. "It is time we were back."

They walked in silence, hand in hand, both in step like a couple in a hornpipe. She tried to guess what this wonderful man was thinking. "Penny for your thoughts," she said.

He stopped and faced her. "A while back you asked me about me. What about you."

"Me? I live with my family on a farm near Beal na mBláth. I play camogie—"

"Tiernan says you are very good at it."

She blushed. "I try. Besides the camogie, I've already told you I love to read Irish history."

"You have."

Should she tell him her dreams? "I'm still in school, working for my Leaver's, so."

"Good for you. I mean it."

She suddenly felt she could trust him. A fellah who wouldn't try to impress a girl, but keep to himself that he was a dancing champion, would know how to preserve a confidence.

"Paudeen, don't laugh, but if I get . . . no, *when* I get my Leaver's, I'm going to take a job as a schoolteacher."

"Are you, now? Well, that would be a thing."

What had Ma said the time she'd explained to Maureen about the sight? "Teacher is it? There's a thing." Paudeen's tone was as sceptical as Ma's had been. Maureen saw him shrug and flick his head to one side. Did he disapprove? "Do you not think I should?"

"It's not for me to say."

He did disapprove. She swallowed. And up to now, tonight had been perfect. She felt the heat in her cheeks. "Why shouldn't I be a teacher?"

He sounded puzzled. "Do you never want to get married?"

"But what's getting married got to do with being a teacher?"

"I don't know about teaching. I know about other jobs, the Civil Service, the bank."

"There's not many women do jobs like that."

"I know, and if they get wed they have to resign."

"They what? I did not know that . . . and it's not right. It is not, so. Miss Toner says—"

"And who's this Miss Toner?"

"My teacher. She says there's no reason women shouldn't have important jobs like men."

Paudeen chuckled. "And I suppose she thinks women should have the vote too?"

"As a matter of fact she does. She says it's only a matter of time."

"She sounds like a right bluestocking to me."

"That's not very nice." Maureen knew how cold her voice must sound. "I'm sorry, Paudeen. I'm getting cross. I shouldn't, but—"

"But what?" There was, she was sure, a conciliatory tone to his words. "What?"

"I want to teach, that's all." She tried to read the expression on his face, but the moon had gone behind the hills, and in the darkness she could not make out his features. "And I'd expect support from a fellah like you when I do."

"You're not in a rush to get married, that's for sure. I'd not want any wife of mine working. Most of the lads feel that way. It's a man's job to support his family, so."

"I am *not* in a rush to marry . . ." Then her words took over. She could hardly believe what she was saying. "And certainly not to a narrow-minded, do-what-the-rest-of-the-lads-do fisherman like you, Paudeen Kincaid. Not one bit of a rush, so." She turned and, her breath coming in short jerks, strode off into the darkness.

She heard him call "Maureen" twice, but did not turn around. If Paudeen Kincaid was half a man, he'd follow her.

She stopped walking and saw just ahead, dimly outlined, the ditch and earthen wall of the *sidthe*, the hill fort. From inside the heaped earth mound, she heard a harpist and a piper. In her mind echoed and sang the words of Yeats's

"The Host of the Air," a poem she had learnt at school. "And never was piping so sad, and never was piping so gay." Was Connor here so far from home?

Maureen sat on the dewy turf at the edge of the ditch. While the pipes rang in her head, it was as if she could peer through the very earth of the fort's wall to the flat sward inside. She saw them: small people, fair of face and light of step, in sets just as she and the others had been this evening. They were dancing a hornpipe. A woman sat at a harp, and a man with a beard to his lap played the pipes.

A young man smiled at her and beckoned her to him.

She shook her head for she knew that humans who danced with the Shee were lost.

Maureen shook as she stood. Her fists clenched and she could feel her nails digging into the palms of her hands. Surely she'd had enough for one day? Foxes with human faces, seeing herself in mourning—well, she was that all right, already bitterly regretting her outburst of moments ago. Why didn't you come after me, Paudeen?

Now this. She didn't want to see faeries. Not now, even if Ma had reassured her they'd do her no harm and would keep an eye out for her. Maureen didn't want to see the future. Knowing it was a curse. A curse. Ma was wrong.

The tarot had predicted love, and the churning in her, the tingling joy she'd felt at his kisses, her pride in his dancing success, his modesty, his sense of fun, those blue eyes, the aching sadness deep in her now that Paudeen was gone, the boiling turmoil in her soul, must be love. She didn't need the sight to tell her that her stupid, pride-ridden words had cost her that love even before it had begun. Her vision and the Death card had meant great change and the death of a love, not a person.

Maureen walked slowly back to the bandstand. The farther she got from the ring fort, the softer the faery music played until she could hear not a note.

Och, Paudeen, she let out a long breath, and straightened her shoulders, can you not understand? I can't give up my dreams. Since I told Fidelma and Ma nearly two years ago, I've worked toward them. Striven. They could come true next year if I do well in that exam. Maureen O'Hanlon would *not* end up working in the mill, desperate to catch a husband, but *och, ochón* . . . och, ochoan. Paudeen, Paudeen.

She hoped he would be waiting for her. She'd apologise, help him to understand, show him she needed him *and* her dream. He'd understand and—she tingled at the remembrance—maybe he'd kiss her again.

But when she rejoined her family, Paudeen was nowhere to be found.

24

Nor did Paudeen reappear in the two weeks that followed, but Maureen could not forget him. Like Connor's spirit, the memory of the fisherman from Ring haunted Maureen. A glimpse of the deep-blue glaze of Ma's porcelain would bring back pictures of his smiling eyes; the mahogany colour of a brick of peat could summon the ebony of his long hair shining in the afternoon sun.

It was Maureen's turn to envy Fidelma, who seemed now, after almost four years, to have put Connor away for good and was walking out with Eamon MacVeigh. It had started at the *céili* and surprised everybody, except Maureen, when Fidelma had refused a ride home on the sidecar and had instead let Eamon run her back in his lorry.

A week later Fidelma had confided to her sister that once you saw past his girth and stutter there was a lot more to Eamon. Looks weren't everything. A lad with a solid head on his shoulders, who played the harp like an angel, who would one day be coming into a forty-acre mixed farm, and who worshipped Fidelma had a fair bit to recommend him, she reckoned. Good for Eamon and fair play to Fiddles. More power to her wheel.

And, Maureen thought, she had better put a bit more power into turning the crank of this barrel churn if she was going to get the butter made. She adjusted her stool and glanced up to where two bright, chaff-dancing rays of morning light streamed through a pair of small holes in the barn's roof. On a day like today it was best to start the churning early, before the heat of the sun made the task impossible.

She'd already separated the cream from the skimmed milk. The watery stuff remaining in the galvanized bucket would go to feed the pigs. She poured the cream into the churn's barrel, closed the lid, and turned the handle. It was a mindless task, and as she cranked she sang to herself,

> Let him go, let him tarry,
> Let him sink or let him swim . . .

And wouldn't sinking serve him right, so, him and his "I've my own boat"? Him and his "Well, that would be a thing."

> He doesn't care for me . . .

If he had, he'd not have said what he had. He'd have tried to understand, and maybe that was what had annoyed her most. It wasn't that he didn't want the wife of Paudeen Kincaid to work; it was because he seemed unwilling to even consider such a state of affairs, and to Maureen that seemed very closed-minded.

And if he cared, he'd have done more than merely call after her when she'd walked away, wouldn't he?

> And I don't care for him . . .

There was the rub. She paused and the clattering of the crank settled. She *did* care. Even after so brief a meeting. All the conflicting emotions she'd felt as she'd walked away alone from the hill fort that night still gave her no peace. She'd think of Paudeen's eyes as she lay in bed. His kisses. She might be reading a book when his face would somehow appear on the pages, and she'd think she heard him saying, "I'd not want any wife of mine working," and she'd purse her lips and growl in her throat. She might see a row of washing blowing on the line, and she'd imagine how light he was, how skillful he been as he'd danced with her.

She cared a great deal, and in losing him before she even got to know him properly she understood now how poor Fidelma must have felt when she lost her Connor. She hoped her sister and Eamon would be very happy and that Fidelma would not be hurt a second time.

Och, well. Sitting feeling sorry for herself would not get the baby a new coat. The handle was more difficult to turn when Maureen went back to work. Soon it would be time to drain off the buttermilk. You had to use it immediately. Buttermilk didn't keep. Ma and she would use it to bake scones with today. She wished she'd not been like bitter buttermilk with Paudeen.

Maureen wondered if there might be some way to apologise for storming off into the *Lughnasa* night, to see if they could give what she felt for him another chance. But how? A letter wouldn't do. A letter couldn't look into his blue eyes nor let him look into hers, and anyway she'd no idea where he lived in Ring.

It was too far to walk there to look for him. What if she took the bus Fidelma used to get to the linen mill in Clonakilty, walked the four miles to Ring—that wasn't far—and went to the harbour? A local would know Paudeen's house or boat. But what if when she arrived he was at sea? Wouldn't she look the right *óin-seach*? Maureen O'Hanlon did not like to be made to look like an idiot.

She set to cranking for all she was worth, feeling the stiffness with each turn of the handle as the butter solidified.

> He can go and get another
> That I hope he will enjoy . . .

She really had to strain to crank. It would soon be time to stop and take off the lid. She had to rest before churning once more; then she put all her strength into the job.

For I'm going to marry a far nicer boy.

Maureen felt the sweat running into her eyes.

"You'll blow a gasket if you don't slow down, Miss O'Hanlon, bye, and I thought marriage wasn't in your stars anyway."

She spun on her stool. Paudeen stood in the barn, propping a Raleigh bicycle against one wall. He stooped to take from his ankles the clips that prevented the cuffs of his trousers from catching in the bike's chain.

Her hand flew to her mouth. She wanted to leap to her feet and run to him, but instead she said, "It is yourself, Mr. Kincaid?"

"It is, bye."

There it was, that "bye" of his. She shook her head and thought about leopards and spots. "Just excuse me for a minute. I need to run off the buttermilk."

She did have to, but she also wanted to collect her thoughts.

"Take your time, now. I'm in no rush." He bent over a wicker basket that sat on top of the rear mudguard and was held to the saddle by thin leather straps.

Maureen poured the buttermilk into a pot, spilling some in her haste. She took a small wooden slat and scraped the fresh butter off the walls and lid of the churn, letting the yellow chunks fall within the barrel. Then she filled a ladle with buttermilk. "Would you like a drink? It's a long uphill ride from Ring."

"I would, thank you," he said. "It is hot after the sun is up, and it *is* a fair ways on an old bike like this. I think I pushed it more than pedaled on the steep bits."

He left the basket alone, accepted the buttermilk, and swallowed half at one gulp. "Begob, that's good," he said, wiping the white moustache from his upper lip.

"I'm glad you're enjoying it," she said, praying that he had come because he felt as she did. She searched for the words that she could use to apologise. She was too shy to blurt out, "I love you."

He finished the buttermilk, gave back the ladle, and looked straight at her. "I came over to see your brother. If the pair of us is going to be a team, we'll need to have lots of practice at the bowling, so, and I never had a chance to talk to him properly about it at the *céili*."

If it's only Tiernan you want, not me, there's no chance *we'll* be a team, and that's all because I never gave you a chance to talk properly that night. "It's Tiernan you're after, is it?" she said stiffly, trying to ignore the prickling behind her eyelids.

"It is." Just a hint of a smile played on his lips. "I know we'd be good together . . . him and me that is."

Was he teasing her? He couldn't be. Even though she knew so little about him, she couldn't believe Paudeen Kincaid would ever be cruel. But if he had come for Tiernan, her initial elation was unfounded. Maureen turned to hang the ladle on a hook and was glad to. With her back to him, he'd not see her face. "He's gone to Skibbereen today, so you've had a ride for nothing. Now if you'll excuse me, Mr. Kincaid?" She started to churn.

"Not for nothing," he said and bent over the basket. "I brought you this salmon. Sometimes they do get caught on the long line, and I thought maybe your family would enjoy this one."

"We will." She didn't want to turn. Not until her eyes were dry. She wanted to talk about making up, but he'd said he'd come to see Tiernan. She had to say something. "Salmon are the fish of knowledge." She kept her voice level with some effort. "They get their wisdom by eating sacred hazelnuts that have fallen into the river from a tree in Ossory." She knew she was prattling, not saying what she really needed to, but she wanted to keep him near. "When *Fionn MacCumhail* ate such a salmon, he became the wisest man in all Ireland." Perhaps this Paudeen was no dozer himself, she thought. Perhaps he was pretending to have come to see Tiernan in case she rebuffed him. He could always salvage his pride if she did by insisting he'd not wanted to see her anyway.

"I know the stories," said Paudeen. He laughed. "But I'm not Finn MacCool, chief of the *Fianna,* the warrior band. I'm *not* a fighting man. I hate fights." He waited.

Maureen heard the asking note in his voice. She dashed her hand over her eyes, sniffed, and turned.

He offered her the fish. Its scales were silver and its eyes barely dulled. He looked long and hard at her. "I just thought that if this fish let me catch it, maybe it wasn't one of the smart ones after all . . ." He raised one eyebrow. "So I decided not to let it get away."

She managed a smile. "Thank you for the fish," she said. "It's kind of you to have brought it . . . and . . . I'm sorry . . ." She wanted to say she was sorry she'd stormed off, but the words wouldn't come. "I'm sorry Tiernan's away, so." She took the salmon and placed it on the table beside the churn.

He laughed his warm chocolate laugh. "I'm not," he said. He moved close to her. "For it was yourself I came to see, Miss Maureen O'Hanlon, to say I'm sorry I didn't come after you that night."

Maureen stood rooted, feeling a glow spread through her. "Och, Paudeen," she said, "it was all my fault. I got way too far up on my high horse. I'm sorry too."

"You had a point to make," he said. "Fair play to you, now."

"And you'd a tide to catch. You'd told us and I'd forgotten. I was just so cross you weren't there."

He nodded. "I think I should have missed it and stayed on."

"No," she said. "You'd your work to go to." Och, Paudeen, Paudeen, she thought. Thank you. "And I've mine, so," she said, filling the ladle again and giving it to him. "Drink up while I finish the churning." She wanted to leap up and kiss him, but Ma was in the kitchen and might see.

Maureen poured cold water into the churn and replaced the lid.

Paudeen drank and she could feel his eyes on her. Somehow the handle seemed to be turning more easily.

"I really did come to see Tiernan as well. I do want to practice with him," he said.

"He'll love that," she said, and she thought, if you keep coming back to see my brother it'll give me a chance to see more of you. "Could you come over tomorrow? I know he'll be here all day."

"I could. The exercise would be good for me, for it is a power of a hill, so."

Her heart sang. "And maybe you'd stay for your lunch today, to give you the strength for the ride home?"

"With pleasure. And I'll be content to sit here and chat with you while you work."

She smiled broadly. "Chat away," she said. "I'll listen."

Paudeen sat on the bale of hay close to Maureen. "Do you know?" he said, "I went off and I thought about what you said about the teaching."

"And do you still think if I did, it would be a 'thing'? It was your word, so." She swung the crank that bit harder.

"Lord Jasus, Maureen O'Hanlon, but you've more spines than a *gráinneog,* a hedgehog. I do *not* think that. I was just surprised, that's all. And before you'd let me explain, you'd snapped at me like a monkfish and run off like a liltie."

"Well, then," she said, churning more gently, "I've said I'm sorry, so explain away now and I'll listen."

"I will." He held out the ladle. "If there's a drop more of that . . ."

"Help yourself."

He did. "Now I confess you flummoxed me, for I hadn't heard of a girl going on after school, and add to that I'd been disappointed myself. I told you I fancied the architecture. I never even got my Leaver's."

She found she was less interested in his explanation for why he'd seemed to mock her aspirations and more interested in his story. "Because you went fishing instead?"

"I did."

"I don't understand. You wanted to be an architect, but you gave up that dream. Is fishing so exciting?"

He sighed and said softly, "Sure I'd been helping my Da at weekends and in the summer holidays since I wasn't more than a chiseller. I've grown to love the sea. It can get a hold over a man like nothing else I know." His eyes had a faraway look.

"Maybe you'd take me in your boat one day?" Maybe I can change your views about what can get a hold over a man, she thought.

"I will, bye. I will, so."

"I'd like that. A lot." So without anything definite having been said about the future, she could feel the rift between them healing over. She decided not to plough the same furrow twice by asking him his opinion on her plans to teach—not today anyway. Better to ask him about himself. "You still haven't told me why you went to the fishing in the first place."

"I told you I'd a big brother and a wheen of sisters?"

"Five, I think."

"Five sisters, it is, and back then all with mouths to be fed. My Da and Casey, my brother, ran the boat until the year I turned fifteen—"

"And you changed your mind about the architecture?"

He shrugged. His voice was flat. "I'd it changed for me. Casey hated the sea. He had a powerful donnybrook with Da one day. It nearly came to blows. I didn't know then how that would affect my plans, but it did. Casey stormed off . . . and the last we heard he was in Sacramento in California." He looked at her.

Maureen wondered if he was thinking about her rushing away into the *Lughnasa* night. "I'm sorry, Paudeen. Family rows are awful," she said and briefly touched his arm.

"They are." His gaze held hers.

Maureen swallowed. "And did you have to leave school to help your Da? I thought you said you went fishing when you were sixteen."

Paudeen shook his head. "You're right, I was. With Casey gone, Da took on a young lad as a deckhand, and lucky enough, Dympna and Myrna got married that year. Da was tickled because with them gone, the money stretched, even if he had to pay a crew."

Did neither of those girls have any hopes of doing more than marrying? Maureen wondered. Probably not, and she had no doubt that Paudeen would have got his ideas about girls and marriage from his Da—and his Da from *his* Da. Ireland, she thought, where things never change, the Land of Saints and Scholars—and minds as closed as steel traps. She frowned. "But if your family didn't need the money, why did you go?"

"Da, God rest him, was washed over in a gale. We didn't find him . . ." Paudeen's voice broke. He took a deep breath. "Until a week later."

Maureen's hand flew to her mouth. "I'm sorry."

He shrugged. "Thank you, but I'm not looking for sympathy. Things like that do happen. Just . . . I still miss him, bye." Paudeen managed a weak grin. "He taught me to bowl, to dance . . . and to fish."

Maureen held her peace.

"Anyway," Paudeen said, "Da's passing made me head of the household with Casey gone, and a living had to be made."

"So you gave up school to take care of your Ma and your sisters?"

He raised both hands, palms up.

"I think you're a good man, Paudeen Kincaid. A very good man." And she meant every word, but still, she thought, maybe if your older sisters, who got wed, had had jobs with decent wages you could have stayed at school. Maureen felt a tightness in her throat. She opened the lid of the churn, spilled out more buttermilk, and poured in cold water. "I think the butter's near done. And I think what you've just told me's very sad."

"Divil the bit," he said. "A fellah does

what he has to, and . . ."—he bent closer and whispered—"I think I'll have to see more of you, Maureen O'Hanlon." He grinned from one ear to the other, and she could do little but lean across the churn, Ma be blowed, and kiss him.

As she moved away Maureen knew she'd been right not to raise the subject of her career. There'd be time enough for that question when she had Paudeen Kincaid as firmly hooked—she glanced at the salmon—as firmly hooked as that fish had been. For hadn't she fallen for him, hook, line, and sinker?

Paudeen stood and smiled at her. "If I'm going to be seeing more of you, Miss O'Hanlon, I still want to have a few lofts of the bullet with that brother of yours too, b—."

"Bye," they said in unison and laughed together in the morning sunlight.

25

Maureen did see more of Paudeen Kincaid. Much more. Unless he had a tide to catch or his gear to maintain, he'd cycle over any day he was able during the school holidays. Once term started, he'd come on Saturdays if he was free, because on Sundays Maureen played camogie for the local GAA team or as a member of the Cork Juniors.

He'd often spend an hour or two practising with Tiernan. But she didn't begrudge him that because when the boys finished, she and Paudeen would walk for miles. They went over the fields or along the roads toward Clonakilty or Ballinvoher or Newcestown.

One late September Saturday when the last of the summer swallows had gone and a single sparrowhawk hovered overhead hunting mice in hedges made brilliant by the orange of the rowanberries, Maureen started looking down the lane for Paudeen's bicycle long before he could possibly arrive, willing him to come sooner. The moment he crested the rise she ran to greet him. His kiss was no longer a butterfly brushing her lips. His arms around her were strong, and she scented the fresh sweat of him.

"I've missed you," she said.

"And I brought you these." He handed her a bunch of heavily scented wildflowers, creamy white honeysuckle, and red foxgloves.

"Thank you. They're lovely." She kissed him again. "Tiernan's helping out over at the MacVeighs today. There's no need to go up to the house," she said.

"But the flowers'll wilt away. Give them back and I'll ride on up and get your Ma to put them in water. You stay here." Paudeen took the bouquet, hopped on his bike, and pedaled furiously away.

She waited, loving him for caring about her flowers.

He was back in next to no time and propped his Raleigh against the fence. "Come on," he said and took her hand. As they strode along the farm lane, Paudeen remarked, "Beal na mBláth isn't far, is it?"

"It's not. Maybe a couple of miles. Why? There's nothing much there except a five-road-ends crossroads and Long's pub." And, she thought, I haven't been up in that direction since the day I went with Fidelma and saw Connor.

"I took a notion I'd like to visit the place. They make a big fuss in Clonakilty about their hometown boy, Michael Collins."

The Irish rebel leader who was shot near Beal na mBláth in 1922, she thought. Maureen frowned and looked at him. "Are you a republican, Paudeen? Paying homage to a dead hero? Is that it?"

He laughed. "It is not, and I am not. Not at all," he said. "I'm a fisherman. I've no time for politics of any stripe."

"I'm glad to hear it," she said. "There's

been too much grief in Ireland over politics. Da said the O'Hanlons should take no sides in the war with the English, the Black and Tan War, nor during the Irish Civil War, the one that's only over for three years."

"Your Da was right."

"Then why do you want to go to the crossroads?"

Paudeen stopped walking, forcing her to halt. He let go of her hand. "I've been reading about those Troubles. Since you told me you're interested in Irish history, I thought I'd better find out a bit about it myself, so I started with a local figure. Collins."

"Just because I'm interested in Irish history, Paudeen? That's sweet." She kissed him.

"Do you know," he said, "some of it's as exciting as anything by R. M. Ballantyne or H. Rider Haggard?"

"I do know."

"Anyway, the Big Fellah—that was Collins's nickname—was born at Woodfield, four miles west of Clonakilty in 1890. He worked for the British post office."

"In London," she said, "and he fought in

the Dublin General Post Office along with Pádraig Pearse and James Connolly in April 1916 during the Easter Rising. I was eight then. I remember Da and Ma talking about it."

Paudeen laughed. "And I thought you weren't interested in politics."

"I'm not, so, but history is very different from politics, and I'm very interested in history . . . everything to do with Ireland from just a while ago and your man Michael Collins, right back to the beginnings. The very start is written down in the *Leabhar Gabhála Éireann—The Book of Invasions*—and Da just about knows it by heart. Since I was wee, I've heard stories from him about all the races who ruled this country from the mists of time until today."

"My aunty Brid knew about *The Book of Invasions* too and tried to tell me, but I was too interested in the sports to pay much heed to her going on about the Milesians or the *Fir Bolg*."

She turned left when they reached the road. "This is the way to Beal na mBláth if you want to go there."

"I do." He shortened his stride so she could easily keep pace.

"And as we go, do you want me to tell you about the Feer Bollug?"

"I do . . ." His eyes twinkled. "Bye."

They both laughed. She kissed him again, loving him for his teasing and his willingness to learn about something that interested her.

They walked through the misty afternoon. The moisture made the air feel touchable and blurred the crests of the hills as if they had been sketched with charcoal, then smudged on a blue-grey paper sky. The road, the drystone walls, and the turning leaves shone damply.

". . . and the Feer Bollug were beaten by the *Tuatha dé Danann,*" she said.

"And aunty told me the Milesians came from Spain, they were Celts, and they did beat the Tooatha, so. Us modern Irish are descended from the Milesians." He chuckled. "Do you think that makes us Spanish?"

"Eejit. It does not, at least not most of us. There's a few folks out on the west coast descended from shipwrecked sailors off the Spanish armada."

"Is that so?"

"It is." She stooped and plucked a piece

of tufted vetch, studded with blue flowers, from a roadside bank. "But you're right, it's the Milesians we're from." Then she asked, "Do you know what happened to the *Tuatha*?"

He shook his head.

"They were driven to live underground into the *sidthe* and became the Shee, the people of the mounds."

He sounded serious when he asked, "Do you believe in the faeries, Maureen?"

"I do." And, she thought, it's been a while since I've seen them or heard Connor.

"Me too." He smiled at her. "Honestly."

"Good for you."

They walked on in silence.

She heard the plaintive cries of a flock of curlew overhead, the bleating of sheep, and smelled the harsh odours of flax being retted in a nearby flax dam. The water softened the plants' stem fibres so they could be separated out and spun into Irish linen.

"You don't get a stink like that at sea," Paudeen said, wrinkling his nose.

"I hear rotting seaweed and dead fish don't get much sales in perfume shops either."

They were chuckling as they turned a corner.

Maureen hadn't seen Connor's cottage for years. She stopped in her tracks. There it was at the end of its short lane. Her laughter faded and she felt an ineffable sadness.

"That's a sad-sorry looking sort of a place," Paudeen said.

"It belonged to a friend," she said softly.

The thatch was dirty brown, mouldy, overgrown with moss and ferns, and half caved-in. Tufts of grass grew from the chimney pots. Brambles, benweeds, and convolvulus snarled in tangles round the windows. The red paint had peeled from the frames, and the panes were smashed, their jagged edges as vicious as razors.

"'Tis an unfortunate-looking spot," Paudeen said. "I hate to see anything wrecked. A good boat up on the rocks with her ribs showing through like the skeleton of a drowned cow always does bring me very low." He sighed and turned to her. "What happened here?"

Maureen looked him in the eye. "Paudeen, you said you believe in the Shee?"

"I do. I didn't use to . . . but since I've taken to the fishing . . ." He stared into the distance.

"Go on."

"You do see strange things in the ocean."

"What strange things?"

"Do you know about the Selkie?"

"The seal women? They're women ashore, but when they put on their magic sealskin they become seals and live in the ocean? I've heard tell. And I've heard of the *Dobharchú,* the sea monster of the Rosses of Donegal."

"I never saw one of those beasts, thank the Lord, but I think a Selkie saved my life," he said.

She shuddered and her eyes widened. Paudeen's outline was now blurred, his voice indistinct. The hill behind him had vanished, and instead there was a wall of white water, roaring, crashing, clawing at him, reaching for him, and then disappearing suddenly, leaving him there smiling, his eyes blue, the hillside behind him grass-green and bracken-brown, and the only water the misty dew on it.

Maureen tried to hide her trembling.

The Pavee woman had shown her a card called the Prince of Cups and said it could have something to do with the moods of the sea. Now she had seen a monstrous wave in an angry sea. She shook her head. What did it all mean?

"Are you all right, Maureen?" She heard the concern in his voice.

It took an effort, but she managed to say, "I'm grand, so. I just felt a bit dizzy."

"Come and sit down."

Together they sat on the one smooth rock on top of a crumbling stone wall.

"I'm fine," she said. "Honestly. It's passed." She forced a smile. "Women do take the vapours once in a while, you know. Now go on, tell me about your Selkie."

She saw the concern in his eyes, how he waited for her to collect herself. She was trying to, she really was, but she'd just watched a wave coming for Paudeen. He said a Selkie had saved him. Maureen connected the thoughts.

For a second, she must've seen the sea that had almost taken him. Did that mean the sight and the tarot worked backward too? That they hadn't been portents of the future, but rather had spoken to her about something from the past of the man she loved? She'd like to think so. She would believe it.

Maureen stopped shaking. "Go on," she said. "I'm fine now, honestly."

"You're certain sure?"

"I am, Paudeen. I'm grand, so. Tell me about the Selkie."

"This is how it was," he said. "I'd gone out on the mudflats at low tide to dig lugworms for bait when from nowhere came this great comber and pulled me out, way out to sea. And I can't swim."

"You what?" Maureen heard her voice rise. "You can't swim? And you go fishing for a living? Are you mad, Paudeen Kincaid?" She almost said, "After what happened to your Da?" but held her tongue. She didn't want to hurt him.

"I am not," he said calmly. "The waters here are so bitter they'll kill you very quick if you go overboard. Being able to swim would only prolong the dying. All the fishermen believe that, so."

"You scare me, Paudeen."

"It was that great big wave that terrified me. There I was, thrashing and choking and drowning. There was nothing but water under my feet and over my head, and I couldn't tell up from down, and my lungs bursting, and the world growing cold and dim, when what do I feel, bye? I feel something shoving me, hard, and I can't see what it is. I put down my hand and there's an animal beside me, silky to the touch. Warm to the touch. And the creature is pushing me. I don't know what nature of beast it is, but I know I'm moving, and I know my feet have found solid land, and my head's out in the air and I can fill my poor lungs. I know if I can struggle a few steps I'll be safe on the strand." He smiled. "And there I was, cold and soaked, but alive and safe. And I couldn't tell if the water in my eyes was salt sea or salt tears."

"Thank God you were saved." Maureen knew now, she just knew, she'd seen the wave that almost took Paudeen. It had been terrifyingly big. That *was* what she'd seen moments ago. Wasn't it?

Paudeen's voice was low. "I mean no blasphemy, but I don't think it was Himself I needed to thank. By the time I'd got my breath and looked out to sea, it was calm as calm, and near to where the wave had taken me was a seal. The animal lifted one flipper and slammed it against the surface. But when the spray cleared, the seal was gone and I never saw her again."

"And you think it was a Selkie?"

"Maureen, I *know* it was." He took her by both shoulders and looked into her eyes. "You asked me if I believe in the Shee? If there's Selkies in the sea, there must be faeries on the land."

"Not too many men today do believe. And few men would confess to a girl that they had been scared of anything. Thank you."

"There's no shame in being scared for the right reasons, and none in the telling of it to someone you trust. And how many men have been rescued by a Selkie? I do believe in other powers." He laughed. "Now you know I do, will you tell me what happened here? Did the Shee have something to do with it?"

"They did. Connor MacTaggart, who lived in this cottage, did not believe in them."

"Lived?"

"Aye. He's gone now. He did a pigheaded thing. Even though he'd been warned, he cut down a blackthorn on the eleventh of November nearly four years ago. The Shee tormented him for weeks, and then he was lost in a blizzard that Saint Stephen's Day."

Paudeen whistled soft and low. "Poor divil."

"He's that, all right. For his ghost haunts this place. He has found no rest. The Shee took him."

"God, have mercy," Paudeen said quietly.

She pointed out beyond the wall. "The branches of the tree he cut are lying on the ground where he left them up there," she said. "Over in that field. Nobody wants them."

"And sensible too. I'd not touch them."

"Those branches," she said, "will lie there until Connor has done a deed that pleases the Shee. When he does, they'll let his spirit go, and the branches will turn to dust." She smiled at Paudeen. "I hope he does his good turn soon. I'd like to see him at his rest. He was a good man and . . ."

She stumbled over her words because

leaning from a window frame, an elbow on the sill, oblivious to the broken glass, was a man's upper body and a face she knew. He had a dudeen in the corner of his mouth, and he was staring at Paudeen and back to Maureen, and smiling and nodding his head.

"Mother of God," she whispered, as her hand flew to her mouth.

Paudeen had his arms round her at once. "What is it? What are you seeing?" His gaze followed hers.

She shook her head. "Nothing." And it was the truth, for now there wasn't anything but the peeling red-painted frame and the broken glass. "Not a thing. Only a ruined cottage." Hadn't Ma told her never to tell anyone about the sight?

"Are you sure you're all right? Do you want to go home?"

She shook her head. "I'll be fine. We're less than a mile from the crossroads. We'll go on, but let's sit for a minute or two longer. I think it was remembering Connor upset me. I liked the man. Indeed, for I was only fourteen when it happened, and I was half in love with him. Fidelma *was* in love with him."

Paudeen pulled her closer, kissed her, and said, his voice husky, "And I've been trying for weeks to find a way to tell you . . . I'm in love with you, Maureen O'Hanlon."

Maureen kissed him right back, hugged him to her, and then laughed and said, "It's taken you a brave while to get round to it, so. I know you're a bit shy and use the humour to hide what you're feeling, but you needn't have worried. Sure haven't I known you've loved me since *Lughnasa* when you kissed me for the first time?"

He tipped his head to the left. "Why didn't you say so?"

"And am I not allowed a bit of modesty too, Paudeen Kincaid? Am I not a woman? And haven't I been in love with you, you great *amadán,* since that kiss too? Now put me down." He'd lifted her off her feet and was spinning round with her in his arms, yelling at the top of his voice, "Maureen loves me, and I love her, and I don't give a gutted herring for who knows. I want the whole world to know. I love her."

"Put me down." Maureen could hardly stop laughing. "It's decent of you," she said, "to cry it to the world when there's nobody around to hear, except that vixen sitting on the wall over there grinning at you. Now put . . . me . . . down."

She wondered if Connor had heard them too. He'd have approved, and even though Maureen couldn't see a woman's face this time, she was sure the queen of the Doov Shee approved too. This time the fox didn't scare her. Ma had said the faeries would watch over her, and Maureen was pleased their queen had seen her with the man she loved.

Paudeen set her gently on her feet, held her at arm's length. His cornflower-blue eyes saw through to her soul, and he held her gaze with his own, never blinking as he said, "Maureen, I love you as I've loved no woman before, and as I'll love no woman after. I love you now, and I'll love you forever." Then he kissed her.

His kiss didn't stop her remembering the Pavee and her cards, the cards she'd been thinking about so short a time ago. The woman had been right about the sea, and her card, the Two of Cups, foretold love. Maureen'd been in love since *Lughnasa*, and now Paudeen had finally plucked up the courage to tell her it was returned.

"Maureen," Paudeen said, "I've seen a lot of your part of Cork. I told you once I'd take you out in my boat. I want you to know everything about me. How'd you like to come into Ring soon, and I'll let you see what I do with myself."

The card, the Wheel of Fortune, had foretold a journey. "I'd love to," she said, and wondered, if the fortune-teller's cards had been right three times, what of the other two? There was no way to prove or disprove the prediction of a long life, but what did the Death card mean? A real death or a huge change?

A thought came on her. She *knew* he loved her as much as she loved him. Unless something completely unexpected happened, he'd soon ask her to marry him. And that could be the transformation the card told.

He interrupted her thoughts by asking, "It'll have to be a Saturday, won't it, like the way it is now?"

She looked at him, his young face, his calloused hands, his blue eyes.

The more she thought about him asking her to marry him, the more she liked the idea.

"Yes, Paudeen, it will, so."

She'd say yes to the other question too. Yes, Paudeen. Yes. Yes. And he'd love her so much he'd encourage her to finish her schooling and go on and be a teacher. That shift in attitude could be the kind of change the tarot predicted. Couldn't it?

He frowned. "It could be a while before we go. Next month's the start of the ling season. My busiest time."

She kissed him and said, "I'll wait for you, Paudeen Kincaid. You're a man worth waiting for."

26

She'd said she'd wait and so she did. Maureen had no chance to see Paudeen until it was nearly November. October had been a very long month because he was at sea every day fishing for the ling.

She missed him, and exchanging letters didn't make up for not having him near.

In his last note, scripted in his strong copperplate, he told her he'd be free on Saturday the thirtieth, and he asked her to meet him on the Ring pier at ten in the morning. Eamon and Fidelma, who often went into Clonakilty on Saturdays, were going to give Maureen a lift in the MacVeighs' lorry.

"Eamon'll not be here for at least another ten minutes," Fidelma said. "I know you're busting to see Paudeen, but telling me to hurry up and finish my breakfast won't bring Eamon any the quicker."

Maureen laughed. "Well, it's lovely out, so. I'm going to wait in the barnyard."

"Enjoy your day," Ma called from near the kitchen range, where she was ironing Da's shirts.

"I will, Ma, and don't let that cup of tea get too cold before you come out, Fidelma," Maureen said sweetly, as she opened the door.

"Get on with you, girl," Fidelma said. "I'm not rushing. I'd get heartburn. I'll be along in a shmall minute, so." Fidelma sipped her tea and buttered another slice of toast.

Maureen closed the door. Outside, it was one of those autumn mornings when the crops were long harvested, the leaves well on the turn. The sky had lost its brassy summer sheen and was a delicate blue like a robin's egg, the clouds as fragile as puffs of bog cotton. The crisp air nipped her cheeks, and she was glad she'd worn a heavy sweater over her thick, ankle-length tweed skirt.

At nine thirty to the minute, Eamon MacVeigh put-putted into the O'Hanlons' yard, waved at Maureen, and honked his horn.

Fidelma came running out, still struggling into her cardigan, climbed into the lorry, and gave a grinning Eamon a kiss. Maureen followed her into the cab. She noticed that Eamon had lost some of his girth. Even his cheeks seemed thinner.

"Right," he said. "All aboard for the MacVeigh sharabang ride. First stop: Ring Harbour."

"You don't mind going that bit further, Eamon?" Maureen asked.

"Not at all. Fidelma and me've all day, so." He patted Fidelma's knee. "Haven't we, pet?"

"We have. Once we've seen to our own shopping and got the messages Ma wants, we can do as we please." She smiled at Maureen. "I told Ma I'd do her errands, for you'd be too busy."

"Thanks, Fidelma."

"Och, sure it's no bother, so."

"Once they're done," Eamon said, driving out of the farmyard, "we'll get a bite, and after I'm taking your sister to the matinee to see Ramon Novarro and Francis X. Bushman in *Ben-Hur*."

"Who's playing Messala?" Maureen asked.

"How do you know his name?" Eamon said.

"I've read the book."

"You and your books, Maureen O'Hanlon," Fidelma said with a smile. "If it's not schoolbooks or tomes of Irish history, it's novels. I'm surprised you make time for Paudeen at all, so."

"I've my Leaver's coming up next June, and I'm still for trying to do what I told you I would."

"Good for you, Maureen. Get your exam. Keep away from the mill." Fidelma leant over and whispered, "I'll be out of there soon." She nodded in Eamon's direction.

For a moment Maureen didn't understand. Then her eyes widened. "You mean . . ."

Fidelma, smiling broadly, nodded. "Aye,

so. We're shopping for the ring today, and Eamon's going to see Da tonight."

"*Fidelma.*" Maureen wriggled round on the bench and gave her sister an enormous hug. "And you too, Eamon. I wish you both every happiness, so."

"Och," said Eamon, "it's only right and proper I make an honest woman of her." Maureen saw the grin on his open, ruddy face. "And," he said, glancing across at her, "we're beginning to wonder when Captain Courageous is going to—"

"Wheest now, Eamon MacVeigh," Fidelma said. "That's none of your business. Don't embarrass Maureen."

"Och—"

"You concentrate on your driving, boyo. I'm going to have a chat with my sister."

Eamon swerved violently to avoid a cow that had ambled onto the narrow winding road, and Maureen grabbed at the lorry's side, feeling Fidelma pressed against her. It wasn't until Eamon had the lorry on course again and she and her sister had got themselves settled comfortably that Fidelma said quietly, "Paudeen's not said anything yet, has he?"

Maureen shook her head, then put her lips close to her sister's ear. She didn't want Eamon to overhear. "But he's told me he loves me, and you know how shy men can be."

Fidelma chuckled and nodded her head in Eamon's direction. "Casanova here had to have a couple of stiffeners in him before he could tell me, and with the stutters of him he hardly got the words out at all, bless him."

Maureen could hear the affection in her sister's lowered voice. She glanced at Eamon, who appeared not to hear their conversation. She said, "Paudeen hadn't had a drop in him, but I know it cost him a great deal to get up his nerve."

"I'm sure he thinks you're worth every penny of it. I've watched the pair of you, even before you danced with him. I saw magic then and I've watched it grow."

"What kind of magic?"

"The kind I had with poor Connor . . ."

Maureen heard Eamon clearing his throat loudly. Maybe he had heard everything, but she realised it really didn't matter.

Fidelma was quick to reassure him.

"And the sort there's between your man here and me." She kissed Eamon's cheek. "Isn't that right, love?"

"True on you, Fidelma O'Hanlon," Eamon said, and for no good reason honked his horn.

Fidelma laughed. *"Amadán,"* she said, then kissed him again.

Maureen said, "I'm so happy to see you're so happy, Fiddles."

"I am, so. I'm looking forward to being a married lady." She hesitated. "What'll you do if Paudeen does ask?"

Maureen wasn't entirely sure. In the excitement of his confessing his love, she had certainly said to herself she'd say yes. But she'd had time to think since, and a question still remained: would he let her teach?

She didn't want to answer Fidelma's question immediately, and so she said, "He told me he'd be down on one knee with a diamond ring."

"So he's a romantic fellah?"

"He brought me a bunch of flowers the day he told me he loved me."

Fidelma shook her head. "You're a lucky girl." She raised her voice. "Eamon here, his idea of romance is to let a girl help him with the haying and then have her cook his tea. Isn't that so, Mr. MacVeigh?"

"And what's so wrong with that?" Eamon asked. "The way to a man's heart is through his stomach."

Fidelma chuckled. "No. The way to a man having a fat belly is through his stomach." She kissed his cheek. "Eamon's been watching his grub. He's lost a fair bit of weight, nearly a stone, and I'm very proud of him, so."

Eamon grinned.

Maureen felt warmed by how comfortable they seemed to be one with the other.

"Maureen," said Fidelma in a lower voice that Eamon probably couldn't hear, "you didn't answer my question. What will you do?"

"If Paudeen proposes?"

"Yes."

"Fidelma, I love him. I love him to my bones."

"So you'll say yes?"

Maureen spoke quietly. "I'm not sure, Fiddles. The night I met him I told him I wanted to teach. Him being a good storyteller's not the only way he's like our Da.

He said he doesn't believe a woman should go on working after she's married, and he seemed pretty fixed about that."

"He'd get no complaints from me on that score," Fidelma said, "but I know you have other notions."

"We had a row about it that night. I didn't tell anybody. Sure for all anyone knew there was nothing between us except tea together, a couple of dances, and a walk in the moonlight. Nobody even knew I'd let him kiss me. But I knew how I felt, and thought I'd lost him then, and my heart did nearly break. It was so wonderful when he came back I haven't dared raise the subject since. I'm scared to. I'd die if he went away again, so."

Fidelma drew in a deep breath. "I know what you mean." Maureen heard a catch in her sister's voice. Fidelma looked over at Eamon, then back to Maureen. "But there are other fellahs. I've been lucky." She touched Maureen's arm. "*A chara,*" she said, "I don't want to interfere, but . . . but do you not think maybe . . . maybe you should have a word with Paudeen? Let him know where you stand?"

"I know I should. Soon. But not today.

It's nearly a month since I saw him. I just want to be with him today, Fiddles. I want to have a bit of *craic*."

"And I hope you do."

"I will. I'm certain sure." She took a deep breath. Just thinking about seeing Paudeen could make her a little breathless.

"But don't you leave the talking too long, girl. It's got to come up sooner or later."

"I know, but I'll wait for the right opportunity."

"Have you two finished your heart-to-heart yet?" Eamon asked. "You're not even noticing the world going by. These cottages round this five-road-ends are Ballinascarthy."

"And what's so special about that?" Maureen asked.

"Henry Ford," Eamon said reverently.

"Who?" Maureen shrugged. "Never heard of him."

Eamon shook his head. "You would have if you liked motor cars. He builds thousands of them in Detroit in America. His Da was born in Ballinascarthy."

"Oh. That's very interesting," Maureen

said, even though as far as she was concerned it wasn't, but she was pleased to see Eamon smile.

She smiled back and glanced ahead. "Would you look at that copper beech? Did you ever see the like?"

The massive tree's russet leaves made a cheerful blaze against the sullen dark of the ploughed field behind it.

"The only other thing I've seen that colour," Fidelma said with a wicked grin, "were your cheeks, Eamon MacVeigh, the night you got a skinful of Archie Bolan's *poitín,* you gurrier." She made a face at him and laughed.

Eamon laughed so hard Maureen could feel the seat shake, and then Fidelma kissed his cheek, and the pair of them were lost in their own conversation.

Maureen didn't want to intrude. She sat back. Fidelma was right. She should have it out with Paudeen. No, that was too harsh a way to think of it. They would talk things over. But when was the "right opportunity" going to be?

Eamon drove past Lios na gCon, and she remembered how slighted she'd felt there three months ago when Paudeen questioned her wish to teach, to go on working after marriage. He seemed to have accepted it more that day he'd come to see Tiernan and she was churning butter. But he hadn't said so. Not out loud.

She could recall the conversation quite clearly. He'd thought about it, he'd said, but she'd never found out exactly what he had thought. She'd let herself be distracted by his story of why he'd gone to sea. And face it, girl, you haven't had the courage since to ask him, have you?

Fidelma was right too about Paudeen going to propose. He would—and soon, she was sure. She longed for him to, but—but she still wanted her Leaver's. She still wanted to teach.

Maybe, she thought, maybe she was being selfish. Maybe she should do what all the other girls did, but she'd been dreaming for years about her career. She'd never wavered in that. She'd worked, and worked hard, toward it.

Maureen had been lost in thought, paying no attention to the surroundings. She sat up to see they were in the outskirts of Clonakilty. Now that Fidelma had raised the question, the need to talk to Paudeen about their future was gnawing at Maureen. She'd have to make up her mind about whether to ask him or just have fun today. And she'd have to make it up right soon.

Perhaps if the opportunity arose she would to talk to him today. He was an intelligent man. Surely when she did broach the subject, explained what she wanted, Paudeen wouldn't let some outmoded notion of pride stand between the woman *he* loved, and who loved him to distraction, doing what she was sure *she* would love.

"Here we are, people," Eamon announced like a tour guide, "in the throbbing heart of the metropolis of Clonakilty, so." He was stopped at a crossroads waiting for a gap in the light traffic.

Clonakilty, she thought, was a name with a musical ring to it, like the nearby villages of Castlefreke, Rosscarberry, and Timoleague. She knew the Irish *Cloch na gCoilte* meant "castle of the woods." The literal translation of *Cloch* was stone house, a structure that had first appeared in Ireland in Norman times.

Maureen looked round. It was the biggest place she had ever been in. To her right and to her left, rows of two-storey terraces lined both sides of the street. Their roofs—yellow thatch, red-rusting corrugated iron, and dark blue-grey slate—looked to her like a row from a patchwork quilt. The church with the needle spire that sat solidly on the far corner to her right must be the Roman Catholic one. She'd recognised the worshipping place of the Anglicans on the road into town.

Eamon turned left and drove slowly along a broad main street. Maureen inhaled. The smells here were not country odours. The fumes of exhaust mingled with a faint aroma of decay that the tang of the nearby sea could not quite disguise.

And it was noisy. Horses clopped on the cobbles. Lorry motors clattered. People seemed to yell at each other, not simply converse.

Pedestrians bustled along the footpaths, going in and out of the shops, and stopped to greet neighbours and chat. She tutted as a scruffy-looking boy finished eating chips and discarded the newspaper and greaseproof paper wrapping in the gutter.

She noticed a greengrocery with fresh vegetables displayed on tables outside the shop window. There was a single-storey whitewashed pub with an advertisement for Guinness on the wall. A simple poster of seven full straight glasses, black as pitch and each with a white clergyman's collar for its head, displayed the words "*Guinness Gách Lá.*" Have a Guinness every day.

Outside two draymen had stopped their big Clydesdale-drawn cart and were rolling a cask down two planks. Making sure, Maureen thought, that the supplies would be on hand to accommodate the urging of the poster.

The noise, bustle, and size of the place had surprised Maureen. "It's very big," she said to Fidelma.

"It is not as big as Cork City, but it's big enough for me," Fidelma replied. "Do you know there's a thousand linen looms here and the mill"—she grimaced—"employs ten thousand workers like me. That's the mill over there." She pointed to a grey-stone, forbidding-looking building that was multistoried and many-windowed. Two high red-brick chimneys towered above the town. "I'll be glad I'm going to be shot of it."

Maureen gently squeezed her sister's thigh.

They had come to another crossroads.

"That place there to our left, Maureen, that's the Old Town Hall," said Fidelma. "It was built in 1696, and on the road to our right, not very far down, is the courthouse. They put it up in 1825."

"One of the nice new buildings," Eamon said with a laugh.

"Don't be daft, Eamon," Maureen said. "It's one hundred and one years old."

"Aye," said Eamon, "but Clonakilty's been here since a fellah called Thomas de Roche got a charter from the English king, Edward I, in 1292 to hold a market here every Monday."

"Has it? Good Lord," Maureen said. That was the kind of Irish history that intrigued her. She knew there'd been a battle at nearby Big Cross in 1798 when the United Irishmen rose. The square which Eamon now drove past was named Asna Square after the leader of the defeated Irish, Tadhg O'Donovan Asna.

Other streets commemorated great

patriots, Emmet, Pearse, Clarke. Eamon was driving along Wolfe Tone Street, which according to a fingerpost led to the road to Ring.

Funny, she thought, the name Ring meant point of land or hill. It was quite the coincidence that she'd be going there today when her sister would be getting a ring of a very different kind. In her heart, Maureen was glad for her sister.

She stared out to see how the way curved round the near shore of a wide sun-glistening inlet.

"This is your first time here, isn't it?" Eamon asked.

"It is."

"That land over on the far side of the inlet's Inchydoney. It used to be an island, but there's a couple of causeways to the mainland now. The tide's in, but you should see this place at slack ebb. Nothing but eelgrass, mudflats, and only a shallow, narrow channel at the mouth near Ring Harbour."

She watched a grey heron standing hunchbacked, rapier-billed, at the water's edge. Its neck uncoiled like a striking cobra, and its beak darted into the water to reappear holding a wriggling silver fish. Two mute swans, snow white and yellow-billed, glided along, stately in the company of their own mirror images.

From across the water over on the Inchydoney side, Maureen heard the strident crowing of a rooster.

Eamon slowed. "That's the pier there," he said, bringing them to a halt.

"Thanks, Eamon." Maureen hugged Fidelma, looked her sister in the eye. "Have a *great* shopping trip."

Fidelma grinned and winked.

Maureen jumped down. "Enjoy *Ben-Hur.*" And, she thought, a bit of a cuddle in the dark.

"We'll be back here at five," Eamon called, engaging his gears and swinging the lorry in a circle.

She waved good-bye as they bounced away. I hope he gets you a lovely ring, Fidelma, she thought, and I wish with all my heart he will bring you happiness.

As she walked along the pier, Maureen breathed in the smells of the sea, of salt, and of seaweed, tarred ropes, and diesel smoke. They were new to her, used as she was to the odours of animals and ploughed land, and scents of gorse blooms and mown hay, and turf fires.

Boats were tied to the stone quay, and Paudeen stood on the deck of one, beckoning to her. Over the grumbling of an engine, the slap of waves against the granite, and the creaking of mooring lines, she heard him calling, "Over here, Maureen."

She saw the smile on his face, heard the gladness in his voice, and convinced herself that she'd spent half the ride here worrying over nothing.

She started to hurry along the pier.

27

Maureen tried to hurry, but found she couldn't run because the pier was cluttered with lines, nets, net floats, and piles of lobster pots. She was warm when she stopped and stood beside his boat.

Paudeen, who was waiting on the granite quay, enfolded her in a bear hug and kissed her. "How's my girl?"

"Grand, so, but I've missed you, pet."

"And I you." He kissed her again. She felt the softness of it, the love in it. They stood apart, he holding her hand.

"And is this your boat?" It seemed to her to be awfully small. The hull was painted dark green with a white strip just above the water. There was a name on the side of the sharp, upcurving front end. *Princess Macha.*

"It is." She heard the pride in his voice when he said, "She's a beauty, so."

Maureen looked at the vessel. A short planked deck, with railings on either side, ran a quarter of the boat's length from the rounded stern to a little wooden hut. It was eight feet high, had a sloped roof, and had windows at the far side, in the front, and halfway along the near side to where a glass-paned door stood open.

The flapper valve of a narrow chimney coming from the hut rattled as puffs of blue smoke escaped.

"Do you like her name?" he asked.

"*Princess Macha*? And her a red-haired queen of all Ireland."

"Like my copper-haired queen." He kissed her again.

She laughed and looked along the boat. "That's the fish hold," Paudeen explained, pointing to a canvas-covered square in front of the hut. "I have the hatches shut."

A mast with two vertical poles held to it by a bewildering array of ropes and pulleys rose from the deck in front of the hold.

"Your boat's not . . ." She could see the way he looked at the vessel and bit off her next words: "exactly the *Mauretania*." Instead, she said, "It's not very big."

"Thirty feet, and a grand sea boat. She was a trawler, but I use her as a longliner. That means I catch fish with a great long cord with baited hooks on it at intervals. You'll see her better when you come on aboard." He held Maureen's hand and helped her over the side onto the rear deck.

The smell of fish and diesel was overpowering. Maureen wrinkled her nose. "You'd not mistake her for a boat that delivers flowers."

"Och, sure," said Paudeen, "if you lie down with dogs you'll rise up with fleas, and if your boat's for the fishing you'll have to learn to live with the stink. It's the ling and the skate and the monkfish that do pay my wage. Now"—he held open the door of the little hut—"this is the pilothouse."

"Pilothouse. Right." She peered in and could see a spoked wheel mounted on a pedestal. "What's that?" she asked, pointing to a cylindrical structure topped by a brass dome that stood in front of the wheel. She could see it had a small window facing the wheel.

"The binnacle. It's where the compass is . . . and see here?" He indicated a flat shelf on which rulers and a set of brass dividers, like the ones she used in geometry class, lay on top of a map covered in small numbers and symbols. "That's a chart of Clonakilty Bay and the waters surrounding. There"—he pointed to a symbol on the paper outside the harbour entrance—"that's the mark on Wind Rock. That's where we're going. The water shallows there . . . see the five? That's five fathoms."

So that's what the numbers meant. A fathom was six feet, so the water would be thirty feet deep. She wondered, just for a moment, how deep was her love for this wonderful man who made his living from this tiny cockleshell of a boat? Was it deep enough for her perhaps to forgo plans to travel to America and settle down as a teacher married to a fisherman?

"You can usually jig up a nice lemon sole for your tea there," he said.

She looked at his smile as he spoke, at his blue eyes in which she saw his deep, honest pleasure at the thought of catching a sole. She felt herself tingle. Yes, she told herself, her love for him was so deep it was unfathomable.

He took her arm and guided her to the back of the room where she could see a set of iron ladders disappearing below a square hole in the floor. "That's the way below to the galley."

"Galley?" She thought of *Ben-Hur* and Roman biremes. "Do people row this thing?"

He laughed. "Galley's what we call the kitchen on a boat."

"Oh." She'd remember that. She never liked to make the same mistake twice.

"I have our lunch ready down there. I'll just need to warm it up, and anytime you fancy a cup of tea sing out."

"I will, so, but I'm not thirsty now."

"A bit past the galley there's a bunk. Sometimes me or the crew can grab a nap if we do be out overnight and have to wait for the right tide to get back into harbour."

"I see." A question formed. "Paudeen, I don't suppose you have a toilet too?"

He shook his head. "I'm sorry. We don't usually carry ladies, but if you need to go, just tell me, and I'll get you a bucket."

"All right." She shrugged. Farm girls weren't prudish about natural functions.

"Now you've had the tour, shall we go to sea?"

Maureen could feel the boat moving under her feet as if impatient to get away. "Aye, aye, skipper," she said and kissed him.

Paudeen left the pilothouse. She was pleased she'd remembered its name. Maureen watched him working with the ropes that ran from rings on the pier to iron posts on the boat. He brought the lines inboard, came back, and busied himself with the familiarity of a man moving about his home.

She moved aside so as not to get in his way.

Paudeen stood, legs astraddle, behind the wheel. He moved a lever on the pedestal, and as the note of the engine rose he turned the spokes so the boat moved away from the pier and out into the short narrow gut lying between low hills.

She could see the open sea of Clonakilty Bay beyond the channel's mouth and past that to the horizon. To her surprise that distant edge was curved where the wide blue sea and vastness of the friendly sky met and melded. She'd never seen the earth's curvature before. Was it such a sight, maybe, that had got Christopher Columbus's mind thinking the earth was round? And she wondered, looking straight up, how beautiful it must be out here on a cloudless night with nothing to block the view of the myriad stars and the planets in their courses.

She was beginning to understand why Paudeen would say that the sea could take a hold of someone. It was wonderful out here, and everything was so new to her.

Maureen turned and gazed at more familiar land, and as the shore passed by she admired the great trees, oak and elm and rowan, and the gorse hedges in bright chrome-yellow contrast to the surrounding soft green of the fields. In one pasture, two roan horses galloped one after the other, for no other reason, she thought, than sheer high spirits. She felt a bit like kicking up her own heels for the same reason and because, she glanced at Paudeen, they were together again.

When she stuck her head outside, the breeze made her hair flutter. Ahead, the sea was choppy and *Princess Macha* swayed gently, one partner in the endless dance of boats and the ocean.

She looked out behind to see twin waves curving away as if the *Princess* were a plough and the water a field being furrowed. Gulls glided on outstretched wings over the wake.

"The gulls," Paudeen said, "are the beggars of the sea. They always follow fishing boats in the hopes of picking up fish that slip overboard, or guts if we're cleaning and filleting before we salt the ling."

As if to mock his words, one bird let go a harsh, screaming, cackling laugh.

Maureen laughed with the bird. "I've never been on a boat before," she said, moving close behind Paudeen and wrapping her arms around his waist. "It's wonderful. Thank you for bringing me."

"I'm glad you like it, bye." He didn't turn

to face her but concentrated on keeping his course. A larger boat was coming in the opposite direction. "Hang on," he said, "your man Willy Cowan's boat there's wake will make us rock a bit, and there's always a chop at the harbour mouth."

Maureen grabbed hold of a wooden rail supported by brass brackets that ran round the wall of the pilothouse. Paudeen waved at the other boat as it passed, and she heard him yell, "Did you do good this morning, Willy, bye?" She saw Willy's mouth opening and closing but did not hear his reply.

The front of the *Princess* rose. Maureen felt herself starting to slide backward. She clung more tightly and looked at Paudeen. He stood braced there, legs apart, both hands on the wheel. He seemed planted as solidly as if he were on dry land.

"The wind funnels in through the narrows. It can screech a bit, but we'll be out of it in a minute. Hang on."

She flinched as spray rattled off the glass of the window in front of her, blotting out the view ahead. She clutched even more tightly as the boat rolled to one side. For a moment, Maureen thought the little vessel would not stop until it had turned completely over. More spray clattered on the glass ahead. She screwed her eyes tightly shut.

This was different from the sea when it was calm, and yet she realised she had found the needle of fear exhilarating too. It was the same feeling she got rushing down on a bigger camogie opponent, knowing a collision could break bones, and slipping past unscathed.

Paudeen probably felt the same sort of thrill too.

She opened her eyes to find the glass in front of her had cleared and the boat was on an even keel. The sun sparkled from a sea where now only a tiny chop disturbed the surface. Overhead, two black cormorants, necks outstretched, flew lazily out to their fishing grounds.

The boat butted its way forward.

Paudeen turned his head and smiled at her. "That's better, isn't it?"

She nodded but did not let go of the rail.

"I'm sorry if it scared you," he said. "I've got used to it."

"It was exciting," she said, and meant it.

"But I don't think I'd enjoy being out in a real gale."

Paudeen grinned. "I'm not so fond of it myself, but the *Princess* is a tough little lady. She has to be, out here in the wintertime."

For a moment Maureen thought the way the boat was moving was preventing her from focusing, or perhaps it was how the sun backlit Paudeen's head. She blinked and rubbed her eyes with the back of one hand.

Here in the shelter of the pilothouse his long black hair seemed to be tossing as violently as willow branches in a high wind, and it was full of white stuff. She frowned, tried to focus her thoughts, to see more clearly, but try as she might, she could not make out whether the white material was blackthorn blossom, snow, or sea spray. She only knew it frightened her more than the day she'd seen the wave behind Paudeen.

She shook her head hard, then blinked, and the picture of a windswept Paudeen faded until there he was, standing at the wheel, head thrown back, mouth wide as he sang:

Just tell me old shipmates,
I'm taking a trip, mates,
And I'll see you some day in Fiddler's Green.

The man was in his element. He was where he belonged. Maybe she'd seen him in one of the gales in this "tough little boat." Maybe—och, blether, she thought. I'll not let it spoil today. "What's Fiddler's Green?" she asked.

"It's a marvelous place, a paradise where sailors and fishermen go after they die.

Where the skies are all clear and there's
    never a gale
And the fish jump on board with one swish
    of their tail.

"An Irish legend says you can find Fiddler's Green by putting an oar on your shoulder and walking inland until someone asks you, 'What's that thing you're carrying, sir?'" He laughed. "I've heard tell that American cavalrymen used to believe they would go to the same place when they die."

She knew she should have laughed

too, made some crack about it sounding like *Tir na nOg*, the mythical Land of Eternal Youth on an island away to the west. But after what she had just seen, this talk about death disturbed her. "I see," she said.

Perhaps he sensed her discomfort and wanted to distract her. He moved to one side of the wheel. "You steer."

"Me?"

"Why not?"

She looked at him hard, accepted his challenge, and stepped up to the pedestal. Paudeen lifted his hands away, and she grabbed the spokes where he had held them. "Now, try to hold a straight course."

"All right." But already the front of the boat was turning to the left. She should stop that. How? Perhaps if she turned the wheel the opposite way? She did, but it must have been too far, for the boat now turned to the right and kept on turning. Maureen gritted her teeth.

This wasn't going to beat her. She turned the wheel a little way left, and to her delight the front stopped moving right and came round left. She moved the wheel back a bit, then stopped. This time the boat was heading in the proper direction. She discovered that each time it wanted to move to one side or the other, if she held the spokes lightly and exerted only a little pressure in the opposite direction, the boat's front stayed moving in a straight line.

"Very good," he said. "Grand, so."

She smiled.

"Now I want you to steer a compass course. Do you see the card in the binnacle?"

She frowned.

"In through the little window under the brass dome in front of you, there's a circular piece of white cardboard."

She looked down and nodded.

"Those numbers around the circle are compass bearings, and them and the spokes going out from the middle to each point are the compass rose."

"Compass rose. Right."

"The card's in a bowl and is free to move. It has a magnet under it, and that magnet always points north; that's shown by the big arrow on the card, so take a good look."

She did. The arrow was nearly pointing

straight at her. "Does that mean . . . Ring's behind us . . . so it's to the north?"

"It does. Well done. Now, do you see outside the circle there's a narrow white rod that sticks out from the edge of the bowl? Straight in front of you?"

"Yes."

"What does the number underneath it say?"

She peered more closely. "One sixty-five."

"All right. So the boat's running on a course of 165 degrees, nearly south."

"I see." She understood. "And," she said, the words tumbling out, "if you know where you want to go is on a course of . . . och, I don't know . . . say 200 degrees, all you have to do is line that number on the card up with the rod, so?"

"It is. Well done yourself, bye."

She looked up, saw the smile in his blue eyes, and thought, you'd not make a bad teacher yourself, Paudeen Kincaid.

"Now if you steer 180 degrees due south, it'll take us straight out to sea."

Maureen bit her lip and concentrated. She moved the wheel and the compass rose swung, but it went past 180 degrees.

She brought the wheel back, but try as she might the card kept swinging, a few degrees too far left, a few degrees too much to the right. "It's not possible."

"No," he said with a laugh, "it's not. The trick is to keep the swings as shmall as you can, and you're doing very well."

"Thank you."

He dropped a kiss on the back of her neck.

"Stop it," she said, but grinned as she spoke. "The boat'll be all over the place if I don't concentrate." She was pleased the way the compass card barely moved.

"We'll make a sailor of you yet, bye," Paudeen said. "You'll love it as much as I do."

"You do love it, don't you?"

He nodded. "The sea can take a hold of you, so, and it has of me. I've told you that."

"I'm glad for you, Paudeen, as I'd be glad for anyone who found what they wanted to do and were doing it."

"Och, sure," he said, "my Da, his Da, and Grampa's Da all fished."

"You're a lucky man, Paudeen Kincaid. You're doing what you love, and you'd not had to upset anybody by making a different choice of a life." The way I may be going to upset you, Paudeen, she thought.

"I might have done just that with the architecture," he said, "if Casey had liked fishing or if Da hadn't . . ." He shrugged.

"I'm sorry about your father, so."

"Och." He managed a smile. "Sure and didn't Da, God rest him, didn't he go doing what he loved?"

She nodded. "I do understand, so. There's enough folks like my sister Fidelma working at jobs they hate. Not like your poor Da . . . and you. I envy you, Paudeen."

He cocked his head, a smile on his lips.

And, Maureen thought, I told Fidelma I'd wait until the time was ripe to talk to Paudeen about my hopes. This might be the very moment.

"You're wandering a bit," Paudeen said, pointing at the compass.

"Sorry. It was my mind was wandering." She turned the wheel and brought the boat back on course. She straddled her legs more widely, gripped the spokes more firmly, took a deep breath, and said, "Paudeen, can I ask you something?"

"What? For the moon? It's yours for only the wanting of it, Maureen O'Hanlon." He kissed the nape of her neck and laughed.

"Not the moon, you eejit. Just a question, and please don't take it wrong."

Paudeen was still smiling. "Go ahead. I'll try not to."

"The night I met you, you weren't too happy about me wanting to be a teacher."

"I remember." His smile was fading.

"When we made up, you told me you'd been thinking on that."

"I had." His smile was gone. "I did tell you that."

For a moment Maureen hesitated to carry on.

The boat pitched and tossed in the wake of a vessel that had gone past. Maureen clung to the wheel until the motion eased. She brought the boat back on course, along with her resolve.

"Paudeen, you never told me exactly what you thought."

"I did not," he said, his voice very flat, "and I did say I'd thought on it. I'll not deny it." He looked deeply into her eyes. "I'd decided that if I gave you time you'd come to love me enough to come round to my way of thinking. And that's why I didn't say more then, was glad you didn't ask me, and I've not mentioned it since in case I might upset you."

Maureen's hands tightened on the wheel's spokes. She sighed and thought bitterly, great minds think alike, Paudeen. So alike, but so differently too. Something gnawed inside Maureen's stomach. Her mouth tasted dry, bitter, and she felt her hands sweaty on the spokes.

As if to echo her turmoil, clouds shut off the sun.

Paudeen shook his head. "Maureen, I've been looking forward to today for a month. Do we have to talk about this now? I don't want a row."

"Neither do I, but I think we do have to talk. I love you, Paudeen . . ."

"I love you, Maureen . . ." Paudeen stared ahead, looked down at the deck, then into her eyes. He said very softly, "I've had a notion, maybe in the new year, to ask you to marry me when you finished your school. I'd want you to finish. I'd wait for you to do that. I would, so."

"And are you asking now? I thought

you said when you did you'd be down on one knee with a ring in your fist." She kept her tone light. She loved him with all her soul, she'd marry him tomorrow, as long as he'd let her—

"I will be, when we've this settled once and for all."

"Paudeen," she said, "I love you. I want to marry you . . . but you don't want me to teach, do you?"

Before Paudeen could answer, Maureen heard a racket overhead like a demented kettle-drumming. Raindrops rattled on the roof, and she saw them ricocheting off the deck. The sea had turned gunmetal grey, and black clouds raced overhead.

"I'll take her," Paudeen said, moving to the wheel. "There's a squall coming. Sailors say, 'Rain before wind, your sails you must trim.' We're in for a blow. We'll have to run for shelter."

28

The wind piled the water into breakers and ripped spume from their whitecaps. Paudeen held the helm so the boat's bows faced into the waves, but still she pitched and rolled. He did something with the engine lever, and the sound of the diesel decreased. The *Princess* slowed, but her bows kept rearing up, then smashing down to hurl up sheets of spray and make her hull shudder. Every time a wave crest rolled under the boat she heaved from side to side.

Maureen clung to the pilothouse railing and stared at Paudeen. She couldn't bear to look ahead at the endless peaks and troughs marching relentlessly toward the *Princess*.

"Maureen." He had to shout to be heard. "I'm going on deck. You steer."

He wanted her to take the wheel? In this tempest? Maureen shook her head, mouthed "no" in a small voice, then said loudly, "Don't ask me to, Paudeen." Her mouth was dry, her palms sweating. "I can't. Please don't make me."

"You must." Paudeen reached out and took her arm, dragging her toward the pedestal.

Still shaking her head, Maureen let him put her hands on the spokes. She took a deep breath, got a tighter grip on the wheel and her fear. Thank the Lord she'd had one short lesson and the wheel gave her something else to hold on to.

"Keep her bows pointing straight into the sea."

She nodded. The spokes in her hands jerked and tugged and she had to fight them. Oh, Lord, she thought, it was bad enough I started a row with Paudeen and now I have to wrestle with a gale too?

The waves were steeper and Maureen

shuddered when she thought what might happen to Paudeen if she let the boat turn sideways onto them. She remembered the wave she'd seen behind him a month ago, then white stuff in his hair not an hour before. "Be careful, Paudeen," she yelled over the incessant racket.

"I'll be quick," Paudeen called back, opening the door.

When the wind swirled inside, she heard things falling from the chart table, heard the chart flapping.

Paudeen darted out and slammed the door behind him.

She watched him lean into the wind to struggle along the deck, past the hatches of the fish hold, his pants plastered to his legs, his long hair tossing like kelp fronds in the storm. He reached the foot of the mast, wrapped one arm round it, and started working with a rope.

She wanted to call out, "Hold tight, Paudeen," but she realized the uselessness of trying to be heard over the screaming of the wind, the battering of the seas. Futile as trying to get this big, strong, gentle but pigheaded man to change his mind. He'd not replied when she'd said he didn't want her to teach. He didn't have to. She knew.

The wheel gave a mighty lurch to the left, and the boat's head began to turn. The *Princess* heeled. Water flowed in over the boat's right side. More loose objects clattered to the floor. Maureen saw Paudeen throw both arms round the mast and stare at the pilothouse.

She thought the muscles in her shoulders were going to snap, but as she strained, the wheel moved and with it the boat's bow. Slowly, slowly, the little trawler turned back on course. Maureen's breath came in short gasps. All those harvests when she helped pitchfork hay onto stacks and hoisted grain sacks into the cart, coupled with her fear for Paudeen, had given her a strength she did not know she possessed.

Paudeen waved once and went back to work. Each pole in turn descended until the poles stuck straight out from either side of the boat and he was able to start struggling back to the pilothouse.

It took Maureen a moment to understand what he had done. While the *Princess* still rode over the crests like the car on a demented roller coaster, the awful tossing from side to side had almost ceased. The poles were acting as stabilizers the way a tightrope artist's long pole gave him balance.

It took both hands and all Paudeen's strength to close the door. He leant against the wall, panting, soaked, and in his hair she saw clots of white spume.

"I'll take her," he shouted. "Well done."

Maureen wedged herself in a corner and grabbed onto the chart table. She watched as Paudeen fought to hold the boat head to a sea more white than grey, as waves crested and crashed and salt spume flew. Spray and rain clattered on the pilothouse roof. The seas broke green over the bows and ran along the decks to stream from the scuppers. When water from a wave bigger than the rest battered against the windows, she flinched, expecting the glass to shatter.

It was cold and she shivered, yet somehow she was not afraid now that she thought she'd understood what her sight had told her. The white she'd seen in his hair was the spume of this storm, and when he'd appeared to her he'd been standing as he was now. Rock solid. Unconcerned. Dealing with the elements as he must have done many times before. Keeping his boat and those on her safe. Maureen was sure she had nothing to fear.

She saw him in profile. The veins of his neck stood out and he clenched his teeth as he strained with the wheel when the boat tried to yaw. Struggling, winning. Och, Paudeen. Paudeen. She loved this man for his courage, for his concern, for the sacrifice he'd been willing to make for his family, for his softness with her, and for the uncompromising way he was battling the sea.

I don't want to fight with you, Paudeen. I'll not overwhelm you the way this gale might. Why, Paudeen . . . why must you be as intransigent with me? Why aren't you prepared to compromise for my sake? Surely to God we could find a way to marry without me having to let go of my dreams?

"I'm going to start putting her across the sea to head for home," Paudeen yelled. "We've not long until we won't be able to get through the gut because the tide will have dropped. I want her into shelter as quick as possible."

She nodded to show she understood.

She saw Paudeen move the lever, and the engine speeded up. "It's going to be lumpy, so hang on."

She took a firmer grip and stood with her legs well apart, the way Paudeen did. As the *Princess* changed course, angling across the waves, the rolling became more violent and each pole tip in turn brushed the water.

It was not just the sea that was in turmoil, she thought. A moment ago she'd been scolding him in her mind for his unwillingness to bend. Wasn't she guilty of the same sin? Yet if she caved in on this, something so vital to her, would she be setting a pattern of having to bow to all her husband's wishes? Lots of girls did after they wed.

But that wouldn't be right for Maureen O'Hanlon.

"We'll be fine," he said, "in about twenty minutes when we get inside the harbour. It'll be calm there."

She nodded, but thought, no, it won't be,

Paudeen. I started something today. And he had said, "Do we have to talk about this now?" Men, she'd learned, were like that, able to put difficult questions in boxes in their minds and think about them at a later date. She didn't want to wait. She wanted this finished today.

She'd once seen Dirk, one of the family's border collies, with his teeth locked in the wool of a sheep that had fallen into a flooded gully. Da told the dog to let go, said he was worried Dirk might be dragged in too. Usually obedient, Dirk hauled until the sodden animal was dragged to safety.

Dirk wasn't the only determined creature on the O'Hanlon farm.

"Another half hour and we'll be alongside," Paudeen said.

But he was wrong. It took nearly an hour of tossing and rolling before they were inside the breakwater, the poles rigged in and Paudeen busy mooring the boat.

By the time *Princess Macha* was up against the quay, sunbeams, the first skirmishers of a watery sun, were forcing their way past the stragglers from the heavy battalions of storm clouds.

Maureen felt less chilled and was

thankful that the deck under her feet had stopped its crazy gyrations.

As soon as he had made the dock lines fast, Paudeen trotted back to the pilot-house. "Jasus, girl, I'm colder than a penguin's paddles, so," he said, blowing on his calloused hands. "I'm soaked through and I'm foundered. I'll only be a minute or six." With that, he vanished down the ladder.

Maureen looked out the windows. The sea in the harbour was a very different creature to the violent enemy it had been outside the breakwater. The water was slicked here and there with rainbows of fuel spills, spotted by the occasional floating can, cork-net floats, and old seaweed. Its surface was ruffled, not boiling.

From below she heard a clattering of crockery and the shrill voice of a whistling kettle. Paudeen appeared in the hatchway. He was wearing a dry jumper and held an oilskin jacket in one hand, the handles of two steaming mugs in the other. "Stick one of those on the chart table—it's Oxo—and put on this jacket for a bit of warmth."

Maureen did, smelling the beefy steam

along with the rawness of the jacket's waterproofing.

She lifted one mug and handed Paudeen his as soon as he was standing beside her. She sipped, feeling the warmth of the beef bouillon spread through her. "That's very good," she said. "Nearly as good as my Ma's beef tea."

"I'll tell you, Maureen, on a cold day a mug of hot Oxo can be a lifesaver, bye." He swallowed a large mouthful. "I'm sorry about today. The weather forecast was good. If I'd known that a squall was going to blow in like that, I'd never have taken you out."

Maureen sipped. When he said, "squall," he meant the weather, which had bothered her less than the disturbance between them. The wind may have dropped, but she hadn't finished yet.

"I was proud of you," he said. "I'd never have got the poles lowered without you, and if I hadn't, it would have been a close call. I know you were scared at first, but you hid it well. A lot of girls would have been much too scared to take the wheel the way you did."

She swallowed more Oxo before saying, "I'm not 'a lot of girls.'" She saw him frown. "But you're right. When you were at the mast and I thought we were going over, I *was* scared. I thought I was going to lose you."

"I was fine. I've been out in worse."

She frowned. "Is it like that often out there?"

He shook his head. "Not usually in October. Most gales come in the winter . . . and if it looks bad we don't go out." He chuckled. "I remember my poor ould Da once when it was howling out there and some city fellah asked him if he was going fishing. Da just looked at him for a shmall little minute; then his lip curled and he said very slowly, 'I may be a Corkman, so, sir, but I'm not *that* bloody stupid, bye.'"

Maureen laughed, then said seriously, "Paudeen, if you are going to go on fishing, heed your Da's advice if it's a long life you want."

"I will," he said, "for it is. I've a lot to live for." He looked hard at her from under a furrowed brow.

"As have I, Paudeen." She set her mug

down on the chart table and took a deep breath. "I want to marry the man I love. I want praties in the pot, herring in the creel, babbies on the rug—"

"That's what I want too, but—"

"But, you didn't answer my question because the storm broke, but I still understood. You simply do not want me to teach if we get married."

"Maureen, you can't have your cake and eat it."

She hesitated, then said, "But I can, don't you see? I still love you, Paudeen Kincaid."

"And I you, Maureen."

"Paudeen, if you'd only . . ." She couldn't go on.

Silence hung, heavy as the storm clouds that earlier had come racing across the bay.

Paudeen spoke. "You are a strong woman." There was sadness in his voice.

"And you a stubborn man, so. I suppose you do have to be when you fight the sea." Her own voice was low.

"Maureen, I have my beliefs. I will have no man say of Paudeen Kincaid that he could not support his wife. That she had to go out to work. I could not bear the shame."

In her mind she heard him say of Beau Geste, "Beau was a man who took his honour seriously . . . as a man should." Was it honour, or was Paudeen another of the men Miss Toner talked about, men who simply wanted women to stay at home and tend to their needs the way Ma and Sinead did, the way Fidelma would?

"I don't understand, Paudeen. Why would it be shameful?"

Paudeen sighed. "I'll say this now, Maureen. It may be a while before I say it again. I love you. I'll always love you. I'll never love anyone else, but sometimes, sometimes when you get that bee in your bonnet, I find it hard to like you. I have *no* reason to think I'd be marrying up, but I cannot have you going out to work."

The silence hung, poisonous as a cloud of mustard gas.

She fought back the tears. He'd not see her cry. He'd not. Finally she said, opening the door, "I think I'd best be getting on."

Paudeen didn't speak.

"Maybe," she said, "maybe we should take a break. The nights are growing in. It's no time to be cycling all the way from here to Beal na mBláth." As she waited for his response, she put her mug on the table and handed him the jacket.

"Maybe," he said and blew out his breath, "maybe we both should cool off a bit, just for a while . . . but I'd still like to see Tiernan . . . if that would be all right?"

That hurt. That really hurt, but she'd not let him see. "It would be, so, but you have him come here or you come to the farm on Sundays when I'll be away."

"I'll see to that." He made no effort to move closer.

Maureen swallowed, then stepped onto the deck. "I'll be running along then. Thank you for taking me boating, Mr. Kincaid." She didn't wait for his answer but clambered up onto the quay.

So now she knew what more of the tarot meant. The Pavee had said that the Prince of Cups signified moods, perhaps of the sea. Maureen had certainly seen the temper of the ocean today. And the Death card? The card that could mean being in love, then losing a lover? And seeing herself in widow's weeds? She felt the tears trickling down her cheeks. She was in mourning all right. Paudeen. Paudeen.

She turned back to look at him, but he didn't see her. He spat overboard once and chucked the dregs of his Oxo into the oily water.

29

There was a distinct smell of oil when Maureen clambered up into Eamon's lorry for the drive home. A bubbling Fidelma told her they'd got the ring and Maureen would see it that night as soon as Eamon had spoken to Da.

Fidelma and Eamon were so wrapped up in each other that Maureen had no need to make conversation and she was grateful for that. She didn't want to talk. Just nurse the pain inside her. She watched the scenery pass by, but the colours seemed muted, the birds' songs tuneless, the air chill and dank.

As soon as they got to the O'Hanlons', Fidelma, Ma, Tiernan, and Maureen waited for Eamon to "have his wee word." Maureen would rather have gone to her room, but she managed to show happiness when Da, with his arm round Eamon's shoulder, came back into the kitchen and poured good whiskeys for himself, Tiernan, and his soon-to-be son-in-law.

Poor Da had no idea how much it hurt when he'd said, clearly in jest with a wink at Maureen and a smile at Ma, "One more to marry off and I'll be able to afford to take you to Dublin for a week, Roisín, so."

Maureen saw Ma smiling. She didn't yet know that there was little chance now of Paudeen Kincaid being the next O'Hanlon son-in-law. Maureen shrugged at Ma and turned away. Tears were close and she had to blink them back.

Ma'd find out soon enough about Paudeen. All Maureen wanted was to bottle her pain inside herself and get away on her own. But it would have been rude not to have stayed for tea, although despite having had no lunch, she'd no real interest in Ma's sausages and champ.

She toyed with her food as Ma and Fidelma chatted about wedding plans. Da wanted to know how Eamon's Da's experiment had gone. He'd recently switched from a herd of Dexter cattle, the tough little beef and milk producers, to Aberdeen Angus for beef only. Tiernan, naturally, wanted to know how his friend Paudeen was. How had the boat ride gone? But Maureen's listless answers soon had him turn to teasing Fidelma and Eamon.

She was about to excuse herself and leave, when Tiernan asked, "When are you seeing Paudeen again, Maureen? It's a brave while since him and me's had a few lofts, and I'd not want to get rusty, so."

She managed to answer, "I'm not sure."

"Doesn't matter," Tiernan said. "I'll be over in Clonakilty next week. I'll nip over to Ring when it's low tide. I'll likely catch him there. I need to have a word with him and see if he'll come out with me on Saint Stephen's as a wren boy, raise a bit of money for the dance that night."

Maureen had no interest in the custom of killing wrens on Saint Stephen's Day. And dances were far from her mind, but she managed to smile weakly at her brother and say, "I'm sure you'll find him."

Inside her a voice whimpered, But *you* won't, Maureen. You'll never see him again.

Next morning, after a sleepless, teary night and a breakfast she'd barely touched, Maureen went up to her room to get ready for Sunday service. She could hardly bear to wear her white-with-red-roses dress, her Sunday best, the one she'd been wearing when she'd met Paudeen. Everything she did, heard, saw, reminded her of him. She adjusted the bow, then turned and stood before the wall mirror, combing her hair.

Maureen turned when Fidelma came in. Her big sister wore the small diamond solitaire that Eamon had slipped on her finger last night with such ceremony in front of everybody.

Fidelma sat on the bed. "I thought you didn't look as if you were yourself at breakfast. Is it well you are, Maureen O'Hanlon?" She heard a softness in Fidelma's question.

Maureen sighed. "It is not, so."

"I suppose you talked to Paudeen yesterday?"

"I tried to." She shook her head. "I tried, Fidelma, I really tried, but I did get no further than him telling me that he'd have 'no man say of Paudeen Kincaid that he could not support his wife.'" She sighed, then let the words pour out. "I'd not concede either. I still want to teach. He can't understand how important that is to me. I never even got time to explain why. Neither of us would give an inch. He said that when I got that bee in my bonnet, he found it hard to like me."

Fidelma flinched.

Maureen sniffed. "I said I'd better be getting along. So we agreed to be taking a break from each other, letting the hare sit for a while, but I know it's not just a break." She looked straight at Fidelma. "I know I've lost him."

Fidelma rose quickly and hugged Maureen, who gave in to her tears and sobbed on her sister's shoulder. Fidelma stroked Maureen's hair and made throaty, soothing noises.

Maureen moved back, sniffed, dashed her hand across her eyes. "I've lost him, Fiddles."

Fidelma frowned and said, "I hope it's not my fault for encouraging you to find out where you stood."

"It is not your fault at all. It had to be said sooner or later. It's his fault for being so thran, but it's mine too. Maybe I should give up the teaching notion?"

"Do you want him back that bad?"

"I think . . ." Maureen made a noise halfway between a hiccup and a sob. "I think I do."

Fidelma pursed her lips. "It's a lot of years you've been wanting the teaching."

"I know."

"I told you, I'm not as smart as you, but I wish I'd stayed at school longer."

"I know." Maureen brightened a little. "He did say he wanted me to get my Leaver's."

"Is that not a step forward?"

"Nooo." Maureen shook her head forcibly. "It's not worth the having if I'm only going to be a housewife." She glanced at Fidelma, hoping the criticism hadn't hurt her.

"Farmer's wife's plenty good enough for me, Maureen, but I do understand." Fidelma steepled her fingers. "Maybe, maybe if you wait, and I know the waiting will be hard, maybe he'll think on it. Come around. Come back like he did the last time. He's probably right now asking himself the same kind of question. Should he give a little? Let you teach for a while."

"He'll not be thinking that, for he does be a very proud man, so." She felt her face crumpling again. "And I love him for that too. I don't think I'll ever stop loving him."

Fidelma glanced at her engagement ring, lowered her voice, and said, "No. You won't. I know that for a fact."

Maureen's breath caught in her throat. "Connor? Connor still?"

"Aye." Fidelma nodded. "Maureen, he was my first love. I don't think anyone ever stops loving their first."

"But . . . but, I thought you were over him, Fiddles. And Eamon. What about Eamon?"

Fidelma smiled. "Eamon MacVeigh's a kind, sweet man. He hasn't a bad bone in his body, and I love him dearly. I'll make him the best wife I can, and I'll never even hint to him that there is still a tiny corner left in my heart that once in a while whispers to me, 'Connor MacTaggart.'"

Maureen didn't know what to say.

"It's all right, *a chara.* I don't hurt any-more, but I'll never forget how much I did, and I'll never, ever forget Connor."

Nor would Maureen, although she'd not seen or heard hide nor hair of him since the day she and Paudeen walked to Beal na mBláth crossroads.

"I'll not forget Paudeen either, Fiddles," Maureen said, "but I hope . . . Lord, I do so hope"—she felt the tears start again—"that the pain will go away, or . . ." She looked more deeply into Fidelma's face, seeking to find confirmation there. "Or that you're right and Paudeen will come back and have changed his mind."

"I pray so, Maureen. I truly do." She handed Maureen a hanky and said to her, as she had when Maureen was a little girl, "Now blow your runny nose."

Maureen took the hanky and blew. "Thanks, Fidelma, and thanks for listening."

"And did you not try to comfort me? Why would I not listen to you now? I only wish I could do more."

"I'll be all right. Honestly. I just need a minute or two."

Fidelma touched Maureen's shoulder.

"You're upset, girl. Do you want me to tell Ma you've a headache and you'll not be coming to church this morning?"

Maureen shook her head. "You're kind, Fiddles, but no thank you. I'll go. I'm sure I'm sadder than I've ever been in my whole life, but I'll not run away from it. I'll not pretend to be sick when I'm not."

Fidelma hugged Maureen and kissed her cheek. "Good girl. Try not to brood the way I did . . ."

"I will, so."

"For if you'll not go to him—"

"I will not."

"He'll have to come to you." Fidelma hugged her again. "And you know he may not?"

"I do."

"Brooding won't change it one way or the other."

Maureen nodded and from below she heard Ma calling, "Come on, girls, or we'll be late."

Maureen smiled at Fidelma and mouthed, "Thanks." Then she called back, "I'll just be a minute, Ma. I need to wash my face."

30

Never mind washing faces, Kinky thought, putting dirty bowls and dishes into the big kitchen sink at Doctor O'Reilly's house. And those were just the start. There'd be a lot more washing-up to do by the time she had everything ready for the doctors' Christmas dinner. She wiped her forehead with the back of her forearm. Lord, it was warm in her kitchen, but the smells were mouthwatering.

Doctor O'Reilly and his friends would be home soon and she had better get on with it. Enough of this reminiscing. Although thinking of those days did bring back good memories, it still saddened her too, and she shouldn't be sad, not on Christmas Day. And wasn't the work a sure cure for feeling sorry for herself? It always had been and it would be now. She'd see to her cooking.

She moved to the counter and lifted the roasting pan containing the presoaked and boiled ham, its fat etched in diamond shapes, each diamond pierced by a single clove. The room was hot, steamy, and redolent of roasting turkey, and became hotter still when she opened the oven door and slid the tray out so she could put the ham in the oven.

It was time now to half boil the potatoes she'd soon be roasting in the turkey fat. She set the pan on a ring on the oven top and heard the *pop* when she lit the gas.

Kinky sliced the peeled onion and began sticking cloves in each cut surface. When that was done, she placed both halves into the waiting bread sauce and put the pan on a gas ring. She'd heat it again five minutes before serving.

She carried dirty plates to the sink and turned on the tap. The old pipes made a clanging-clattery-thumpety noise. Doctor

O'Reilly was always threatening to get a plumber in, but sure, did not the road to hell be paved with good intentions, so? The rackety plumbing in the kitchen was as familiar to her as . . . as the chimes of the grandfather clock in the O'Hanlon farmhouse and, she cocked her head, the ringing of the front doorbell of Number 1 Main Street. Who was it this time? she wondered, turning off the tap and wiping her hands on a convenient towel.

"Merry Christmas, Mrs. Kincaid." Archie Auchinleck, the milkman, was wearing a gabardine raincoat, heavy muffler, and woolly hat with a pom-pom. He handed her a brown paper bag. "Just a wee thingy for the doctors. A wee thank-you for fixing my back last summer, like."

"Merry Christmas, Archie, and thank you. Now run you away on home, so. It's snowing to beat Banagher."

"I will, Mrs. Kincaid." Archie turned his shoulder to the snow and strode off.

She closed the front door and took the gift into the dining room. The sideboard was getting cluttered. When her doctors came home, she'd ask them to take some of the bottles to the upstairs lounge to make room in here for the Christmas-dinner side dishes.

Outside the window the daylight was fading, and still soft, fluffy flakes fell, covering the earlier prints of pedestrians on the footpath and hiding the tyre tracks on the road. She drew the curtains and hoped her family, for that was how she'd come to think of Doctor O'Reilly and those close to him, would have no trouble getting home from the marquis'.

Back in the kitchen, Kinky glanced through the windows before she pulled the blind. Snow had always worried her, ever since Connor MacTaggart had been lost in a blizzard. She tugged the blind string, sat, and thought back to another snowfall, on Saint Stephen's Day in 1926. So long ago.

The day before, the O'Hanlons had celebrated a family Christmas. Maureen had wondered if she might hear from Paudeen, thought maybe he'd send a card. But there'd not been a word. Nor had there been since the day she'd left him on his boat.

She knew he had been coming to see Tiernan, but always while she was away.

Her sports and her studies, now that she was more determined than ever to be a teacher starting next year, kept her busy. The farm chores filled more hours and stopped her from brooding about Paudeen Kincaid—most of the time. But it was hard not to at night, after she'd blown out her candle and could, in the silence of her room, think on him, ache for him.

When Eamon came over on Christmas Day to exchange gifts with Fidelma, Maureen had been happy for her sister, but inside she was close to tears because Paudeen wasn't coming with something for her. And he'd not be getting the gansey she'd been knitting for him since September. She'd spun the raw, untreated *báinín* wool herself on the spinning wheel she'd been given for Christmas four years earlier. The strands, rich in lanolin, would be waterproof and ideal for wearing on the *Princess Macha.* Och, well. The knitting of it hadn't gone to waste. Tiernan had been delighted to receive it on Christmas and was wearing it today.

She'd overheard her brother telling Da that he'd be meeting Paudeen at the road up to the peat bog. She'd no idea how

Paudeen would get there from Ring, but that was none of her business. The pair of them would be going wren hunting, and Tiernan already had blackened his face with burnt cork.

The hunting was for later. Now Malachy and the O'Hanlons, Tiernan, Da, Ma, Sinead, Fidelma, and herself were assembled in the kitchen waiting for Da to tell his Saint Stephen's Day story, an annual ritual as well observed in the O'Hanlon household as the lighting of the Yule log the day before. There'd only been one Saint Stephen's that Maureen could remember when Da hadn't told the tale, nor had there been any wren hunting that year either.

She unbuttoned the front of the green cardigan Sinead had given her. With the range and the stove both lit, the room was toasty warm. Sinead's three-month-old daughter Maeve was asleep in a crib on the floor. Finbar, who sat on Sinead's knee clutching a stuffed dog, pointed at Tiernan's daubed face and gurgled.

Hurry up, Da, she thought. Every year he'd tell the story of why young Irishmen blacked their faces, hunted wrens, and

used them as a device to collect money
for the hooley that would be held that evening. His story was as familiar and comforting as the chimes of the clock. And
she wanted to be comforted. Mind you,
she thought, the wrens did get no comfort, so.

They were little, rich brown—coloured
birds, all of four inches from the tip of their
beaks to the ends of their short, cocked
tails, which they would flick continuously.
A wren weighed four ounces. Wrens had
been hunted on this day since Celtic
times. She felt sorry for the little things,
the poor wee crayturs.

"Will you get a move on, Finbar?" Ma
said. "New Year's Eve will be over before
you tell your tale."

Maureen smiled and wondered how often Ma had heard *all* of Da's stories, but
she would still listen out of love for the
man.

"I will, as soon as everybody's sitting
down," he said, settling his duncher more
comfortably on his bald pate.

Maureen, Tiernan, Ma, Fidelma, Sinead,
with Finbar on her lap, and Malachy all sat
round the table with Da at its head. He be-

gan to tap his foot and sing. Tiernan and Malachy joined in.

> The wren, the wren, the king of all birds,
> On Saint Stephen's Day was caught in the
>   furze,
> Although he is little, his family is great,
> I pray you, good landlady, give us a treat.

Tiernan smiled at her as Maureen mouthed the words. She'd heard Da and her brothers sing the song every year on this day for as long as she could remember. She wondered if big brother Art was singing it in far-off Philadelphia, then realized he'd probably still be in bed.

Da said, "That's the first verse of the song the wren boys sing from door to door as they collect money for food and drink for tonight's wren dance.

"Why the wren? And why a *céili*? Well, I'll tell you.

"This is what it was. Before Saint Patrick came here to Ireland, the Celtic people believed that the robin, who stood for the New Year, had to slay the wren, who stood for the old year, before the year would turn. So they killed wrens and celebrated that with a great feast on the night after their *Alban Artuan,* their Christmas. The whole thing is that old.

"Once Christianity came, the Celts were told that they had to give up their superstitious ways." He chuckled. "Silly, wasn't it? If you'd a good excuse for a hooley, why give it up?

"The new priests said this was to become the feast of Saint Stephen, a martyr who was stoned to death shortly after the Crucifixion. And do you know what your forebears did?" He paused, then said, "Come on, you tell us, Maureen. You've all the makings of a *seanachie* yourself."

She blushed at the praise. Telling instead of listening would keep her from thinking on Paudeen. She carried on with the story the way Da would have.

"It is what it was, so. Just because the Celts were pagans didn't mean they were stupid. Hadn't Saint Stephen tried to escape from his pursuers by hiding in the bushes, and hadn't the chattering of a wren betrayed him? Well, now, with *that* as a good Christian excuse for retribution, they blacked their faces like Tiernan there so no one would recognize them, and exactly as they had done in the old days, they went out, killed a wren, and collected money to pay for a great ta-ta-ta-ra that night the way they always had. But they persuaded the priests that they were honouring Saint Stephen."

"And," said Sinead, clearly not wanting to be outdone by her little sister, "there was soon another good reason to kill the wren. When the Vikings were pillaging Ireland, before Brian Boru threw them out in 1014 at the battle of Clontarf, a wren gave away an Irish raiding party that was sneaking up on a Viking camp.

"It started pecking at crumbs on a drumhead and the *rat-tat-tat* of its beak on the drum skin woke the camp, and the Irish were all killed."

"Aye," said Da, picking up the thread, "and it does be said about a wren alerting Oliver Cromwell's troops the same way when he was ravaging this country in 1649. I think myself that that's more likely. I don't think Vikings used drums." He shook his head. "But no matter what reason you give to justify doing it, to this day groups of boys, aye, and men like your brother black their faces and go wren hunting." He hesitated. "I only re-member one Saint Stephen's when they did not."

"We all do," said Malachy. "Four years ago."

Maureen shivered.

Da continued. "They kill a wren, tie it to the top of a pole, and decorate it with rib-bons. Then away they go from house to house." Da began to sing.

My box would speak, if it had but a tongue,

The men joined in.

And a penny or three would do it no wrong.
Sing holly, sing ivy—sing ivy, sing holly,
A drop just to drink, it would drown
    melancholy . . .

Da laughed. "There's only another forty verses. Will we go on?"

"You will not," said Ma. "If you have to sing today you can give us a couple of your come-all-ye's at the party tonight."

"Fair enough, Roisín," he said. He

winked at her, then continued. "So there it is, the story of the Saint Stephen's Day wren."

"And if we're going to get one, I'd best be on the road." Tiernan rose.

"You take care, now," Ma said softly. "Do not be going onto the high pasture."

Maureen glanced at Fidelma and saw the frown on her sister's brow. Saint Stephen's Day was always a trial for her.

"We'll take care all right. Never you fear, Ma," Tiernan said. "And I'll even take care of the salty sailor man who doesn't understand the land very well."

Och, but he does understand the sea, Maureen thought. I only wish he could understand me.

Tiernan lifted a cudgel from behind the door and opened it. Bright sunlight spilled into the room. He called, "None of you worry, now. We're only after going to hunt the wren. The bushes up by the peat bog will be full of them, and we'll have our bird in no time." His voice grew serious for a moment. "And don't worry, Ma. We'll not go near the high place."

"Good," said Ma, with a glance at Fidelma. "And don't stay too long for I think it might snow, and if it does start, get you off that hill as fast as you can."

"We will, so," Tiernan said. "Eamon's meeting us at the crossroads with his Da's lorry, and we'll be off to Clonakilty in no time to collect the wren money." He looked out into the brightness of the day and said, "I don't think we need worry about snow today." He was laughing as he closed the door.

Maureen had to strain to hear Ma saying in a very soft voice, "But we *are* expecting snow," and her mother's face in that warm kitchen was the only one that didn't smile. Ma rose and went to the range. "I'll make us some tea."

Thinking of Ma boiling water for tea in the cosy O'Hanlon kitchen brought Kinky right back to her own kitchen at Number 1 and the tatties she had half boiled not very long ago. It was time to put them on to roast and to give the bird another basting.

She busied herself and managed to raise a small blister on her right wrist when it brushed against the hot oven. As soon as she'd finished holding it under a stream of cold water from the tap, her mind went back to Da saying to Malachy,

"Will you give me a hand in the byre? I want to move two of the beasts."

"I will, so."

She had watched the two men leave. They were coatless and hatless. The day was warm, so if Ma had seen snow it must be coming later. By the time it did, the boys would be snug in Eamon's lorry, the one she'd ridden home in after her row with Paudeen. Och, blether, she told herself, stop moping and give Ma a hand.

Maureen rose and crossed the floor. She took down a tin and started putting pieces of Ma's homemade Scottish shortbread onto a plate.

The morning passed quickly. Once they'd enjoyed their tea and shortcake, it was time for her to help Ma with the turkey carcass and hambone, which were being boiled to make stock. Then she made a start on the "Dear Aunty" letters.

Fidelma had gone to her room for something and Sinead asked Ma and Maureen to keep an eye to Finbar, who was now playing on the floor. Sinead took her howling baby, Maeve, to be changed.

Maureen was always amazed by how much noise a small baby could make. She smiled, but her smile soon fled when she heard a very different noise. It was wind howling through bare-branched trees. The walls of the kitchen became blurred, the range and stove vanished, there were no cooking smells, only a chill in her nostrils. Maureen saw flakes, whirling and flying, and small sheep huddled against a gale. A vixen stalked over a drift. A vixen with the face of a woman.

31

Maureen felt an arm round her shoulder. "What is it, *a chara*?" Ma asked quietly.

Maureen stood and buried her face in her mother's bosom, seeking to be comforted like a very small, scared child. She took three deep breaths, then straightened and looked into Ma's eyes. "I saw snow too, lots of it, Ma, and sheep and the vixen."

"The fox-woman?"

"Aye, so."

Ma held Maureen more tightly. "You saw more than me, girl. There were only a few flakes for me. I didn't think too much of it then, so. Not enough to forbid Tiernan. Only enough to warn him so he could tell Paudeen when they met, but—"

"And now you think I've seen something dangerous?" Maureen stepped back. Her hand went to her mouth.

"We both watched it snowing . . ." Ma lifted an arm, hand palm up, in front of her. She gestured at the sun-dappled hillside. "You'd not think it could snow on a day like today."

"And four years to the day after Connor was lost." Maureen clenched her fists. Paudeen. Tiernan. She thought of the Death card she'd seen last August, the white stuff in Paudeen's hair. Maureen looked up to where clouds were forming, dark they were and heavy, and the sky's once-smiling face now scowled.

Ma lowered her arm.

"And"—it cost Maureen a great deal to talk about him, but she ploughed on—"I've seen Paudeen before with white stuff in his hair. I thought it was sea spume, but now I'm not so sure. It could have been snow. But I don't understand about the sheep." Or the vixen, she thought. Maureen shivered and hugged herself.

Ma's eyes narrowed and she shook her head. "Nor me." She pursed her lips, then said, "I think we should send Da and Malachy after Tiernan to tell him and Paudeen to come back at once."

Maureen swallowed. She'd no idea at all what she'd do if they brought him here today. What would she say to him? That didn't matter, she realized. She just wanted him safe. She wanted him back.

"You stay with the child," Ma said. "I'll go for the menfolk. Better so, for there's still no need for you to let on you are fey like me. I told you before, the less folks who know the better, and even in families tongues can wag. I'll tell them I've seen a blizzard coming, and they'll understand what needs to be done."

"Go quick, Ma. Hurry."

Maureen sat alone at the table and waited for Da and Malachy. She watched her nephew playing with his stuffed doggie, chewing its ear, gurgling, quite unaware of the terrible worries of his aunty as the clouds outside spread and dressed the sky in mourning. "Hurry up, Ma," she whispered. Maureen didn't hear Fidelma come back.

"Why do you want Ma to hurry up?"

Maureen turned to her. "Ma's seen more snow coming. Look out there."

"Mother of God." Fidelma stared out the window. "Not again. Not on another Saint Stephen's." She sat at the table and held her head in her two hands.

Maureen stood beside her sister and rested a hand on her shoulder, remembering her sister's pain when Connor disappeared, her overwhelming grief when his body was found. And now Tiernan and Paudeen were in peril on the very same day and in the same circumstances. Were the O'Hanlons cursed? Had someone looked at them with the evil eye?

Ma and the men returned. The sunlight had been snuffed out, and the first flakes were falling.

"Ma's right," Da said. "Right it was going to snow, and right to send us after them. If the blizzard she's seen is starting, the sooner we get them off that hill the better. I don't know about Paudeen, but Tiernan's not dressed for the cold."

Ma said, "I'll heat some beef tea and put it in a thermos while you're getting ready. Finbar, get you a knapsack, and the whiskey. Malachy, there's a hurricane lantern on that shelf; grab it."

Maureen could see, as she had many times, where Sinead had learnt her way of organizing things.

Da grabbed the bag, stuffed in the bottle of John Jameson, pulled the men's coats and hats from pegs behind the door, and chucked Malachy his.

Ma looked at the cow-clap lumps that had fallen off their boots in her clean kitchen. She tutted, but Maureen understood why they hadn't wasted time worrying about the floor.

Maureen rose. "I'm coming with you." And she would brook no denial. "I'm going to my room to get dressed warmly. I'll only be a shmall minute, so wait for me, Da."

"I will not," he said. "It does *not* be a job for a girl, so."

"And why not? Why not, Da? Tiernan's my brother. Paudeen's . . ." She shook her head and felt the prickling behind her eyelids. He's the man I still love, she thought, but she couldn't say it out loud.

She saw Da's eyes soften and fill with understanding as he said quietly, "We'll wait, *muirnín,* but hurry."

Maureen fled upstairs. She sensed someone behind her and turned.

Fidelma stood on the landing. "I didn't go out the last time," she said. "I've rued it to this day. I'm for coming too."

"Bless you," Maureen said. She hugged her sister before heading for Tiernan's room, where she lifted a pair of his heavy pants and an old necktie and then went to her own room.

She heard Ma calling, "Girls, one of you bring four blankets from the hot press when you come down." Fidelma answered, "I will, so."

Outside the window, great flakes were being blown horizontally past. Maureen could hear the branches of the sycamores rat-a-tatting against the windowpanes. There was a piercing whistling that she knew of old. It always happened when a strong easterly wind blew over the chimneys and played on them as if the row of pots were the devil's ocarina.

She put on a string vest, like the one she'd once grumbled about writing a thank-you letter for, a woollen shirt, a light jumper, and a heavy sweater. She remembered that Tiernan was wearing the raw wool one she'd knit for him, and she hoped it was keeping him dry and less cold.

His trousers were too big so she used his tie as a belt. The pants legs were soon tucked into thick woollen socks. She started to sweat, but one look outside to where the snow was already starting to drift chilled her inside.

When Maureen came back into the kitchen, Ma and Sinead, holding Maeve, stood together as Da helped Malachy into the straps of a knapsack. Her brother-in-law carried a hurricane lantern. Fidelma, bundled up like Maureen, was distributing blankets.

Maureen rapidly crossed the room, but as she passed the table she felt a chill as if she were in an icy pocket of air, even though the rest of the room was toasty warm. The hairs on the nape of her neck rose and she shuddered. The temperature plummeted and goose pimples stood out on her forearms. Her teeth chattered.

The chair, the very one Connor had knocked over in his haste four years ago, clattered to the floor, though no one was near it save a wispy shapeless mist. She

458   Patrick Taylor

wasn't seeing him clearly this time, but she knew he was there.

She picked up the chair and said to the others, "Clumsy of me. Sorry." But under her breath she whispered, "I know the Thevshee can move things. Connor, do this house no harm . . ." Then as an after-thought she added, "And if it's true that ghosts have to obey the commands of the living, get you up to the high pasture where you belong and watch over my brother and Paudeen."

"What?" Fidelma asked.

"Nothing," Maureen said. "I was just talking to myself." She dragged on a pair of Wellington boots and swathed herself in a scarf, overcoat, gloves, and a woollen hat.

"Here." Fidelma handed her a rolled blanket. She slung it over her shoulder and tied the ends together over the opposite hip the way Da, Malachy, and Fidelma already had theirs.

She saw Da put one of Tiernan's caps in his coat pocket. "Have you anything of Paudeen's?" he asked.

Maureen shook her head. "Nothing." Nothing at all, but he still had her love.

"Pity," Da said. He looked at Ma. "Don't worry, Roisín; we'll be home soon, and we'll have the boys with us."

How can you be so sure? Maureen wanted to scream, but taking her cue from Ma and her sisters, she said nothing.

"Come on then." He headed for the door and, from a collection of walking sticks leaning against the wall, he gave them a heavy blackthorn each and took one for himself. He managed a weak smile. "I did ask permission before I cut these."

He opened the door and an icy blast roared in.

Maureen followed outside. The last thing she heard over the gale, before Da closed the door, was Ma calling, "You'll come home to me, so. All of you. Safely now."

32

How many times, Maureen wondered, had mothers, wives, and sweethearts spoken those words when loved ones were going in harm's way? For herself she felt no fear, but for Tiernan and Paudeen she trembled and tried to imagine how they would be faring.

Already she was cold despite her layers of clothes. The boys would be chilled through. Tiernan wasn't dressed for these conditions, and she guessed Paudeen would be lightly clad. Ma was right about bringing the beef tea and whiskey and blankets to them.

She heard Da's shrill whistle over the wind's keening.

The two O'Hanlon sheepdogs, their fur rippling, ice rime already forming on their eyebrows, piled out of the barn.

"Heel, Kris. Heel, Dirk."

The dogs obeyed Da's curt commands.

Maureen pulled her hat down on her forehead and covered her mouth with her scarf, but the wind sliced at her cheeks, and she had to screw up her eyes to peer ahead through the driving snow. She could barely make out the gate in the low wall of the barnyard. For every step she had to haul her foot out of an ankle-deep drift. She felt Fidelma's mitted hand reaching for her own, took it, and half turned to smile as her sister plodded gamely along.

It might be a bit deeper higher up the hill, but the boys should be able to tramp through the drifts. Tiernan was a big strong man. Hadn't she seen him working with a pitchfork, tossing more hay into the hayloft in an hour than any two other men? And wasn't Paudeen—a man who had been as gentle with her as a nursemaid with a newborn—wasn't he a man who, when playing road bowls, could loft a twenty-eight-ounce bullet as far as Tiernan himself?

It would take more than this blizzard to hold them up long, for in the time Tiernan'd been gone they couldn't have walked very far. It would take more than a bit of snow to stop them, she reassured herself, although it might well make their progress slow. They'd probably meet the search party long before the four of them reached the turnoff up to the peat bog.

But, she shivered, it was cold, and the sooner they got to the boys, brought them hot drinks and blankets, the better. She tugged on Fidelma's hand and lengthened her stride.

The farm lane ran from west to east, and they were tramping directly into the teeth of the wind. When they turned south onto the road to Clonakilty, the wind would be blowing on her left shoulder. Maureen would welcome that respite, especially in the unlikely event they didn't meet the boys but had to turn east again and start climbing up to the bog.

Not a word was spoken as they marched forward, Da and Malachy taking it in turns to go first to break a path. Maureen felt a burning in her chest and her breath turning into tiny ice crystals in the wool scarf. Despite her gloves, her fingers were numb.

She glanced again at Fidelma and squeezed her hand. The squeeze was returned and Fidelma thrust her shoulder into the wind. Together they plodded on to the open gate to the main road where Da and Malachy stood waiting.

"Are the pair of you still for going on?" Da called, his hand cupped round one side of his mouth. "There'd be no shame in it for a girl if she turned back."

"I'm going on, Da," Maureen shouted and looked to Fidelma for support.

"Tiernan's as much our brother as you, Malachy, and I love you both, so," Fidelma yelled. "I left one man out there when you went to search for him. I'll not sit at the farm chewing my nails and waiting for you two to come back . . . and nor will Maureen."

Bless you, Fidelma, Maureen thought. You understand, I know.

"You'd not have too far to go from here to get home," Da said.

She gritted her teeth. "Da! We're going

on." Maureen crossed the main road, followed by Fidelma, and found what little shelter there was to be had in the lee of the hillside. It was less windy there and perhaps not snowing as heavily as it had been when they set out.

As she trudged along, Maureen could see downhill to the fields, where a blanket of white was punctured here and there by stark trees, clumps of whins, their branches dark where the snow had not lain. The drystone walls had white capstones of snow, and those cows unlucky enough to be outside huddled in the corner of two walls seeking what shelter they could. Their breath clouds were blown to shreds. One heifer lowed. It was a deep mournful cry.

"Can you see our farm in the valley there, Fidelma?"

"I can."

"It's like a castle under siege. Look at the way the chimney smoke's getting knocked flat."

"But the walls aren't. They'll let nothing in that's not supposed to be let in. It's solid, reliable. It's our haven and the lights from the windows are beacons." Fidelma moved closer to Maureen. "And those lights'll guide us back home . . . all six of us. You'll see."

"Do you think so? That we'll find the boys?"

"I know it." Fidelma sounded so certain, it comforted Maureen. "We'll find our brother . . . and we'll find your Paudeen."

"I pray you're right."

"I have to be right. What happened to Connor couldn't possibly happen again four years later to the day. It couldn't. Not again."

At the mention of his name, Maureen thought she heard a sound. Was it the wind in the trees, or was it a tune on the *uillinn* pipes? She shook her head and trudged on, and even as the sound grew fainter she strained to see. If it was Connor she might catch a glimpse of him, and more importantly she hoped that at any minute two men would appear from out of the murk.

But as they tramped along, nothing came save the swirling snow.

Maureen could make out the familiar gateposts, but no gate. It had been removed years ago. This she knew was the start to the road up, but apart from two narrow, lower strips at each side—those would mark the ditches—the hillside was barren, unbroken white stretching up to the not-very-distant horizon. No dark figures broke the featureless expanse.

Her heart sank in her.

As Maureen drew level, Da called, "I don't see any footprints here, so the snow must have come on after they headed up. Judging by how long it is since Tiernan left home, we should see them soon. I'm certain they'd have turned to come down when the snow started to fall."

"Please. Please," Maureen mouthed into her scarf.

"We'll keep going up to meet them. Get something hot into them," Da said.

Maureen nodded. Ma's beef tea would revive a frozen ox.

"We should see them anytime, but . . ."—Da avoided looking directly at Maureen—"if we don't in fifteen . . . say, twenty minutes, and it's still a howling gale . . ." He shook his head.

Maureen understood. The boys could appear any moment if they'd gone up the road, turned, and come straight back. Another fifteen minutes with both groups walking toward each other should certainly allow plenty of time for them to meet. If they hadn't by then—and she cringed at the thought—then the boys must have lost their way and be wandering out there, somewhere, anywhere.

She screwed her eyes shut and tried to look into herself, tried to summon the sight to tell her exactly where Paudeen was, but nothing happened.

Maureen clenched her gloved fists. What use was the gift if it couldn't tell her what she so desperately wanted to know?

"Malachy," Da said, "get the lantern lit."

Maureen waited, stamping her feet and flailing her arms across her chest, willing Malachy to get a move on.

Fidelma moved closer and put her mouth close to Maureen's ear. "I understand what you're feeling."

Maureen nodded. Of course Fidelma understood, more than anyone could.

"It's awful," Fidelma said, "but they'll be all right. We're going to find them. Any minute. You'll see."

Maureen nodded, wishing she could believe it, knowing Fidelma was doing everything in her power to keep her sister's spirits up.

At last the lantern's yellow beam was reflected from a myriad tumbling flakes, but its light barely penetrated the clouds of falling snow. It might have been a pretty sight, she thought, if viewed from indoors, but here it only served to emphasize how difficult finding the boys might be.

"Right," said Da, "follow me . . . and nobody leave the road."

As if to give emphasis to his words, the wind increased, hurling great walls of snow so Maureen's world shrank to a tiny sphere of weak, paraffin light.

She had no idea how much time had passed when Da called another halt. Maureen, bent over, put her hands on her knees and hauled in great, throat-burning lungfuls of frigid air. She coughed until the paroxysm passed and she was able to hawk and spit. She straightened up.

Fidelma had turned her back to the wind and stood by Maureen's side. Da was on his hunkers in front of Dirk and Kris. He held Tiernan's cap under each dog's nose.

Maureen wished she'd had something

of Paudeen's to give to Da. She hoped Paudeen would have something of himself to give to her when they found him. And she wished they would meet the boys, and that Paudeen and Tiernan would be safe. How she wanted them both to be safe.

Even if—after they'd got back to the farm and the snow had stopped and melted—even if Paudeen went away to Ring and never came back, she would be content, she thought, simply knowing he was alive.

Da stood and pointed to his right. "Seek, Kris."

The collie tore off, across the ditch— and vanished into the falling snow.

"Seek, Dirk." Da pointed left.

The other dog ran into the left ditch, up, and across the far field.

Da moved closer to Maureen and put his arm round her shoulder. "I'm sorry, *muirnín*, I'm sorry, but there's no point us going any further."

"I know, Da. I wish I'd had something of Paudeen's for the dogs."

"Never worry," he said. "The boys'll have stuck together. When one of the dogs finds Tiernan, he'll find Paudeen too."

Maureen took comfort from Da's "when" not "if."

"Thanks, Da, I—"

"Wheest!" Da snapped and held up his hand. "What was that?"

Maureen strained to hear.

Nothing. Nothing. Then as the wind momentarily dropped, she heard the faintest, *"Hellllp."*

"Bring the light." Da, with Malachy at his side, strode off in the direction of the sound. Fidelma and Maureen followed. She was grateful for the way the two men's bodies made a small windbreak.

"Hellllp."

They stopped, and Maureen stood still, trying to pinpoint exactly where the cry had come from.

"Kris," Da yelled. "Kris. Come in. Come away in."

The dog came charging back from out of the swirling snow. He was panting like a steam engine with a boiler leak; his tongue lolled from his gaping mouth. The collie ran up to Da, turned, and looked over his shoulder before starting to lope back the way he had come—the direction from which Maureen was certain she could hear the cries for help.

"That's Tiernan," Da said, a great smile spreading over his frost-chapped face. *"We're coming, son,"* he roared. *"Hang on."*

And Paudeen would be with him. Maureen hugged the thought.

She and Fidelma followed the hurrying forms of Da and Malachy.

She could make out something small running at an angle toward her. It must be Dirk, she thought. But as the animal came closer, she saw its brush held just above the drift and its narrow muzzle and piercing eyes changed into the face of a beautiful, smiling woman. Then the fox changed direction and vanished into the swirling snow.

Maureen stopped in her tracks, trying to understand. Why had the fox-woman appeared now? What was she trying to say?

"Are you all right?" Fidelma shouted.

Maureen nodded. "Just a bit short of puff," she yelled, before starting off again. The Shee were here. That *had* been the pipes she'd heard back on the road, so Connor was here too. But why? Why?

Before she could try to answer her own question, she saw Kris, and there was no mistaking him for a fox. He was sitting over the body of a man who was half covered in loose snow and lying in a deep part of the ditch. As she drew closer she recognized the coat Paudeen often wore.

Thank the Lord he was safe. And surely Tiernan couldn't be far away, could he? It *was* Paudeen, wasn't it? Please God. She knew, she just knew, that Connor *had* watched over them, and she wondered whether the Shee were watching Connor.

Da and Malachy scrambled down into the ditch.

Maureen waited on the road.

"Tiernan," she heard Da say. "Thank Christ, son. Are you all right?"

Tiernan? She moved closer to the edge of the ditch. Her father was helping Tiernan to sit, brushing snow from his shoulders. Tears welled up in her eyes, tears of joy that her brother was safe and tears of anguish for Paudeen. Maureen strained to look all around her but saw nothing that resembled the shape of a man. Her man. Where was he? Why was Tiernan wearing Paudeen's coat? Where was Paudeen?

"All right is it, Da?" she heard Tiernan say. "I am not at all. I didn't see the ditch in the snow. It was about half an hour ago. I fell in and twisted my ankle. It won't let me stand. At least . . ." She heard him manage a weak laugh. "At least I'm so bloody foundered that it dulls the pain a bit."

Poor Tiernan. She could still remember the pain of twisting her own ankle last year playing camogie. At least she'd been surrounded by teammates and officials who carried her to the clubhouse. Tiernan had been out here with no one but Paudeen—and where was he?

"Hang on," Da said. "We'll oxtercog you out of here." He and Malachy got Tiernan up, and each draped one of his arms over their shoulders. They hauled him, hopping, floundering, and grimacing, onto the road. Then they laid him down, and Da, Malachy, and Fidelma pulled their blankets free and covered him. Maureen took hers off and used it as a pillow for her brother.

He smiled up at her. "Thanks."

She could see him shivering, saw how blue his lips were.

Malachy opened the knapsack and pulled out the thermos. "I'll get you a mouthful of hot beef tea, so."

While Malachy fiddled with the cap of the flask, Maureen knelt beside Tiernan and asked, "Paudeen?"

"He was waiting for me when I got to the road to up here. I blacked his face for him and we set off together. We turned back the minute the snow started. We'd not come far when I took my tumble." Tiernan drew in a deep breath. "When Paudeen saw what had happened, he climbed down in there. He tried to help me get out, but I couldn't. I told him to leave me, to go and get help, but he wouldn't hear of it."

If he had, we'd've met him coming down, Maureen thought. Where was he? He was a stranger here and even locals could get lost in a blizzard like this one.

"Did he finally go?"

"Aye. That Paudeen Kincaid's a brave man, so. I told him to follow the road, not get lost, but he just smiled."

Smiled was it? Maureen thought. She

imagined his blue eyes twinkling. "Why? There was nothing funny about it."

"He grinned and pulled out a funny-looking yoke from his pocket, a thingummy like I'd never seen. It looked like a big pocketwatch with only one hand. 'That,' says he, 'is a compass. I should have got it out sooner, but I reckoned you knew the way, bye. I can find my way with it.'"

"He can," she said. "He's got one on his boat."

"Aye, so. Them fishermen do be quare and smart about some things. Anyway, he offs with his coat and puts it on me. 'The walking will keep me warm enough,' says he and climbs out."

"'*Slán*, Tiernan,' says he. 'I'll be back in no time with help.' That was about twenty-five minutes ago, maybe fifteen before you folks arrived, but—"

"But he wasn't on the road," Maureen said. She heard her voice rise and felt Fidelma's hand gripping her shoulder.

Tiernan shook his head. "He'd only gone a few steps when I heard him swear, and Paudeen Kincaid is not a swearing man. 'What's up?' I yelled at him. 'Buck eejit that I am,' he yells back, 'didn't I drop my compass and tread on it with my boot while I was looking for it? It's bust,' says he. 'About as much use as last year's tide tables. Never worry, I'll be grand, bye,' and that was the last I saw or heard of him."

33

Pray God, it won't be the last anyone else sees of him, Maureen thought. We have to find him. We must.

Da looked her straight in the eye and slowly shook his head. "I know what you want, girl, but we can't. It'll take Malachy and me all we've got to help Tiernan home, and I will not have you and Fidelma out here on your own. Is that clear?"

"It is, Da." Whenever he asked, "Is that clear?" there was no point arguing. She felt the tears start, dashed them away with the back of her glove, and managed to say, "I understand." But deep inside she didn't want to give up. She wanted to ignore the reality and keep trying as long as there was breath in her body.

"Good lass. We'll have to get started back down," Da said. He whistled loudly and roared, "Come in, Dirk."

She heard Malachy say, "Get that into you, Tiernan, now. It's Ma's beef tea, so."

Maureen could see that the warmth of the blankets had helped Tiernan. The blue tinge had left his lips. Now he held the cup in both hands, blew across the surface, and sipped from it. "Lord Jasus," he said, "that would put life back into a frozen corpse."

She tried to ignore the thoughtless re- mark.

Dirk appeared. His breath came in white puffs as he ran to Da and sat by his leg. He'd not have done that if he'd wanted to be followed out into the snow. No one fol- lowed him out of the blizzard.

"Good boy," said Da and patted the dog's head. Then he made both collies sniff Paudeen's coat. "Seek, Dirk. Seek, Kris," he said. The dogs raced off.

"Here." Tiernan gave the thermos cup back to Malachy. "Thanks."

"I'll pour you a cup, Maureen," he said, "and you're next, Fidelma."

Maureen took the beef tea gratefully and drank, feeling the heat of it warming her insides. The tea and the glow of the hurricane lamp standing on the ground where Malachy had set it were the only warm things in an icy world. And somewhere out there, beyond the lamp's pool of light, somewhere in the snow that was falling more heavily, was Paudeen.

Her heart ached for him.

"I'm sorry, Maureen," Da said, "but when Fidelma's had her beef tea we'll have to head home."

She nodded. She understood, and not just why Da was making them go back now. It had been clear to her why, four years ago to this very day, he'd said searching for Connor would have to wait until the weather improved. Da'd been too wise then, as he was now, to risk more lives on a hopeless quest.

"I know, Da," she said, thinking that at least back then Fidelma and the rest of the O'Hanlons had been able to cling to the hope that Connor either had got home or had taken the warmth from his sheep.

He hadn't, poor man, but he might have. There was nothing on this hillside today to shelter Paudeen but some angle between two walls, where at this moment he could be crouching like the cattle she'd seen earlier. He'd be growing numb.

Another tear slipped from the edge of Maureen's eye. It was a particle of ice on her cheek before it reached her scarf. She finished the beef tea, refilled the cup, and tried to hand it to Fidelma. "Here."

Her sister was stooped, her back to the gale, as she lifted and folded two blankets. She turned to Maureen, straightened, accepted the cup, and drank. "Thanks."

In her own aching, Maureen felt for her sister, who must be reliving that other Saint Stephen's. "I'll have my blanket," Maureen said, taking it from Fidelma and putting it over her shoulder, "and the knapsack and the lantern." She shrugged into the straps and picked up the hissing lantern.

Da and Malachy got Tiernan up on his good leg.

"You and Fidelma lead, Maureen," Da said.

They started off down the road, the

wind now at their backs. She willed the dogs to find Paudeen. Guide him back to safety. Guide him back to her.

Maureen turned and looked up the hill. She held her arm above her eyes to protect them. Da and Malachy had the blanket-draped Tiernan between them. In the snow she thought they looked like figures from a picture in one of her history books. A picture called *The Retreat from Moscow.* The two men supported the third as he hopped, slowly, one hop at a time. Even the collies, who had returned, looked dejected.

It was going to be a long journey home.

It was. The men had to stop frequently to let Tiernan catch his breath and rest. Every so often, Fidelma would take Da's place helping Tiernan. Malachy curtly refused all offers of respite.

Maureen's heart stumbled when she saw something black moving over the snow, keeping pace with them. It wasn't a fox, and when she heard its *toc-toc-toc* drifting on the wind, she knew. She trembled, and not only from the bitter cold. Were the Shee tormenting Paudeen out there as they had Connor? Why were they taunting her? She'd not harmed them. The fox-woman had smiled when she'd seen Paudeen with Maureen.

"Go away," she yelled.

"What?" Fidelma called.

Maureen turned to her sister. "That raven over there," she said, but when she looked back the bird had vanished. She sighed and said aloud, as she had in the farmhouse when he'd tumbled the chair, "Connor MacTaggart, if you are out there, watch over Paudeen, for my sake."

But no shape appeared in the swirling snow; no pipes hummed over the gale.

And as if in mocking answer, she heard from overhead *toc-toc-toc*.

By the time they got to the main road, the hurricane lantern had sputtered and died for lack of fuel, but still Maureen refused to let her hopes die with it. But of Paudeen they had seen neither hide nor hair.

Halfway between the hill road and the farm lane, Da and Malachy sat Tiernan on the top of an ancient milestone. "Clonakil" was all that remained of the original directions chiseled into the granite.

"Would you look in the knapsack, Fidelma?" Da said and coughed. "There's a bottle of whiskey." His chest wheezed as he inhaled.

Maureen felt her sister working behind her to get the whiskey out.

"Here, Da," Fidelma said.

Each of the three men took a swig and wiped the neck before passing it on.

"Here, girls." Da handed Maureen the flask. "You've earned it."

The neat spirits were raw in her mouth, but she swallowed them down, feeling a tiny explosion in the pit of her stomach and a tingle spreading through her. "Thanks, Da." She gave the bottle to Fidelma and waited for her to drink and return it to the knapsack.

They set off again. Progress was slow, but at least the blizzard was abating. The power of the wind was weakening, the fall of snow less heavy. Maureen and Fidelma trudged ahead, occasionally looking over their shoulders to make sure the three men were following.

Maureen was too weary to talk to her sister. She felt her lips growing number, her teeth chattering, her legs heavier to lift with each stride, and her heart chilled within her.

It was only the sight of the lights in the farmhouse windows—beacons, Fidelma had called them—that kept her going until at last she stood outside the back door.

Ma must have been watching from the uncurtained window, for she threw the door wide. "Fidelma. Maureen. Are you all right? Come in out of that, the both of you."

"We're grand," Fidelma said.

Maureen didn't bother to answer.

The heat inside the house was over-powering. As she started to get rid of the lamp, the knapsack, her blackthorn, and her outer garments, Maureen heard Ma welcoming the others, and Da saying in a hoarse voice, "I'll put the dogs in the barn; then I'll be back."

By the time he returned, Maureen was down to her shirt and trousers, Malachy was sitting beside Sinead, holding her hand, Ma had set a tray full of steaming mugs of tea on the table, and Fidelma, also rid of her heavy outer gear, was passing them out.

Ma knelt before Tiernan. She had taken

off his woolen sock, examined his swollen, bruised ankle, and pronounced there were no bones broken. Now she was winding black wool round and round the sore place and chanting in a low voice:

> The Lord rade and the foal slade.
> He lighted and He righted;
> Set joint to joint and bone to bone,
> And sinew unto sinew.
> In the name of God and the Saints,
> Of Mary and her Son,
> Let this man be healed. Amen.

"You'll have to lie up for a few days, son, but you'll be lofting bullets in no time, so."

"Thanks, Ma." He looked hard at Maureen. "And maybe, God willing, Paudeen will be with me."

She took a very deep breath.

"I'm sorry I let him go off on his own. If we'd stayed—"

"It's not your fault, Tiernan." Maureen shook her head. "You didn't know we were coming. Paudeen was right to try. He's not a man who'd give up without trying everything. He's out there somewhere still struggling. I just know it, and even if he's got himself a bit lost, it's not your fault."

He managed a weak smile. "Thanks, Maureen."

"Maureen's right," Ma said. She smiled at Tiernan, then looked at Da. "Finbar, I am glad to see you all home, for I did worry, so. I'll be happier still if Paudeen sticks his head round our door."

Maureen knew Da was not a demonstrative man, but she could feel for him as he bent and kissed the top of Ma's head. "I am glad to be home, Roisín. I am glad that our Tiernan's home with us all." He moved to Maureen and squeezed her shoulder. "And I am sad too that there's been no sign of Paudeen yet."

She closed her eyes.

"He may very well show up yet," Da said, and she knew he was trying to comfort her. "It could happen."

She covered his hand with her own. She couldn't speak for the lump in her throat.

Da looked hard at Ma. "Have you seen anything?" he asked.

Ma rose. "I have," she said softly, looking directly at Maureen. "I saw more snow, and I saw a fox in the snow and a raven soaring above. I know they were the Shee, but what they were after, I know not."

"Maureen saw a raven when we were on the way home," Fidelma said.

"And a fox on the hill," Maureen said. She thought back to what had happened in this kitchen before they had left—the chill, the chair toppling over, the wisp of smoke she was sure had been Connor MacTaggart. "Watch over Paudeen," she had said then, and she had repeated the invocation on the hillside. She stole a quick look at Fidelma before asking, "Did you hear any music at all, Ma?" If Ma'd heard the pipes it might be a sign that Connor *was* watching over Paudeen.

"I did not, *a chara*. Not a note."

Maureen let her head droop. She sighed but she had to accept what Ma said. Maureen prayed that Ma was wrong about more snow. Although blizzards could be fierce here, they rarely lasted long, and the thaw was usually quick. There was still a chance Paudeen was sheltering somewhere on the hill. He'd be cold, thirsty, hungry. He might even get frostbitten, but he was tough and used to foul weather—what fisherman wasn't?

The little daylight filtering through the falling flakes was fading outside, and Maureen knew the bitter night would soon be on him. How much longer he could hold out didn't bear thinking about. And his chances of finding his way here in a fresh blizzard would be slim.

The others were talking in low voices, leaving her to her own thoughts, she assumed. She heard a low moaning, and then she saw the windowpane shiver as a gust hit the house.

Outside the window, in the glow from the kitchen lights, the snow was now flying more thickly and whirling past more ferociously than it had earlier in the day.

Despite the warmth of the room Maureen felt her heart turn to ice within her. She felt arms round her and looked up. It was Fidelma. With tears in her eyes, she looked into Maureen's and whispered, "I know, *muirnín*, I know. But maybe the storm won't last for long."

34

The storm did not let up. Maureen had gone to bed before she'd half finished her mug of tea, too tired to eat, too exhausted to do anything but crawl under the bedclothes and worry about Paudeen. But despite the turmoil in her and the raging of the blizzard outside the window, she soon tumbled into a dreamless sleep.

When she awoke she blinked at the pale grey light filtering into her room. Down below, the grandfather clock chimed the hour, then struck eight. From outside she heard the *rat-a-tat* of the branches on the pane.

She pulled the curtains back. Snow. Thick swirling flakes.

She washed, brushed her teeth, and was surprised to see something strange in the mirror. There were a few silver strands among the chestnut of her hair. She examined them more closely. No mistaking it. Silver. She sighed. Everyone knew worry could start a body's hair greying, and she'd been worried enough for two since the blizzard started.

She dressed and went down to the kitchen. "Morning, Ma. Fidelma." Her voice was flat.

"Morning." Fidelma's smile was forced.

"Morning, Maureen. I hope you slept well," Ma said, throwing more rashers in the pan.

"I did."

"So did everybody else. Only Sinead, Fidelma, and myself are up. We've eaten. Sinead's seeing to the chisellers upstairs, so."

Maureen felt a gust hit the house. "With that out there, the men might as well all stay in bed and keep warm." She sighed and said, "I don't suppose . . . ?" but didn't bother to finish. They'd have told her at once if somehow Paudeen had found his way here.

She smelled the aroma of the bacon frying, heard it sizzling. You were a grand man for the pan, Paudeen. You'd have enjoyed what Ma's cooking. "I'm not very hungry, Ma," Maureen said.

"You'll eat what I put before you," Ma said. "After yesterday, you'll need to build back your strength, so."

There was no point arguing. "Yes, Ma." Ma was right, she should eat, but she had no appetite. Only a pain inside her, a bottomless ache with no borders.

She sat at the table across from Fidelma. Maureen shivered, although as always the kitchen was toasty. Her eyes widened. She felt the hairs on the nape of her neck tingle. The same icy air as yesterday had come back. The chair beside where Fidelma sat rattled gently on the tiles.

Fidelma might not have noticed, Maureen thought, but from the barn came the racket of Kris and Dirk barking. She wished they'd shut up, but like all border collies they were excitable and would rant at any rat that scuttled across the barn floor.

Still the dogs barked. They didn't usually keep it up for so long. Maureen frowned. Then she rose, went to the door, opened it, and looked out. Snowflakes whirled into the kitchen. She saw a man coming toward her, staggering as if drunk. He was not ten yards away.

She ran to him, made him lean on her shoulder for support, and helped him back into the kitchen and onto a chair. *"Dear God, is it yourself, Paudeen?"* she yelled.

His head nodded, but Maureen could not tell if he was agreeing or simply too exhausted to hold it up.

She hardly noticed Fidelma closing the door to shut out the storm.

The man's clothes were snow-caked, his eyebrows rimed. He had no coat, and flakes clung to his heavy gansey. A cap was pulled low over his eyes, and a scarf swathed the bottom of his face. His eyes were screwed up, and she could barely see their colour, but they were blue. Deep blue.

Maureen's hand flew to her mouth.

He smiled with his eyes and mumbled through his scarf, "Maureen."

My God. My God. "Paudeen. Paudeen." She held him at arm's length. "Take off that scarf. Now. *Now*." And the minute he did, ignoring the streaks of yesterday's blacking on his face, she kissed him. His lips were dry, cracked, and icy. "Paudeen. You're safe." Her heart climbed from its abyss.

"He'll be safer," Ma said, "if you'd let the poor man get out of his snowy clothes, a chair under him, and up to the oven for a bit of heat. You must be foundered, Paudeen."

Maureen grabbed his frigid gloved hand and tried to tug him toward the range.

He laughed. "Just a shmall little minute, Maureen. Let me get some things off." He removed his gloves, cap, and his sweater.

"Let them lie where they fall, Paudeen," Ma said, "and go over there to the warm. I'll get you tea when you're ready for a cup. It is welcome you are in this house, so."

"Thank you, Mrs. O'Hanlon. And it's very glad I am to be here for I am cold as all of Antarctica, bye."

Maureen helped him over to the oven and Fidelma brought his chair.

Paudeen sat heavily. His eyes were bloodshot, the skin of his cheeks scarlet where the blacking had worn off, his lips slatey blue, and when he held his hands over the range top they shook.

He looked at Maureen. "Is Tiernan home all right?"

"He is," she said. "Da and Malachy brought him back in one piece."

"With help from Maureen and Fidelma here," Ma said. "I'd have had to lock them in their rooms to stop them going, they were so bound and determined to look for you."

"Thank you, Maureen. Fidelma." He nodded to each in turn. "And thank God Tiernan's safe home for I *hated* to leave him with his ankle out of kilter, but somebody had to go for help."

"It's all right, Paudeen. You did the right thing," Maureen said, "and you're safe too." She skipped on the spot, then said very softly, "You're safe, my Paudeen."

"I am that," he said very deliberately, and from his voice and the way he was looking at her she knew *exactly* what he meant. She skipped again. My Paudeen.

"Maureen," Ma said, with laughter in her voice, "stop flaffing about and give the man another kiss."

Maureen moved to him, and when he stood, she held him round the waist, felt his arms round her, his lips on hers. She didn't care who was watching or listening, and when he took his lips away, she said, "Paudeen Kincaid, I love you, and I thought I'd lost you forever, so."

"And I love you, Maureen, and I'll never be far away from you again, bye. Never ever."

"Good for the pair of you," said Ma. "Now, if you're a bit warmer, go you and sit down at the table, Paudeen. And you, Maureen, get your man the cup of tea I promised him."

Paudeen sat across from Fidelma while Maureen poured his tea.

Ma said, "I've the pan on. How many eggs, Paudeen?"

"Four please, and could you put in a few more rashers, maybe some black pudding, sausages, and a couple of potato cakes?"

"You've a good appetite, I'll say that." Ma grinned and started putting slices of black pudding into the pan.

Maureen smiled at Ma. Nothing gave her more pleasure than cooking something that was appreciated—and she'd passed that trait on to her daughters.

Paudeen said, "It's not just for me. I hope you don't mind, Mrs. O'Hanlon, but the fellah who brought me here, I asked him to come in, and I know he'll be famished too." He accepted the cup of tea Maureen had poured. "Thank you."

She sat next to him.

"A fellah? Huh?" Ma cocked her head. "If someone brought you here, I certainly don't mind feeding him. I don't mind one shmall little bit."

"Where is he now?" Fidelma asked.

"In your barn. He said he'd see to his flock and his dog first. What's keeping him, do you think?" Paudeen sipped his tea. He smiled. "I don't know much about sheep."

His flock? Maureen wondered why anyone in his right mind would be herding sheep in this weather. Yet hadn't she seen sheep yesterday in her vision? She shivered.

"Is it someone we know? Maybe Eamon MacVeigh, my fiancé, from the next farm over?" Fidelma wanted to know.

"It wasn't Eamon. I'd have recognized him. Didn't I meet him at *Lughnasa*?" Paudeen frowned. "It's funny that he never gave his name. Mind you, at the time I didn't care. All I remember is that when I left Tiernan, bedamned if I didn't hear the pipes and I wanted to see who was playing."

Fidelma breathed in sharply. Ma turned from the pan. Maureen glanced at the empty chair beside her.

"Like an eejit, I'd broken my compass and I thought I might get lost without it, but then I reckoned I was having a bit of good luck because if I followed the sound of those pipes I'd find the piper. I just knew that whoever he was he'd know how to get to safety and he could give me a hand with Tiernan too.

"I didn't see him at first because of the snow; then I did. He was only about a hundred yards up the road, sitting on a wall. A great big fellah with a border collie at his feet. He had snow on his caubeen, a dudeen stuck into the middle of the biggest, blackest Old Bill moustache I've ever seen. He'd a red stain on the left side of his face. I thought it was a birth-mark . . ."

Maureen looked at Fidelma sitting with her hands outstretched on the table in front of her. She was crying quietly.

Paudeen didn't seem to notice. ". . . and his elbow going ninety on the bellows to blow the bag. I knew the tune. It was 'The Star of the County Down,' and your man was a quare hand with the pipes. How his fingers worked in that cold I'll never know. He even had an audience. A vixen and—"

"A raven," Maureen said quietly. She saw Fidelma picking at the skin round her thumbnail.

"That's right," Paudeen said. "You know him?"

Fidelma nodded and took a deep breath.

Maureen glanced at Ma, who said, "We all do." She put her hand over her sister's. "Go on, Paudeen."

"He stopped playing. 'Dirty day, even for the time of year it's in, so,' says he.

"I asked him to come and give me a hand with Tiernan, but he smiled, and says, 'Tiernan O'Hanlon? Never worry about him. His folks are looking after their own. They're sound people. Sure, I'm in and out of their place all the time.'"

Maureen squeezed Fidelma's hand. He was here today. He'd been there yesterday. He'd heeded her plea to go and care for Paudeen. She looked at Paudeen's weather-reddened cheeks and his blue, blue eyes. God bless you for that, Connor MacTaggart, for I do love this man so much.

"Your man goes on: 'His Da and brother-in-law and sisters are coming to find him. I saw them an hour ago. They'll get him home.'"

Connor had seen their preparations when she'd spoken to him in the kitchen yesterday morning.

Paudeen hesitated and looked at Maureen. "'Is the youngest coming?' I asked him. 'She is, so,' says he, and I nearly ran off down the hill there and then."

"We've been worried silly about you, you *amadán*," Maureen said. "If you'd gone back to Tiernan, we'd have found you too yesterday."

Paudeen hung his head. When he

looked up, Ma was setting a plate in front of him. "That should have been your breakfast, Maureen."

"I can wait."

"Eat up, however little much is in it, Paudeen. I'll get Maureen's ready now, but I'll not cook a plate for your friend until he comes in." She looked straight from Maureen to Fidelma.

"Thank you, Mrs. O'Hanlon. You're right, Maureen. I should have gone back to Tiernan. I'm sorry you had to worry for an extra night. I wanted to go back down, but the snow was thicker by then. You couldn't see your hand in front of your face. I asked your man to guide me, but says he, 'We'll be better staying put. Don't you worry. I'll see you right.' And, by God, didn't he just?"

Paudeen filled his mouth with bacon, chewed, and swallowed. "That's grand, so, Mrs. O'Hanlon. It hits the spot."

"How did he 'see you right,' Paudeen?" Maureen asked.

"'We'll have to go uphill first a ways,' says he, and he leads me right to almost the top. He'd a fair-sized flock up there, every sheep as far as I could see with a dollop of blue-grey dye on it. 'They'll keep us warm tonight, for it will be safer to go down in the daylight tomorrow,' says he. 'There was a while back there I'd have welcomed the chance in a snowstorm to get back to my flock, but I was too far down a shortcut on my way home.' He sounded a bit rueful.

"I didn't understand him, and he gave me no chance to ask him what he meant.

"'I'm sorry I've nothing to eat up here . . .' says he, and I did think it was odd that a shepherd would be out with his flock on such a day without at least a heel of bread in his pocket or a couple of *crúibins . . .* maybe a wee half-un in a shmall bottle." Paudeen filled his mouth with potato cake dripping with yellow yolk. "But he said he didn't eat much at all these days. I thought perhaps he was ill but he looked hearty enough."

Ma, back at her stove, turned and sadly shook her head as she looked from Paudeen to Fidelma.

Paudeen stabbed a piece of black pudding, chewed it, then said, "We huddled up with the sheep all night. They're like big hot-water bottles with all that wool.

Then this morning I never saw a thing like it. He and his dog—he called her Tess—got the flock moving, and they were like little snowploughs making a path for us. When the ones at the front got tired, he put new ones in the lead and let the tired ones rest at the back." Paudeen ate a piece of sausage.

"Once in a while we saw his old friends, the fox and the bird. I suppose some landsmen attract wild animals. I have a friend who has a great way with seals. They come for miles just to see him when he's out in his boat."

"Do you think they could be Selkies, Paudeen?" Ma asked.

"Women in seals' skins? They could," Paudeen said, "I suppose."

Maureen remembered his story. This wasn't the first time the supernatural had intervened on behalf of Paudeen Kincaid. The man must be charmed.

He swallowed a great mouthful of tea and said, "It seemed no time at all until we were in your yard. I noticed one strange thing as he headed for the barn. The birthmark on the side of his face . . . it had completely vanished."

Fidelma gasped and glanced at Ma, and Maureen saw Ma nod and smile. She knew the red was the mark of the faeries the way the blue-grey dye on the sheep was Connor's mark. Now it was gone.

Paudeen, who must have been unaware of this byplay, looked out the window. "Glory be," he said. "The snow's stopped."

It had.

"I'll put my sweater on," he said, "and go and see if your shepherd man needs a hand, for he's taking forever."

"I'll come with you," Fidelma said, rising and grabbing her coat from its hook as she went to the door.

When they'd gone, Ma said quietly, "Do you think the Shee like your Paudeen, Maureen?"

"You told me the faeries like me because I have the gift. The day he first told me he loved me, there was the vixen."

"And did she give any sign she'd heard?"

"I didn't see the woman's face that time, but I'm sure the fox grinned at us. Connor smiled that day too. He understood about Paudeen and me."

"It's clear to me," Ma said. "I think they like Connor's rescuing of Paudeen. They do approve when a Thevshee does a good deed for a stranger, and Paudeen wasn't from these parts and didn't know Connor. If I'm right they've taken off their spell. Lord," she said, "I do hope so."

"Maybe," Maureen said, "maybe when I saw them yesterday they were trying to tell me Paudeen was going to be all right?"

Before Maureen could answer, Paudeen and Fidelma came back. He carried a crook. Fidelma smiled weakly. "There's sheep hoofprints all over the yard, boot marks, and dog tracks right up to the barn door, but all we found inside was—"

Paudeen held up the crook. "I yelled for him, but divil the bit reply did I get. He's vanished like . . . like snow off a ditch." Paudeen shook his head. "I . . . I'd not have believed it if I hadn't seen it with my own eyes, bye."

"It was Connor, Ma, wasn't it?" Fidelma went to Ma to be held in both arms.

"I do believe so, daughter," Ma said. "And I do believe because he brought you home, Paudeen, he found favour with the Shee. And if he did, their spell will be lifted and we'll hear no more of the Saint Stephen's Day Ghost, for Connor will have found his rest."

"Thank you, Ma," Fidelma whispered. "Poor Connor, I let you go a year or so back when I met Eamon, so I'm not holding you by caring too much. May the Doov Shee have released you too."

Paudeen, still frowning, still looking baffled, asked, "You're all talking about the Connor MacTaggart who folks round here say is the Saint Stephen's Day Ghost? And *he* rescued me?"

"We are, and we are sure he did," Maureen said. "You'll remember I told you Connor's story outside his ruined cottage?"

"I do, and I remember I told you I loved you then, and I'll tell you again, I love you now." He moved to her and put his arm round her shoulder. "I've no ring, and my knees are too stiff to bend, but if you'll have me, Maureen O'Hanlon, and before you ask, after we're wed you can teach away to your heart's content. I'll speak to your Da as soon as he gets up."

35

And she had loved him, her Paudeen Kincaid. Loved him dearly.

Kinky sighed and got down from her stool. It was time to set the brussels sprouts to boiling and baste the turkey again. She busied herself with her tasks. When she opened the oven door to pull out the bird, she noted how golden and crisp the skin of the turkey looked, how the praties were roasting beautifully, and how well the ham was doing on the rack below.

She'd told Doctor O'Reilly to be sure to have his party home by five, and she knew he was a man of his word. It was still snowing, so they might even leave the marquis' party early. Well, she'd kept her word too. Dinner would be ready exactly on time, despite the interruptions of gift-bearing patients.

Telling the kiddies how Connor had been turned into a ghost, then having a wee shmall rest to herself and a nice cup of tea, hadn't interfered with her timing, although she needed to get moving now.

And she did, and as she worked so she remembered.

She'd enjoyed that cuppa and the trip back into her memories of how she'd met the man she would eventually marry in 1927, the man Connor's ghost had saved, and by so doing had found release for himself.

Kinky patted her chignon. From that second Saint Stephen's Day onward, the silver in her hair had spread. At first she hadn't liked it. But she had refused to dye it, she thought with a smile, because Paudeen said he admired the colour.

The change in her appearance wasn't the only thing different after that day. No more was ever heard of the Saint Stephen's phantom. And no strange sheep with blue-grey markings were ever seen on the high pasture, nor were the sounds of the *uillinn* pipes heard with no one there to be playing them. There were no more pockets of chill air in Ma's kitchen, and the chair never budged from its place again.

But there was a last chapter for her and Paudeen.

In March 1927 spring had come early, and a good thing too, for she and Paudeen were to be married in a double wedding with Fidelma and Eamon on Monday, the twenty-first. Paudeen had come over on his bicycle two Saturdays before. It had been a glorious day. Trees were in bud, the yellow gorse flowers reflected the spring sun, birds darted through the hedges, cocks pursued the hens, and in the low pasture ewes nursed their lambs.

They'd gone for a walk and before long they'd found themselves outside Connor's deserted cottage. They'd not gone in, but Paudeen had peered through the windows. He'd been surprised to report that despite how derelict the place was, there was not the sign of a spider's web.

They'd climbed over the stile and up into the field where Connor had felled the blackthorn. It was as Ma had said it would be. There was nothing left of the branches but flakes of rotten wood. If proof were needed, there it was. The faeries had indeed lifted their spell.

A single huge boulder stood among the decayed wood, and in its shade a vixen kept watch over her cubs, while in the field beyond a pair of ravens strutted, their agate eyes aflash as they spoke. *Toc-toc-toc.*

The lid on the pan of sprouts was knocking. She tipped it to let the steam escape. Kinky sighed deeply.

She'd sighed because she remembered, word for exact word, what Paudeen had said that day beside the decayed blackthorn.

"I never thought I'd ever meet a ghost, but I'm glad I did, for without him I'd not be getting to marry you. I'd have frozen to death. I did tell him so, but he just laughed and he said, 'No you'll not, Paudeen Kincaid. You've the face of a man who was born to be drowned.'"

They'd laughed about that then. With the spring sun and their young love warming them, their wedding only days away, there was no need to talk of death, unless it was to joke about it.

Kinky used the hem of her apron to brush away a single tear. "I miss you yet, Paudeen Kincaid. I miss you yet."

To save money they moved into his mother's house once they were wed. Maureen Kincaid had to change schools to one in Clonakilty, and she didn't mind the walk there and back every day. She had passed her Leaver's with distinction that June, but she never did get to teach, even though Paudeen had wanted her to. There were no positions in Clonakilty that year, but the headmistress had assured her that an older teacher was to retire next year.

So she kept house for Paudeen, laughed at his pet name for her, "Kinky," because he said he'd never heard of anything as kinky, as odd, as her way of cooking *drúishin*—and sure didn't Kinky fit well with her new surname? In her turn, when she found he was as good at the footracing as he was at the bullets, she called him her *giorria mór*, her big hare.

She went fishing with him in the summer to save paying a deck hand's wages. She wished she'd not taken time off in

August to visit her family. She wished, how she wished, she, instead of the hired-for-the-day man, had been with Paudeen when the freak summer gale had washed her love overboard. She cursed the sea that had taken him forever.

Kinky sighed. She'd lost him, and it was poor consolation that from the day of Paudeen's death, the sight had come to her more powerfully than Ma's own, just as Ma had said it might if something enormous happened. Now she saw and she understood what she saw.

She could foretell now, but she hadn't been able to discern her own future back in 1927.

It would have been grand to have been a teacher, but her other ambition had been to travel and there was no chance of a teaching job in Clonakilty until the next September. In early 1928, weary of living with her grief, needing to get away from County Cork and all its memories, she'd gone to see Ireland as she'd promised herself one day she would. She'd fully intended to come back and teach, but, och . . . Kinky smiled and looked around. Wasn't it the grand job she had now?

All of Paudeen's sisters were helping support their Ma, and even Casey was sending home money from California. Maureen took the boat, everything he'd owned and could leave to her. With the money from its sale she'd travelled the West through Kerry, Limerick, Clare, Galway, Mayo, Sligo, and on north into Donegal. She'd crossed the border near Strabane into the recently constituted province of Northern Ireland.

Her funds had run out in Belfast, and still not wanting to go back to Cork, she'd answered an ad in the *Belfast Telegraph*.

The skills Ma had taught her made her eminently suited for a housekeeping position, and Ballybucklebo seemed a short-term port in a storm. But it had turned into a true haven and had given her a satisfying job and a home. The stop gap had lasted thirty-six years, and sure hadn't it been grand here? And wasn't she content? And now with all the years gone by, there was no point feeling sorry for herself.

Feeling sorry for herself had never been Kinky's way. She took a deep breath, then lifted and drained the brussels sprouts.

She heard the front door open and voices in the hall.

She left the kitchen. Doctors O'Reilly and Laverty and Miss Kitty O'Hallorhan were hanging up their coats.

"You're a bit ahead of yourself, Doctor O'Reilly, sir," Kinky said. "You'll have time for a drink before dinner."

"Lovely," he said, beaming. "We'll all go upstairs."

"And I need room on the sideboard, so will you take up the bottles Archie Auchinleck and Mr. Coffin brought to wish you doctors a merry Christmas?"

"We will." O'Reilly beamed. "And His Lordship wishes you a very merry Christmas."

Kinky smiled.

"It was a grand party and I was for staying a bit longer, but Kitty thought we'd better get home because it is snowing so heavily."

"It is, so."

"I'll bet you've never seen snow the likes of it down south in County Cork, Kinky."

"Och," she said, smiling to herself, "you'd be surprised, sir. You'd be surprised."

AFTERWORD

Much of this story is based on Irish mythology. Some readers may wish to learn more about this subject. My own interest came about because of one remarkable woman, Miss Maud Tipping, my primary-school teacher. Her knowledge of Irish history and folklore was encyclopaedic. She always set aside ten minutes after each of her British imperial history classes to make her pupils familiar with their Irish heritage. Please remember, I grew up in Northern Ireland, which was and still is a part of the United

Kingdom. We had the same curriculum as kids in England.

In those precious ten minutes, Miss Tipping would read to us from a book called *The Knights of the Red Branch*. It told of the adventures of the great Irish hero *Cúchulain* (Kuh-koo-lin), and of his and his Ulster warriors' struggles with the forces of Queen *Maebh* (Maeve) of Connacht.

Queen Maeve had set out to steal *Donn* (Dunn), the great brown bull of Ulster. In this story, great themes are all told lyrically. In her quest and the battles of resistance by *Cúchulain* and his Red Branch knights, you will find heroes and villains, gods, goddesses, and demons. Great themes are there: loyalty and betrayal, love and hatred, and life and death. It is an epic to equal the *Odyssey,* the *Iliad,* the *Chanson de Roland*.

I was eight years old—and hooked for life.

I later discovered that *The Knights* is an English retelling of the great Irish epic, the *Táin Bó Cualgne* (Tawin bo Cooley), or *The Cattle Raid of Cooley.* It is Ireland's oldest recorded saga.

If I have piqued your interest, let me recommend an amazing work written in 1920, *Visions and Beliefs in the West of Ireland: Collected and Arranged by Lady Gregory, with Two Essays and Notes by W. B. Yeats.* In it you will find all the tales of the supernatural you could desire. From it comes this wonderful quotation referring to things ghostly: "There's no doubt at all but that there's the same sort of things in other countries. . . . But you hear more about them in these parts, *because the Irish do be more familiar in talking of them*" [my italics].

When I came originally to create Mrs. Kincaid, it was the influence of my childhood experiences that let her emerge as a woman who is fey. And her having the sight drove me to ask how she got it, and ended up with this telling of her story.

Kinky is also a superb cook, as readers of earlier works will know, so I have, as with all the Irish Country series, included some of her recipes here.

I hope you enjoy them. I certainly do.

Irish Recipes

LEEK AND POTATO SOUP

1 chopped onion
3 leeks
4 potatoes
knob of butter
vegetable stock
10 fluid oz / 1¼ cups cream
salt and pepper

Fry the onion gently for about 10 minutes until cooked but still transparent. Add the well-washed, trimmed, and chopped leeks. Cook for another 5 minutes. Then add the chopped potatoes and enough vegetable stock to cover them. Season and cook for about 20 minutes until potatoes are done.

Add cream, and garnish with chopped parsley.

POTATO APPLE FADGE

450 g / 1 lb / 2 cups cooked potatoes
115 g / 4 oz / ½ cup plain flour
1 teaspoon salt

115 g / 4 oz / ½ cup butter
1 large apple
a sprinkle of sugar

Mash the potatoes while they are still warm. Sieve flour and salt together; add to the potatoes and work in the butter.

Form into a round, and roll out on a floured surface to about ¼-inch thick.

Grate or thinly slice the apple, and cover one half of the circular, rolled-out potato mix with it.

Depending on how sweet the apple is will determine the amount of sugar needed.

I like to use Bramley apples grown in the beautiful orchards of County Armagh. These are quite tart apples and do need a little sugar.

The entire circumference of the pastry is moistened and the empty half folded over the half with the apples. This will seal the edges.

Lightly grease or oil a heavy frying pan, and cook slowly on both sides over a medium heat so that the apple inside is cooked.

Serve hot, spread with extra butter.

COLCANNON

---

675 g / 1½ lbs / 3 cups mashed potatoes, still hot
225 g / 8 oz / 1 cup savoy cabbage, cooked and chopped
125 ml / 4 oz / ½ cup cream
125 ml / 4 oz / ½ cup milk
small bunch of scallions, chopped
55 g / 2 oz / ¼ cup butter
2 slices of cooked bacon, chopped

Combine the potato and cabbage in a serving bowl.

Cook the chopped scallions in the milk until soft. Add the cream and seasoning, and mix into the hot potato mixture. Add the chopped bacon. Dot with butter and serve.

STEAK AND KIDNEY PUDDING

---

680 g / 1½ lbs chuck steak
225 g / 8 oz / 1 cup ox kidney
a small onion
salt and pepper
30 ml / 2 tablespoons plain flour
140 ml / ¼ pint / ¾ cup beef stock

Suet Pastry

400 g / 14 oz / 1¾ cups self-raising flour
200 g / 7 oz beef / ⅞ cup or vegetarian suet
½ teaspoon salt
black pepper
285 ml / ½ pint / 1½ cups cold water

First make the pastry by sifting the flour together with the black pepper and salt.

Then add the suet, and mix it in with a knife. Gradually add the water until you have a doughlike consistency. (Indeed you may need to use extra water as some flours need more than others.) Now use your hands, and work the mixture till you have a nice smooth dough. Roll out the dough, and line a pudding bowl with about three-quarters of the pastry.

Cut the steak and kidney into small little cubes. Toss the meat in seasoned flour and put the flour-covered cubes into the pastry-lined bowl. Then add a chopped onion and enough beef stock to almost cover the meat.

Now roll out the rest of the pastry to make a lid. Dampen the edges with water to make a good seal. The next step is a little tricky because the pie must be covered, but the covering has to leave room for the crust to expand during cooking.

I use greaseproof, that's waxed paper, to cover it. Take a sheet and fold it in half. Now bring the upper fold back, but refold it two inches from the first fold to form a Z-shaped pleat. This will allow for expansion.

Alternately butter one side of aluminum foil and pleat it in the same way.

Now cover the bowl. If you use buttered foil, put the buttered side toward the pastry.

Cover the bowl and its "lid" with brown paper tied on with string. Once the string has been tied round the top of the basin, tie the long end of the string to the opposite side of the basin, making a loop to use as a handle.

If you own a steamer, use it. If not, a saucepan filled with water can be used if the pudding is set in the pan on a trivet or even an upturned plate. Remember to keep an eye on the water level and keep topping it up so the pan does not boil dry.

To serve, turn the pudding out on a

plate, and cut it into wedges. I like to serve it with peas and mashed potatoes.

FROCKON (BILBERRY) JELLY

900 g / 2 lbs / 4 cups bilberries
900 g / 2 lbs / 4 cups sugar, warmed

Place the washed berries in a preserving pan or a saucepan or stockpot large enough to enable the fruit to be cooked without boiling over, and bring slowly to the boil.

Stir and press the bilberries to break down the fruit and release the juice.

As soon as the fruit is cooked (about 10 minutes), add the warmed sugar and stir until dissolved. Then bring the mixture to a rapid boil, and boil for about 10 minutes.

Now you can use either a muslin jelly bag or a sieve lined with gauze placed over a bowl.

Pour the jelly mixture into it, and let it drip through. If you don't mind not having a completely clear jelly, you can press to extract as much juice as possible.

Pour the juice into warmed jars and cover when cold.

This makes two one-pound jars, but the process is exactly the same for a larger quantity.

GLOSSARY

The earlier Irish Country works have been set entirely in north County Down. The dialect spoken there is rich and colourful, but it can be confusing, so in each of the earlier books I provided a glossary.

An Irish Country Girl takes place both in Ulster and County Cork. The children in the early part of the book are from north Down and naturally speak in the idiom of that part of the world.

Readers have been kind enough to say that they found it helpful to have the translations of expressions Ulster folk use, like "He wouldn't come within a beagle's gowl of it." This is not only because the expression is opaque and requires explanation, but also because "gowl" is spelled correctly. It is not a typographical error for "growl." When a beagle dog gives voice, its gowl can be heard a very long way away.

In the present volume, the focus shifts to Mrs. Kincaid as a young woman called Maureen O'Hanlon, from County Cork. The accent and syntax there are very different.

Ireland is a country where someone familiar with the speech patterns and accents can easily differentiate between the inhabitants of the Lower Falls Road in Belfast and those from the Upper Falls, never mind those from County Down and County Cork. Professor Henry Higgins would have had a field day—and that's just with the English language. And Higgins's creator was an Irishman, George Bernard Shaw.

Irish is also spoken by many people, particularly in the Republic of Ireland. Indeed in the *Gaeltacht* (galetack) in the west of Ireland it is the first language. Where I felt it added authenticity, I tried, if it did not interfere with the narrative, to give both the Irish word and the phonetic English spelling in the text. Where the phonetics would have been intrusive, I beg your indulgence and hope you have consulted the glossary.

Many readers of the earlier works have wanted to know the meaning of the Irish names of the characters. They are appended here in a separate category called "Names" with their Anglicised spelling and, if necessary, their pronunciation. Connor, the Anglicised version of *Conchobar*, pronounced "Connachoor," and Patrick, the Anglicised version of *Pádraig,* pronounced "Pawdraig," are but two examples. Where no English version exists—for example, for *Finnbheannach,* the name of a mythical bull—the pronunciation is given.

This glossary, though just as wide-ranging, is different from its predecessors in that a lot of the more colourful expressions in the previous books were scatological and would not be used by the characters inside these covers.

I hope this glossary enhances your enjoyment.

a chara: Irish. Pronounced "ah kara." My dear.

acting the goat, lig: Behaving foolishly.

Alban Artuan: The earliest Irish celebration of the winter solstice. Replaced, post–Saint Patrick, by Christmas.

amadán: Irish. Pronounced "omadawn." Male idiot. See *óinseach*.

Angelus: Short daily period of devotion celebrating Christ's incarnation. Repeated morning, noon, and evening at six. Marked by the tolling of a bell.

anorak: Parka.

an poc ar buille: Irish. Pronounced "an puck ar bwilla." A mad goat.

ants in your pants: The inability to sit still. Constantly fidgeting.

arse: Backside (impolite).

at yourself: Feeling well.

aunty, auntie: Not necessarily a relative but a title of respect used by children to female family friends. See *uncle*.

aunt Fanny Jane, my: Nonsense.

away off and chase yourself: Go away, or I don't believe you.

away off and feel your head: Don't be ridiculous.

away on: I don't believe you.

babby, babbies: Baby, babies.

bad cess to you: Bad luck to you.

báinín: Irish. Pronounced "bawnyeen."

Raw wool rich in lanolin and hence waterproof.

Banagher, to beat: Far exceed any reasonable expectations.

banjaxed: Exhausted or broken.

bank (of a fire): To cover the hot coals with small pieces called slack or turf, which slow the rate of burning. Usually done overnight or if the house will be empty.

Bean Sidhe: Irish. Pronounced "banshee." Literally "woman of the mounds." A female spirit whose moaning foretells death.

Bealtaine: Irish. Pronounced "bye-ol-tan-na." Celtic May-first festival celebrating the beginning of summer.

bap, to lose the: To lose your temper.

barmbrack: Speckled bread (see Mrs. Kincaid's recipe on page 340 in *An Irish Country Doctor*).

beagle's gowl: Very long way; the distance over which the cry ("gowl") of a beagle can be heard.

Beal na mBláth: Irish. Pronounced "beeuh nuh blaw." Literally, the mouth of the flowers. A five-road crossroads in West Cork where Long's Pub stood in the

1920s. In August 1922, Michael Collins, chairman of the provisional Irish government, and commander in chief of its armed forces, was ambushed near there and shot dead.

beasts: Cattle.

bee in your bonnet, have a: Be obsessed with.

bee on a hot brick, like a: Running round distractedly.

blether: Useless talk. Sometimes used to express frustration. "Och, blether."

bletherskite: Nonstop talker.

bluestocking: Originally an eighteenth-century women's society fostering the education of women. Came to be used pejoratively of women with feminist ideas.

bodhrán: Irish. Pronounced "bowrawn." A circular handheld drum.

boke: Vomit.

bollocks: Testicles (impolite). May be used to express vehement disagreement or to describe a person of whom you disapprove. "He's a right bollocks."

both legs the same length: Standing around uselessly.

boul': Bold.

bound and determined: Absolutely set on a course of action.

bowler hat: Derby hat.

bowsey: Drunkard.

Bramley: A tart cooking apple.

Buck eejit: Imbecile.

cailín: Irish. Pronounced "cawleen." Girl.

camán: Irish. Pronounced "cumawn." Hurley. Stick with flat curved head used for playing hurling.

Carrageen moss: An edible seaweed.

cast in the eye: Squint.

caubeen: Traditional Irish, unpeaked, soft bonnet.

céili: Irish. Pronounced "kaylee." Party with music and dancing.

certificates*:* In the Irish education system, two national examinations could be sat for: the Junior Certificate, when the student was about sixteen, and the School Leaving Certificate, two years later. Possession of either in 1926 guaranteed the holder some form of lesser white-collar work. The Leaver's, as it was known, was required for university admission and for entrance to professions like nursing and teaching.

cess: A contraction of "success." Luck.

champ: A dish of buttermilk, butter, potatoes, and chives.

chancer: Devious person.

chips: French fries. In Ireland, potato chips are called "crisps."

chiseller: Dublin slang for a small child.

clabber: Glutinous mess, usually of mud or of mud and cow-clap. See *Lady Muck*.

clatter, a brave: A large quantity.

clearing: A ritual to prove one's innocence or persuade others of your veracity.

Cloch na gCoilte: Irish. Pronounced "Clonakilty." Castle of the woods. Clonakilty is a town in West Cork.

clot: Idiot. Royal Air Force slang that crept into common usage.

Clydesdale: Huge, powerful breed of plough-and-dray horses.

colcannon: A dish made of mashed potatoes, butter, cream, cabbage, scallions, and bacon. Traditionally made from the first pulled new potatoes and eaten at *Lughnasa*.

come-all-ye: Traditional Irish narrative song that starts with the bidding "Come all ye." For example, "Come All Ye

Dry-Land Sailors," or "Courtin' in the Kitchen."

come into: Inherit.

coney: Rabbit

coortin': Paying court to. See also *walk out with*.

cow's lick: Tuft of hair that sticks up, or hair slicked over to one side.

cracker: Excellent. See also *wheeker*.

craic: Irish. Pronounced "crack." Fun. Good conversation. A very good time was had by all, often fuelled by several drops of the craytur.

Crannóg: Fortified man-made island reached by a causeway. One at Lough-brickland dates to 400 B.C.

craytur: Creature. Equivalent to North American "critter."

craytur, a drop of the: Whiskey.

cross: Very angry.

cross as two sticks: Furious.

crúibins: Irish. Pronounced "crubeens." Boiled pigs' feet, served cold and eaten with vinegar.

culchie: An Irish man or woman who does not live in Dublin. A hick or rube. Used pejoratively by Dubliners. See *jack*.

cure, wee: Hair of the dog. Hangover cure supposedly accomplished by having another drink.

dab hand: Skilled at.

Dáil Eireann: Pronounced "doyle airann." The Irish parliament.

damper: Device for restricting the flow of air to a coal or turf fire to slow the rate of burning.

dander: Literally, horse dandruff. Used to signify either a short leisurely walk or anger. "He really got my dander up."

dead on: A strong affirmative or excited acceptance of good news. Equivalent to "I totally agree" or "That's marvelous."

Dia dhuit: Irish. Pronounced "deeat gitch." Hello. Literally, God save you. The reply is *Dia is Muire dhuit* (God and Mary save you). Pronounced "geeas mwurrah gitch."

divil: Devil.

divil the bit: None. For example, "He's divil the bit of sense." (He has no sense.)

Dobharchú: Irish. Pronounced "duvarchoo." Literally, otter, but also used to describe a mythical sea monster.

doddle: A short distance or an easy task.

dolmen: Megalithic grave of three standing stones and a capstone.

donnybrook: Fight. Donnybrook, now a suburb of South Dublin, was the site of an annual fair renowned for its drunkenness and violence.

dote: *v.* To adore ("I dote on her") or to be utterly confused ("He's doting").
n. Something adorable.

do with the price of corn: Irrelevant.

dozer, no: No fool.

drop of the pure: Drink of whiskey.

drouth, raging: Pronounced "drewth." Thirst. Also, an alcoholic.

drúishin: Irish. Pronounced "drisheen." Dish made of cow's blood, pig's blood, and oatmeal. A Cork City delicacy.

Dubh Sidhe: Irish. Pronounced "doov shee." The dark faeries.

dudeen: Short-stemmed clay pipe.

dulse: A seaweed that is dried and eaten like chewing gum.

duncher: Cloth cap, usually tweed.

dunder: Forcible thump.

dungarees: One-piece coveralls.

Dun Laoghaire: Port near Dublin. Pronounced "dun leary." Literally, Leary's fort.

eejit: Idiot.

-een: See *-in*.

eye to, to keep an: To watch over, either protectively or with suspicion.

fadge: A flat fried pancake of potato, flour, and salt. Fruit such as apples may be added. (See Recipes, p. 295.)

fair play to: Good luck to or in all fairness to.

faugh a ballagh: Anglicised spelling of the Irish *Fág an Bealach*. Pronounced "Fawk a bollah." Clear the way. Originally an old Irish war cry. Adopted by the Royal Irish Fusiliers and in America by the Irish Brigade of the Union Army.

Feile na Marbh: Irish. Pronounced "fayle na marev." Celtic festival of the dead celebrated on November 1.

féis: Irish. Pronounced "Fesh." Music and dancing competition.

fey: Possessed of the second sight, the ability to see the future.

Fianna: A band of legendary soldiers. Their name survives today in *Fianna Fáil* (Finnuh-Fal). Soldiers of Destiny. One of the major Irish politic parties. The other is *Fine Gael* ("finnuh gale"), the clan of the Gaels.

finagle: Achieve by cunning or dubious means.

Fir Bolg: Pronounced "feer bollug." One of the early races believed to have inhabited Ireland. Probably invaders of the *Belgae* tribe from Gaul. Displaced by the *Tuatha Dé* (see entry).

fist of, to make a good: Do a fine job.

fit to be tied: Furious.

flaffing: Carrying on excitedly and to no useful purpose.

flies, none on: Smart. Streetwise.

fleadh: Irish. Pronounced "flah." Festival.

florin: A silver two-shilling coin, one-tenth of a pound sterling or a *punt*, the Irish equivalent. The Irish florin, stamped with the image of a salmon, was not introduced until 1928. Maureen's coins were sterling. In 1926, a florin would have been worth about 40 U.S. cents. In 2009, 120 florins, about $24, would be required to buy the same amount of goods a florin purchased in 1926.

Formorians: A race of demons who inhabited Tory Island.

for it: In line for punishment shortly.

football pools: A weekly English sporting lottery where gamblers try to pick eight soccer matches that end in draws. The payoffs can be spectacular.

footpath: Sidewalk.

fornenst: Beside.

fortnight: Contraction of "fourteen nights." Two weeks. A se'nnight (seven nights) is a week.

foundered: Chilled to the marrow.

Free State, Irish: In 1922, the United Kingdom granted partial independence to 26 of Ireland's 32 counties. The 26 counties, later to become Eire and then the Republic of Ireland, were known first as the Irish Free State.

fraochán: Irish. Pronounced "frockon." Berry of shrubs of the genus *Vaccinium*. Known as bilberry, blaeberry, whortleberry, and European blueberry.

furze: Gorse. See also *whin*.

GAA: Gaelic Athletic Association. Organisation fostering Irish sports like hurling and Gaelic football.

gander: Look at.

gansey: From the Irish *geansaí*. A jumper (sweater). Used in the Anglicised form by Irish and non-Irish speakers.

garsún: Irish. Pronounced "gossoon." Boy.

gas, great: Good fun. "It was great gas" or "He's a gas man" (he's great fun).

giorria, giorria mór: Irish. Pronounced "geara (more)." Hare, big hare.

give off to: Scold.

give over: Stop it.

glipe, great: Stupid or very stupid person.

good man ma da: Expression of approval to someone.

Go raibh míle maith agat: Irish. Pronounced "go ra meeluh maw agut." Thanks very much.

go way on out of that: "I don't believe you" or "You're making it up."

grand man for the pan: One who really enjoys fried food.

gráinneog: Irish. Pronounced "grawinnyog." Hedgehog.

great: The ultimate Ulster accolade; can be used to signify pleased assent to a plan.

gub, a good dig in the: Mouth, a punch in the.

gumboil: Dental abscess.

halfpenny: Unit of currency of which there were 480 to the pound. In 1926, worth less than 1 U.S. cent. In 2009, 60 halfpennies (about 50 cents) would be required to buy the same goods a half-penny bought in 1926.

half-un: Small measure of spirits, usually whiskey.

hard row to hoe: Very difficult.

hard stuff: Spirits, usually whiskey.

harrier: One who uses packs of dogs and follows on foot to hunt hares.

have your cake and eat it: Try to enjoy two mutually exclusive options.

having me on: Deceiving me.

head in your hands: Having been severely chastised or heartbroken.

head staggers: Behaving very stupidly. Literally, a parasitic disease affecting the brains of sheep and causing them to stagger.

heart of corn: Very good-natured.

heels of the hunt: Finally.

heifer: Young cow before her first breeding.

hide nor hair: No trace. Nothing.

high horse, up on one's: Declaiming about a pet topic of little interest to anyone else.

hiring fair: Meetings that workers would attend in the hopes of finding work.

hirstle: Chesty wheeze.

hit the spot: Fill the need.

hooley: Party.

hurling: Very fast, fifteen-a-side team sport played with a *sliotar* (slitter), a hard leather ball, and a *camán* (cumawn), or hurley, a curved wooden stick like a field hockey stick but with a broader, flatter blade.

hurricane lamp: A cylindrical metal-and-glass paraffin-fueled lantern. It is constructed so that it cannot be extinguished by high winds.

I'm your man: I agree to your plan and will follow it.

-in: In Irish, *ín* (pronounced "een") attached to the end of a word signifies little, as in *Roisín*, or little rose. It is often attached pejoratively to an English word, as in "maneen" to signify "little man."

in soul I do: Emphatic.

jack, jackeen: Slang for a Dubliner. Used by natives of Ireland from outside Dublin, who themselves are called "culchies" by Dubliners.

jar: An alcoholic drink.

jaunting car: An open, high two-wheeled vehicle. Also known as a sidecar because the passenger accommodation was two benches, arranged along either side so the passengers sat with their backs to the cart bed. By the 1960s, it was rarely seen, except in the most rural parts of Ireland or as a tourist attraction.

jigs and reels, between the: To cut a long story short.

Junior Certificate: See *Certificates*.

keening: High-pitched women's moaning at wakes and funerals. Keeners were often professionals.

knackered: Very tired. An allusion to a horse so worn out by work that it is destined for the knacker's yard, where horses are destroyed.

Lady Muck, Lord Muck: In full, Lady Muck from Clabber Hill. People having pretensions well above their social class. See *clabber*.

lapwing: Green plover. *Vanellus vanellus*. Also called a peewit because of its cry.

Law and the Prophets: Alpha to omega

on any subject. Usually said of a long-winded person.

Leabhar Gabhála Éireann: Irish. Pronounced "lyow-ar gavawla Erin." *The Book of Invasions*. A collection of poems and stories recounting the history of the various races, mythical and real, who have conquered Ireland.

Leaver's Certificate: See *Certificates*.

length and breadth of it: All the details.

lepp: Leap.

let the hare sit: Leave the thing alone.

lift ("Can I lift you?"): Offer of a free ride in someone else's vehicle. If applied to police action, *lifted* means "arrested."

like the sidewall of a house: Huge, especially when applied to someone's physical build.

liltie: A madman. An Irish whirling dervish.

Lios na gCon: Irish. Pronounced "lish na gun." Hill fort of the hound.

long drink of water: Tall and skinny.

lorry: Truck.

lough: Pronounced "logh," as if clearing the throat. A sea inlet or very large inland lake.

Lucht siúil: Irish. Pronounced "luck shul." Literally, "the walking people." Gypsies, also known as travelling people or travellers.

Lughnasa: Irish. Pronounced "loonassa." Harvest festival celebrated on the Sunday closest to August 1 to honour one of the gods of the *Tuatha dé*, Lugh (loo) of the Long Hand.

lugworm: A member of the phylum *Annelida.* A ragged-edged marine worm that lives in burrows under tidal sand or mud. Much prized as bait. Harvested at low tide by digging close to the creature's blowholes in the sand.

lummox: Stupid, clumsy creature.

MacGillicuddy's Reeks: Mountain range in County Kerry.

main: Very.

marrying up: Ireland had a rigid class system. A person from a lower class marrying one of a higher social stratum was said to have married up.

mavourneen: From the Irish *mo mHuirnín.* Pronounced "mahvourneen." My beloved.

melodeon: A button accordion.

messages: Errands or shopping.

Milesians: The name originally given to the Celtic invaders who displaced the *Tuatha dé* (see entry). They originated in what is modern Spain. Some believe the Milesians were originally the lost tribe of Israel.

moping: Indulging in self-pity.

more power to your wheel: Very good luck to you; encouragement.

mud guard: Mud flap. Narrow curved metal strips fitted over bicycle wheels.

muffler: Woollen neck scarf.

muggy: Hot and humid.

muirnín: Irish. Pronounced "moornyeen." Darling.

mullet, stunned: To look as stupid or surprised as a mullet, an ugly saltwater fish.

nines, done up to the: Dressed up in one's best clothes.

no goat's toe, he thinks he's: Have an overinflated sense of one's own importance.

nose out of joint: Miffed.

not a patch on: Not nearly as good.

not at yourself: Not feeling well.

ochón: Irish. Pronounced "ochoan." Alas.

óinseach: Irish. Pronounced "ushick." Female idiot. See *amadán*.

old ones: Older adults, usually grand-parents.

onion, cut to the: Wounded very deeply.

Ossory: Pronounced "ossory." Ancient Irish kingdom of *Osraighe*, comprising parts of the modern counties of Laois, Kilkenny, and Offaly.

ould goat: Old man, often used affectionately.

out of kilter: Out of alignment.

oxter: Armpit.

oxter-cog: To carry by supporting under the armpits.

paddy hat: Soft-crowned tweed hat.

pan, the: A fried meal consisting of any or all of the following: bacon, ham, eggs, sausages, black pudding, white pudding, tomato, soda bread, potato cakes.

pan loaf: Loaf of ordinary bread.

paraffin: Kerosene.

peat (or turf): Fuel derived from compressed vegetable matter.

pipes: Three kinds of bagpipes are played in Ireland: the great highland pipes (three drones), the Brian Boru pipes (three drones and four to thirteen keys on the chanter), and the *uillinn* (elbow) pipes, driven by small bellows under the elbow. There are keys on both the chanter and the drones.

plough ahead: Please get on with the story or the task.

poitín: Irish. Pronounced "potcheen." Moonshine. Illegally distilled spirits, usually from barley. Could be as strong as 180 proof (about 100 percent alcohol by volume).

pop by: Make an unannounced visit.

powerful: Very.

power of: A great deal of.

praties: Potatoes.

province: Ireland is divided into four provinces: Ulster, Leinster, Munster, and Connacht. (See map on page 13). Each province contains a number of counties. Beal na mBláth in County Cork is in Munster. "Ballybucklebo" in County Down is in Ulster.

purler: Severe fall.

pussyfoot: Waffle about.

quare: Irish pronunciation of "queer." Very or strange.

quare hand at: Expert.

quiff: A hairstyle worn by men in which the front of the hair is brushed up.

Radio Éireann: Irish. Pronounced "rad-deeo airann." Irish state radio network.

Radio Telefis Éireann: Irish. Pronounced "raddeeo telluhfeesh airann." Irish state television network.

range: A cast-iron kitchen stove fuelled by coke, coal, gas, or turf. In rural Ireland it was used for heating the kitchen and the water, and for cooking food.

raparee, rapparee: A seventeenth-century bandit or robber. Now used pejoratively.

raring to go: Eager and fully prepared.

rasher: A slice of bacon from the back of the pig.

right enough: That's true.

right enough?: Is that true?

run-race: Quick trip to, usually on foot.

Samhain: Pronounced "saun." November festival of the end of the harvest.

scunner, take a scunner at or to: Dislike someone intensely and bear a grudge.

seanachie: Irish. Pronounced "shan a kee." Storyteller.

Selkie: Mythical women. When they put on a sealskin, they become seals, and they revert to being women by removing the skin. Brought to popular attention by the film *The Secret of Roan Innish* (*Rón inis*, or seal island).

sharabang: Mispronunciation of *charabanc,* a motorised, four-wheeled open vehicle with many benches. Popular in the 1920s for party excursions.

shebang, the whole: Lock, stock, and barrel. Everything.

shenanigans: Carryings-on.

sheugh: Bog.

shillelagh: Pronounced "shi-lay-luh." Blackthorn club used in stick-fighting sports or as a weapon.

sidecar: See *jaunting car*.

Sidhe: Irish. Pronounced "shee." Faeries. Literally, the people of the *sidthe*. See also *Tuatha dé Danann*.

sidthe: Irish. Pronounced "shee." The burial mounds and hill forts that litter Ireland. The faeries and spirits who inhabit them are the people of the mounds and include the *Bean Sidhe* (banshee), the spirit of death; *Lenan Sidhe,* the spirit of life; and the *Dubh Sidhe* (doov shee), the dark faeries.

skate: A fish of the ray family. Once common, now endangered.

skinful, to get a: To get drunk.

slagging: Mutual verbal abuse, but used humorously and with affection.

slán: Irish. The one leaving says *"Slán agat"* (slawn agut). The one staying says *"Slán leat"* (slawn lea).

slane: Special narrow-bladed spade for digging turf.

sliced pan, best thing since: Presliced and wrapped pan loaf was reintroduced after the Second World War. To be better than it was to be the acme of perfection.

sliotar: Irish. Pronounced "slitter." Hard leather ball used in the game of hurling.

slip jig: Traditional dance in nine-eighths time.

slobber: Salivate sufficiently to drool.

slough about: Laze around.

snib: A metal catch for keeping a door, lid, or shutter closed.

sodger: Soldier.

soft hand under a duck: Gentle or very good at.

soft soap: Flattery.

sound man: A good, reliable man.

spalpeen: From the Irish *spailpin,* originally an itinerant farm labourer. Now used to denote a ne'er-do-well.

Spoil Five, or Maw: A four-hundred-year-old gambling card game where the object is to gain three of five tricks or prevent any other player from doing so, in which case the stake was added to the pot of the next hand.

sticking out: Very good.

sticking out a mile: Absolutely the best.

sticking plaster: Primitive Band-Aid.

stiffener: A drink, usually whiskey, taken to give false courage.

stirabout: Porridge.

stocious: Drunk.

stone: Measure of weight equivalent to fourteen pounds.

stook: When grain crops were reaped by hand, bundles of sheaves were made and then stacked leaning vertically against each other. These stooks stood with the grain-bearing ends at the top to dry prior to threshing.

stout: A dark beer, usually Guinness or Murphy's.

sums: Mathematics.

suppurate: Become infected and leak pus.

sweeties, sweets: Candies.

Tá fáilte romhat: Irish. Pronounced "taw fawlcha ro-at." You're welcome.

Taidhbhse: Irish. Pronounced "thevshee." Ghost.

Táin Bó Cualgne: Irish. Pronounced "tawin boe cooley." *The Cattle Raid of Cooley,* the first great Irish saga.

take a gander: Look at.

take a grip: Pull yourself together.

take a hand out of: Fooling someone to make them appear stupid.

take a shine to: Be attracted to.

take your hurry in your hand: Wait a minute.

taking the mickey: Mocking someone to make them appear stupid.

tall around: Rotund.

taste, a wee: Amount. Small amount, not necessarily edible.

ta-ta-ta-ra: Dublin slang. Party.

tea: Term used for the main evening meal, as well as for the hot drink.

telt: Corruption of *telled*. Told.

terrace housing: Row housing.

thick as champ: Very stupid.

thole: Tolerate or put up with.

thrawn or thran: Bloody-minded.

thruppence: A coin worth three pennies,

one-eightieth of one pound sterling. In 1926, about four U.S. cents. In 2009, it would take sixty such coins—about $2.50—to purchase the same amount of goods.

tinker: Itinerant tinsmith who mended pots and pans.

tinker's damn or cuss, don't give a: Could not care less.

Tir na nOg: Irish. Pronounced "teer na noag." The mythical Land of the Young where no one dies, sickens, or ages.

toffee apples, unable to do something for: To be completely useless in the pursuit of something.

toty: Small.

toty, wee: Very small.

tousling: Roughing up. Can be verbal, physical, or both.

townland: A village and its surrounding farms.

travelling people: Gypsies.

tried, to get: Become agitated about.

trilby: A soft, narrow-brimmed, fedora-like hat. The name is derived from George du Maurier's 1894 novel, *Trilby*.

Tuan Mac Cairill: Irish. Pronounced "tooann MacCarol." A Partholonian, an early race inhabiting Ireland. He under-went a series of transformations, end-ing as a salmon, which was eaten by a woman who gave rebirth to *Tuan* as a child.

Tuatha dé Danann: Irish. Pronounced "tooatha day danann." One of the early mythical races to inhabit Ireland. They displaced the *Fir Bolg*, but were them-selves defeated by the Milesians. The *Tuatha* were driven underground to live in the *sidthe* and became the People of the Mounds.

uillinn: Irish. Pronounced "uhlin." Elbow. See *pipes*.

uncle: Not necessarily a relative. A title of respect used by children for a male family friend. (See *auntie*.)

United Irishmen: An allied group of Catholics and Reformed Protestants who tried to free Ireland from English and Anglican rule. Their rising in 1798, aided by a French regiment, was crushed by British troops led by Gen-eral Lord Cornwallis (fresh from his recent defeat at Yorktown).

walk out with: Go steady.

wean: Pronounced "wane." Child.

wee: Small, but in Ulster can be and is used to modify almost anything without reference to size. A barmaid and old friend once greeted me by saying, "Come on in, Pat. Have a wee seat and I'll get you a wee menu, and would you like a wee drink while you're waiting?"

Wellington boots, wellies: Knee-high rubber boots patterned on the riding boots worn by the Duke of Wellington.

Wenclesslass: Usual Ulster corruption of Wenceslas (the Good King).

wheedle: Cajole.

wheeker: Very good.

wheen: A number of.

wheen, brave: A large number of.

wheest: Be quiet.

wheest, hold your: Keep quiet or shut up.

wheezle: Wheeze in chest.

whin: Gorse.

whippet: Small, fast racing dog like a mini-greyhound.

whisky/whiskey: Scotch is "whisky." Irish is "whiskey." Both derived from the Irish *uisce beatha*, water of life. The earliest licensed distillery (1608 by James I) is in Bushmills, County Antrim, Northern Ireland.

wisewoman: Witch. Shaman.

won't butter any parsnips: Will make absolutely no difference.

worse for wear: Drunk.

worser: As bad as it is possible to get; much more so than worse.

yes and no: Although both words exist in Irish (pronounced "sha" and "knee ha"), they are rarely used. Instead, sentences are constructed as follows: "Do you understand?" "I do" or "I do not." "Would you take a jar?" "I will"—or much less commonly—"I will not." This construct usually appears when English is spoken.

yoke: Thingamabob. Whatchamacallit.

y-o-o-o-oh: Cry of approval by Ulster children used instead of the upper-class "hooray."

your head's a marley: Your head is as small and as dense as a child's marble.

your head's cut: You are being very stupid.

your man: An Irish version of "What's his

Glossary

557

name?" or a confirmation that everyone knows who is being described.

youse: Plural of "you" in Ulster and other regions.

Names

Ailell **(m):** Pronounced "ayill." A legendary king of Connacht.

Art (m): Bear.

Barry (m): Short form of Finbar. (See below.)

Brid (f): Pronounced "breed." Old Irish goddess.

Caitlin (f): Kathleen.

Casey (m): Brave.

Cathal (m): Strong in battle.

Clodagh (f): From the name of a river in Tipperary.

Connor (m): Lover of hounds.

Cúchulain: Pronounced "Kuh-koo-lin or "Koo Hullin." A famous Irish hero from Ulster.

Dermot (m): Free man or god of arms.

Donn **(m):** Pronouced "dun." A legendary brown bull.

Dympna (f): Irish saint who could cure epilepsy.

Emer (f): Wife of *Cúchulain*.

Fidelma (f): Champion.

Finbar (m): Fair top.

Fingal (m): Fair stranger.

***Finnbheannach* (m):** Pronounced "Finn vannock." A legendary bull.

Fionn MacCumhail: Finn MacCool. Legendary Irish giant who was chief of the *Fianna*. Building the Giant's Causeway near Bushmills, County Antrim, was one of his many heroic deeds.

Mac an tSagairt: Irish surname. Pronounced "mock on taggart." Anglicised to MacTaggart. Son of the priest.

Macha (f): Of the plain.

Maeve (f): Pronounced "Mave." She who intoxicates.

Malachy (m): Pronounced "Malacky." Michael.

Myrna (f): High spirited or beloved.

O'Echtigerna: Irish surname. Pronounced "O'Ekteegurna." Anglicised to Aherne. Literally, "grandson of the lord of the horses."

Patrick (m), Patricia (f): Noble.

Paudeen (m): Pronounced "Pawdeen." Diminutive of Patrick.

Roisín (f): Pronounced "Rowsheen." Little rose. Rosebud.

Seamus (m): Pronounced "Shame-us." James.

Sinead (f): Pronounced "Shinade." Jane.

Tiernan (m): Lordly.

*Street Names in Clonakilty**

Wolfe Tone: Theobald Wolfe Tone, a leader of the United Irishmen revolt in 1798.

Emmet: Robert Emmet, leader of the revolt of 1803.

Clarke: Thomas Clarke, a leader of the Easter Rising in 1916.

Pearse: Pádraig Pearse, a leader of the Easter Rising in 1916.

*All of these men died for their cause.